Five Heaven On Earth Stories

Francis William Bessler

Spanning from 1974 to 2007.
Compiled in this book in 2015.

Featuring one person's
liberated view of life:
*"Life is Good as it is
Because an Infinite God
Must Be In It. "*

ISBN: 1511779578
ISBN 13: 9781511779579
Library of Congress Control Number: 2015906247
CreateSpace Independent Publishing Platform
North Charleston, South Carolina

Summary of My Five Stories

My Spiritual Stories
by
Francis William Bessler
Laramie, Wyoming

Note:

All of my stories feature characters who believe that God is in Nature and that the key to the good life is to embrace – not only God in Nature – but God in ourselves as part of Nature. None of my principle characters are caught up with sin where sin is defined as a separation between God and man. All of my characters believe that Christ really taught the Immanence of God in all things – not the traditional doctrine of sin. All of my stories feature characters fond of life as it is and thus embrace nudity as an ideal merely because nudity is only embracing the real Divinity of life. All stories were originated in the 1970s and 1980s, but revised and concluded in 2005 - except one - PEACE ON EARTH - which was written in 2007.

1. **ALL'S WELL WITH THE WORLD** – Started in 1975 and revised and completed in 2005, this is a spiritual novel about a young couple, Tom and Molly, who decide to set aside a weekend to discuss the meaning of life. In their discussions, they decipher much that could be called *Natural Spiritual Doctrine* and decide for themselves their own *Natural Ethics* – or

Spiritual ethics based on the evidence of Natural truths. Several years later, they encounter Naturalist friends, Joe and Liz, and their eight year old daughter, Elise. Tom and Molly have a son, Kerry, who at the time of this later encounter is almost seven. Both families meet at Tom and Molly's and later visit the next door neighbor, Sam, age of sixty, and his grandson, Tony, seventeen, and Tony's girl friend, Julie, seventeen. They enjoy their time educating Julie about how they see life and Sam hosts a barbecue and includes them all in a Naturalist Toast to God.

2. **THE SEVENTH RECORD** - Written in 1980, this is a short story about an elderly couple facing end of life considerations. The old man - age 82 - decides he wants to be on the "other side" when his wife of many years eventually passes on. To assure that he is there to welcome her, he plans a way to go before her. Does he succeed? You need to read the story to find out.

3. **FROM THE DARK – INTO THE LIGHT** – Started in 1980 and revised and completed in 2005, this is a spiritual novel about a minister's daughter – Priscilla – who is asked by her father to close his traditional Christian church and release his parishioners to find their own ways. Priscilla attends the last service with her Naturalist family, including her husband and three children, and delivers the closing sermon which she entitles – *The Wedding Garment.* Later, one of the parishioners, Lance, visits Priscilla at her home and Priscilla & Lance discuss the relationship between God and man.

4. **SUMMER TOWN** – Started in 1986 and revised and completed in 2005, this is a musical screenplay with 10 songs that tells the story of a Naturalist (nudist) town called *Summer Town*. Like one of the characters, Julie, says, *Summer Town is the way the world should be.* Started by David and Linda, reared near the Big Horn Mountains in Northern Wyoming, an early scene flashes back to David and Linda in the Mountains and tells of their beginning. Narrated by one of *Summer Town's* main residents, Frank, this screenplay attempts to show how delightful a town like *Summer Town* could be. All songs are of a Spiritualistic Natural vein.

5. **PEACE ON EARTH** - Written in 2007, this is a short story about a grandfather and his 17 year old granddaughter. The granddaughter visits her grandfather and the two of them discuss the meaning of life - as each sees it.

Preface

Welcome to this *Idealist's View of Life*! I am 73 as I write this Preface - born in Powell, Wyoming - or outside thereof on a tiny farm - on December 3rd, 1941. Perhaps it was on that tiny farm of about 70 acres that I first began to practice the ideals I have chosen in life. I do admit that my practices were mostly from intuition, I guess, as opposed to due to any youthful learning; but nevertheless, I think I began to practice my Idealism on that tiny farm - unbeknownst to any of my family or relatives or friends.

I grew up Catholic. I think I loved the idea of God that my church taught; but I did not know at the time that I would live to continue to embrace a love of God, and that, in time, I would change my opinion as to what that God really is.

God & I were one, though, in those early years - even though that God was seen as a Person - somewhat like me. I mean I was a *person*; and God was a *Person* - kind of like *Father* and *son.* Know what I mean? My Dad in real life was just an older and larger form of me; and my God was seen as just an older and larger form of me too. Together, God & me played on our tiny farm. I'd do something and look over my shoulder and say - *How was that, God?* God never answered back, but I always imagined that He was looking and I always imagined that He was smiling and taking some degree of delight in me, His son.

It was a good beginning! A very good beginning! So I am thankful that my parents and my church taught me that God is a Person. It did not hurt at all; and it sure made life on our tiny farm a really wonderful experience.

In time, though, I grew up and as I did, I began to suspect that God is not really a "Person" because God must be Infinite. **How could Infinity be a Person?** So, in essence, I decided to part ways with my church - Catholicism - and make my own way according to my own view of God; but I held onto my view of God as being a *Delightful Friend* - even though I decided that My Friend was not the Person I loved as a kid.

It sure was nice, though, that I had viewed God as another person when I was young because it took away any kind of burden of having to deal with God as other than a person - or to capitalize the notion, Person. In order to help me try to work out another view of God, I began to write stories about other people trying to do the same thing - finding God in their own way.

In 1975 or so, I wrote a story called *DAVID & BELINDA* in which I had my characters - a young husband and wife - researching a meaning of God and Life on their own. Like me, David & Belinda had grown up believing in a Personal God because that is how they were taught; but like me, they came to outgrow the notion of a Personal God. In *DAVID & BELINDA,* I had my characters discuss life and find some answers in doing so.

Later, I changed the name of my novel to *NEVER BE ASHAMED TO LOVE* - and printed a few copies of it to share with family and friends. In this work, I am repeating, for the most part, that story in Part 1 of something I call *ALL'S WELL WITH THE WORLD.* Part 2 of *ALL'S WELL WITH THE WORLD* deals with David & Belinda - changed to Tom & Molly - for that work - engaging with other people as they go about acting out life according to their "new view." Part 2 of that story was written in 2001 and enhanced in 2005 when I finished compiling Part 1 and Part 2 as a single story.

Actually, my first attempt to rationalize life happened in 1963 when I was studying for the Catholic ministry in Denver, Colorado. In my junior year, I wrote an allegory I called *WISDOM;* but unfortunately I did not make a copy of that and later I lost the original.

ALL'S WELL WITH THE WORLD became my second attempt to explore a rationalist view of life, but it did not end there. In this work, I am featuring all of the stories I have written down through the years - as noted in the previous page. We will begin with *ALL'S WELL WITH THE WORLD* and simply go forward in the order in which each work was begun - including the various Introductions as each work was completed - in 2005 with the exception of my final short story - *PEACE ON EARTH* - which was written in 2007.

Let me leave it at that for now. Enjoy my efforts as you can. **I do believe that life is good as it is because an Infinite God must be IN it. When I was young, I believed in a "Good God," but I saw that Good God as being outside of me. Now, I believe that Good God is not outside of me or anyone simply because that Good God must be Infinite - and as such must be IN everything and everyone. Accordingly, if God is truly IN all, that makes all equally sacred. It is indeed a simple view; and it's the view of all of my characters - or at least, most of them.**

Also, I have written many essays and songs about my view of life. If interested, check them out in my writings website, listed below. In 2014, I published a book called *WILD FLOWERS* that contains many of the blogs of essays and songs that I have added to the blog section of my website since I started that website in 2012. I am planning now to compile and publish a *WILD FLOWERS # 2* in August of 2015 that will feature many of the blogs I have written since the completion of the first *WILD FLOWERS*.

If interested in any of that, you can go to my website and follow an Amazon link to those works there - though, of course, at this time, **WILD FLOWERS # 2** is a planned production and is not yet available. If you liked what you read in the first **WILD FLOWERS**, more than likely you will like what is coming in **WILD FLOWERS # 2**. If you do not like my writings in one work, be it **WILD FLOWERS** or any of my works, you probably won't like any of my works. I guess if you like one, you will probably like them all. If you do not like one, well, as the French would say, *se la vie!*

In parting, I would like to thank all of those who have helped me to *"practice my ideals"* in life. Practice is so important. **Having an ideal is good; but practicing it is better.** Without practice, I think, one can't be sure an ideal is more than just thought. I have lived well in this life, I believe, but thanks so much to so many who have allowed me to do so.

One particular person comes to mind - my friend, *Nancy Shaw,* who is my latest companion; but Nancy is only one of many who have helped me live my life as I think it should be lived. Thanks to Nancy Shaw - and to everyone who has been there along the way. Others of importance to me will be noted in the Introductions of the various works I am including.

Welcome to my **HEAVEN ON EARTH STORIES!** If you wish, try imitating some of the characters - and perhaps find that in such imitation, as one of the stories says - You will pass **FROM THE DARK INTO THE LIGHT** - and realize that we really do have - or can have -

HEAVEN ON EARTH!

Thanks!

Francis William Bessler
Laramie, Wyoming - www.una-bella-vita.com
April 17th, 2015

Contents

All's Well With The World

By
Francis William Bessler

— A Spiritual Novel —

Originally written in 1975.

Rewritten & Enhanced in
2001 and 2005.

Contents

Introduction

- The Way It Should Be -

This is a work of love.
It is a story about love;
and it is a story about lovers.

Tom and Molly are no ordinary couple; but they should be. They are a couple who feel that man has been endowed with all the intelligence necessary to determine by reason alone how man should live. They believe in God, but they believe that God has endowed them with all the reason or rational faculties necessary to determine what is right and wrong for a soul. They think things out and they act things out. They act as they feel they should based on their thinking things out because that is why they wanted to think things out in the first place – to determine how best to live.

Not being bound by a lot of irrational hearsay type of instruction, Tom and Molly are free to live their lives according to their own norms. This is their story and how they impact their friends and neighbors; but I refuse to allow any enemies into my stories because I do not believe in them. So Tom and Molly have only success in their dealings with others. No conflict is offered because I hate conflict and see little value in it.

Accordingly, you may be in store for a boring story. Can life without a villain be interesting? Well, I am not interested in providing villains just to keep you interested. If you need villains to find life interesting, then you will not find them here. My joy in life is to live it without conflict. It has always been my dedication – to live life without conflict. That dedication has driven me to walk away from a lot of relationships that, in time, have discovered and insisted on conflict. That is life, I will admit; but it should not be the way it is. We should not have to live in conflict – and so if I am going to write a story about life, I want to write about it the way it should be – not the way it is. Maybe by reviewing a story without conflict, some who read this story can see how very useless conflict is. I hope so.

My characters who are being refused conflict find themselves respecting norms that most who insist on conflict would consider outrageous. I think the norms offered in my story would be considered outrageous by many because of the need for conflict – the very thing that I refuse in life and the very thing that I refuse to allow my characters. You see, my characters are me. What you see is what you get. What you read in them, you will find in me.

Thus, in a way, this is a biographical story. I allow my imagination to invent characters who perform my norms, but essentially I offer reality as I know it – or at least want it. Can any of my own personal norms be useful to anyone else? Well, that remains to be seen. Who knows? I offer my story mostly to share where I have been in terms of thought in my life. I have already lived it. It has been really good for me. Maybe others can find some worth in it too.

Actually, I started writing this story in 1975 or so and called it *NEVER BE ASHAMED TO LOVE.* For the most part, the earlier story is reflected in Part 1 of the current story. In 2001, however, I wrote a good deal of the Part 2 of the current story; and now, in 2005, I am finally finishing it. I did not like the way I ended my story of 1975. I think that is because I had not lived long enough to know how to end it. Sometimes, it takes living out a story before you can tell it. *ALL'S WELL WITH THE WORLD* is such a story. I had to become a sixty year old and experience some of the changes of post potency days, I guess, to be able to finish my story.

As noted, this work is being split into two parts. Part 1 is a highly philosophical discussion that I call **Rationalizing Existence** – just as I have actually done. Many readers may want to skip Part 1 and proceed to Part 2 which I call **Rationalizing Life – The Way It Should Be**. Reading Part 1 should be very useful, but it features mostly an attempted study of existence in general. Unless you find a discussion of general notions like *goodness, unity, and truth* appealing, you may find Part 1 of this work terribly boring. If so, just bypass Tom and Molly's meandering in Part 1 and go directly to Part 2 where Tom and Molly have much more exciting things to do than just discuss existence. I'd hate to skip Part 1 myself, but to each, his or her own.

Part 1 offers a lot of discussion about rational morality, though. It may be boring, but it has been my life. It is part of the reason I have been able to live life without conflict. So, if a conflict free life is at all entertaining, the discussions in Part 1 may prove interesting.

Part 2 is mostly showing life lived in freedom after determining in Part 1 that it should be lived in freedom.

May I wish you a happy adventure in looking at life as one man thinks it should be; and, like me, I wish you luck in patronizing the characters of this personal revelation and carrying forward the personal liberties defined within.

See you in Paradise!

Thanks!

Francis William Bessler
Laramie, Wyoming – U.S.A.
March 27th, 2005

All's Well With The World

Part 1

Rationalizing Existence

1

Virtue Through Understanding

This would indeed be an unusual weekend for Molly and her husband, Tom. It would come about from their desire to probe deeper into the true meaning of life and the purpose of man's existence on this earth.

Tom and Molly possessed deep spiritual beliefs as to what life is all about; and they felt they could very easily live their lives simply believing there is a God and an immortal existence; however, they could not bring themselves to accept the idea that God would want them to merely believe. Why, they questioned, would God endow mankind with intelligence if He preferred that His human creatures blindly accept the word of another? While it takes a certain amount of intelligence to believe, it takes more to be able to reason things out. Man, they felt, has been endowed with reason and the processes of reasoning; and it seems almost sinful to deny him the freedom to make use of these talents.

Tom and Molly were young, intelligent, and very much in love. They found it hard to believe that their sort of love relationship isn't more common in the world. After several years of marriage, love was easy for them, but it hadn't always been that way. It had taken time to develop their present relaxed and fairly uninhibited relationship.

Before their first few years of marriage, before their son, Kerry, was born, they had each suffered numerous hurts – due simply to their many differences. At the start, Tom saw man's role as ruler of the roost, with the wife being totally subservient to her man and grateful for the opportunity. Molly, on the other hand, saw marriage as a cooperative venture, with the husband at least occasionally assisting her or serving her in the same way he might expect her to serve him.

Although disagreement on the roles of husband and wife caused their major difficulties, there were additional contrasts. The loud music he liked was "noise" to her. He liked to tease, but she had a more serious nature. He was fond of going natural. She was much fonder of dressing in the current fashion.

Through an uncomfortable period of adjustment, however, they had remained together, determined that their apparent incompatibility should not be allowed to lead them into defeat. They loved each other now far more than they had ever thought possible. Painful as the necessary adjustments were, the light now shone through, and the promise of a beautiful future lay ahead. Whenever they commented on their present state of happiness, Tom's usual comment was, "Sweetheart, the best is yet to come."

Endlessly enthusiastic, Tom censored little of himself in a fierce drive to know himself. His love of life boundless, he refused to be intimated by the world at large, which would have him apologize for his thirst after full expression of his nature. The society in which he had thus far matured often looked with great disrespect, if not total disgust, upon the sexual members of the human body, especially those of the male. Seeing everything about his humanity as vibrant, alive and natural, he became irritated to the point of anger whenever anyone would accuse any member of the human body of ugliness.

Tom was convinced that such irreverence could only lead to a terribly unwholesome atmosphere, completely unsuitable for mutual love communication between the sexes. Dedicating himself to the thwarting of all damaging social misconceptions of human nature, he was determined to act without inhibition – to the frequent dismay of his much loved wife.

Tom and Molly had done a lot of growing up since their marriage vows. He had come to accept her somberness; and although she had frequently complained in those early days about his uninhibited behavior, she had since learned to appreciate his openness and natural honesty. She even learned to love his endless teasing and often took the initiative in launching what she referred to as "loving attacks" on him as he read the paper or some enticing romance novel he may have been reading. To him, these were "joyful irritations."

Kerry, their pride and joy, was a real bond between them. Now three years old, he was their special blessing. They gave thanks daily to God for His precious gift; and they planned for the day that they would add to their family. Kerry was fast becoming like his father. Naturally outgoing, he was becoming quite a tease too. Both parents spent considerable time with their little prince; and, as a result, he was unquestionably spoiled. But in keeping with their realization that a full and open expression of love is essential to happiness, the little guy was learning early in life the lessons of loving and being loved. There were limits to the spoiling, though, for he was also learning that being disciplined is another way of being loved.

Having put in a full days work at the office, Tom was glad to be home. As usual, Molly had prepared an excellent dinner; and, as usual, he had eaten a bit too heartily. After dinner he had helped Molly with the cleanup detail and both had enjoyed playing with Kerry before tucking him in for the night.

Molly, relaxed with drink in hand, looked thoughtful. "Tom, we have always had pretty firm beliefs about the meaning of life and man's purpose for living. Don't you suppose," she went on, "that we could come to a better understanding of ourselves and the world in which we live if we really applied some logic and sound reasoning to the question of what life is all about?"

Tom was not sure where this thought had come from, but he was intrigued by it. "I don't really know, Hon, but maybe it would be worth some thought." Tom recalled that Molly had often compared man to a puppet, although man, she reasoned, was created without strings attached since he, unlike the puppet, had been given the ability to think and act for himself. But man, like a puppet, must perform in all ways designed and intended by his maker or not realize his full existence.

A man fashions a puppet with the ability to perform in various ways; and, if after certain of its strings are pulled, it doesn't react accordingly, its maker must be somewhat displeased, although he would have to look toward himself to correct the deficiency since the puppet has no power to act itself.

Man, on the other hand, given talents and intelligence by his maker, is expected to perform on his own power as designed. If he fails to react with all his given functions to the utmost of his ability, his maker, too, must be somewhat displeased, although the fault lies not with the maker. Unlike the puppet, man was created with the ability to correct his own deficiencies. So, it would seem logical to assume that his maker expects him to do so.

Like a puppet, man was not made for himself, but rather for the gratification of his maker. Only if he acknowledges this can he understand what he is all about; and understanding himself, he can therefore appreciate himself far more than he otherwise could.

Both Tom and Molly felt that the key to accepting life and being happy with it could only be through understanding. Since man was made to know, he must seek knowledge. Since man was made a creature of reason, he must practice reasoning. Since man was made to understand, he must demand nothing less.

It's easy to see, however, that man must not yet have come to an understanding of himself since the whole world seems to be in conflict. Conflict is possible only when there is misunderstanding between two peoples – when one or both of any given pair simply do not appreciate themselves because of their failure to understand what they, themselves, and the world around them, are all about.

Such people can only flail at the wind in attempting to solve their problems because, not knowing who they are, they could not know where they should be going; and not having a worthwhile goal, they would only be able to travel down a path having no end but emptiness.

It didn't take long for Tom to adjust to Molly's suggestion. "Hmmmmm, sounds interesting! We could only gain by doing as you suggest, Molly. Just spending time together would be gain enough, but if we could really explore our lives and reveal some truths of which we are unaware, it would be mighty nice, I think. Do you have some specific thought in mind we could explore?"

Molly smiled. "Nothing in particular. Maybe we would do more rambling than anything else, but that would be nothing new. Would it? I mean we do a lot of rambling anyhow. Right?"

"At least I do," Tom responded. "You are always catching me questioning myself out loud. If that's not rambling, what is?"

"There's nothing wrong with questioning yourself, Honey – just don't answer yourself." She giggled a little.

"But I do, My Dear! I always answer me."

"Let me answer you for a change," Molly replied, "and let you answer me."

"I'm game," he said. "We need to think about how to get started with our musing. I will give it some thought; but in a couple of weeks, I'd love to give it a try."

Molly was pleased that Tom reacted so enthusiastically to her proposed project; *and thus was the idea launched that would lead them to one of the most enjoyable and beneficial weekends of their lives.*

2

Existence – A Starting Point

During the days that followed, both Tom and Molly devoted considerable thought to the matter of a starting point for their search for man's purpose in life. Meanwhile, their family routine went on as usual with Tom keeping at his job during the week and Molly tending to home duties and Kerry's care.

Their free time was, as always, spent in family oriented activities. One weekend occasion involved a day long fishing excursion. Another day found them swimming with Kerry in a neighborhood pool. Tom was grateful that his son seemed to love the water.

As a child, Tom had little opportunity to go swimming. Consequently, he had grown up with a fear of water which had taken him years to overcome. Although he especially enjoyed diving and swimming under water, he still had a feeling of uneasiness in deep water.

He was thankful that he could give Kerry an opportunity to learn to swim and enjoy the water early in life and thereby be free of a fear such as his own. You have to learn to be afraid like you have to learn anything else, he argued, and he wanted Kerry to appreciate the water and learn to cope with it before he could learn to fear it.

Back in their living room on an evening a few weeks later – and after Kerry had gone to bed – Tom asked Molly if she had come up with a suitable starting point for their planned mind project.

"I do have an idea I've been tossing around in my head," she responded. "I think that a good starting point would be to assume that life is beautiful. We could assume this to be so and then proceed to reason why it is so."

Tom's first response was in regards to a saying that was stated all the time at work – *to assume something is only to make an ass out of u and me.* He was forever being told by his boss that he should never assume anything when it came to under-standing what is to be done. Don't assume. Know. That was the constant dictation. So, Tom was not too keen on Molly's suggestion of a starting point. Facts were demanded at work; and he mused that their project should start with a fact too.

"I disagree, My Love," he said, without going into the defi-nition of 'assume' at work. "I don't think our starting point should be an assumption. In my opinion, our starting point should be a fact that's obvious to anyone who can reason. Your idea is more a conclusion than a starting point. We should be able to conclude after our discussion that, without the slight-est doubt, life is indeed beautiful; and our argument should be so cogent that even the hardest agnostics would have to agree. Not everyone would accept an assumption, but only a fool would deny an obvious fact." It was clear that Tom had pondered the matter considerably.

"And I suppose you have such a 'fact' in mind," Molly remarked.

"That I do."

"Well, what is it?"

"Existence!"

"That's your starting point?" she questioned dubiously. "You feel that existence is a fact no one can deny?"

"Unless he is a fool," he answered.

"You know, Tom, there are a lot of people who say we can't be certain of anything, even of our own existence. They would say that we may be figments of our own imagination."

"Alright, then," he said, "for the sake of argument, let's say we are figments of our own imagination. To be that, we must have imagination to begin with, and, therefore, this thing called imagination exists and, as such, has existence. I'm not trying to prove what things are or aren't, but simply that things are something and, therefore, have existence. Can anyone really deny that?"

"Only if he were a fool, as you say," she said.

"OK, then, that would be a good starting point. Don't you think?"

"I'm not so sure." Molly was still uncertain. "Where can that possibly lead us? At least to say that life is beautiful would provide us a fairly strong and particular principle. The fact of existence, I think, would be too general and I don't really see what we could prove by it."

"I'm not sure either," he replied, "but whatever it might be, it would have to be totally rational and intellectually acceptable by all open minded people. I simply cannot see using as a starting point something that can be disputed. The beauty of life is certainly something you and I believe, however, lots of people would deny it. If we are to be rational in our discussion of life, we must start out with fact, not assumption."

"Maybe you're right, Tom," said she. "After all, what can we lose? If we don't prove anything worthwhile using your fact, we can go back and play our little game based on my assumption."

"I take it you agree, then, that our starting point should be existence – or the fact thereof?"

"For now," she replied, "let me say, 'no argument,' just as long as you agree that if we don't get anywhere using your idea, we try mine."

"Certainly," he said. "That's fair."

"Well, it's getting a bit late, and I don't think either of us has a clear idea of where we're going from here. Why don't we think about it for awhile before we continue?"

"I'm all for that," he replied. "Right now, I'm a little too tired to do much creative thinking anyway. What do you say we take a bath and relax for the rest of the evening?"

She agreed, and soon there could be heard the splashing of water and the bubbly voices of two people very much in love. They didn't know exactly where their quest would lead them, but they felt they had to at least try to use their God-given intelligence to figure out the puzzle of life. They knew that existence has meaning, but they weren't sure how to explain it.

So, this was this their plan: *to allocate some time, perhaps a weekend, and try to find for themselves a reasonable explanation for the meaningfulness of existence.*

3

Finding A Trinity

Existence! That would be their starting point. During the next few days, Tom and Molly spent considerable time thinking about what 'existence' really means. They were caught up in their intriguing quest and decided to leave Kerry with Grandma and Grandpa the following weekend to allow them the freedom they desired to delve into their project without interruption.

Actually, this would be the first time in a long time that they would leave their son with a baby sitter. Neither Tom nor Molly believed much in leaving little ones with baby sitters, although Grandma often begged for an opportunity to keep her grandson for a few days. They realized, too, that there must be some exceptions to their rule; and this was one they considered right.

Friday night soon arrived and they were eager for the weekend that lay ahead. As planned, Kerry was left with Grandma and Grandpa; and Tom and Molly were free to pursue their goal. Soon enough, however, each could play Socrates, but for a beginning – no thinking.

With a glint in her eyes that meant, "you can't get away from me now," she pursued her pleasure. Tom was ready for her 'joyful irritation' and succumbed to her assault without resistance.

If she had not started their evening in this aggressive way, he was prepared to be the tiger. This time, however, she was the aggressor; and it pleased him that she felt free enough to occasionally make the advances.

On those occasions, she would often say, "Satisfaction guaranteed!" More often than not, she had lived up to that pledge admirably. Now and then she'd give her guarantee of satisfaction the moment he arrived home from work. He recognized this as her 'love code' and would bathe early in anticipation of a delightful evening, knowing he could look forward to her most intimate love acts. It had become her way of saying, "I'm in the mood, Honey! Be ready!"

On this night, with no duties but to themselves, they loved a little longer than usual. It was not late, however, when they, relaxed and refreshed, launched their planned search for answers. ***Enter the Socratic Twins!***

"What quality best defines existence?" asked Molly, as she sipped a cup of fresh coffee.

"Certainly, anything that exists has a 'being ness' about it, so to speak," Tom replied. "If something exists, it is in a state of being. However, I don't think that simple knowledge advances us any."

"I agree. There must be something that would tell us more."

"Maybe we could help our cause if we answer the question, existence is a statement of what?" suggested Tom. "What logically would follow if something exists?"

"I think I have an idea!"

"Alright," he said, "what is it?"

"Truth!"

"Truth?"

"Yes, truth," she said again. If something exists, it can be said to be true or have truth. Isn't that so?"

"I guess it is, but where does that lead us?"

"I'm not sure," she replied, "but I think it's something substantial."

"It may well be," he agreed. "When you think about it, it says a lot more than being ness. Existence and being are really the same thing, but truth is definitely a distinct idea from existence, even though they must exist simultaneously."

Molly desired a definition. "What is truth? I mean, in your opinion, what is truth?"

"Truth, " he answered, "can be nothing more than a fact of existence."

"Fact of existence?" she questioned. "Maybe so, but I think a better explanation would be an affirmation of existence." Molly was pleased with her Socratic sound. She had so enjoyed the discourses of Plato as offered by Socrates a few years back. To her, that may be how Socrates would have described truth – an affirmation of existence.

But Tommy Socrates wanted her to clarify such an opinion. "Why do you say that?"

"Because, Honey," she replied, "when you say that something is true, you affirm it to exist or say that it does. Anything that exists is affirmable. Therefore, truth must be an affirmation of existence."

He pondered her answer for a moment – and then, "Sorry, I disagree. Would you say that an act of affirmation is an act of an intellect?"

"Yes, I guess I would."

"And that an affirmation process presupposes that there is an agent around to do the affirming?"

"Yes," she said.

"Then accordingly," he replied, "nothing can be affirmed unless there is someone to affirm it. In that case, only those things whose existence is affirmed by some intellect can, in reality, be true. No, My Dear, I can't buy that. It seems to me that truth cannot be made dependent upon someone's intellect.

"Things must have truth of themselves," he continued. "To say that your cup of coffee doesn't exist or isn't true unless you or I or someone else actually affirms that it's so is just not acceptable. That cup is true regardless whether or not anyone is around to acknowledge it. To define truth as a fact of existence does not make what is true dependent upon any intellect."

"I guess if you really analyze it," Molly responded, "what you say is correct. Actually, there aren't many who would stop to analyze it."

"No, there aren't; and we would have been among the multitude if we hadn't decided to go on our quest."

"We may have gained an inch or two," she said, "but merely coming to a greater understanding of truth doesn't mean much."

"I'm betting, though," he responded, "that this little discovery, if you wish to call it that, will lead us to more significant notions about life and its meaning."

"I certainly hope so. Where do we go from here?"

"I think we could probably delve into what makes a thing true, or what makes it what it is," he replied. "Have you ever thought about that? For example, if we were to analyze a salad, what could we say makes it up? It seems to me if we know the answer to that, we can know why it exists as a salad and not as something else – like a rock. What contributes to the truth of a salad? Am I getting through to you, Honey?"

"I think so," she replied. "You want to know what it is that causes a thing to be identified for what it is. Using your example, a salad is what it is because it contains a mixture of certain ingredients, namely fruits or vegetables or both. A salad exists as a fact of existence, or as a 'salad truth,' so to speak, only when this condition is present."

"Very nicely put," he responded, "but I'm after something more general than that. I think maybe I could say it this way. As I see it, a thing is what it is or is true in its own identity when the necessary goods of its identity exist in the conditions necessary.

"Getting back to the salad," he continued, "let's say that we have available some lettuce, tomatoes, and cucumbers. When these elements are mixed together in a cut fashion or condition, we have what is called a 'salad'. Without these elements, our particular salad couldn't exist. This idea pertains to everything, though, not just a salad."

He continued. "A rock is what it is because of the goods or properties of its specific matter, combined with a principle of adhesion – or cohesion. A given life is what it is because of certain elements of matter or flesh, along with a particular principle of life. Regardless what you name, it can be said that it is true in its totality and specific identity only if possesses its necessary goods or goodness."

"Correct me if I am wrong, Tom, but I get the message from that last comment of yours that you're equating the terms of 'goods' and 'goodness'."

"You're reading me right, My Dear. Don't you think they should be equated?"

"To tell you the truth, I'm not sure," Molly responded. "It seems to me that 'goods' has a different connotation than 'goodness' in that goods refers to specific parts or properties, and 'goodness' refers to the idea of the rightness or value of a thing in relation to something else. 'Goodness' expresses an entirely different notion to me than 'goods'."

Tom paused a moment. "Goodness, in the realm of moral judgment, does mean rightness and benevolence and kindness and a host of other things, but goodness in the scope of my interpretation can be correctly understood as the state of a thing having its necessary goods, as the goods or properties of a thing taken together.

"I think it's entirely proper to say that if a thing has its goods, it has 'goodness' like a thing has 'trueness' if it's true. It's in that sense that goodness must be understood in the context of my argument. When I say goodness, then, I am speaking not of moral judgment, but of a thing's goods or properties, collectively understood."

"In that light," she remarked, "goodness is what makes a thing go, what makes it tick, what gives it its being in the first place. It is not the value of a thing after it is made, but rather the composition of a thing before it becomes what it is."

"That's right, Sweetheart. Goodness is, as it were, the first principle of being because only if a thing's goods exist in their proper relation, can identities flow."

"You know, Tom, now that you've explained your idea of the nature of goodness, I find myself liking your explanation much better than the preconceived notion I had of it. It sure simplifies things to think that achieving goodness as a goal in life is really based on possessing the necessary tools in life, so to speak, to allow the fullest possible existence.

"It stands to reason that people are good, not because of what they've done, but because of what they are. And what they are is entirely dependent upon their having it all together, upon their seeing things in proper perspective, upon their disposing themselves to be open to gratefully experiencing the many blessings of life.

"Goodness," she added, "is what you possess before you act virtuously, not what you express because of your virtue. You don't act virtuously and therefore are good. You are good and therefore act virtuously."

"Molly, I can't tell you how gratifying it is to me that you've obviously grasped the meaning of goodness as I refer to it. It's important that we both understand our terminology in the same way. Otherwise, we will end up batting at the breeze."

"That's for sure," she agreed. "Alright, let's go over what we have determined so far, to put our discoveries in proper perspective."

"OK," he said. "We started with the idea of existence, from which we subsequently deduced the notion of truth, which in turn we defined as a 'fact of existence'. Then we concluded that in order for anything to exist and be true, it must have its proper goods or goodness to exist specifically in its own identity. That's where we are at this point."

"Now," pondered Molly, thinking out loud, "if a thing has the necessary elements to be what it is, it must therefore possess a resulting identity, a specific oneness or unity about it. Right?"

"Unity," mused Tom. "That does seem to be another distinct idea, completely separate from truth or goodness. Certainly if a thing has the necessary goods or elements to exist in its own identity, those elements must be unified. I'll buy your idea of unity being an essential characteristic of existence – or of an existing thing."

"Given your acceptance of unity as a third distinct characteristic of existence," Molly continued, "what would be our next consideration?"

Tom thought a moment. "Fundamentally speaking, I don't think there is anything more. I don't think we can be more complete about a thing in general than to acknowledge that it has its necessary properties, or at least a necessary property, or goodness, that it has a specific unique identity or oneness, and that it is a complete fact of existence in the totality of its unity and parts. In other words, we have determined that the three basic elements of existence are goodness, unity, and truth. Can you be more complete than that, considering that we are trying to find qualities that must be true of all existence?"

"How about beauty?" Molly questioned. "I realize that was my original suggestion for a starting point and I may be a bit prejudiced, but can you deny that everything is beautiful? Don't you think that beauty can be attributed to all that is?"

"You have heard it said, Dear Spouse, that beauty is in the eye of the beholder. I think that's true."

"Oh, do you now?" she quipped. "You don't think I'm beautiful of myself without someone else having to say it?"

"You can think it of yourself, alright, but don't you think you are a little biased?" he said, gently poking her in the ribs. "Anyway, regardless of whether you are beautiful or not, beauty can still be no more than a characteristic attributable to existence, not an essential element thereof.

"Beauty, like color, for instance, is a quality not inherent in an existent thing, but rather something that may be attributable to that entity by some outside source. Color is not in the thing seen. Rather, it is in the eyes seeing. Likewise, beauty is not in the thing valued, but is in the eyes of the one making the judgment. Otherwise, there would be no such thing as color blindness. Red would come out as red, no matter who is seeing it.

"Unlike beauty and color," he added, "the qualities of goodness, unity, and truth are inherent in an existent, and not at all dependent upon some outside source. Therefore, they are not mere attributes of existence, but rather essential elements of existence. Do you understand what I am driving at?"

"I think I'm beginning to," Molly replied, "and I'm also beginning to see the wonder of it all. You know I did not understand until we discovered it for ourselves why some of those old thinkers called the qualities of goodness, unity, and truth the 'transcendental' attributes of being. That's a good word and very meaningful when you think about it. Goodness, unity and truth are transcendental attributes because they transcend the importance of all attributes simply because they are inherent to all being, whereas no other attributes are."

"I'd say that is a pretty keen observation," he said, "but I think I would quarrel with those old thinkers, as you call them, for even referring to the qualities of goodness, unity, and truth as attributes. An attribute, by definition, should mean 'something bestowed,' although it is used much more loosely now. The transcendental qualities, as you call them, are not bestowed by another, and, therefore, are not mere attributes. They are essential, elementary, and inherent in anything that exists – in a word - elements."

"I don't know about that, Dear. I think you are splitting hairs there. What difference does it make if we call them attributes or elements?"

"You're right, Molly. It really matters not – just as long as we have a better feeling for existence because of them. I think our discovery of what might be called the *trinity of existence* could well serve as an appropriate breaking point. What do you say we hang it up for tonight?"

Molly was not ready just yet to retire. "Do you suppose it's the same for God?" she asked. "I mean, shouldn't God have the same trinity of elements as anything?"

"For sure, My Dear. For sure!"

"What a beautiful thought!" remarked Molly. "God and everything are all linked together via the same elements of Goodness, Unity, and Truth. Isn't it marvelous?"

"Yes, it sure is, Honey," he said. "Perhaps that trinity is the exact same as the so called *Blessed Trinity* in God. It would seem so. Goodness as the eternal source of all that is could be equated to the Father. Unity could be equated to that which comes from the Father – The Son. And the togetherness of Father and Son, of Goodness and Unity, could be seen as emerging as Truth – the so called *Holy Spirit*."

"I'd bet it's so, Tom! It is not so difficult to understand. Is it? Do you suppose that our enjoyment of life should be inspired by the existence of a trinity in God and man and everything?"

"If only we humans would pay attention to the beauty of it all," her husband replied. "Rather than hurt our fellow man, just be aware that he or she has goodness, unity, and truth. The notions are so clear and yet men hate each other because of thoughts of inequality. Wouldn't it be nice if people realized that Heaven is really and truly at hand because we all share in the ultimate Goodness, Unity, and Truth of God – a very real Trinity?"

"Or at least we share in the same notions," Molly commented. "We all have goodness, unity, and truth – God, you, me, everyone. It seems to me that we all should rejoice in that. Tom, let me bow down to that trinity in you. I will love you even more now than before – knowing that we share in such a *Blessed Trinity*!"

Tom smiled and reached out to embrace his lovely Molly – and then he kissed her and said, *"and Blessed be the Trinity in you too, Sweetheart. And Blessed be the Trinity in you!"*

4

Expression and Identity

Surprised to find herself awakening at such a late hour, Molly could hardly believe it was already past 9. Late as it was, she decided to let Tom sleep while she went to the kitchen to make coffee. Both she and Tom loved to start each morning with a cup of coffee. Tom was sold on the necessity of at least eight glasses of water a day and had two before he had his first cup of coffee, but Molly generally started her day with coffee. They had only been married nearly six years, but Tom was confident that, in time, he could persuade Molly to adopt his water regimen too.

Molly couldn't help but turn her thoughts to her son, wondering if he had given his Grandma any trouble the night before. It was, after all, the first night in a long time that he had spent the night away from home. There had been other occasions, but only a few.

Molly was grateful. Except for Grandma's willingness – and eagerness – to keep Kerry for the weekend, they would have had to find some other way to conduct their intellectual quest; however, good friends, Joe and Liz and their five year old daughter, Elise, would have been more than happy to take Kerry as well. Then there was Sam and Nellie next door who would have been extremely happy to take Kerry too – or at least, Sam, as Nellie was seriously ill, suffering from the debilitating disease of diabetes. In truth, Tom and Molly would have had a lot of baby sitters, but they chose Grandma and Grandpa this time.

With the coffee brewed, Molly delightfully light of heart, returned to the bedroom and her sleeping husband, carrying a tray with two hot, steaming cups, warm rolls and butter.

Sitting by the bed, Molly nudged him, suggesting that he share coffee and rolls with her. The aroma of the coffee almost made him forget his ritual of several glasses of water before breakfast, but he was quick to recover and hurriedly skipped off to the bath to complete that act before returning to his lovely Molly and her early morning presents.

As usual, Tom was naked. He never slept with a stitch, regardless of how cold it might get. Molly had come to enjoy the naked state as well, especially since the birth of Kerry three years before when the sight of her naked baby made her want to be naked too, however, she was also fond of pajamas. As he returned to the bed and stretched out, sitting up enough to consume Molly's offerings, she enjoyed looking at his body. Reflecting back on the night before, the trinity of goodness, unity, and truth seemed to make that body seem so much more. It was almost as if a good fairy had slipped into Molly and touched her with a wand that allowed her to see Tom as she had never seen him before. It was almost as if God Himself was present in her bedroom and lying right next to Tom; and, of course, it was true. God was there in the two of them.

Molly had been lying in the bed waiting for Tom to return from his early morning watering, but as she looked upon her naked partner, she rose and slipped out of her pajamas. "You look too good to be alone like that," she said. "I trust you could use some company." Then the two of them were naked; and God was still there, embracing both.

"You look so good, so unified as the one you are, and so true," she remarked. "It just doesn't seem right that I should overlook that remarkable trinity in you." Then she lay down next to him and the two trinities bonded as one as the two sipped their coffee and munched on the hot rolls – and each other.

Before long, the breakfast was over and Tom and Molly showered together, then cleaned up the few dirty dishes from their meal, and retired to the living room to continue their quest. It didn't seem right to have God at a distance and try to hide from Him. So, out of respect for the Divine Trinity in their presence, they remained unhidden. Of course, two fresh hot cups of coffee accompanied them, which were settled nicely on the coffee table in front of them.

Molly started the session. Leaning forward to look into his eyes, while letting her hand fall where it may, she asked the big question. "Why?" she asked.

"Why? Why what?" he replied.

"Tom, we tried to research what things are last night. Perhaps we should try to research why things happen today. I mean, why do people act as they do? Why are some people like you and me, loving? Why are some others, like Hitler and his crew, hateful? Why do we act as we do? Why do people hate? Why do people love?"

"That shouldn't be too hard to figure out," he replied. "I must admit I think it is a powerful notion to resolve. Why do we do things? Since you are the one to suggest it, do you have any idea how to begin?"

"Yes, I think I do," she answered. "I think we can logically determine the answer to this question if we ask the question of ourselves in causing something to exist. We talked about existence last night. In a way, all things that exist are made to do so. Maybe we can find out why people do things by finding out what motivates them to create, what motivates them to make things exist."

"What do you mean, things?" he asked

"Things, anything, tangible and intangible. Why do I make a tangible thing like a car? Why do I make an intangible thing like love – or hate? It seems to me that all things that exist are made to exist by someone or something."

"You are right there, My Dear," Tom responded. "You know we don't ordinarily think of love or hate in the same way we think of a car. We make cars. We admit that. But we don't see ourselves as making hate or making love. But I guess we do because they exist – and they can't exist unless they are made. That is absolutely brilliant. I am proud of you to realize it."

"Well, I don't know if it's brilliant or not, but it is an observation. If I make a dress, why would I do it? The answer to that may be that I make it because I want to or because I need to."

"That's good for a starter," he said. "Let me cite several more examples. For one, I am going to build a house. For another, I am going to write a song. For another, I am going to fry a chicken. Accordingly, I might build a house, like you made your dress, because of simple desire or because of necessity – or maybe for both reasons. I would probably write a song because of desire also, as well as fry a chicken, although I might do both of those things out of necessity. If song writing is my business, I guess I would have to write songs."

"It seems to me," Molly expressed, "that almost anything we do to cause something to exist could be either from desire or necessity or both. We couldn't say, however, that either desire or necessity could be dictated universally as reasons for being. Maybe there isn't a single reason that could be applied to all existence."

"Perhaps, but maybe there is some universal character that could be applied to both the reasons of desire and necessity. It could be said, could it not, that both desire and necessity are expressions? If I say I need something, I am expressing the fact that I cannot do without that something; and if I say I desire something, I am expressing a wish."

"Maybe you have something there," Molly agreed. "It would seem that whether a thing exists because of necessity or simply because of desire, it would definitely exist as the expression or outgrowth of something else. Regardless of the source of the expression, it can definitely be said that the reason any given thing exists must be because it is the expression of something else."

"I am not so sure that what we say is true," suggested Tom. "I mean, let's take the case of an accident. An accident, as an unintended happening, may be neither a necessity nor a desire. Therefore, it may not be the expression of anything."

"Couldn't you say, Honey, that an accident may be due to the weakness of the subject causing the accident? Therefore, it could be said to be an expression of the subject's weakness."

"Yes, I guess you could. That would seem to indicate that we were wrong when we determined that all existence had to be due to either desire or necessity."

"That is not important, is it?" commented Molly. "The only thing of significance is that, even though there are many particular reasons why things might exist, the universal and general reason is that they exist as expressions of outside agents, and nothing, absolutely nothing, except for maybe 'expression' itself – if there can be such a thing – can defy that law."

"That means you and me, too," he added. "We also exist because we are the expressions of something else. But what does that really mean? What is the significance of being the expression of something else?"

"To answer that, I think we have to know what we are an expression of." Molly was sure they were making some progress, as she paused and took in the expression of the sight of Tom's body. Nature was doing well, expressing herself through

Tom. She did not say it, but she thought it, as she smiled at him. "The particular thing that expresses us," she continued, "should indicate our significance."

Tom caught her smile and knew immediately that she was thinking on two separate rails at the moment – one of her was thinking about the subject of discussion and another of her was thinking about the expression of his masculinity as it had received a momentary glance a moment ago – though she was now focused on his eyes. He returned the smile, letting their smiles meet in agreement that the expression of Nature is mighty fine. "Maybe so," he remarked, "but I think the way to go about it would be to analyze what our expressions mean to us, and then maybe we can understand what we might mean as expressions of something else."

She agreed. "That seems fitting. Alright, you artist you. You ask me to pose for you in the nude, since that is the way you like me best, and then you try to recreate me on canvas. In other words, you are expressing yourself through the medium of a painting. Why would you want to do that?"

"Sweetheart, the reason is pure and simple. I love you and therefore I want to decorate the house with you. Since you won't fit on the wall and on the couch at the same time, I have to find another way to spread you around. For that reason, I paint you so that I can see you in more places than one. For me, it would be an expression of my wanting you more than I can have you."

"Then you would say that you would paint a picture of me because you love me and your painting would be an expression of love?" she said.

"Absolutely!"

"Suppose I call you a bum, and taking it to heart, you get angry and clout me one. What would you be expressing in that instance? It certainly would not be love."

"No, it certainly wouldn't. In that case, my action would be an expression of anger – or maybe even hatred. Hatred and love are both expressions, even though they are opposites."

"True enough," she replied. "It seems to me that the eyes of the beholder determine the expression. The way I see you is the way I will react toward you. If I see you as offensive or ugly, I won't want to tolerate you, even though in reality, you may not deserve the reaction or expression I give you."

"That may well be true," he commented, "but it could also be true that I may do something offensive that would cause you to see me as something unworthy and ugly. Therefore, it is both the subject and the object that determines the expression."

"But, Dear, you will have to agree," she said, "that the prime determinant of an expression is the subject, simply because, in our example, in the end you will see me in the way you have been molded to see me – but it will still be you, in spite of the many influences, that will be doing the seeing and the expressing."

"I can't disagree with that," he replied, "but where is this discussion leading us?"

Molly did not hesitate to answer. "I think into something significant. You said you thought that in order to understand what we would mean as expressions of something else, we would have to analyze what our expressions mean to us. So, we have determined that our expressions mean to us what we have been molded to make them. Basically, it seems to me, expressions as products of a given agent could qualify as characteristics of hate or love."

"Maybe so," he replied, "depending upon what you mean by hate and love."

"To put it as simply as I can," she said, "to hate something is to want to destroy it. To love is to want to build or be constructive. Hate is destruction. Love is construction. If you love something, you want to at least maintain it, if not generate more of it. If you hate something, you do not want it to exist in the slightest degree. You want to eliminate it altogether. Depending on the way I have been molded to see you, I will either love you or hate you in some degree."

"Alright, I accept that, at least for the moment," he replied. "Are you not trying to say that if we can determine ourselves as expressions of love or hate, we can know something about our expression, and, therefore, why he or she or it would want us to exist? It follows that if we can know why we are being expressed, we will know the reason for our existence."

"Oh, sage of sages," she quipped, "you have hit the nail on the head. Now, if you can, tell me why I exist. Am I an expression of love or hate?"

"According to your line of thinking, My Dear, it would be impossible for you to be an expression of hate since it is obvious that you are not being eliminated from the realm of existence, but rather allowed to exist. Evidently, you are an expression of love since your expresser made you into something and maintains you in that existence."

"But who is my expresser?"

"In general terms, I guess you might say Nature," he replied. "You are a product like everything else we can touch and see and feel of Nature."

"Nature must indeed love us since she allows us to exist in the first place, then maintains us as her expressions," she added.

"I think it would be more aptly put to say that Mother Nature loves, and therefore she expresses something positive, and that something positive includes you and me. She couldn't be expressing hate since she is not seeking to eliminate us. Since we exist, we must obviously be expressions of love."

"I'm not sure we can go that far, Honey. Can we really say that everything that exists, by virtue of its very existence, must be positive, and therefore an expression of love? How about pain or sorrow? Can we say these are expressions of love?"

"Maybe we can't," he replied, "but Mother Nature, the true expresser, can."

"You will have to explain yourself on that one."

"Look," he said. "To us, pain is something negative and not at all a love expression, but Mother Nature does not take into account the way we might feel things. A germ to us would be considered offensive because it causes discomfort, but to Mother Nature, a germ must be just another facet of her positive expression."

"You know," Molly retorted, "I have never thought of it that way, but I'll bet you're right. Mother Nature expresses herself in individual existences, and it may make no difference to her that those individual existences are sometimes at odds with each other."

"Alright, then," said Tom, "we have determined that we are expressions of Mother Nature, whatever that might be. We haven't come to any realization of the exact reality of Mother Nature, but merely that, whatever she might be, we are given reality as her expressions. How we are fashioned is not important, only why we are fashioned. We have determined that we are fashioned because Mother Nature loves, and therefore, expresses herself necessarily by way of construction, or maybe, 'creation' – and we are simply manifestations of that love or creation."

Molly, looking a bit puzzled, commented. "That summarizes this discussion fairly well, My Love, but one thing bothers me. If we can be said to be expressions of Mother Nature, does it not follow that for this to be so, she has to exist as an expression itself? And if that's the case, of what might she be an expression?"

"That is indeed a good question. It would seem that, since she is obviously being maintained in existence rather than being destroyed, she must be a love expression of something else."

Molly countered. "But since we really don't know the exact reality of Mother Nature, how can we possibly know the expresser of which she is herself an expression – other than she has to be an expression of love?"

"I don't know," he answered, "but let's not tackle that problem until later, if at all."

"I agree. We have covered enough for one morning session, especially since we got started so late. I really think our quest is yielding a lot of fruit, though."

"I think so too," he replied, "but it's sad that more people don't go on similar quests. Our minds are really very powerful, but few people use them to think things out for themselves. The riches of the mind are unfathomable and are rarely tapped to any appreciable degree."

"Riches of the mind, riches of the flesh," Molly remarked, "are really one in kind. We see the mind and flesh as somehow separated and at odds with one another, as if challenging each other for expression, but it seems such a waste to me."

"To me too," Tom enjoined. "Philosophy would have us believe we are all one, being equal expressions of a common expresser, but religion would often have us believe we are all separate, some deserving of happiness and some not. It's too bad people do not think for themselves a lot more than they do. Then they would not be subject to so many ups and downs and pressures from those who think we are unequal."

Tom bent down and kissed his wife in her middle; and while talking to her middle and not her eyes, he said, "Molly, I love you. I love all that is you. I love all that Mother Nature offers in you. I love the mystery of your womanhood – and the scent of it too."

"And I, you, Sweetheart," she said, as she gently pushed his head further into her middle. *"You like it there – and I like it that you like it. Taste it, if you like, while I close my eyes and think of God."*

5

Packing God into a Little Hole

And thinking of God was good. While Tom made love to Mother Nature through Molly, Molly meditated. Her meditation was quiet – with none of the ordinary chants of ecstasy. It was not so much a personal thing she and her husband were doing, but rather a natural thing. Molly was not thinking so much of herself as some isolated entity within Nature, but as one – just one – of the numberless little stars of the universe. It all meant so much to belong.

One of many. That is the thought that occupied Molly's mind as her husband was being familiar with her. I am one of myriads of girls in this world – all alike and the same in everything that matters. Sure, Molly delighted in her uniqueness, too, but being different, though nice, was no more of the total pie of life than one piece of ten. Molly felt that nine tenths of the pie of life was about being the same as all others; and only one tenth, at most, should deal with being different.

Tom was thinking along the same lines as he pressed his tongue in between the folds of Molly's vestibule of life, but he was making love to womanhood, not just Molly. They often commented to one another that when they made love to one another, it was like doing it for the world – especially for the world of humans. Each of them represented their gender making love to the opposite gender. It was very personal, but it was also very impersonal at the same time. They felt that they were representing couples everywhere in honoring the wonder of life.

Tom often argued that involvement with life and feeling the flesh for the sake of the soul should be like a mandate for every human. Souls occupy bodies for a reason – and that reason is to use the body to know the soul. How could any-one know their soul by ignoring the body? That seemed to be the prescription of the ages – know your soul by avoiding your body. At one time, Tom had believed it; but that was before he became liberated by his thoughts of reason. Molly also believed it before her marriage to Tom, but talking with Tom and adventuring with Tom while always talking about it in intellectual and spiritual terms had liberated Molly as well.

In time, Tom finished nipping on nature's buds and Molly finished with her meditation. They had enjoyed their various refreshments and were ready to go another round with their thinking things out.

"It's been good so far," Molly commented, "but where do we go from here?"

"Would you believe, infinity?" Tom suggested.

"Infinity?"

"Yes, infinity, or the endless or the whole or whatever."

"The whole?" she replied. "The whole of what?"

"The whole of existence," he answered. "You and I are part of the whole of existence. Maybe we should investigate that for a bit. Who knows what we will find?"

"I suspect you have an idea where this is leading. I sure do not," she said, "but I'll play along. You seem to be equating the whole with infinity. Is that correct?"

"Yes, that's right. I'm just thinking that maybe we should try to investigate that which we call 'God' since we failed to do much with it in our last session. Maybe by analyzing the infinite, which God supposedly is, we can come to understand more about God."

"Like I say, Honey, I'm game," she replied. "Oh, Master, continue! But if we don't get anywhere with this, I have a little story to tell you about God. OK?"

"OK," he said, with a bit of a grin. "Let me give it a shot. When I say infinite, My Friend, I'm really meaning all that is. All that is – is the infinite. Given that definition of infinite, no one can quarrel that there is such a thing as infinite because no one can quarrel with the idea that there is an everything. Existence is infinite in that it includes all that is – without exception. Let's just say that existence cannot limit its membership. All things that are must be included; and no thing that exists can be excluded."

"So we know that existence, in general, must be infinite," she responded. "What does that mean to us?"

"It means for one thing that, as products of existence, we must eventually trace ourselves to being expressions of this infinity called 'existence'. It seems to me that if we can understand our relationship as finite beings to the Infinite Being, we can come to know why that Infinity chooses to express us. Then we can know the reason for our existence."

"I'm all ears," she said. "Go on."

"I think that to determine our relationship to the Infinite as an expression of the Infinite, we'll need to determine what any expression does for its expresser."

"That's true," she agreed, pondering out loud. "If I express myself through a puppet I make or a portrait I paint, that expression could be called a reflection of me, could it not?"

"Yes."

"And if I eat a meal or swim a lake, I am also reflecting something about myself. In one case I might be reflecting my ability to eat or my desire to eat; and in the other case, I might be reflecting ability or desire too, as well as enjoyment or any number of other things. Essentially, what I express reflects me in some way."

"So, you are saying that an expression essentially reflects something of the expresser." Tom thought a moment. "Would you also say that an expression adds something to the expresser?"

"Not necessarily, but I guess that would depend on what you mean by that. If you were to say that an expression changes the expresser insofar as there is something about him after the expression that wasn't true before the expression, then you could probably say that the expression added something.

"However, at the same time," she went on, "you could lose something because of an expression. For instance the expression of sorrow could cause you to lose a tear at the same time that it was adding a different mood to your life."

"Maybe a better word would be 'modification'," he replied. "It could definitely be said that to some extent, an expression, whether it adds or detracts, modifies or changes the expresser."

"Yes, I think you're right," she agreed.

"Dealing with us in relation to existence, then," he said, "you would have to say that existence as our ultimate expresser underwent a modification because of those expressions, and undergoes modification any time and every time a new thing comes into being."

"That would definitely seem to be the case," she responded, "but it seems to me there's a contradiction somewhere."

"Oh! What might that be?"

"Did we not agree that existence cannot limit its membership and therefore is without limitation, or in other words, is infinite?"

"Yes, we did agree."

"Existence is limited to what is, is it not? I mean it can't take in what will be – or even what was. It can only take in what is now."

"Are you questioning the existence of an absolute infinite being that cannot be limited, even by the past or future?" he asked.

"Yes, I am – or at least I am saying that existence defined as 'all that is' can't possibly be that absolute infinity since it is definitely limited to the now."

"Alright. For the sake of argument, let's assume that position. If there is no such thing as an absolute infinite being, then the contrary is true. There only exists finite beings. To my understanding, if something is finite, it necessarily is limited. Finite means 'limited'. If it is limited, it is therefore dependent for its very existence upon something else. And if it's dependent upon something else and not completely self-sustaining, it must have had a beginning."

"I agree so far," she said. "Continue."

"If everything finite has a beginning, wherefrom could the finite world ultimately come? It can't come from itself, or else it would be self-sustaining, which by its very nature, it is not. It can't come from another finite world, since we are talking about the ultimate in finite existence, and you can't go further back than that. So, My Dear, to whom or what must the ultimate finite existence, which by its very nature must have a beginning, owe its existence?"

"As you have so cogently illustrated," responded Molly, "the answer to that question cannot possibly be another finite existence – since no finite existence can meet the necessary condition of ultimately being its own cause."

"Exactly!" he chimed. "Does that not prove the need for an absolute infinity?"

"Yes, I guess it does, but we still don't know what the existence of absolute being means to us."

"That we have yet to establish," he replied.

"So, establish it if you can."

"Alright," he said. "We know that because the finite world exists, it does so because it is an expression of an absolute infinite being. Therefore, as part of that limited finite existence, we must be reflections of that being."

"And as a positive reflection or expression, we must somehow add to the character or glory or something of the Infinite," commented Molly. "Yet, that seems to be contradictory. If something is without the ability to be limited, then it must also be without the ability to change – because change, by its very nature, suggests limitation."

"I'm not sure I follow you," Tom said.

"Look," she explained, "does not change or modification suggest to you the notion of a beginning and an end?"

"Yes," he replied, "as a matter of fact, it does; and I think I can see what you are getting at. You're saying that because, by definition, an infinite being is without a beginning and is eternally self-sustaining, it could not possibly undergo change in any way. The objection is that to do so would be to impose limits on that infinity – and thereby destroy it of its infinite character."

"Correct!" she said. "Furthermore, the Infinite Being could not be involved with time because time is an effect of change. How, then, does the finite world have meaning if it is not an expression of the Infinite?"

"I guess I will have to admit that we are getting into territory we can't handle, Honey. We can know so much about our world and our meaning by applying our minds, but trying to figure out infinity, other than being assured it must have a Blessed Trinity of elements like everything else, we just can't go there."

"That doesn't mean we can't be enthralled with the idea of the Infinite and God," remarked Molly. "We can love God as something we know must exist – even as we realize we can't know what we love."

"I think you are right, My Love. The Infinite is such a mystery and will always be a mystery. No one can explain it – and anyone who claims some kind of dialogue with the Infinite should be ignored. So many get themselves into so much deep water by believing some who suspect that they had an encounter with the Infinite. At least, we know where to stop. The last thing I would do to Kerry is to try and tell him I know about the Infinite – because I don't."

"Nor do I, Dear Tom. Nor do I."

"Molly, you said that if we did not succeed to figure out the Infinite that you would have a story to tell. Well, we haven't. So, a story is in order. Let's hear it."

"It's a story my Dad told me a long time ago," she offered. "The story is about a little angel, disguised as a little boy, playing on a beach. Watching the little boy was a man who was pondering God. Of course, the little angel knew what the man was trying to do – explain God to himself. The man observed the little boy taking trips between the ocean and his little hole in the sand. With each trip the little boy would empty his bucket into the hole and go after another. After watching him for some time, the man who was pondering God couldn't help but become fascinated with the little boy. He finally asked the little boy what he was doing. The little boy told him that he was emptying the ocean into his little hole. The man told him that such a thing was impossible.

"The little angel boy just looked at him and said: *Sir, it would be easier for me to empty the ocean into my little hole than it would be for you to figure out God."*

6

Exploring Eternal Life

Her story about the little boy angel complete, Molly noticed that Tom was smiling. Her story was quite a good tale and it did what it was intended to do – satisfy Tom that *loving God does not require knowing God – just knowing about God*. What a wonderful thing it is to realize that we are part of an Infinite Being or Reality without really knowing what that means. Being part of Infinity – it meant everything to Molly. Maybe her Dad had satisfied her with that tale about the little boy on the beach and the pondering man long ago. Maybe it was at least partly because of that tale that she had the tremendous love for God that she had – a love she knew Tom shared.

Knowing that life is so full of God, how can one who loves want to keep their hands off of it? Molly often wondered why people who claim to love God and who offer that existence is created by God often treat life like it comes from something other than God. Molly had no reservations now about that. She knew that God was present – and that in some wonderful inexplicable way, both Tom and she were like gifts of that God. There was no stain in their relationship. How could there be if God was in it?

As Tom had done to her in the last break, Molly wanted to do now. Kissing her Tom and her God-send ever so warmly, she bent down and took his masculinity in her mouth. It was not a sordid thing she did. It was an expression of love – far deeper than any act of abstinence could possibly have been. The mystery of God was in her mouth. How could she not be exhilarated by that?

It did not have to go further than that. It never did between Molly and Tom. Somehow they realized that each of them was complete and they did not have to link to tell each other of a love they knew was already complete. Love is so easy when you do not complicate it with a sense of needing completion. Molly knew that – and so did Tom. Molly was holy. Tom was holy. Neither needed the other to become holier; and neither needed the other to feel complete.

It had not always been that way, though. At first, Molly felt that she needed to have Tom in her to feel completed – and Tom felt he needed to go into Molly too; but not for long. This was a couple who became caught up with the sense of the individual. They could not quite put their finger on it, but the simplicity of love without coitus somehow nurtured a sense of individual wholesomeness between them. **They had become as much brother and sister as husband and wife – allowing actual coitus only when an act of conception was desired.**

It sure did simplify life. Some might call it abstinence for lack of copulation, but Molly and Tom knew different. There was no abstinence between them. They loved freely and without inhibition, never having to concern themselves with unwanted pregnancies or timing or maneuvering that most couples have to confront. It was free and easy – and it was always with God in mind. Theirs was a Divine love as well as a human love. Somehow, Molly and Tom could not tell the difference. Was it

Divine? Was it human? For their love of God and their love of themselves, they knew it was both.

In only the second year of their marriage, Molly had lost her father. She had been extremely close to him, but so also had her mother. With her father's death, her mother became devastated. It was something about that scene that told Molly that she should never come to depend on Tom like her mother had depended on her father.

When two people love each other too much, they can lose a needed sense of solitary holiness. The key to knowing one is complete is to never completely depend on another. Anything that another can give is part of the one to whom it is given. There is no need to depend on another for any sense of individual completion. After Molly's Dad's death, that lesson became quite apparent to Molly; and she confided in Tom that she never wanted to become as dependent upon him as her mother had been on her father.

Molly and Tom had talked about it – and had decided on independence in marriage. They even marked the day as a kind of second anniversary – what they called their own Independence Day; and each year for four years now, on March 9th, they celebrated their independence from one another. Their real marital anniversary was September 3rd, but both saw March 9th as equally important.

Brother and sister! A rather liberated brother and sister, but that is how they lived – unless it was time for a little co-creation. Little Kerry had been co-created using the normal act of copulation. They were more than willing to make an exception. It was just that their independence of spirit dictated the regimen they chose for a normal course. It was all so simple; and Molly and Tom had the happiest of any lives of which they were aware.

Perhaps it could only work for some. Molly and Tom realized that, but they also realized that most married people never even consider being brother and sister in marriage. Maybe if they did, more husbands and wives would follow that course. It was not for Molly and Tom to concern themselves about what others do or do not do. They had long ago decided their own course. They told others about their decision, but it was for others to make of it what they wanted or could. Once told, it was enough to let others do as they chose.

Molly always enjoyed the intimacy of her mouth on Tom's unique parts, but when it was time for him to come, he was to let her know and her hand replaced her mouth on his virility and her mouth went to kissing. Once the kissing took over, she almost never looked at what was happening in the lap area because kissing was really important. Let what happens happen in the lap area, Molly argued, but never did she want to miss kissing while it happened. Molly loved all the acts of love making, but nothing pleased her as much as kissing. Other ways of loving could come between the kisses, but kissing was like bookends for Molly. She always wanted to begin and end any intimacy with a kiss.

And now the act had been completed with the kissing. It was time to resume the discussion. "I suppose that Mr. Socrates could use a fresh cup of coffee."

"You bet, Mrs. Socrates, but first I have to pee." All the water that Tom drank earlier was pressing for release.

"Me too," she said.

Following their bathroom break, Molly retreated to the living room to fetch their coffee cups for refill as Tom stepped out back for a few minutes. They had a back yard that lent itself to privacy and they spent a good deal of time out back when they could, watching the squirrels munching on the sunflower seeds that the birds would drop to the ground from the bird feeder Tom had attached to a tree limb.

It was springtime. The weather was comfortably warm and it was a real joy to be out with Mother Nature. Tom found immense pleasure in just being a part of it all and knew that the wonderful God that the man in Molly's story could not fathom was there present in all the trees and evergreens that populated their little landscape. Mother Nature is God's child. We are Mother Nature's children. So, that makes us God's grandchildren. It is a way of looking at the big picture.

Soon Molly joined Tom out back. "I see you are watching the birds and squirrels again. I knew you would be. I see no reason why we should not continue our quest out here. We could even add to our suntan while doing so."

So, the mini convention to discuss the meaning of life was moved to the outdoors. It was still early enough in the day that hot coffee would not be out of place. Later, they would resort to coke, but for now, it was still coffee time. They had a small patio in the back, with a gas grill to the side. They would probably use that grill later in the day and fix some steaks for an evening meal. But for now, Tom and Molly settled down around the round tin table in their back yard and began to add another round to their fantastic quest.

Molly had been thinking about what she would like to talk about. "Honey, do you think we might be able to discuss human conduct – or what it should be, using reason alone to define it?"

"That may prove to be some order," he said, "but what have we got to lose?"

She continued. "It seems to me that we have determined that the nature of the Infinite is simply to exist, and that it would be impossible for the Infinite not to exist – or to effect nonexistence."

"Agreed," he replied.

"You might say that the Infinite wants existence, and anything that would counter that wish would necessarily be contrary to that wish or act, and could be considered improper conduct – or conduct not in accord with existence or the Infinite. As we said before, the act of creating or constructing or making something is an act of love, whereas the act of destruction or negation of existence, so to speak, is an act of hate. Therefore, to be in accord with our reason for being, we should cooperate with the act of the Infinite – or simply, love."

Tom responded. "Anything which is not in accord with the nature of the Infinite – which, for all practical purposes, is simply, existence – would be considered improper conduct. That's your argument. Right?"

"Yes, it is," she replied. "That may be oversimplification, but does it not illustrate by the use of unaided reason what proper conduct should be?"

"I might agree that it might determine the essence of good behavior, but so what? Your argument does not demonstrate a preference for virtue or good conduct. What difference would it make if I choose to violate the rules of good behavior?"

"Maybe none," she replied, "but would you agree that if reason can explain the basis for unhappiness, reason could also dictate the basis for happiness?"

"Yes, I think I would agree with that, although I don't see how such a discussion would tie into our study."

"Come now, Tom! You don't really think that happiness is irrelevant. Do you?"

"Of course, it's relevant," he responded. "It's just that happiness is not objective. Happiness is simply being comfortable, and different people seek comfort, and therefore, happiness, in different ways. Happiness is not something you can dissect. It's like to each, his own. Certainly what might make you happy may thoroughly irritate me – and vice versa."

"Happiness, in general, could be determined to have somewhat of a specific nature, though," Molly argued. "You said it yourself. Happiness is comfort; and if that is so, unhappiness must be discomfort."

"Alright," he said. "I'll play your game. What can we say is the nature of comfort?"

"Being at ease with a specific situation," she replied, "or being disposed to accept or enjoy a specific circumstance or reality."

"And if you are not so disposed, you'll experience discomfort and unhappiness. Is that what you are saying?"

"Yes, it is," she answered, "but what is more important is that if you're indisposed to a given circumstance, you can't but be frustrated in any attempt to identify with it."

"Would you mind explaining what you mean by that?"

"Not at all," she responded. "Let me give you an example. Let's say you have a dislike for a certain food, although you know that by eating this distasteful item, you will benefit with better health. You realize, then, that theoretically at least, it would be to your advantage to eat the item, in spite of your dislike for it."

She continued. "Your indisposition, or close mindedness, toward eating the item may cause you to react in one of two possible ways. You may flatly refuse to eat it, and therefore feel frustrated that you will not benefit from its potential – or you may choose to eat it and experience frustration only momentarily from the taste while waiting to benefit from its effects. Either way, you will be more or less frustrated because of your discomfort.

"The wise man will choose to eat the item," Molly said in conclusion, "and if he practices this act regularly, he may eventually overcome his dislike for the item and completely erase his previous frustration, turning an uncomfortable action into a comfortable or happy situation. Do you understand my argument?"

"Yes, I think I do," he replied. "You are saying that reason dictates that the basis for happiness is the lack of frustration. Therefore, the basis for unhappiness is frustration. If you are frustrated, you are naturally unhappy. Consequently, if you want to be happy with something, you have to overcome the frustration related to it, if there is frustration accompanying it. That's fine as an explanation of happiness, however how does this relate to reason alone providing incentive to act in accord with the Infinite?"

"As long as one is aware of the Infinite," she responded, "not to act in accord with it would simply make one live a frustrated, and therefore, unhappy life. If you realize you need the Infinite to make any meaning out of your life by accepting that Existence is Infinity, but then fail to act in accord with it, you can't lead anything but a frustrated existence. Reason alone can tell us this."

She added. "The way I see it, life is like taking medicine. I may not like the taste of some healthful potion, and if I choose to refuse to accept the initial discomfort of taking it, I may never attain the good health it might effect either. Reason would tell me that knowing the need of the medicine, but not taking it, would be much worse than accepting the initial discomfort for the promise of lasting health afterwards. Is that not so?"

"As a general rule, yes," he replied, "however one exception would be that it might be more worthwhile to refuse needed medicine because of the discomfort than to take it, if you knew that your life expectancy is short. For instance, a man who knows he is to die shortly of cancer would be better off not to undergo an operation for some other ailment. It simply wouldn't be worth it."

"I'd agree with that," she responded, "although I don't see what that has to do with anything."

"Let me assure you, it has a lot to do with it," he replied. "I'm arguing that a man might be better off finding his own choice world of happiness, even if that means acting contrary to our imagined wishes of the Infinite, simply because life is too short to care about how one finds happiness, just as long as he finds it. Acting in accord with the Infinite – or simply admiring existence – might be validly compared to undergoing an operation, in spite of imminent death from another cause. If death ends it all, why care about how you find happiness before death? Acting in accord with the Infinite could then, not only be useless, but foolish as well. Why waste away life by trying to be good if it's more fun to be bad? Do you think that reason alone could provide an answer to that?"

"Yes, I do," she answered. "Reason could prove that approach to be the approach of a fool – merely by proving that life is not terminal, but rather, immortal. Death does not end it all. It merely provides a transition from one mode of consciousness to another mode of the same."

"You mean to tell me that reason can prove that life is immortal?"

"Yes, I certainly do."

"Now that indeed should prove interesting," he said. "Let's hear it."

"Don't you think, Honey, that death could not come to something having merely one vital process or function, but only to something that has many vital processes – that is, having a vital process that's interdependent among many other processes? Know what I mean?"

"No, can't say that I do," he answered.

"Let me give you an example," she explained. "The function of the heart would have no meaning as a vital process of life if there were no vessels or arteries, which are certainly other vital processes for that same life. And the vessels would have no meaning if it weren't for the flesh to which they give form."

"I'll grant you that," he responded.

"If one vital process ceased, then the whole unit of which the ceased function is a part would cease as well – or, in other words, it would die. What I mean to prove by this," she continued, "is that, in order for a thing to die, it would necessarily have to have parts or functions – of which one is interrupted. The heart is a necessary part or function of human life as we know it; and if the heart is interrupted in its vital process, death will result to that life."

"I follow you there," he said, trying to be patient to see where she was leading with all this.

"If death can only come to something with a composite of functions," she argued, "it would be correct to say, then, that death is impossible to a non-composite existence. If something is not made up of functions, but rather is its own function, it would be incapable of breaking down, since it is already as far down as it can go, existing as it is as a simple unit, rather than as a complex unit. If it can't be broken down or divided, it can't undergo death or cease to exist as the simple unit it is."

"Maybe so," he agreed, "but so what? You're still not out of the woods in proving that life is immortal. Granted that simple existence is incapable of normal death and is, except for possible annihilation, immortal, you have not proved that, in fact, there is anything about human life that is simple. It seems to me that, on the contrary, the human being is very much a complex being, and, as such, cannot possibly be capable of immortality. As a matter of indisputable fact, we must die and do die."

"As human beings, yes, we do die," she replied, "but that does not necessarily mean that everything about us dies. Maybe one of our parts or functions is a simple existence, and, therefore cannot sustain death. If so, then even though as human beings we are not immortal, something about us is."

"I'll go along with that," he responded, "however I fail to see what part of us could be defined as simple and incapable of death – though I suspect you are talking about the soul. Right?"

"Of course," she replied. "It's the soul. At least most would call it the 'soul'. I think it might be better described as a 'consciousness,' however."

"Alright, call it 'consciousness' if you like. Our consciousness is immortal, you say?" he questioned. "Right off hand, I'd say that is not so – just to play the devil's advocate – merely because our consciousness is entirely a product of our brain; and if the human brain dies, so also must that which is dependent upon it."

"But is our consciousness solely dependent upon our brain?" she asked. "Might not somewhat the opposite be true? Maybe the brain is dependent upon our consciousness."

"I hope you can support that theory with reason," he replied.

"Answer me this," she said. "Can a complex thing produce – or effect – a simple thing?"

"Why not?"

"It seems to me, Tom," she replied, "that anything produced by a complex thing must also be complex or comprised of parts. The only tools that a wholly complex thing has are also complex in themselves, and therefore anything produced by us, as complex human beings, must also be complex."

"So?"

"How do you explain the existence of ideas?" she asked. "Or don't you think that ideas are simple realities?"

"Are they?"

"I think so," she replied. "For everything that exists of which we are conscious, we attach a particular notion. Even though the subject matter may be complex, the idea we form from it – or for it – is simple. For instance, if we have a salad set before us, it exists as a particular unity or identity to which we attach our notion of 'salad'. Long after that salad has been digested, and after it has lost its original identity, the notion of 'salad' still exists. That notion is simple, and, as such, once produced, it is indestructible."

"Let's back up a moment," he said. "You can't tell me that salad is simple. It's made up of the various ingredients that compose it, and is very much a complex thing."

"I didn't say that a salad is a simple existence – only that the notion of 'salad' is. The notion or idea of salad is the indivisible thing. Notions bear the test of simple realities by virtue of the fact that, once formed, they are indestructible. Long after the complex item has passed out of existence, the notion produced by the mind in relation to it still lingers. A salad is corruptible, but a salad notion or idea is not."

"I am not sure I agree with you, but assuming I do, what does that prove?"

"Wholly complex things can only produce complex products," she explained. "Yet, clearly, to my mind, the human being produces simple products in the form of the notions it expresses. Therefore, there must be something essential about the human being that is simple, since it produces simple products.

"If that's the case," she went on, "there must, then, be something about the human being that cannot die and that is immortal because of that simple existence. In effect, that which is responsible for producing notions or ideas must be immortal. In other words, our minds, not our brains alone, which work only in conjunction with our minds, are immortal – since, in fact, they are responsible for the notions we produce."

"I must admit that is one fantastic notion by itself," he conceded. "If your argument is correct, after the brain and the mind have ceased producing notions, the mind still holds those notions in reserve. The brain may die, but the mind, as simple, and the notions, as simple, live on. Apparently in some inexplicable way, the mind, even though simple, must cooperate with the brain in producing notions. As such, before the brain is deceased, we had better be storing good notions, so to speak, because after death, we are going to have to live with them."

"Exactly! The Infinite would have us love because that is what It does," she continued, "because that is Its Nature, yet we often choose to violate our reason for being and hate or kill simply for the sake of destruction. The disposition that we condition ourselves to at the time of death, reason would say, is the disposition that we will live with forever after death – or at least until we can be reborn in another incarnation. That means, if we know we should act in accord with the Infinite, but don't, we'll be frustrated until we do, knowing we are violating the meaning and the expression of existence."

"It would also stand to reason," Tom added, "that one who, before death, is never conscious of the intended meaning of life, whether or not he fails to act in accord with love, would never attain the degree of happiness that one conscious of the meaning of life would – that is, of course, if the one aware of his meaning, did, in fact, concur with the Infinite. By the same token, one not aware of his true meaning could not suffer the frustration that would a violator, aware of his meaning.

"In a sense," he went on, "it could be correctly argued that the hell we have in eternity would be due to the notions we instill in ourselves in this life. After death, we would no longer be capable of attaining our notions by ourselves. Before death, we are the makers of our own destiny, with no one but ourselves to blame for failure. After death, we are no longer the makers of our own destiny, but must then live the destiny we created for ourselves when we had the chance."

"That's true," Molly responded. "Solely from the standpoint of reason, then, it can be seen that it is very important for us to immediately develop a good, loving disposition that we can take into eternity. To wait until tomorrow would be a very foolish thing to do – since there is no assurance that we will have a tomorrow with which to work.

"It would be entirely correct, then," she continued, "to say that the hell we have in eternity is simply an extension of the hell we have here. If we are not in hell here, we won't be in hell on the other side of mortal life either."

"I agree. You know, Molly, the concept of good disposition or good thoughts must clearly be the one thing that determines our achievement of Heaven or Hell. Psychologists have long advanced that the key to mental health, which is what we are really talking about when we talk about good disposition, is to think good thoughts. For such a simple resolution, there sure haven't been many who have actually succeeded in capturing the process and using it to its fullest degree."

"No, there haven't, Honey," she said, "although it's encouraging to me to know that, in spite of living amidst confusion, I can scale the heights of the good life simply by a sort of positive meditation or concentration on the good things that are mine."

"Oh, Lovely One," he enjoined, "that indeed should be the number one goal of each of us – to think good thoughts and not harbor negative ones that can only lead to despair and self-destruction. Clearly, the human mind cannot concentrate on opposing thoughts at the same time. So, since we have an inherent power of concentration, we can avoid any bad feelings and bad disposition merely by thinking good thoughts about ourselves and our world."

"Furthermore," she added, "it's not possible to have good thoughts about something or someone and not want to love that something or someone. To love, then, is to be grateful and to enjoy what is loved. *Love is not so much a duty as an inspiration.* If we do not feel inspired to enjoy, we are not loving. We may be obliging, but we are not loving. If I say I love you – and have pain in my heart toward you – it is a lie."

"For sure, I agree," he said. *"Love is an activity of the heart that reveres the Infinite and all that the Infinite creates.* It seems to me, as it does to you, that it's extremely important for us to use, now, to the fullest extent possible, the gifts of our expresser. Indeed, we should practice gratitude without inhibition every hour, every minute, every second. To put our talents under a blanket under the pretext that they deter us from our end is tantamount to telling our Infinite Father that we don't appreciate His gifts, and that we have a better way to please our Infinite Benefactor."

"I know you are saying 'Him' out of convenience and not out of correctness, My Dear," remarked Molly, "but allowing for that reverence, I could not agree with you more. The kind of pride that says that the gifts of God are not good enough to embrace in the sunlight and in the nighttime should certainly be damned. In fact, acting like the life we have from God is not good is damnation, even if we think we are directing a prayer to God, while striking our breast and pledging unworthiness. We humans are such fools to think that such can be correct behavior for any soul wanting to attain Heaven."

"Again, you tell it like it is, Honey," he responded. "Speaking of Heaven, how about letting me kiss my angel?"

"Anytime, My Dear! Anytime!"

Tom stood in front of Molly and assisted her to her feet in front of him. They embraced and kissed; and then Tom turned his angel around with her back to his front. She closed her eyes and had some wonderful daydreams as his hands massaged all they could reach. Indeed, Molly thought, it was nice to be at Home in Heaven.

After a few moments of his loving hands touching her loveliness where they would and could, Molly opened her eyes and looked at a tiny pink and blue bird resting on the limb of a tree in front of her. It was easy to see that her little bird somehow had sensed by instinct what it had taken discussion for Tom and Molly to realize. Her little bird was at home in Nature. Why shouldn't it be the same for humans too?

"You know, Tom, I think we have really discovered a very important idea," she said as she kept her eyes on the little bird in front of her. "In a very significant way, the concepts that we emphasize in that which we call our souls are probably the prime determinants of how we spend time and eternity. My life is so full as I am in your embrace, but that which is really fulfilling me is the thought or notion of kindness I am experiencing. And if for some reason you were not here and I was alone, I could reflect back on the time you were here and recreate, as it were, the kindness I am feeling now. In a very real way, you are assisting me to create the images and the notions I can take with me into eternity. I am like that little bird I see in front of us. *I am getting ready to fly.*"

"Me too," Tom replied, as he turned his love around and looked into her eyes. Then he lowered his mouth on hers and kissed her sweetly. Having kissed her, he pulled back and again looking into her eyes, he said, "I agree, Molly. Kindness is probably the best disposition. I am glad you feel a sense of kindness with me."

"If kindness is the ideal, perhaps we should just take a moment to reflect on the less than ideal, " Molly responded. "Besides kindness, Tom, what do you think are the basic dispositions we could have?"

"I am reminded of that song that Daniel O'Donnell sings, Honey. I think he calls it *Yesterday is History – Tomorrow is a Mystery'* or something like that."

"Yes, I think he does call it that. I know we both enjoy it; but refresh my memory. What disposition are you thinking about that he offers in that song?"

"One of the verses offers that *it's best that we forget all the things that we regret.* I definitely believe in that, but it's that word 'regret' that comes to mind as one of the basic dispositions of which any soul is capable."

"How so?" she asked

"Well, it seems to me that one can't hold both regret and kindness as dispositions at the same time. I can see that regret may be a step toward kindness in the end, but just speculating about it, I can't see how I can focus on regret and kindness at the same time."

"You mean you don't think one can regret what one has done and be kind at the same time?"

"No, I don't. Do you?"

"No. I guess not – not at the same time."

"So, there it is," he said. "Like Daniel sings in his song, *it's best that we forget all the things that we regret.*"

"But how can you forget all the things that you regret without overriding your regret with something else?"

"That's just it. You can't. If you have regret in your heart, there can be no room for anything else – be it kindness or whatever."

"I think you're right, Honey," she said, "but if regret can be overridden with kindness, what else might override it?"

"Meanness."

"Meanness?"

"Yes, meanness, Molly. It seems to me that one can go one of two ways from regret. One is kindness and the other is meanness. One is down from regret and the other is up from regret."

"I'm not sure about that, Tom. Are you telling me that the three basic dispositions of a soul are meanness, regret, and kindness?"

"It seems so to me," he replied.

"What about justice?"

"What about it?"

"I am not sure, but at first hand, it seems to me that justice should play some kind of part in the picture."

"As I see it, My Love, meanness, regret, and kindness are justice. I don't think justice should be considered in itself as a disposition of the soul. As I see it, justice is only the state of a soul for choosing one of the three basic dispositions. *Justice for a soul is only having to continue a state of mind.* If I am kind, then my justice is that I will continue to be kind. If I live in regret, then my justice is that I will have to continue to live in regret – at least until I override regret with kindness – or Heaven forbid, meanness. If I am mean, then my justice is that I will have to continue to be mean – at least until I override my meanness with regret."

"You don't think one can go from meanness to kindness without having regret first?" Molly anticipated total agreement with what her husband was to offer.

"No, I don't. I think that if I am mean, in order to be able to change to kindness, I have to go through a state of regret for or from my meanness first."

"There are a lot of people about, Tom, who do not regret being mean."

"Exactly! Did you hear what you said – do not regret being mean? That is exactly my point. How can you go from meanness to kindness if you do not regret being mean first?"

"Wow! I like the simplicity of that," she replied. "It's like a roadmap for a soul. If one is mean, then to change to kindness, regret for that meanness must be experienced first. It makes it all so simple."

"Yes, it is simple, Honey. We both know that – or at least, we both suspected that because we entered this weekend thinking that reason could tell us how to live well all by itself.

Our reason is telling us that there are three basic possible dispositions or attitudes of a soul – meanness at the bottom, being the most negative, regret for meanness in the middle, and kindness at the top, being the most positive. One cannot focus on but one of those three at any one time. As one lives, one will probably die. There are probably very few so called deathbed conversions. That would make the state of our soul before the time of death to be the justice we will take with us beyond death."

"Hmmmmm, that's delicious, Sweetheart," she replied. "It is delicious because it makes it all so simple. I love it because it makes ideal conduct so clear – as you say, by reason alone. But maybe we should ask, what is meanness?"

"It's a lot simpler than we think, My Dear. It is the complete opposite of kindness. Being kind is only wishing or doing any neighbor well, no matter what any neighbor may have done to you because it is an attitude. You can't want ill for someone and injury to them at the same time. It should not depend on what another does or does not do. True kindness must be a constant disposition – or else it would not be kindness.

"On the other hand," he continued, "meanness must be a constant disposition too. Meanness is only wishing or doing another ill – again not depending on what another does or does not do. It's an attitude; and being so, if one has it, it is simply dispersed over everything one does. I suppose you can pretend to be kind to some and mean to others, but that is all it is - pretense."

"I am not so sure about that, Tom. I don't think I agree with that. I think I can wish one well and be kind to him or her and wish another ill and be mean to him or her. Maybe I can be mean and kind at the same time."

"Not at the same time, Honey. Since the mind can only really focus on one disposition at a time, in reality, if there are two dispositions in a person, one is probably a pretend disposition and not a real disposition. It is only the real disposition that amounts to anything in terms of the justice of a soul – or for a soul. One can't pretend he's being kind. He either is or isn't."

"Again, I am not sure about that," she responded. "But do you think that one can be mean to another without actually doing them ill?"

"Of course. I don't have to literally hurt you to hurt you in my mind. It is not so much what I do to you as what I do to me in my mind. Attitudes exist only in the mind and soul – not out there in the world. I am responsible for what I think because how I think and what I think shapes my attitude. It is attitude that is our judgment – in terms of our souls – not what someone else might do to us."

"I certainly agree with that," she said. "Like I say, it makes it all so simple. But it seems to me that we are making all forms of punishment an expression of meanness because if we want some one to be punished for some act or crime, we are actually being mean to them in our mind."

"That's the crux of it, alright," he replied. "Wanting someone hurt is to be mean to them in the mind. It almost makes me feel sorry for anyone in the so called 'justice system'. Just being part of it almost handcuffs them to have to be mean because the normal mind almost instinctively wishes harm to those who do ill. How can you avoid being mean, then, if you constantly put yourself in a situation where you have to wish another harm or pain?"

"There's always regret," Molly offered. "It is probably the only way out of such a mess, but I doubt that many who are mean really think of themselves as being mean. So that does not give them much of a chance to regret their states of mind. Does it?"

"It certainly doesn't," he agreed. "Well, at least we are aware of what we have to do in order to practice the ideal, which we think is kindness. We can't mess around with mean-ness and we can't even dally with regret. Like Daniel sings in his song, *it's best that we forget all that we regret*; but the only way we can forget all that we regret is to override it with kind-ness. What a wonderful way to go for those of us who can go that route."

"And sad for those who can't," she replied. "Why can't we see what we are doing to our souls?"

"It takes thinking to know what we are doing, Honey, and not many people take time to think. Thus, they continue to pay the price that justice of soul demands – they have to con-tinue with the attitudes they possess."

"Thank Goodness for your kindness, Sweetheart. It is oh so sweet – and for that I have no regrets."

"You better not have, Honey, because if you did regret kind-ness, there would be only one way to go – and that would be meanness. You do not have a mean bone in your body, Molly. Thanks so much for being you!"

"And thank you for your being you, My Prince of Kindness, My King of No Regrets!" But Molly was still pondering regret. "Regret – or the notion of regret – seems a bit confusing, Honey. We think we have a handle on meanness and kindness, but what do you think is regret?"

"Wishing you were mean or kind, I guess," he replied. "I suppose one can go from mean to kind or from kind to mean, but either passage has to be through regret. Regret is like some middle ground where real meanness or real kindness are only pondered. From a state of kindness, it is far inferior. From a state of meanness, it is far superior."

"But you think one can always go from one extreme to the other through regret?"

"I suppose it is possible. Why not? But somehow I doubt very much that it is very likely to go from kindness to meanness because once one experiences the true liberty of kindness,

I can't imagine being able to give that up for something as unfulfilling as meanness. Can you?"

"Not really," she responded. "Do you think that one would have to spend a lot of time in regret – or what I might call a state of limbo – before being able to go from meanness to kindness?"

"I like your referring to regret as a state of limbo, Molly. I think that is a great characterization of it. In answer to your question, maybe yes, maybe no. I think it is possible that one who has previously been mean of heart could realize the insanity of the state of meanness almost instantly and switch from meanness to kindness almost instantaneously, spending almost no time at all in regret, but I don't think it is likely."

"No, I don't suppose it is likely," Molly said, "but it sure is comforting to think it could happen. Maybe it is the bleeding heart in me, Honey, but I want everyone – no matter how mean they have been – to be like us instantly. I want Hitler to realize he was wrong almost instantly. I want him to realize he can become an angel of kindness very quickly if he would put his mind to it. I don't want anyone to suffer either hating or being hated. I want kindness for everyone."

"That is why you are kindness itself, Honey," Tom replied, "and you are not alone. At least, I share your sympathy. I want kindness for all too."

Molly was still not finished. "Tom, what about sorrow?"

"What about it?" he responded.

"Do you think it is an expression of regret?"

"I guess you could consider it to be so. One needs to feel sorrow for one's meanness before one can actually wish that one were kind, I guess. So, it could be considered to be a lower stage of regret; but, you know, Honey, I really prefer to think of sorrow as being a higher stage of meanness rather than a lower stage of regret."

"Why do you think that?"

"I just see sorrow as still being mean. I don't see it as stepping up to regret at all. I think people are sorry all the time for being mean, but that does not stop them from being mean. It is a step in the right direction, but it is not regret. I suppose Hitler was sorry for his meanness, though he probably did not see it as meanness. He probably saw it as some form of justice. He may have thought about being sorry for having to execute all the undesirables, as he saw it, but that did not stop him from doing it. No. I don't think sorrow deserves to be considered regret. Regret is much higher than sorrow. People are sorry all the time for what they think they have to do in terms of being mean to others, but it does not stop them from doing it. Does it?"

"No, I guess it doesn't. It's true. When you analyze it, if one regrets what one has done, it is like they have stopped doing it. They may have not yet proceeded to be kind after they have stopped being mean, but at least they have stopped being mean – or have no desire to continue being mean. When one is only sorry for being mean or having to be mean as they see it, then it is true, they may still continue being mean. They are still blinded within meanness and being sorry for having to be mean will not necessarily release them into regret for what they have done. So, I think you are right. Sorrow, though a step in the right direction, is not true regret."

"And forgiveness, Molly? How would you see that?"

"As a higher stage of regret, I think, Honey. It may well be the last stage before you can say goodbye to the world of no kindness and say hello to the world of kindness. I think forgiveness is really only closing the door on a previous world of meanness. It is saying I am ready to go forward with kindness. It is saying I am finally through with meanness and I never want to experience any of it again. Don't you think?"

"Yes, I agree," he replied. "I do not think it is thought of that way, but I think you are right. I think most people think of forgiveness as something another does for you rather than what you must do for yourself. You know our love for Jesus, Honey, and I think he would be agreeing with most of our sentiments about life and love and kindness. I think he would also agree with our notion of forgiveness. It is not Jesus forgiving another. It is one forgiving himself for a life of past error and telling himself – I am ready now to go on. That's true forgiveness."

"Exactly!" she exclaimed. "If people ask for forgiveness for what they have done from an outside source, chances are they are not ready to stop doing what they are sorry for. If they see forgiveness only in an external sense, thinking they need forgiveness from another, more than likely their forgiveness is not really forgiveness but only sorrow – which has not even passed into the stage of regret yet."

"Yes, I think you are right there, Honey," he replied. "Forgiveness is very often equated with Jesus. Jesus and forgiveness are often seen as one, but they should not be. Jesus cannot forgive another for a past meanness. There is only one way that meanness can be forgiven; and that is by stopping it. But forgiveness of self is probably necessary to get it all behind you. Like you say, it is probably the last stage of regret. Once you have really forgiven yourself and you are really ready to move on, presto, like Daniel sings in his song, *it's best to forget all the things that you regret.* I think forgiveness is really only finally saying goodbye to regret."

"Correction," she responded. "*We* think that forgiveness is only saying goodbye to regret. We are in this thing together, Honey. You do not need to forgive me of anything and I do not need to forgive you of anything – even if you had done something gnarly and offensive. You need to forgive yourself and

I need to forgive me; but I doubt that either of us needs any forgiveness. We have passed far beyond regret and the need for forgiveness has long been behind us."

"I agree, Molly; and so I think would Jesus. Perhaps it's time that this world started seeing Jesus right, even as Jesus could not have offered us any more than what we have offered ourselves today. In Jesus, we have a brother, one of kindred thought, but not a master or lord as so many want to make him."

"Yes indeed, Tom – we are our own masters. We are our own lords; but neither of us is lord or master of the other."

"Nor we of Jesus or Jesus of us," he responded. "We are all only *spiritual siblings* of one another."

Molly looked up into his eyes and gave him a great big smile. Then she closed her eyes and buried her head in his chest, thinking about the little pink and blue bird that had probably already flown away; and as she pondered it all, she was thinking that *she was flying too – with kindness in her heart and soul and no regrets in her mind.*

Note: That is the end of Part 1. Stay tuned for Part 2. I let Tom and Molly call achieving happiness Heaven because that seems to be the common consensus; however, in fact, I am of the belief that Heaven is only the Presence of God. We are all in Heaven no matter where we are because we are all in the Presence of God. Personally, I do not believe Heaven should be tied to any kind of meriting process, but for the sake of my story, it does not hurt to act like Heaven is being at peace with life and treating it like an achievement.

Part 2

Rationalizing Life
- The Way It Should Be -

7

A Different Ethic – Natural Discipline

Life – unbelievably simple, though mankind generally makes it inexplicably hard. Tom and Molly both saw it that way. Several years had passed since Mr. & Mrs. Socrates spent the weekend they had dedicated to pondering life and its meaning. It was another Saturday and Liz and Joe were coming over with their eight year old daughter, Elise. Kerry would be celebrating his seventh birthday in about a month. It would be good for Elise to provide some kid company for Kerry as the grownups carried on as well.

The grownups, Joe and Liz, had been informed in detail – to the best of Tom and Molly's recollection – about the deliberations of that monumental weekend. They had been thoroughly educated by Tom and Molly – Mr. & Mrs. Socrates – to the best of that couple's ability – and had more than once expressed a wish that they had been included at that *University of Higher Learning*. Tom had offered that he and Molly had attended *UHL* that weekend – a thought that came to him after that weekend. When Joe asked what the heck is *UHL?* Tom chuckled and replied: *The University of Higher Learning*.

Liz and Joe were special friends of Tom and Molly on account of a strange beginning. Liz and Molly had worked together in the arena of insurance before both had married and started their respective families with Joe and Tom. As it happened, before Tom met Molly, Tom tried his hand at trying to sell the Rainbow Vacuum Cleaner door to door; and one of his casual potential customers turned out to be Liz and Joe.

Tom was only a neophyte salesman when they had first met, with Tom knocking at the door of Liz and Joe and being told that they did not want to buy anything, but they would be open to having Tom practice his spiel – as Joe had called it – on the tenderfoot, Tom. Joe could tell almost immediately that Tom was only beginning; and from his own failed personal experience of trying to be a door to door salesman earlier in life, he recognized a beginner's awkwardness and out of compassion for a fellow salesman, he offered to let Tom practice on him and his wife.

Later, Tom and Molly would meet at a church bazaar and fall in love. Of course, the first friend that Molly wanted to introduce to her new love, Tom, was her good friends, Liz and Joe. Imagine the surprise when the old acquaintances of Molly turned out to be Tom's guinea pigs of some months back. When they all came together, it was like they had all known each other before – and they became great friends.

Poor Molly! At their first dinner out as a foursome after they met, Molly felt mortified by Tom when he told Liz and Joe that he believed in going naked for the rightness of it. He said he felt they should know that so that if they just happened to drop in like friends often do, they would not be surprised. Joe responded with – to each, his own – and felt no problem with the declaration. Liz, however, wondered in silence about this new wild and crazy friend of theirs, as Molly had sputtered to Tom – "Tom! Whatever prompted you to say something like that?"

"It's my belief," Tom had answered, "and friends should be aware of each other's beliefs if they want to remain true friends. So why not tell it like it is? It cuts to the quick of things and everyone knows at the outset where everyone stands."

Molly had responded, "Yeah, Tom, it's good to be honest, but you don't have to tell all. You think Liz and Joe care what you believe?"

"It's not for me to care if they care or not," Tom had managed as a reply, "but it is for me to care about being truthful. I mean it's OK to withhold some little truth like not liking fried potatoes or the like, but it's not OK to withhold a principle truth like that reflected in a spiritual belief. People should care about one another's spiritual beliefs in order to relate the best they can because spiritual beliefs should be the very core of living. How can you attempt to communicate with people if you avoid talking about your very insides – about what makes you tick? People try it all the time – and live their lives as strangers because of it. I don't care to be a stranger to those I love." Such had been Tom's argument.

At that moment, Joe had turned to Liz, showing a wide open smile. "How refreshing!" had been his response; and then he took a slice right out of the movie, **CASABLANCA,** and raised his glass of water as a toast to Tom and Molly and said, *"Louie, I think this is the beginning of a long and lasting friendship!"* To the quip, Molly had frowned and questioned Joe. "Who is Louie?" she asked.

"You mean you have never seen the wonderful movie with Humphrey Bogart and Ingrid Bergman called **CASABLANCA**?" Tom had seen it and knew immediately all about Joe's fantasy character named Louie.

"No – sorry, I missed that one," Molly responded at the time.

"Then we will have to share it with you sometime," Joe had said. "It's a wonderful movie and we have it in our video library.

Until we get the chance of sharing it with you, let's just say that Louie is just another term for friend. OK?"

"OK," Molly had said.

And that happened nine years before. After that, Tom was caught on numerous occasions without clothes when either Liz or Joe or both of them came over without invitation – which happened quite a bit. Tom had made it clear at the outset that they should never feel like they had to ask to come over – and though Molly was not sure she liked the proposition of anyone catching her unaware and unprepared, she went along with Tom in his open invitation.

In time, Joe began to relax as well; and if Tom came over so that the two of them could go golfing or something, he would not hurry to dress – and neither would Liz. Little Elise was also encouraged to be free when the *Family Socrates* visited – and she loved it. When Liz saw the love of life reflected in her little one by just flitting about and flirting about au natural, she became a great believer that life ought to be that way. First came Tom's example about being open – then Elise's. Anyone with an open heart could see that both reflected a wonderful thing called 'innocence'. No one can beat that.

Elise acted like a big sister to Kerry whenever she could and pretended that Kerry was her little boy, however Kerry had grown up since those early baby days together and did not feel comfortable in being the baby any longer.

Liz had come to look forward to a visit by Tom. She knew there was a good chance the two husbands would get naked – either before an outing or after it; and she loved to see the two guys together. How admirable they both looked! Tom's middle appendage was a good bit smaller than that of her Joe, but unlike the greater population which cared about such things, neither of her two men did.

And Tom made it so easy to get along because of his **'Ethic of Natural Discipline**,' as he called it. Tom had long argued that the biggest reason people can't be free with one another is most choose to violate the standard of Natural Discipline – which he insisted should be capitalized in print. Nature made sexual intercourse for making babies, not wild and loose orgasms. If any two opposites of a relationship respected that truth and did not engage in intercourse except to make a baby, then any two opposites could trust one another to keep a relationship safe. Life is unbelievably simple, he argued, if we just pay attention to some basics; but if we don't, then we have to pay the piper with the consequences of complicated behavior.

In the nine years they had known each other, Tom had not once suggested other than his Natural Standard. The result was that Joe could trust his Liz with Tom, naked or otherwise, because he knew his friend, Tom, would not challenge his right as husband to be a co-parent with Liz. The two could hug and be affectionate – and they often were – with nary a consequence to their behavior. *Life is so simple if we just act according to Natural Discipline.* Liz and Joe and Tom and Molly were living testimonies to that.

"They're here already!" Molly exclaimed, as she heard a car drive into the driveway. "I didn't expect them this early."

"Great!" was Tom's response. "I hope they have not had breakfast. It has been awhile since I cooked one for the six of us."

"It just so happens we have plenty of eggs, Honey. That would be just fine if we could treat them to breakfast."

Elise was the first to enter, as she bounded out of the car and ran to the door. Kerry was naked, as were his parents, but was eager to open it. "Hi, Elise! Come in!" the little host enjoined.

"Why of course, My Young Prince!" was her reply, as she giggled and hurried in. The two of them went bouncing off to Kerry's room, with Elise patting Kerry on his fanny and giggling some more.

"It's nice to hear them giggle so," Molly said, as she glanced at Tom and smiled.

"Come on in!" Tom said to his friends, as they opened the door and entered. "It sure is good to see you. Make yourselves at home. We are."

"Sounds like a plan to me," offered Joe, as he smiled and began unbuttoning.

"We got the pictures developed of our outing last week," Molly said. "Would you like to see them?"

"Of course," Liz responded, as she joined Joe in disrobing. "I like clothes, but it's always nice to get out of them too. Thank God for the two of you. We do not know another soul we could do this with."

"Yeah, I know," Molly replied, "and isn't it sad?"

"Isn't it?" Tom agreed, and then he reiterated his standard comment. *"Life is so unbelievably simple, but we make it so inextricably hard."*

"Why do you believe that is so?" Joe questioned, looking at Tom.

"Why do people make it hard?" Tom repeated the question. "I think it's because most see God as outside of life. It's only a matter of perception. If you see God as outside of life, you tend to make of God a judge – and then you have to come up with some arbitrary rules that such an external God must impose on his subjects. If you have God as outside of you, then you have to see God as a judge because who else is there that should judge? But if you see God as inside of life, then God can't be seen as a judge. It is really as simple as that. Don't you think?"

"At least we think it's that way," Molly added. "I mean, for example, look at Joe's erection." Joe smiled and felt proud that he was the object of everyone's comfortable gazes. "And then look at Tom. He's soft." Tom smiled and knew well what Molly would say next. "If you see God as outside of life, the tendency is that God is going to have to agree with one of our guys and disagree with the other because they are different. But if you see God inside of Joe's hardness and inside of Tom's softness, there is no problem. Both Tom and Joe are seen as good because both have the same God inside of them. When you put God outside of you, you have to look for approval and disapproval. And I think that is what troubles society so."

"Lady, you are right there," Joe said. "So many religious zealots claim to love the same God, but then denounce each other in the process. Why? Because each of them see a different God outside of them. It's like people actually have different gods when God is seen as outside of them. Even though in words every religious person claims to honor the same God, by having to define a God as outside of them, they are quite apt to define different gods – and the real God that is in all is simply missed."

"And that is exactly what happens," Tom agreed. "Just look at Moses and the Pharaoh of Egypt. Moses saw or knew a different god than did the Pharaoh and the Pharaoh saw or knew a different god than did Moses. The result was the Moses had his god or gods challenge the god or gods of the Pharaoh and the Pharaoh had his god or gods challenge the god or gods of Moses. If both Moses and the Pharaoh had respected only one God and realized that the one God is in both of them, there would have been no quarrel between them."

"I think it's true," commented Liz. "People quarrel because they feel they have different gods when all the time the same God exists in all. It's pretty stupid. Isn't it?"

"As stupid as it gets, Honey," Joe agreed. "As Tom would argue, look at me, look at Tom. We both have God inside of us. I'm harder than Tom right now, maybe because I just got out of restricting clothes and the new flow of blood to my penis is causing an erection – whereas Tom has been naked and relaxed for awhile. Anyway, on another occasion, he will be harder than me. So what? The only matter of importance is that both Tom and Joe are enjoying life because the same One and Good God is making it happen."

Just then, Elise, who had joined her young host in his state of the natural, came running in. "Mommy, Kerry says his dad is going to make breakfast for us all. Can we stay?" Actually, Joe and Liz had intended on asking their hosts out to breakfast; and that was why they had come so early. Tom and Molly were expecting them, but had not expected them until after breakfast.

Kerry followed Elise into the room; and the reflection of all six could be seen in a large mirror on the wall. "We are going to have them for breakfast, aren't we, Dad?" asked Kerry.

"That would be nice, Son, if they would agree. Would you mind joining us here for breakfast?"

"That would be delightful!" Liz remarked. "We wouldn't have to get dressed so soon if that were the case. Actually, we planned to treat you out for breakfast. That's why we are earlier than we planned to be."

"We have plenty of eggs for all of us," Tom replied, "and plenty of bread and butter for toast. Molly may even have some jam or jelly. If that's fine, we can handle breakfast for all. If you want more than that, we will have to go out."

"Eggs and toast sounds fine," Liz responded.

"And coffee and orange juice, too," added Molly. "Tom and I already had a cup of coffee this morning, but there's plenty left. Would you like a cup?"

"Sure," Joe said, "with milk if you don't mind."

"The same for me," Liz said, "as if you did not already know how we take our coffee."

"Kids, would you like some orange juice?" Molly asked.

"Please," responded Elise.

"Me too." Kerry was quick to agree.

Tom then proceeded to fetch the coffee for the adults – including for Molly, who always drank her coffee black as Tom preferred the altered taste of a milked down version. Molly grabbed some glasses from the cupboard and filled them with orange juice for the kids. Elise and Kerry thanked Molly for the orange juice and sat down at the kitchen table, chatting kid talk as they did. Kerry was a bit intentionally sloppy and spilled some of his on himself. Elise took advantage of the opportunity to play the mother and quickly grabbed a dish rag from the rack on the sink and watered it down some. Then she took the wet rag and moved to wash her friend.

"You don't have to do that," Kerry pretended to shrug, fully aware his intentional spill was designed to get him the attention Elise was providing. When people know each other, they also know what an action might prompt. This was a game these kids often played – as do a lot of adults. Why not? It's fun.

Elise then pursued her task like a real grownup, washing Kerry wherever the juice had spilled. Elise could not tell if the juice went to her friend's middle, but this little game was scripted to have her wash the area. She was intent on exploring her little friend, as he was intent on being explored. Curiosity is a wonderful thing, especially when it can be satisfied so openly.

Of course, Kerry was too young to expand from the attention, but Elise enjoyed touching him just the same. Now she was like Mommy who constantly touched Daddy and made him big. Elise was wise enough, however, to know that little boys are not supposed to get big when they are touched. She was as innocent as a lamb about such things – as were Liz and Joe who encouraged her.

As for our prince of the moment, Kerry, he enjoyed the attention – as any normal person would. Tom and Molly taught Kerry that it is OK to accept a kiss or hug or any attention if it is offered, but it is not OK to ask for attention. He was told that to ask for attention is to chance imposing on another person; and young as he was, he knew what imposing on another means.

It means putting another in a position where they might do something with which they disagree – just to please that someone. Kerry was only nearly seven, but he was old enough to know that love is not asking another to do for you, but to do for another. If that other wants to do something in return, that should be up to them; and a real gentleman would not ask a lady to please him. Accept if offered, maybe, but never ask for attention. Enticing with a hint, like intentionally spilling orange juice on yourself, is not out of place to open a door, but actually requesting attention is not proper. If someone takes a hint, fine, but let it go at that. Always make it easy for another to respond. Never make it hard.

This was the ethic that worked for this small group of six; and none of this ethic would have likely become that if Tom had not been so mildly blunt so many years ago when they first met. He had testified that he often went naked at his house for the rightness of it. It was that honesty that first intrigued Joe and Liz to wonder about this strange man who seemed to lack the shame that most hold close to themselves.

Tom tried not to offer any disrespect for other beliefs, but early on had mimicked those who think they are sinful and unworthy of life by beating his bare chest and repeating the words in jest that so many repeat day after day in earnest. He knew the chant well, as earlier in life he had practiced it.

"Oh, woe is me, unworthy beast that I am!" he had mimicked, pounding at his chest with clenched fists, as others do who think they are unworthy of God's love. "Of what sense does it make," he argued, "that God Who is making his chest would approve of our rejecting the gift? *How can man be unworthy of life if life is a gift of God?*"

It made no sense to him; and deep down, it made no sense to Liz and Joe either as both had welcomed the suggestion that a contrary conduct in life should be the norm, not the exception. So they had become the masters of their own lives, starting out as a couple of students eager to learn and to attend what Tom called *The University of Higher Learning.* And like Tom and Molly were doing for their Kerry, Liz and Joe were doing for Elise. Attending *The University of Higher Learning* is simply to go into the heart and mind and make sense of the world about you. No books are needed – just an eager, willing mind.

Kerry and Elise had become students of *The University of Higher Learning* too; and a principal course was the ethic of "accept, but don't ask." People need openings, however, and it's OK to do things to open doors – as long as one does not insist that another must go through an opened door. Open a door, but never reach out to pull another through it. Kerry had intentionally spilled the orange juice on himself to provide an opening for Elise to react as she, in fact, did – and as he expected, knowing her as he did; but it would have been wrong for Kerry to ask Elise to wash him down. Besides that, it would not have been 'manly' either.

It's OK to tell someone that your back hurts – as long as you don't ask for a back rub in the process. To say that your back hurts and then leave it to your partner to offer a back rub is just fine, but to tell your partner that your back hurts while also commanding attention is out of order. Always approach a partner, armed only with suggestion and never petition. That way, life remains simple for all and people don't get into making all sort of demands upon one another. To repeat, open the door for another, but don't insist on pulling him or her through it. Do that and your world will always be filled with love because you will find yourself always seeking to do for another and not be the recipient of another. It's OK to receive gratefully from another, but only if that other offered out of generosity first.

For sure, our youngsters, current students of **The University of Higher Learning**, were very much aware of the ethics of their parents – and the ethics of their parents were being adopted by themselves as well.

Elise knew what she would do next. She would provide a curiosity opening for Kerry as Kerry had provided one for her, but what could she do that would not be an imposition? She decided her course of action and went about it, while the four adults watched the little play going on before them with hearty approval. How could they not? They inspired the writing of the script being rewritten by their two students.

Elise returned her used rag to the sink and went back to Kerry, stretching her hand to him, palm open. Of course, that was an invitation to stand and go with her to wherever she was planning to lead them. "Let's go look at ourselves in the mirror," she suggested. Elise suggested the mirror activity because she wanted to give Kerry an opening to look at her; and looking at themselves seemed like a good idea. The mirror she was talking about was the huge mirror in the living room. Taking her young lover by the hand, she led him to the mirror. Without shame, they stood there for awhile, freely looking at one another's body.

And what a beautiful sight they were to one another – and to the adults, too, who had followed them to watch the little play unfold as it did. Given the ethics of this small band of human beings, there was no need for privacy. Kerry and Elise did not feel they had to go someplace else to look at each other. They knew their parents would approve because their parents frequently did the same thing. They only left the kitchen because there was no mirror in the kitchen. Tom and Molly planned to install a mirror in the kitchen, but had not yet done so. So the kids went to the living room to find a mirror there.

"Look at us, Mom!" offered an excited Elise. Somehow, 'Mommy' would not have been the grownup thing to call her mother on such an auspicious occasion; and so, Mommy became Mom. "Look at us! Aren't we beautiful!"

"You certainly are, Honey!" was Liz's response.

"Yes, we all are," Joe added, as he led his wife to stand beside the kids in front of the mirror. Joe had hair in his middle and had a rather firm penis to present in front of the mirror whereas little Kerry was still bald and still very little, though his penis did point out a bit rather than hang as Joe's did. It must be the weight, Kerry thought, as he compared himself to Joe. I guess when you get older, you get bigger, but you must also get heavier.

"I can't wait to grow up!" exclaimed an excited Kerry. "Joe, do you think my penis will be as big as yours?"

"Probably not, Kerry. Yours will probably be more like your dad's than mine. Children often inherit the features of their parents. As your dad is much smaller than me, you will likely be that way too."

"However you turn out, My Little Prince, I will like it!" Elise gleefully offered.

Kerry just smiled and knew that it would be that way too. The problem with other people's ethics is that they accept others only according to size and not content of the heart. Kerry was taught that he was a very unique child of Nature; and though he may take after his dad a lot, he was still different. People should enjoy one another based on their general similarities, but they should also enjoy one another for their specific offerings as well.

One of the great joys of life should be that we come in all different manners – some small, some big, some in between. If we were all alike, the world would lack variety. With all of us being different, variety is a given. Yet instead of celebrating how different we are and finding tremendous encouragement in that, we often act like being different is a reason to sub-merge oneself behind some false claim of modesty. Our variety should be seen as a blessing; yet we often treat it like it is a curse.

Molly felt an urge to join the others in front of the mirror. "Come on, Tom! Let's join the kids!"

Then all six were there, bunched in front of the mirror, able to gaze at one another without gawking. Mirrors are really wonderful things in that you can look at yourself or another and not worry about being seen doing so. So often, people don't care to be gawked at. So the advantage of a mirror allowed each of this group to look and not gawk.

"Honey, as much as we are enjoying looking at the beauty of Nature in us all," Molly said, "perhaps we better get on with making breakfast for our guests."

"I agree," Tom responded. "Kids, why don't you go out and play a little with Tybee? We will call you when breakfast is ready. OK?"

"OK, Dad," Kerry replied. "Come on, Elise."

With that, the kids went out the sliding glass door at the back of the house as Tom and Molly proceeded to prepare the breakfast.

Kerry and Elise always enjoyed playing with Tybee, who had a great life as a yard dog. Molly was allergic to dog fur; and that's why Tybee had to live outside. If Tybee had not been a dog with so much fur, she might have been allowed as a house dog, but Tybee was a cross between a Labrador Retriever and a Chow, making her a rather large dog at seventy pounds with a heavy coat of fur. Tybee did not mind being a yard dog, how-ever, and she had a very nice shed to stay in when the weather was a bit inclement.

Surrounded by a high privacy fence made of oak panels and populated with large evergreens, the back yard was a gem of privacy. Though Tom and Molly would not have required any privacy, they knew that the neighborhood might require it of them if they became aware of their natural beliefs and conduct. So, a privacy fence was installed immediately upon purchasing the home some nine years back. Kerry and Elise were free to play naked in the back yard without anyone noticing, although almost everyone in the neighborhood knew that Tom and Molly and 'the kid' were Naturalists.

Tybee was an extremely friendly mutt and always enjoyed the frequent attention she received at the hands of Kerry and family and any guests who might drop by. Sitting on a chair by the picnic table on the back patio, Elise called for Tybee to come – which she did promptly. Elise couldn't help but wonder out loud why it is that dogs seem to be so happy. With just a small bit of attention, they respond like the petting they just received was the only thing in the world they need – and enthusiastically, their tails wag, equivalent to the spark in their eyes. Dogs are so easy to please, thought Elise. Why couldn't humans be that way?

Kerry was eager to show Elise how big the 'mystery plant' in the back yard had grown since she last saw it a week ago. "Let's check out the mystery plant," he said. Actually, there were two mystery plants in the back yard. One was in the middle of a path to the back woods behind that back yard and the other was just over a fence off an area for a garden. A garden was never planted, as evergreens were planted instead, but the rather decorative wood fence that was to corral the garden was still there.

The mystery plants first occurred in the back yard out of the blue about five years previous. At first, no one knew what they were – but one friend of Tom's thought they were 'mosquito plants'. How in the world a 'mosquito plant' should just start to grow – if that's what they were was a big mystery. Tom and Molly would later find out that their mystery plant – or plants – and the two plants were the same – were not 'mosquito plants,' however. Tom took a sample leaf to a neighborhood nursery and his plants were identified as something called a Royal Paulownia or some such. It is native to China and is called also "The Princess Tree" in China. Tom and Molly lived in a suburb of Atlanta, Georgia. How in the world a tree native to China became entrenched in their yard was quite a mystery, but they had two of them.

The first year of their existence, they grew only to about two feet. Each succeeding year, they seemed to double in size from the previous year – even though Tom would cut them down to the ground in the fall. Last year they grew as tall as sixteen feet or so. It was anybody's guess how tall they would grow this year. More than likely, initially, the seeds of the Royal Paulownia were carried to the yard by the winds; but regardless of the origin of the seed, the resulting plants were as beautiful as they became tall. Their leaves grew very large, some extending a foot in width and another foot in length. Tom liked to call them 'elephant ear leaves'.

Part of the huge mystery about Royal Paulownia seeds taking root in Tom and Molly's yard is they seemed to be alone. No one in the neighborhood had ever seen such a plant. So why did the wind choose Tom and Molly's place as a destination for the seeds? Molly conjectured that maybe other yards received the seeds, but the owners just hoed out the plants thinking they were weeds. Tom and Molly, however, took care to nurture their unknown weed; and it grew into a beautiful plant. They figured that the lesson of it all was that one ought not to be so quick to think of an unknown plant as a weed. It may just turn out to be a "Princess Tree."

"Wow!" exclaimed Elise, as they approached the plants. "That thing is already taller than me!" And it was only early summer. It was quite a sight – two lovely, innocent, naked kids measuring themselves according to the mystery plant. A week prior to this, Elise was taller than the plants. Now, she was considerably shorter. "It will be fun to see how tall they grow this year," she said to Kerry.

"Yeah, it will be," responded Kerry, with Tybee jumping about between them and barking for joy.

Then they heard a voice beckoning them to come quickly. "Breakfast is ready, Kids. Come and get it."

Molly had been showing the recently developed pictures of a previous outing to Liz and Joe. "Want to see the pictures of a week ago, Elise?" Molly asked, as the two hungry kids came rushing in.

"Yeah!" was the reply.

"Here they are," Molly said, as she handed the envelope with the pictures to Elise. "Why don't you and Kerry go to the couch and look at them. We will have breakfast when you finish. OK?"

"OK," Elise responded. "Come on, Kerry."

The pictures were of an outing the six of them and the next door neighbor, Sam, enjoyed a short time ago. They had gone to a wooded area about fifty miles from home where they knew they could enjoy a picnic au natural. A good time was had by all; and the pictures captured the event. There were several of Tom and Joe and Kerry, naked except for sneakers, trying to climb an old tree. That had been a hoot. Only Joe managed to reach the third branch up. They had to admit that they didn't know much about climbing trees, though both Tom and Joe had climbed a lot of trees when they were Kerry's age. Sam decided he was too old to even try.

Sam had just reached sixty last December. He and his wife, Nellie, some thirteen years older than Sam, moved into the house next to Tom and Molly about a year before Tom and Molly moved to the neighborhood. Nellie had diabetes and died a couple of years ago, but before she passed, she and her husband insisted on Tom and Molly and Kerry having a Sunday evening meal together almost every week; and after eating, they would play cards – sometimes canasta and sometimes hearts. With this, Kerry was quite bored and almost always chose to watch TV instead of play any ole boring card games. Now, if Elise had been at the table, that would have been a different story – but to play cards with a bunch of boring adults was no fun at all.

Nellie was not at all comfortable with going naked; and she suspected that if she were to visit at Tom and Molly's, they would embarrass her by going naked. So she never visited at Tom and Molly's, even though she insisted that they visit her and Sam. On the other hand, Sam had no problem visiting the naked neighbors – and whenever Nellie was away and the neighbors were home, he would find a reason to borrow something or other. Until Nellie passed, however, he had never participated in going naked in his own home beyond the bedroom and bathroom, even as he admitted to those who did that it was probably a good thing. He did, however, go naked at the neighbor's home with the neighbors as often as he could – the neighbors being Tom and Molly - and sometimes, Joe and Liz.

And then Nellie passed. After the funeral, he decided it was time for him to change and adopt the naked ways in his own home that he sometimes enjoyed in the neighbor's home. He even allowed for going naked both inside the house and outside of it around a seventeen year old grandson, Tony, who visited every summer for a couple of weeks. School had just finished for the year; and more than likely, Tony would soon be coming for his annual visit with his grandparents, though it was now only with Grandpa, being that Grandma Nellie was deceased.

Within the current set of pictures, there were pictures of Sam carrying some wood for the fire and some of Sam holding weenies over the fire and some of Sam playing kick the can with the others when Sam was caught alone in the middle. It seemed for some reason that most of the pictures that Elise and Kerry were enjoying on the couch in the living room were of Sam – but there were a few of Liz and Molly, too, sitting on an old wood stump, and one of all of them, except Tom who took the picture. Tom caught one of them all wading in the rocky creek that wandered through the area. And in all the pictures, only sneakers were worn.

The kids finally finished their review, laughing especially at the ones of 'Ole Sam' as they did. "Mommy, Ole Sam is so funny, isn't he?" Kerry liked the old fellow a lot.

"Yes, he is, Dear," replied Molly. Why don't you and Elise go and say hello to him after breakfast?"

"OK," was the reply.

"Let's all sit down for breakfast now, though," Tom said.

The table had been set. A hot bowl of scrambled eggs was in the middle of the table – and a couple of plates of warm cinnamon rolls had been prepared instead of the toast that had been planned. Each had a glass of orange juice setting beside his or her plate. There would have been ham or sausage or some kind of meat had there been any available in the house, but that which was handy was quite satisfactory to all.

"Those cinnamon rolls sure look good. Smell good too," Joe said.

"And they probably eat as good as they look and smell," responded Tom, "but before we eat them, let us offer a word of thanks for the meal at hand."

With that, they all joined hands. Some of them bowed; and some of them kept their heads high, looking mostly at the food in the middle of the table. Kerry and Elise sat next to each other and enjoyed the little affection they were sharing – and the adults were no less pleased. Tom offered the words.

"Blessed Nature, we thank you for what we are about to enjoy – the meal before us. Without wheat, there would have been no flour. Without flour, we could not have made cinnamon rolls. Without sugar, there would have been no icing for the rolls. Without chickens,

there would have been no eggs. All that we have before us comes from you, Blessed Nature – and we are grateful for it all. And we are grateful for ourselves as having come from you as well. Without you, Blessed Nature, none of us would be here today to enjoy this meal – or each other.

"As God is to you, Blessed Nature, you are to us. You come from God. We come from you. God is only the mysterious energy out of which Nature is born. It is not for us to insist on knowing how it all came about. It is only for us to enjoy that which has come about. And so, Dear Nature and Dear God, we embrace your gift of life as we enjoy each other. We thank you for the Blessed Trinity of Goodness, Unity, and Truth in us all."

After his blessing, Tom looked up and nodded his head and said, "And now, wonderful friends at this table, let's eat."

And the six said in unison – *Amen!*

8

Becoming A Believer

"Hello, Sam!" Kerry and Elise arrived at Sam's door. The main door was open in front of a closed screen door. They could see Sam at the far end of the house in his kitchen, wiping the dining room table. He had probably just finished breakfast, too, like they just had.

Sam's heart quickened its beat, as he always enjoyed the kind of company that the neighbors next door represented. They were so generous and kind. How could he not like them – from the parents to the kid; and he enjoyed Kerry's friend, Elise, tremendously too – as well as Elise's parents. On a good number of occasions, he had encountered them during visits with Tom and Molly; and often, Joe and Liz and Elise would come by to say hello with the neighbors.

"Well, Hello!" he said, as he hurried to the door to open it for his young guests. "Come on in and make yourselves at home!" Since Nellie's passing, Sam had fully embraced the neighbor's naturalism – and as was customary for a day at home, he was naked. The kids expected that as they knew Sam from his many visits to Kerry's house. Not all of Tom and Molly's guests were comfortable with their host's way of life, but Sam was one who was; and Sam knew he was welcome to drape his clothes on the rack by the front door. If Sam came over to visit rather than just ask a favor or offer a message, often he would join his hosts in their comfort.

Sam bent over and hugged his shorter visitors and kissed Elise on the cheek. Sam was 6'1" and much taller than the kids. He also had a bit of a paunch where his stomach was – and he enjoyed making fun of it. He claimed that his gall bladder surgery of fifteen years ago weakened his stomach lining and caused his belly to push out a bit. "Take heart, Kids," he said," as he groped his belly. "Maybe when you are as old as I am, you'll be lucky enough to grow a pillow like me too. Nellie told me that if I ever got rid of my tummy, she would have to find another just to have a pillow to lean on." And he chuckled at his own joke.

Sam was always laughing. His laughing often made the world brighter for Molly when she visited – and she felt like skipping home, even if she had walked over. It was good to hear Sam laugh.

"Are they still there?" he laughed, referencing his genitals often hid below his belly.

"Of course they are, Sam, you silly one, you," retorted Elise.

"That's good to know," he laughed again.

Elise giggled. "Oh, Sam!"

Kerry had moved to the back of the house and was looking out the open door to the back yard. "Elise, come quickly! Sam's birds are so pretty!"

Elise hurried to the site. Pointing at a red one, eating from Sam's own bird feeder, Elise asked, "Is that a cardinal, Kerry?"

"I think so," he said, while noting a blue jay scouting the ground for seeds dropped by the others. "Sam, I wonder why blue jays never use the feeder? I have watched your birds and our birds and I have never seen a blue jay perch on our hanging feeder - or yours. Are they scared of the feeder or what?"

"I don't know, Kerry," was his reply. "If they are scared of a feeder, that would seem to be out of character. I can't see them being scared of anything. They seem to be a rather bossy bird and drive the other birds away from the bird bath out front when they come. That's a good question. Why aren't they as bossy when it comes to feeding from a bird feeder?"

"I guess it's one of those 'Nature's Way' things," offered Elise. "Dad says there is so much we can't figure out about birds and animals. If we can't understand why something does what it does, just chalk it up to 'Nature's Way'."

Unawares to any of the three of them watching the birds and squirrels, Tony, Sam's seventeen year old grandson, had come up behind them. "Nature's Way! Yeah, that sounds good as an explanation for it all."

Elise jumped from the surprise. "Tony, I did not know you were here!"

"Yeah, came in last night with Julie."

"Who's Julie?" asked Kerry.

"Ah, she's just a girl friend," he said.

"Just a girl friend, huh?" remarked another newcomer. Julie had heard the voices and was intent on investigating.

"Ah, you know what I mean," Tony replied. Julie just smiled and gave Tony a hug.

"Julie, I want you to meet Kerry from next door and his 'girl friend,' Elise." Tony put a fun emphasis on 'girl friend' since he had spoken of Julie as his own girl friend.

"Hi!" Kerry said, as he gave Elise the eye. "And my 'girl friend' says hello too." Kerry took special delight in taking advantage of the opportunity and calling Elise his girl friend.

Elise chanted, "Hello, Julie! Hello, Tony! Good to see you again, Tony!"

Like his grandfather, Tony was naked, though Julie had not become accustomed to the new freedom as of yet. She was wearing a blue bathrobe that Nellie had worn for twenty years before her death a couple of years ago. Tony had grown considerably since his visit last year – and that included his masculinity. Kerry and Elise both noticed the change."

"Wow!" exclaimed Kerry. "You have gotten so big!"

"Just call it 'Nature's Way,' Kerry. You will get big too when you get as old as me." Tony snickered a little as he said it, seeing himself as really old, compared to six year old Kerry.

Indeed! Call it for what it is – Nature's Way. Julie was much too much of a neophyte of the **Natural Way** to be sure that this little rendezvous was at all proper, but it was very comforting to be referred to in such a polite term – Nature's Way. That was a lot like 'Nature's Child'. Makes everyone feel like they belong. That was nice. Why would anyone object to being Nature's Child?

Tony had seen Grampa naked often – even before his liberalization after Gramma's death. Nellie never went naked before her grandson, but she tried to accept Grampa teaching Tony the ropes. Even so, before Gramma died, Grampa did not mind sleeping in the raw, but he did not go about the house in the raw. Tony saw Grampa naked in his bedroom, but before Gramma had passed, he had not had the privilege of seeing Grampa naked in the kitchen or living room or out back.

Sam was grateful for his friendship with an angel, Molly. She had known of his acceptance of their own natural behavior when he visited and knew that he considered it the right way, but it took a little encouragement from Molly to go that extra step and become a practitioner of the **Natural Way**. Molly had followed a similar path a few years after her marriage when Tom convinced her that it was the right way to go.

Molly's conversion came as much from Kerry, however, as it did from Tom. Like Liz experienced with Elise, when Molly saw her naked baby frolicking with her naked and loving husband, she became a believer that natural freedom ought to be the ideal. She had been reluctant at first because of her upbringing that taught her that nakedness is of the devil and estranges the heart from God.

Tom, of course, had overcome the same teaching and did all he could to gently help Molly overcome her own bad vision. She struggled through the bad vision of her upbringing until Kerry was born – and then it was like a light came on. If Kerry was pure as a baby – with no taint of being soiled in sin – then, as Kerry's mother, she could not be tainted with sin either. *For how could it be that a son could be untainted while the source of that son was tainted?*

So, with Kerry's babyhood, she took off the bad vision glasses and threw them away. Every chance she got after that rebirth, she encouraged friends to follow the path. Most ignored her, but some, like Sam, heard.

And after Sam heard from Molly and Tom, Tony was awarded the same encouragement. Perhaps by this time next year, Julie will have heard the same encouragement, and she, too, will have adopted the *Natural Way* and feel right at home being just another of Nature's Children.

Tony had come to notice that the board holding the bird feeder had come loose from the pole to which it was attached. Grampa had nailed a two by four to a pole he had cemented into the ground that was to serve as an anchor for the bird feeder. The squirrels loved to scamper on the pole and board and try to reach the bird feeder from a wire holding the hanging bird feeder to the two by four. Apparently, the activity of the squirrels over time had caused the two by four to waver and become loose. Tony noticed it.

"Grampa, how about I fix that bird feeder for you?" Tony asked.

"Go ahead," Grampa replied.

Tony then fetched the step ladder from the shed out back, along with hammer and nails from Sam's tool chest in the shed and placed the ladder next to the pole. Then he climbed up the ladder to a point where he would be above where the two by four met the pole. Feeling the ladder as a little on the unsteady side, he asked Grampa to hold the ladder – and then he proceeded to add some new nails from the top down to better secure the bird feeder.

"I ought to get a picture of this," offered Julie. "What a sight you two are fixing a bird feeder, naked as the blue jays over yonder!"

Elise giggled. "I wonder if Sam is ticklish," she said to Kerry.

"I heard that," replied Sam. "In answer to your question, no, I'm not ticklish." But he chuckled as he said so. Sam's laugh always gave him away.

"Shall we see if that is true?" Julie sniggered to Elise.

Elise giggled again. "Yeah!"

Kerry joined the two of them and they all ganged up on Sam, while peering up the ladder and seeing Tony's middle attachments hanging down. The ladder was over a place laden with pine straw. So, if Tony did fall, he would not fall on anything hard.

After trying a few minutes to get a reaction from Sam by tickling him under the arms and getting no response, Julie decided to see how ticklish Tony was while Kerry and Elise kept up the attack on Sam. Sam laughed at the effort, but not as much from the finger tickling as from being tickled in the heart.

It wasn't a smart thing to do, going up a rickety step ladder to pursue a laugh, but Julie went two steps up and then decided she would not try to tickle Tony. She could not reach that high to get to his underarms. She would pretend that she was falling and then grab hold of his penis to keep her from falling. It had lost its earlier erectile state, but it was still big enough to grab.

"I'm falling," she pretended. Then she reached out and grabbed Tony's right thigh with her right hand and his penis with her left hand. With the grab, Tony's penis began to swell again, as an excited Julie shouted, "I'm OK! I'm saved!" And then she roared with laughter.

Seeing Julie hanging on to Tony as she was, Kerry and Elise joined in the laughter – and then Sam joined in with the loudest laughter of all.

"What's all the laughter about?" Tom and Molly had come over and seeing no one in the house, but hearing noises in the back, entered the house, knowing they would be welcome. The plan was for Liz and Joe to come over later, but for a little while, they wanted to make love in privacy in the home of their dear friends, Mr. & Mrs. Socrates.

Tom proceeded to the back while Molly took the liberty of slipping out of her dress and getting naked while still in Sam's kitchen. She knew Sam would appreciate the surprise; and she loved surprising Sam, however, she did not know Tony had come. So, Molly would be in for a surprise as well.

"Daddy, we're fixing Sam's bird feeder," Kerry said, as he continued to poke at Sam's ribs.

"Does it take all four of you to do that?" replied Tom, knowing full well that far more than fixing a bird feeder was in process.

Kerry and Elise stopped their fun with Sam and turned their attention to Tom. Kerry said, "We were just having fun with Ole Sam, Daddy!"

"I'm glad you were, Son," Tom replied, "and you, too, Elise, and you, too, Tony."

Tony had finished his nailing task and turned around to greet Tom. "Hello, Tom! Good to see you! May I introduce you to my girl friend, Julie?"

"Pleased to meet you, Julie. I see you have become somewhat accustomed to Sam and Tony and do not seem to be minding their ways."

"Tom, is it?" Julie responded.

"Yes," Tom replied.

"Glad to meet you, too, Tom – and yes, I am enjoying Sam and Tony for their ways. I would have never guessed I could be so comfortable around naked people, but I'm loving it. Do you practice their ways too?"

"Do they practice our ways?" offered Sam. "Julie, they are our ways. Tom and his wife, Molly, introduced me to their natural ways."

"Oh! Is Tom, Kerry's dad?"

"Yes, he is," Sam said.

"And he is my husband!" Molly had completed her disrobing and was talking from behind the back door screen. "And a mighty fine husband he is too!"

Of course, Sam recognized the voice. "Is that you, Molly? Come on out and give Tony a hug and meet Julie."

Molly considered putting her dress back on since she had not expected any newcomers, but she gained her composure immediately and knew that greeting Tony and his girl friend without pretense was the right thing to do. Molly had become very dedicated to taking every chance she got to testify as to her adopted belief that the **Natural Way** is the best way. So what better thing to do than to show Tony how special it was and to illustrate the beauty of it to a new acquaintance? She could not do such a testimony on the street, but in her friend's house, she knew it was right. She stepped out onto the back porch and into the morning light.

Sam was indeed a little surprised, but not a lot. Molly had gone natural with him many times – with and without Tom. "It's wonderful seeing you, Molly – and I love your wardrobe!" Then he chuckled. "Bet you did not expect my guest and guests. Surprise, surprise!"

"I'll say, 'Surprise!'" responded Molly. "Hi, Tony! I was trying to surprise Sam, but it looks like I have surprised more than Sam – including me – and Julie, is it?"

Julie had let go of Tony's penis upon Tom's first announcement of himself, but was still holding on to his thigh. She let go and stepped down from the ladder. Sam and the kids had already backed away. What do you say to a naked lady? Julie was confronted with a most unexpected situation. She responded admirably, sensing immediately that there was no threat here. Walking up to Molly, she gave her a big hug – like she had always known Molly and was greeting an old friend. Molly responded in kind and embraced Julie eagerly, then turned her face to hers and kissed her warmly, gently, and firmly. It was like a reunion time – even though no previous union preceded it.

"Good to meet you, Molly!" Julie said, "but talk about a surprise first meeting! This one takes the cake!"

"Then you were not put off with my liberal ways?" asked Molly.

"I must say I was a little embarrassed at first," she replied, "but - put off - no, not in the least. Tony told me about Sam and you guys. So, I am not totally unaware of your beliefs. And from what I have seen so far, I can't help but wonder why the rest of the world doesn't believe."

"It's a wonderful belief, Julie, to believe that all is right with you and that you belong just as you are – without pretense and with tremendous love in your heart – not only for yourself, but for everyone around you. It's what dreams are made of, Honey, and it belongs to any who have the courage to say yes to it."

"You are absolutely wonderful!" Julie replied. "I think I am becoming a convert."

"May I?" gestured Molly, gently tugging at the tie around Julie's bathrobe?

"Yes, Yes, Yes!" was her quiet, but eager, reply.

And then before Tony and Sam and Tom and Kerry and Elise, Molly untied the cincture to Julie's robe. Then with the care of a great lover, she loosened the robe from around her shoulders and let it fall. Behind the robe, there had been nothing. So Julie was naked, even as she felt clothed like she had never felt clothed in her life. Yes, she was without clothing, but now having joined her friend, Tony – and Sam and Molly and Tom and Kerry and Elise – she felt like she had joined a real family.

Tony was still on the ladder, though his attention had been on the amazing scene below. "I told you that you would be in for a nice surprise," offered Tony, as a tear of joy fell down his face. "I told you! Now, do you believe?"

"Yes, Tony, I believe!" she exclaimed, wiping her tears away with her hair.

"Kids, it seems as if we are the only nonbelievers here," said Tom, feeling truly wonderful by all that had gone on here in his friend's back yard. "What do you say we become among the believers?" Then he sat down on a picnic chair that was available and began to untie his shoes. *Soon, he, too, would join the believers.*

9

A Lesson in Love

Six year old, Kerry, and eight year old, Elise, did not hesitate to help each other join the believers. Neither knew how profound a belief in the **Natural Way** could become, but both believed in their parents who believed. Elise suggested to Kerry that she should help him undress and that he could help her undress. It just seemed like a right thing to do – to assist each other out of love – though like Julie could have disrobed herself, they could undress by themselves too. Elise knew Kerry would like to agree; and so she knew she was not imposing to offer her suggestion.

First came the shoes, then the socks, then the pants, then the little briefs, then the shirt. Like an artist going from one part of a scene to another, she filled the canvas with a naked boy. All the adults had gone in upon Sam's suggestion that he take out some steaks for a cookout later in the day. He had gone in, but all the others had followed, perhaps sensing that the kids needed some time to themselves.

Little Kerry with his sparkling eyes and slim body stood before a fully clothed Elise. Being reminded of the scene with Tony and Julie, Elise felt comfortable with touching Kerry all over, as she drew him close and hugged and kissed him, with her little hand feeling the little fellow's genitals. It wasn't sex. It was better than sex as only a child, perhaps, could enjoy it, not having progressed to the sometimes tumultuous feelings that can be unleashed when raging hormones assume control of some after puberty. What better time for a child to experience affection while he or she can still reach out spiritually. Then when puberty happens and all those raging hormones come into play, having known spiritual affection as a child, love would continue and penises and vaginas would not take over. Minds would be in control because minds started the direction.

Greater civilization would not approve, but greater civilization approved of all sort of things that were not proper – like theft and murder and war. What was greater civilization that it had the right to determine that love among the young is improper – even as it did condone hate and anger among adults? If all the Elises in the world could feel love for all the Kerrys in the world, would not this be a better world? Why should love among the children be denounced? And who denounces it? The many who find God above and beyond life. That's who. Elise was finding God inside of Kerry and inside of herself; and the two were becoming a prince and princess of kindness in a world that knows mostly hate and prejudice and envy.

"My Handsome Man, I adore you!" she said, as she stood before him. "Now, it's your turn."

Kerry then pursued his part of the deal. He removed her clothing in the same way she had removed his. And then they were both naked. "Let me feel you like you did me," he said, as he took his hands and felt his way around her body, becoming spiritually aware of the possibilities of purity as he did so.

"OK," she agreed, "but don't go in my vagina with your fingers because Mom says little girls are too young for that. She says little girls should grow hair around their vaginas before they are old enough to do more. Mom says, *first let there be hair, then you can do more."*

"And little boys should grow hair around their penis before they can do more too," he added.

Neither the little boy nor the little girl knew exactly what 'more' meant, but they were content on not having reached that stage, whatever it meant. Too many parents refuse allowance for little boys and little girls to get to know one another on their own levels because of a fear of 'more'. They fear that little kids should not investigate one another because they will follow the adults and try to experience the more that Liz told Elise she should not try to experience until later. But at her age, Elise had no desire to learn of the 'more' that would come about later. She was content on being a child, knowing that she was unique in that. Why put away her childhood too soon when her parents enjoyed specifically that aspect about her so much? There would come a time for older loves. Now was a time for Mommy and Daddy to enjoy her being a child. Why should she want to do that 'more' thing and lose her childhood when her childhood meant so much to her and her parents?

In truth, if kids are left alone to themselves to investigate as they can and will – with a little safe direction from their parents about staying away from the 'more' thing, they will grow to become loving adults who will want to do the 'more' thing. Kids are smart enough to know that 'more' should not come until hair prepares the way. It is Nature's Way. First, let there be hair, then you can do 'more'. If adults would approach their children with that simple little directive, little children could live and play in the world like it is the Paradise it is. But when parents refuse to let their kids learn on their own level as Nature would have them know the lessons of life, then girls grow up having skipped childhood and boys grow up having skipped it too. In the end, all become adults without ever having enjoyed their childhood.

But to let children be – that's to make childhood wonderful; and no child would want to become an adult and leave all their fun behind. In time, they would take their place as adults because it is *'Nature's Way,'* but having such wonderful memories of their freedom loving childhood, they could only become freedom loving adults. And wouldn't that be wonderful? But all too often, for fear of 'more,' parents live in fear themselves – and teach their children more of the same.

"I like you, Elise. Isn't God wonderful for making something so pretty as you?" Kerry was repeating what Daddy said to Mommy all the time. Kids learn by what their parents say and do.

"I like you too, Kerry," she replied. "I like you a lot, but I'm thirsty. Let's go see if Sam has a coke we can drink?"

"Me too," Kerry responded.

And so she took him by the hand and they went inside where all the adults were.

"Hi, Mom! How do we look?" asked Kerry of Molly.

"Splendid, Sweetheart, just splendid!" Molly replied.

Sam was quick to agree. "My Dears," he said, "you children do the whole world proud – and all of us adults are very proud of you too."

"Yes, we are, Kids," Tom added. "We are very proud of you, but very few in the world agree that to go natural is to go Godly. So, until the world changes a good bit, you need to keep this thing of going without clothes just between us here. OK?" Tom hated to have to offer a warning at a time like this, but being a parent, he felt the urge.

"I know that," Elise replied. "Mom and Dad always tell me to go naked only with those who agree that it is good and Godly and do it themselves. She says, you can know who agrees with going naked by how they talk. If they make fun of going naked, then they probably don't do it. If someone asks you to take off your clothes, but they have their clothes on, then they probably are a bad person and only want you to take off your clothes so they can hurt you."

"It's too bad there are people out there in the world who want to hurt others," Molly offered, "but unfortunately, there are a lot of people who do not care about others and love to hurt them. It's too bad, but that's the way it is – at least for now. Someday maybe the world will learn to love much better, but right now, we need to be careful."

"But why would anyone want to hurt me?" Kerry asked.

"Because they have been hurt by someone else, Honey," replied Molly, "and they are only trying to get even. Someone who has been hurt by someone else thinks that to make it all even he or she has to hurt someone too. That's why someone might want to hurt you, Kerry. That's why someone might want to hurt you, Elise."

"If you know someone who has been hurt and you think they may be looking to hurt someone else to get even, be sure and stay away from them," added Tom.

"But shouldn't I be friendly with someone who has been hurt?" Elise asked. "I thought I am supposed to love everybody."

"You can love everybody, Sweetheart, but you can love everybody without getting in their way. Just wish everybody well and that's loving them. OK? Love is only wishing another well." Molly knew it is more than that, but she also knew that hate in the world cannot be controlled.

If another is out to hate because of being hated or hurt, then they will do hurt to those closest to them at the time. Every parent frets about their child being the victim of one who hates, but it is not good to live life afraid of those who hate either. If one lives afraid to act like one should for fear of being the victim of one who hates, then that one's life is damaged. The best defense in life is not to fail to love out of fear, but to love in spite of fear, and as much as possible, stay out of the way of those who hate. But how do you tell that to a child who only wants to love? How do you tell that to anyone? All anyone can do is just do the best they can by good example – and hope for the best.

Elise had been satisfied with the short definition of love she had received. "Molly, I wish you well. So I guess I love you. And I wish Kerry well. I guess that means I love him too. And, Sam, I wish you well. And, Tom, I wish you well. I guess that means I love you all. It's nice to wish you well and love you. It's really easy to love. Isn't it?" Then she shouted to Tony and Julie, who had escaped to the living room - "And, Tony, I wish you well too, and Julie, I wish you well. That means I love you!"

As it happened, Joe and Liz picked just that moment to check things out next door from where they had been enjoying themselves – at Tom and Molly's.

"Looks like we are joining a love fest," Joe said to Liz, as they heard the voice of their dear little one shouting how she loves everybody while coming up the walk to Sam's front door. Having reached the front door, Joe yelled in jest, "Anybody home?"

Elise was the first to respond, as she ran to the door and opened it wide for Mom and Dad to come in. "Mommy, Daddy, I wish you well. That means I love you!"

Before Mommy and Daddy could answer, they looked in and saw that Heaven was at home at Sam's too. Liz just opened her eyes wide as if they would pop out of her head as she viewed all the naked people in one little house. Mr. & Mrs. Socrates had surprised her and Joe a lot in the years they knew each other, but not like this.

There was Sam over there standing by his sink, and there was Tony and some young stranger sitting on the loveseat, and there was Tom and Molly sitting at the dining room table, and lastly, there were the children, Kerry, standing next to Molly at the dining room table, and her own Elise, hugging her at Sam's front door. And everyone of them was naked.

Joe was surprised, but not shocked. Staring at the scene before them, having stepped inside, he shook his head and said, "What a wonderful surprise! But it looks like we have been missing something!"

"And we have been missing you," Tom said, "but you don't have to miss anything anymore and we don't have to miss you. Come on in to Sam's house!"

Sam was elated as Tom knew he would be. Tom would have never assumed the right to ask another into Sam's house – except that he knew Sam.

Sam exclaimed. "What a wonderful family you are to me, everyone! I feel like this is Father's Day, multiplied by eight, because of the eight of you who are here. I only wish my Nellie could have been here with us." Then he turned to the ceiling as if Nellie was sitting on the lamp over the dining room table and said, "Nellie, Dear, see what you are missing?"

Liz squatted to the level of her hugging daughter and said with tears flowing freely," Elise, of course, we know you love us! And you know we love you too!" Then she looked across the room to Kerry and bid him to come. ***"Come over here, Kerry. I'm in a very hugging mood!"***

10

Making the Body a Paradise

"Looks like we are the odd ones," Joe remarked, looking into the eyes of his love, Liz. Then he looked over to Sam and said, "Sam, awfully good to see you again. I see that Tony has arrived for another summer visit. And who might I ask is the lovely lady sitting next to Tony?"

"I'm Julie," Julie volunteered. "I take it you are the Joe and Liz Tony has told me about. Now I guess I have met you all."

"Good to meet you, Julie." Then he went over to where she and Tony were and bent down and hugged Julie. "Hi, Tony," he said. "Brother, have you grown in one year!" And he reached down and hugged Tony as well. "Come on over, you two, and meet my wife."

"No," Liz said. "Let me come over there to you." Liz then walked over and hugged both Julie and Tony, who had risen to hug Joe better.

"Liz, I see by your reaction that you approve of all this," offered a comforted Julie.

"I certainly do," she said, "and I can't wait to join you all. Life is such a wonderful blessing. I guess you could even call it a feast. But trying to love life with clothes on is like trying to eat a steak through cardboard."

"That's an interesting way to put it," Julie responded. "So you see life as a feast, huh?"

"Don't you?" asked Liz.

"Not until recently – until I met Tony and all of you," she replied, "but I am beginning to see life in a different light."

"Tom and Molly and us are all so very close," commented Liz, while starting to undress. "That which makes us so close is our shared vision that our bodies should be a Paradise. It's just the way we look at things."

Joe had already stripped to his pants – and when they came off, his penis was erect. Julie glanced at it and then glanced at the others in the room, seeing that none of them seemed embarrassed. Noticing that Julie was a bit surprised, Joe moved to offer an explanation. "It happens that way sometimes, Julie. It's **Nature's Way**. This group of friends do not constantly question our reactions like so many others do. It's important to accept life the way it is – and our bodies are our lives. So why not accept them for what they do?"

"But there is a perfectly normal explanation for it, Julie," added Liz. "You will find it out with Tony if you haven't already. When a guy has his penis tucked into his pants, it is kinda squashed in there. So when the little guy – or big guy as the case may be – gets out, he feels sudden freedom and sometimes springs to a stiffened state. At least that is what Joe tells me," she added, as she laughed at her own reference to a guy's penis as a little guy or a big guy.

"You can call that a normal explanation if you want," countered Joe, "but the real explanation is that when a penis is set free from being smothered behind clothes, blood rushes to it. That's what makes it come to life, as it were. I guess what we are saying by being so blunt is that we shouldn't make erections as personal as we do. They are far more natural than personal. If we accept our responses on a natural level, then we won't get all hung up with the personal."

"It sounds like you don't think much of the personal," Tony remarked, from his sitting position on the couch. He had sat back down after giving Liz her hello hug.

"We like being personal alright, Tony," Tom replied, having been silent on the sidelines for a bit. "We even love being personal, but we realize that the key to really enjoying the personal is to enjoy it only within natural bounds. It's proper that Julie enjoys seeing Joe's erection, but she should not make that a personal thing in that she may have caused it. People give themselves credit for reactions that are strictly natural – and that is foolish because it is often not the case."

Then Tom turned toward Julie and spoke to her. "Now, look at me, if you will, Julie. I have been out of clothes for some time and my penis is relaxed. Does that mean I am not excited about life or that I have suddenly become bored with life? Of course not, but people often think that if a man's penis is limp, that is a sign of his lacking excitement around those he is with. That, too, is a lot of personal nonsense. When we get too hung up with being personal, we lose sight of the real world. Why would anyone want to lose sight of the real world when the real world is Paradise?"

He continued Julie's education. "Keep in mind, Julie, that if I were alone in this room, the reaction of my penis would not be much different than if the most loving lady was touching it. Of course, I must mean by that, Molly – as she is the most loving lady of my life." He glanced at Molly and Molly smiled in return. "It is really important to keep a proper perspective – always try to see what is happening, first, as natural, and then only secondarily, as personal."

Stroking his penis, it began to rise. "You have seen it in Tony. You know what happens when I do this. My penis is getting hard because by stroking it, blood is rushing to it and through it, making it firm. But, you see, I am doing it – not

Molly – or rather, Nature is doing it, not Molly or me. It's *Nature's Way*."

From his sitting position on the couch, Tony found himself amazed that he was actually enjoying Julie's education. It was as much an education for him as it was for Julie because Tom was showing it just exactly as it happens to him. He, Tony, had been guilty in his young life of seeing too much of the personal in him – and he was grateful that Tom was showing just how untruthful that could be.

Molly wanted to add something. "Julie, we in this room believe that the body should be Paradise because we believe that the mysterious spirit we call God is in us all. That makes us sacred vessels of God. We don't understand how God does, only that God is doing – and God is doing us. We are happening now because of God and God is making us happen. We should see our bodies as our Paradise because it is ungrateful to God to do otherwise. Keep in mind that it is only a perspective.

"Nature in all its unfathomable wisdom," she continued, "as the handmaiden of God is happening through us. It is not primarily a personal thing. It is primarily a natural thing, though our enjoyment of it should be personal as well. Nature is impersonal – and so should we be as much as possible. *If we get lost in Nature and embrace ourselves primarily as Nature's Blessings, then we can see it clear to enjoy what we are.*"

"Molly's right, Julie," Tom said – and Julie turned in Tom's direction and saw that he was still gently stroking his genitals. "This that I do is a wonderful feeling, but it is Nature's offering far more than my own. I am not some independent one outside of Nature. I am only doing what Nature is giving me to do. It feels good, but it also feels right. It's convenient.

"My hands fall naturally to my middle; and the natural thing for a hand to do is touch what is closest. That is *Nature's Way*. So by designing mankind as Nature has, man is invited to touch himself – or in the case of you ladies, herself. I mean, my design is such that I do not have to go out of my way at all to reach my pubic area. And, in fact, if I do not touch myself and enjoy Nature's Blessings, then I do have to go out of my way to avoid things. Why would Nature design me with hands that reach my middle and then command that I avoid the middle? Only one who does not believe in Nature's design could possible believe that my handling myself is not by design. If it's by design, then I should do it."

Noticing Julie trying to make contact with Elise, Molly decided that it would be best if the children were not brought into the discussion at hand – simply because it might be too confusing with so many people around. Molly moved to exclude the kids from the discussion at hand. "Kids, how about taking your cokes and going outside to watch the squirrels or the birds?"

Kerry was eager, but Elise felt a suspicion that they were being excluded on purpose. Of course, it was about what Tom did or was saying. She was smart enough to know that, but she knew she could ask Mom and Dad later for an explanation if she was still interested. So, off the kids went into the backyard so the adults could be alone.

Sam had been in the kitchen since Joe and Liz arrived, busily doing this and that, but he was aware of all that was being offered to Julie – with his full approval. He had no way of knowing anymore than anyone else of what Julie and Tony would think when it was all over, but he felt quite strongly that they should at least hear the side of life as believed by the group in this house. After the kids had gone outside, he moved over to the discussion going on in the living room. It was now his turn to talk.

"Julie and Tony, I hope you have enjoyed Tom's demonstration if you want to call it that. He is only trying to offer that we should be comfortable with our bodies and what they do."

Pointing to a movable mirror, he said, "See that mirror there. My favorite time of the day is to sit naked before that mirror and meditate on the wonder of life. Tom and Molly bought me that mirror when Nellie died and told me it could become my best friend – and it has – next to them, of course.

"Now, don't get me wrong. I am not someone who thinks he is some outstanding looking guy. I am not. I am just ordinary – from head to foot – but when I look upon myself in Molly's mirror, as I like to call it, and see God's good graceful creation looking back at me, then I know that God is being good to me. Molly and Tom knew from the way I enjoyed looking at myself in their living room mirror that I enjoyed seeing something about me; and so they bought me that mirror which I can set in front of a chair to be able to look at Nature in me in my meditation.

"Looking at any body should prompt the same reaction," he continued, "and I enjoy looking at other bodies. But I'm mostly alone now and the only body I can look at is my own. It suffices quite well as a body to review because it is like any other body. I am not looking specifically at my body when I look at myself. I am only using me to see all of Nature – and I love it. The body is filled with the wonder of God – and yet mankind so often thinks it can override that wonder and even legalize the suppression of the natural. Mankind's greatest sin, I think, is its false pride that it has the right to make all the rules. In doing so, it often overrules normal conduct of the body. The body's rules should be seen as God's rules for the body, but humankind often thinks it can outlaw various functions of the body because of being embarrassed by those functions.

"As Tom often argues, though, Honey," Sam continued, "we should do nothing in private that we should not be anxious to do in front of another. Nothing about life is primarily personal. It's mostly natural; and in loving Nature, we should not feel ashamed about anything that Nature does. When I sit in front of Molly's mirror and see life reflected in this still half vibrant sixty year old, I feel like I am celebrating Nature and God. I am seeing the gift of my body as my own passage way to Heaven. God must be in it because God is making it – not me."

Sam's offering mellowed Julie's confusion a bit, but she was still uncertain. "Tom, may I ask you a question?"

"Anything at all, Julie," he responded.

"Sam says he feels the same as you in that we should do nothing in private that we should not like to do in public – or something like that. Is that right?"

"Almost," he responded. "That is almost correct. I would prefer to say it like this. I should do nothing in private that I would be ashamed to do in public."

"Would you have intercourse with Molly in public?" she asked.

"I would not mind that in the least," he answered.

"He means he would not mind in the least if it were for the right reason – and neither would I," Molly added.

"And what is the right reason?" Julie questioned.

"To begin a child," Molly said.

"You mean you would have intercourse only if you want to conceive?" Julie asked.

"That's right, Julie – only if conception is intended," Tom replied.

"I am under the impression that you are liberal," Tony commented. "That is hardly liberal."

"Let me try to explain," Tom said. "You see, Molly and me and Joe and Liz – and even Sam – believe that we should respect *Nature's Way*. When and where it is clear that Nature would have us do one thing and we do another, then we are not being faithful to Nature – and not being faithful to Nature and Nature's design, we are not being faithful to God – from whence Nature comes. It is clear to us that Nature intends intercourse only for conception – even though societized man often chooses to disregard Nature's design. From the viewpoint of Natural Design now, when a penis enters a vagina, it is intended to release the male's seed. Keeping with respect for Natural Design, if I should enter Molly, it should be for releasing my seed. So, if I do otherwise and try to avoid the consequence of natural intercourse by withdrawal or contraceptive or condom or whatever, then I am not being a true disciple, as it were, of my belief.

"Now, one of the good things about practicing restraint," he continued, "is that we avoid all sort of unwanted consequences – like conceiving an unwanted baby or catching some venereal disease. By not having sex – in terms of intercourse – except to have a child – we are really protecting ourselves. We belong to Nature and if we respect that to which we belong, more often than not, Nature will protect us. We just won't suffer the many consequences that societized folks do. Know what I mean?"

"Societized?" That's a new word to me," said a puzzled Tony. "Just what do you mean by that?"

"To become societized," Tom replied, "is to rule your life by what society does, regardless of how dumb it might seem. Sometimes we do the dumbest things and do them only because everyone else around is doing them. Society says to do this and you do it – whether you agree with it or not. That's being societized.

"Society often teaches that God is outside of life, rather than in it. Anyone who believes that believes it by virtue of someone in society who first thought it was – or is – right. Now that one in society may have been under the impression that he was receiving a ruling from God, but since God did not speak directly to any of us who have been given the ruling, we can only rightly conclude that the one in society who thinks he spoke with God is probably wrong.

"I mean if God really intends us to follow some rule or ruling of His, then it stands to reason that God would instruct us all directly on an individual level. It makes no sense whatever that God would speak to an Israeli and not speak to a Brazilian. It makes no sense that God would speak to an Israeli in the year 2000 B.C. and expect that Israeli to tell some Brazilian 8,000 miles away of the conversation – especially if what God told the Israeli is necessary for salvation.

"Any ruling that someone in society has levied is a societized ruling – even if it is claimed to have come from God. That is how I see it. We believe we should rule our lives by virtue of our interpretation of Natural Design – not by virtue of what anyone in society may think is right. I think that which has corrupted mankind the most is its false sense of a bestowed spirituality – or a spirituality that is not interior to its being, but one that must be given in addition to its being. In other words, mankind has been misled by itself to believe that God must come to it when in reality, God is already in it.

"Now, the problem with the view that mankind is not already whole and Godly is that the door is left open to all sort of misbelievers who are absolutely positive that someone who speaks to them and gives them some outside ruling is God. Entire structures of societized man have been built on a false sense of spirituality because those who started the structures had false impressions of life in terms of placing God outside of life. If you don't believe that God is in life, then you look for answers outside of life and leave yourself wide open to those who claim they spoke with an external God.

"In truth, most of our religious tradition is actually based on the false perception that life is unholy or ungodly. When the foundation is so poor, being based on error, then the entire building built over the foundation is at risk of falling. Societized man is so caught up in the web of its own misbegotten rules based on an idea that God is exterior to life rather than interior to it that it has been long lost in confusion."

"Once again, Tony," said Sam, "we emphasize natural over social. What comes from society is social. What comes from Nature is natural. We believe that it is best to go with what is natural."

Joe had been silent for a good while, but was now ready to contribute. "Kids, you might think that restricting intercourse to conception is harsh, but you could not be more wrong. It is because of that restriction upon ourselves that I can trust Tom with Liz and he can trust me with Molly. By virtue of our belief – and our faithfulness to it – we are free to play and enjoy without ever suffering the many tragedies that society suffers. Our regimen makes us free and allows us to trust one another.

"Now if I were to make an exception with my wife, Liz, and have intercourse with her while using a condom, then she would have reason to believe that I might make another exception too – like with her friend, Molly, for instance. Then in not being able to trust me, she might become suspicious, whether she has reason or not, and then our marriage would suffer and her friendship with Molly would suffer and my friendship with Tom would suffer.

"By voluntarily restricting ourselves to intercourse for conception only, we are free to play in front of the children and know that the children will not be hurt by doing something we should not be doing. If we have intercourse outside of conception, then there is no reason why our children should not do the same. And, in the end, chaos results and no one is happy."

"You see, Tony and Julie," offered Sam, "it's like we belong to a club that has dues. The dues we pay are to restrict ourselves to conduct within Natural Design; and some of the many benefits we receive are healthy lives. But if we are unwilling to pay the dues of the natural club, then we can't enjoy any of the benefits either. Keep in mind that conduct in the ***Conduct by***

Natural Design Club is totally voluntary. No one makes anyone join. It is entirely up to each individual."

"Do you think Kerry and Elise will join your club?" asked Julie, wanting to hear how all of this liberal conduct might be affecting them.

"Not our club," corrected Liz, "Nature's club. But we realize that is a good question. The answer is that we think they will, but we don't know. When Elise and Kerry become teenagers, they will undoubtedly be pressured to act societized, as Tom calls it. As their parents, we hope they will pay attention to our example, but they may not – and if they don't, well, it's their lives."

"I'm curious as to what the kids think about what went on here today," commented Julie. "Do you think it will hurt them?"

"They haven't seen anything today that they haven't seen before," Tom said, "but in terms of our open conduct, there will be some hurt, yes. It will hurt them a little because it will confuse them. They know that what I call societized man will not approve of open conduct of adults before children – or they will come to know it. By our doing what we do and main society now disagreeing with what we do, that will confuse them for sure. But, in time, if our example is constant, they may agree more with us than with societized man. So, yes, it may hurt them a little by virtue of the confusion they will experience as children, but, no, it will not hurt them overall because, in the end, our examples will save them from making so many of the mistakes that so many do who have no regimen such as ours."

Julie continued. "Tom, do you think that adults should relate to children in matters of sex?"

"Ideally, no," he replied. "Kids should do with kids as adults should do with adults, but one should not do for or with the other. At least using Nature as the source of the instruction, in

Nature, never do you see adults getting sexual with children – or children with adults. From that standpoint, it is clear that humans should not act contrary to the regular format within Nature. And yet societized man violates that rule a lot. We in this group do not."

"Kerry is allowed to see us loving one another," added Molly, "but he is not encouraged to join in. We tell him that he can join in with his friends and do with his friends what Nature allows of them, but he should not play with adults. Adults have their own play and children have theirs, but the two should not mix."

"Do you think he understands?" asked Julie.

"Yes, I think he does," answered Molly. "Being open like we are, it is clear to him that his body is different than his dad's. He can handle that because he can see it for himself. He doesn't have to wonder if it is so, even if he does wonder why it is so."

"How do you handle Elise's curiosity, Joe?" questioned Tony. "Does she ever want to check you out?"

"Of course," Joe replied. "She has touched me to see what happens – and I let it happen to satisfy her curiosity, but she knows that adults and children should not engage each other as a standard practice. She knows I will never touch her, even if she asks, in a genital way, because she knows from what we tell her that only children should play with children and only adults should play with adults. It has never become an issue; and we don't ever expect it to become one."

"I hope you are right," responded Tony. "I could imagine that a prolonged obsession could become an issue."

"Obsessions are only for those who are not allowed to entertain curiosity, I think, Tony. Once a curiosity is satisfied, it goes away. We allow curiosity on the part of Elise, but we also rule by what we see as the rule of Nature in not encouraging adult-children behavior, even though adults and children can be in the same room as they play. It is not the play that is wrong. It's the unnatural interaction."

"We are not so fragile as we might think," commented Molly, "if we leave ourselves to established patterns in Nature to make the right choices. That's what making the body a Paradise is all about – letting Nature make the rules by doing what it does in the animal kingdom. *All we have to do is observe her ruling and act accordingly.*"

"Let me play the devil's advocate," suggested Tony. "If you think that looking at patterns in the animal kingdom should be the basis of our own rules, look at a den of lions. Sometimes they fight with each other and kill each other. Is that to say that we should take from that observation that men should fight with each other and kill each other?"

"No, Tony," Mollie replied. "We are not talking about patterns as established by just one species, but about patterns that are common to all species. Some animals kill each other and some don't. You can't deduce an ideal from just one animal – but from all animals taken together. *It's only where there is a common conduct among animals that we humans should be wise to conclude that if it right for the rest of the animal kingdom, then it should be right for humans.*"

"Exactly!" chimed Tom. "In the issue at hand of how humans should conduct their sexuality, there is, in fact, a general pattern in the animal kingdom that indicates that other animals only have sex to co-create. We kid about fast human males who conduct sex on a 'slam, bam, thank you, Ma'am' basis. Well, in the animal kingdom, that is true. Generally speaking, animals mate quickly without regard to any lingering pleasure. That's not to say we humans should not take the time to enjoy sex, but it is to say that sex in the animal kingdom is for co-creation – or procreation – only. Accordingly, in the issue of sex, Nature does provide an answer by virtue of a common pattern within it."

"That's cool when you think about it," commented Tony. "I can see now how you could consider such a ruling as gospel, so to speak."

"Yeah, it is cool," Liz replied. "I mean it takes all the guess work out of deciding what is right."

"And when you consider how important an issue sex is for the human race," added Joe, "by deciding the issue of sex as we have, we have eliminated most of the concerns that human beings face relating to one another because so much of our interrelations deal with sex in some way. And it was there all the time for us to know. All we humans have had to do was to study Nature and conclude our ideal conduct based upon a general pattern in Nature. If it's good for all, then it's good for any within that all. Since humans are within the all of the animal kingdom, since it is good for all the other animals, then it must be good for us too. Simple, huh?"

"It seems a lot simpler than I thought it would be," commented Julie. "This reference that I have heard several times of making the body a Paradise seems so much more correct now that I have heard your explanation. We really can trust ourselves to find ourselves and attain Paradise by observing Nature. I really am amazed. Thanks so much for taking the time to point it out. I have really enjoyed this discussion."

"That goes for the both of us," offered a satisfied Tony. "We sure did not expect this, but it has been a wonderful surprise. We may just join that club of yours, Grampa."

"Nature's club," Sam corrected, "not our club. We hope you do. You will be in great company if you do. *Just make of your bodies a Paradise, keeping in mind that all is well with the world of Nature. Give yourselves to Nature and by so doing, give yourselves to God Who is in Nature. When you can, look toward Nature for the answers. Belong to Nature and seek its counsel – and by so doing, find peace.*"

"I think I will, Sam," replied Julie. "I think I will."

11

A Special Love Offering to God

"Let us offer a toast with the children!" Sam exclaimed.

It was early evening and the day was coming to an end. Sam was there with all his guests in his own back yard. The gas grill had been reduced to low, just hot enough to keep the steaks hot. All the guys, even little Kerry, liked their steaks medium rare. Julie liked hers well done, but Molly and Liz like theirs medium rare too. Elise was not particular. She said it didn't matter to her.

Molly had mixed a salad from the vegetables she and Tom provided for the affair. It was a simple salad made up of lettuce, tomatoes, cucumbers, and green pepper. At Sam's request, the salad, like the steaks, had been left off the large picnic table in the back. Sam planned a special toast and he said it would take the whole table. When asked what could take a whole table, he had just smiled and said, "You'll see."

When Nellie was alive, her kids came around often, including Jason and Helen, Tony's parents. Jason was one of Nellie's kids. Sam actually had no kids of his own, but had married a young widow with three kids, ranging from four to ten. Nellie's husband, Steve, had been killed in an auto-pedestrian accident that had claimed his life at the age of thirty-three. Sam was a much younger brother to Philip; and Philip had been Steve's best friend. Sam and Steve and Philip went fishing quite often; and Sam had come to know and love Nellie via that friendship.

When Steve was killed, Sam became a real comfort to Nellie. Philip had to be away quite a bit due to business after his friend's funeral. So he asked his younger brother, Sam, to look in on Nellie from time to time. It was due to his looking in on Nellie that he came to fall in love with her. Though only twenty at the time of Steve's death, he and Nellie got married about a year later. He was twenty-one and she was thirty-four.

Sam had wanted to go to college, but with a quick family of three kids and a wife, he had to go to work. So he hired on with the Postal Service and remained with that job throughout his marriage. After the family of two girls and a boy had been raised, he and Nellie were mostly alone – except for occasional visits by the family. For thirty-five years, Sam worked with the Postal Service, delivering mail to all on his route while also delivering a friendly smile to all he met. Sam was well loved by family and everyone.

At the age of fifty-seven, Sam decided in favor of early retirement so that he could be on hand for his ailing wife. For the last ten years of Nellie's life, she was down as much as she was up. Her diabetes took its toll. About two years before Sam retired, Nellie had to have a couple of toes on her left foot amputated. Finding it hard to move around, she came to depend a lot on Tom and Molly when Sam was away at work. More often than not, either Tom or Molly was at home when she needed help; and a quick phone call would bring them to her aid. Sam really loved Tom and Molly for helping them through that dire time. Nellie's kids all lived far removed from Sam and Nellie and were told that they needn't worry about Nellie. Sam and his friends would see to her; and so it happened.

Grandma and Grandpa loved all the kids and their kids, but special to them was Tony. Whenever he could, Tony liked to stay with his grandparents; and Jason and Helen always arranged for a summer stay for little Tony. Tony was special because he came around much more than the other eight grandchildren, but he was also special because he was one that Grampa felt he could confide in.

Being uncomfortable with her own nakedness, Nellie chose not to visit the neighbors, Tom and Molly, who were always talking about how wonderful it is to go naked and free for the love of God. Sam, however, made treks over to his neighbors often and fell in love with them and their ways. He never confided in Nellie that he often went naked with the neighbors because he thought it might upset her, though she probably knew it. It did not seem to matter to her. It was making Sam happy, even if it did not comfort her all that much.

But little Tony – he received an earful from Grampa. To Tony he could tell it like he had come to believe it. "Tony," he would say, "we human beings are just not doing right by the gift of life that is being given to us. How do you think I would feel if I were to give you a bright new fire truck to play with and you would discard it? That must be what we are doing to God. He gives us these wonderful bodies to enjoy and we hide them, not only from ourselves, but from God Himself. Or at least we try to hide them. Now that can't be the right thing to do. We need to try and get it right as best we can, just you and me, and maybe we can help change things."

And little Tony would reply, "Yeah, just you and me, Grampa!"

Grampa told little Tony that he could always go without clothes in his room and Grampa would do the same in his. Grampa would try to leave the door open, too, so that Tony could come and visit anytime. And Gramma never seemed to mind that Grampa was naked and little Tony was naked when they came together in Gramma's bedroom, but it was clear to both Grampa and Tony that Gramma did not think it was proper anywhere else.

"I think a toast with the children would be nice to start this meal," Sam said. "We are all in agreement here that God would have us naked all the time if God could command us – because God would have us grateful for His gifts of life. I think it would really be nice if we adults could offer to God the youngest of us here, a boy and a girl. Kerry and Elise, could you both step up to the table and get on it?" Then he helped Kerry and Elise on to a couple of chairs, then on to the table.

Kerry and Elise had no problem with this. They liked it that they were the center of attention; but the adults were pleasantly amazed by Sam's action. They all knew Sam and knew he could only do something wonderful, but they could only wonder what that something wonderful was.

"If you don't mind," Sam began, "I'd like to command just ten minutes of your time. During this ten minutes, we will be conducting a very spiritual exercise because we will be doing it with God in mind. We will be revering God by or with an attitude of gratitude for the wonderful gift of life. I consider such to be prayer in its most excellent form.

"Kerry and Elise," Sam said, as he directed a warm smile toward the children, "you can look where you want – at us or the sky or at each other." Then he glanced around at the others standing around the table and added, "but I would like all the rest of us to look at the children and study them in silence for a whole minute. I will tell you when that minute should start and when it ends. And then I would like each of you to study the person next to you and hug and kiss each other, while feeling the other's body. That goes for Kerry and Elise too. When I tell you to start, I want you to hug and kiss and feel each other all over. OK?

"During the first minute," he continued, "I would like silence. Just look at the children in silence and listen to your heart and mind for what it is telling you. Knowing all of you as I do, I know there is only the right kind of love in you. So I know your thoughts will be of a kindly nature. Then after that first minute, while you are loving each other, I will be offering a prayer to God. I think this would be a very nice way to begin our meal – to start it with a prayer and a love offering such as God probably never receives. During your lovemaking to the one nearest to you, imagine your partner as being God Itself, because, in effect, it's true. Since God is making your partner, then it could properly be argued that your partner represents God. So be intimate with your partner like he or she is God."

"Sam, what a wonderful idea!" exclaimed Molly.

"How fitting!" offered Liz; and they all agreed.

"Let us begin our minute of silence, then," he said. "Let no one bow their heads. Just keep your heads up, your eyes open, and look at the children."

And thus began the loudest moment of silence since time began. It resounded with the chirping of birds in the background as all looked at the kids in the center. There was God's naked little boy, Kerry, with his stout little body, looking around to see what the others were looking at. Standing there, they beheld his little penis and testicles – so full of the love of God – and so promising to hold the beginning of some life some years away.

Tom saw him as bold, while Molly saw him as handsome, as Joe saw him as gentle, while Liz some him as cute, while Tony saw him as playful, while Julie saw him as pure – and they were all right. And Sam, he saw him as perfect; and he was the rightest of all.

There was God's naked little lady, Elise, with her lovely hair falling down her back. Sam offered an option of looking at the sky; and that was the option that Elise chose. While

life we have is from you and in you and for you and by you. And we thank you for it.

"Dear Wonderful Creator, we reach out and touch you by touching and hugging and kissing each other. You deserve to be touched and hugged and kissed for all the wonder that you are giving us. Our earth is a Paradise and the air and water and soil and all that it allows to grow are our salvation. Without them, we could not live. Without them, we could not be here today to say anything. But we are here today and we do have the wonder of your gifts – and your wondrous gifts. We want to thank you by offering this very special toast."

While Elise was making love to Kerry, Kerry began to respond. His little hands stroked her hair as she was bending down to his middle. Her little mouth on him was nice, but he was much more interested in stroking her hair, and then when she stood up, he did as she had done and caressed her body with his hands. It was nice, too, to kiss her lips as she had his and bend over and kiss her little chest. He had watched Daddy do that to Mommy a lot; and so he knew what to do. But when he reached her little vagina, that would need some practice; but give him time and he'd get that right too.

It was nice to hear the words Sam was speaking. They said what they were all feeling.

Tom looked into Liz's eyes and saw the warmth spring back to him. "This is nice," he whispered. "You are nice. Thank you so much for sharing your gift of life."

Liz responded, "You are welcome, Tom. It's not my gift, though, Honey. It's Nature's gift."

"Yes, I know," he replied, as he stroked her and kissed her all over – and she, him.

Joe was embracing his friend's wife. Molly was fully aware of the intent of the embrace. Like Sam was saying, it was to offer human purity back to its origin – the Creator. As she felt Joe's penis, having reached the hard state from brushing up against her body, she knew she was feeling Nature's penis. Joe was only renting that penis for a lifetime, but the idea of a penis belonged to Nature for all time. So, when Molly took Joe's penis into her mouth, she was taking all creativity with it. By taking Joe, she was taking God – and she knew it. It was just like Sam said. She was making love to God.

And Joe was equally knowledgeable about what was happening. As he took Molly's nipples into his mouth, he was aware that from those breasts came milk to nurture little Kerry; but more than that, those breasts represented all the breasts in the world that nurture the young. "Bless your sweet breasts, Molly," he said. Nothing could be more appropriate for this time of prayer than a loving mouth on her vagina. Once again, it was not just a vagina he was kissing. It was the vagina of the world. It was the only vagina that ever existed and ever will exist. It represented the very origin of life. "Bless your sweet vagina, Molly," he said. And she replied, "Thank you, Joe."

Julie and Tony were falling in love. If there had been any question of it before this day, there would be none after it. "Tony, you are so good," she said. "And so are you," he replied. And the two of them took a moment to glance at the kids so engrossed in their own offering. "Tony, I love you. Would it be possible that we could have a couple of those?" she asked, nodding toward the kids. "Julie, anything is possible between us," he responded.

Sam continued his prayer. *"Dear Wonderful Life, we who are here applaud you. We thank you for your wonderful mystery. May we always be proud of ourselves because we were first proud of you. May we be lost within the folds of your Infinite Sanctity and find salvation in the warmth we exchange.*

"Dear Wonderful God, we are so proud to be sons and daughters of God and sons and daughters of Nature. All are sons and daughters as all come from you. You have no only son. You have only many children; and we are so proud as to be numbered among those children. We find our salvation of heart and mind and soul in the reverence we feel for your astounding love and gift of life. We share

so much of you when we share with each other. Thank you, Dear Infinite Energy of all that is."

And then Sam moved to embrace each of the couples and kiss each on the lips. Lending a hand to the children, he helped them step down from their altar. Raising his arms into the air, he called their attention, saying, "Let us all close our eyes for a moment and say thanks in the depth of our own silence – and then, let's eat."

And so it was.

Sam's benediction had ended and Sam and Tom were fetching the steaks from the outdoor grill. "Sam, Molly and I have been present for many a fine prayer – mostly our own – but none have been better than our prayer today."

"Thank you, Tom. I agree. We have experienced so many wonderful moments together – your family and mine – but this day has been as good as it gets, even as I know it will be repeated many times in the future. We are just too full of love – the right kind of love – and too full of admiration as a group to restrict such happenings to one time."

"Perhaps there will come a day, Dear Sam, that offerings of children like you devised will happen all over the world. The children of the world, like the adults of the world, are all the same. Kerry and Elise are not the only innocents in the world. They are only two of billions. If only we could let the billions love. Then there would be no room for hate. What a dream, huh?"

"A dream only for so much of the world, Tom, but a reality for us."

"Come on, Grampa, let's eat," yelled a hungry Julie.

This was the first time she had heard her call him Grampa. It had always been Sam before.

"OK, child, keep your pants on. We're bringing the steaks," Sam replied. Realizing his reference to pants, he could not help but break out in laughter. The outer world used that expression a lot in his younger days. He thought to himself that he was going to have to come up with another expression with this group because it did not wear pants.

The steaks had been delivered and all were enjoying the simple feast.

"Grampa, this is really good!"

"What happened to calling me Sam?" he asked

"You have become my Grampa now," Julie responded. "You have gained my consent to your beliefs with your prayer. Somehow, Sam just doesn't fit anymore – especially if Tony and I become another couple in your life."

"Sam will always fit, Sweetheart, regardless of your joining the family or not."

"How about I call you Grampa Sam, then?"

"That would fit just fine. Welcome to the family, Julie!"

Then there was lots of chatter and everyone fully enjoyed the meal, talking about this and that, but mostly about God. This was a group that was in love with love and the very definition of love is God. There were almost no dishes, but what there were, Molly and Liz cleaned them and put them away.

By the time the cleanup detail had been finished, night had fallen – and it was dark. Joe and Liz and Elise decided to accept Tom's invitation to spend the night. So no one was anxious to slip into clothes for the brief trip home next door. They would go naked so as not to interrupt the spiritual event – under the cover of a mild darkness. It was not totally dark, but the yard light was low and they felt they could slip back home without being seen. So they decided to take the chance and do so.

Sam had enjoyed their visit – and was a little sorry to see them go – yet he was also a good bit tired and needed to 'hit the hay,' as he called it. Sam had been raised on a farm and farm people never go to bed. They 'hit the hay'.

There was no way he was going to let them go without a fond embrace. "Kerry, I sure do enjoy seeing you. Come over anytime. You know that. How about a hug for ole Sam?"

"Sam, I love you – and thanks for the day," he replied.

Then they hugged and next up was Elise. "Sam, I love you too!" Elise exclaimed. "You are so neat!"

"You're neat too, Sweetheart. I love to see you. Come over anytime."

Then they hugged and kissed and next up was Joe. "Goodbye, Joe. Thanks for coming over. I can't tell you how much I enjoyed it. It is so special to have friends like you who don't howl every time someone mentions the word 'God'."

"Especially when God is found in the raw," he replied. "Not many find God in life, but so many try to find God beyond life. But like you and I know, it just can't be done. Can it?"

"Nope! To think you have to find God outside of your very being is like insisting that a butterfly be frozen in crystal to be viewed."

They hugged and shook hands and next up was Liz. "Liz, what a wonderful lady you are. Thanks so much for spending some time with an old widow – or is it, widower?"

"You are far from old, Sam. In fact, I don't think you will ever grow old. You are a beautiful man and a beautiful soul – and I am so proud to call you friend."

"Thank you, Honey! That means a lot to me."

They embraced – and Liz kissed him gently while whispering in his ear, "God Bless you, Sam."

Then came Tom. Tom was the one who started it all – and Tom would always be special. "Tom, what can I say? We did it again. It seems every time we get together, it's always the same. It never grows old – like our friendship."

"You are right there. It can't get old, I guess, Sam, because what we do is based on truth as we all see it. We all love life for the same reason – because it is a gift – and until it ceases to be a gift, I guess we will always want to unwrap it and enjoy it."

"Yes, Tom, there is no doubt of that." Then Sam and Tom hugged; and waiting for a goodbye was Molly.

"Molly, how wonderful to have you here today! It is always a treat. I feel like I have just eaten a luscious banana split every time you go because every time you come, you come with such love."

Molly then hugged him firmly and kissed him, while letting her hand trail to his middle. "Sam, next time I come over we will pray together again. You know how much I appreciate the type of spiritual exercise we enjoyed earlier today. You are mighty fine, Sam, even if you have become impotent, as they say. It is particularly sweet to know someone older who does not pine for his youth – like so many older people do. In you, Sam, soft is fine."

"I see life as continuous, Molly. How can I regret growing older when all the time I am only getting closer to being a baby again and doing life again?"

"That's a good thought, Sam – and I believe it too – but even if we don't get recharged with some new life after this one, we sure are fools not to enjoy the one we have."

"And I intend to live out my days – however many they are – fully enjoying the life I have, Molly."

"I know you will, Sam! Goodbye for now!"

Sam watched them as they moved from his front porch to across his front lawn to their own. It was beautiful seeing them going home as they enjoyed the day – dressed in all of God's glory.

Sam sat down in his easy chair in front of the TV. Tony was already sitting on the loveseat.

"Grampa, it's been such a good day!" exclaimed Tony. "We have really enjoyed it!"

"And I, you, Tony. Where's Julie?"

"Brushing her teeth."

"Well, I suppose we all better get a little shuteye," Sam remarked. Then Julie joined them.

"Grampa, I would like to sit on your lap and give you a hug," she said.

"What's stopping you?" he replied.

"Not a thing," she responded. Then she dropped her naked body onto his naked body and said, "Now do you think this is the way it is supposed to be?"

"Yes, My Dear, Yes! But it can only be this way if we throw out the old and bring in the new. We must throw out the old sexy ways and bring on the new sensual ways without sex thrown in. Tom and Molly are so correct in saying that voluntarily dedicating yourself to an intercourse free life unless a baby is desired is the only way to really be free."

"Yes, Grampa. I see the light. Can I make a confession to you?"

"Is this a confession I can hear too?" asked Tony.

"Of course! You know there are no secrets between us, Tony. Grampa, I have never had sex – and I don't think I will have sex unless I want a baby."

"I think that is the smart way to go, Honey," Sam replied.

"She wanted to, though, Grampa. She tried to get me to have sex with her. Didn't you, Julie?"

"Yes, I did, but Dear Ole Tony here refused – said that maybe we should visit you first. I told him I would love to meet you – because he's always talking about you. He said that you and he have some kind of pact – that you and he are going to save the world or something."

"Hardly save the world, Julie – only save ourselves," Sam responded. "But, yes, Tony and I are a team. Aren't we, Tony?"

"You bet, Grampa!"

Julie wanted to continue. "Grampa Sam, I never knew someone could talk of God in such easy to take terms. I can't tell you how much I like that. Everyone else I hear talking about God is always talking about God as some kind of judge, but you talk about God like He is a member of the family. There is no notion of threat when you talk about God – only love. Like I said out there in your backyard, I think you have made a convert of me. I'm going to talk to God like a friend forever more. Thanks for giving me a real loving God, Reverend Grampa!"

"I may have helped to open your eyes, Dear One, but I have not given you God. You have had God all the while."

Julie wanted to get back to her confession. "Grampa, back to my confession. I have never had sex – in terms of intercourse, that is – and because of what went on here today and listening to you guys talk about things, I don't think I will until I want to have a baby." Then she turned to Tony and said, "Sorry, Pal, you had your chance when I tried to get you to lay me, but now you will have to wait until you want to give me a baby."

"I think I can handle that, Baby," Tony responded, offering emphasis on the 'Baby'. "Baby, when you want a baby and I want a baby, we may have a baby – and we can call it 'Sam'."

"Or 'Samantha,'" Julie replied.

"I am so pleased to have a baby named after me. I will look forward to rocking your baby to sleep," said Sam.

"Speaking of babies, I hope I am not crushing yours," chuckled Julie, referring, of course, to his genitals.

"No, but you are squashing them a little," he replied.

"Well, we can't have that," she said, as she got up. "Thanks for letting me sit on you, even if I did squash you a little."

"My balls are just fine," he responded, while letting out one of his famous Sam chuckles.

"May I kiss them just the same?" she asked

"If you feel so inclined," he answered.

"I do, Reverend Grampa. I do."

Then with Tony looking on, she bent down and kissed him on his genitals, fingering them a little as she did. Tony felt no threat in this. After all, he and Grampa had a pact; but now it was not only the two of them. It would be Grampa and Tony and Julie.

And the beauty of it all was that in this innocent act of young female chivalry, innocence remained. Because Sam had committed himself to a holy abstinence, there was not the slightest danger of copulation, even if Sam had not been impotent. Freedom truly abounds in those who respect Nature and its design, including its design of sex.

Tony joined the two to make it three. After all, they were adding one to their pact. While Julie fingered and kissed the Reverend Grampa, Tony kissed and fingered Julie wherever he could reach by moving around the two.

"I could go all night long like this," uttered a very flattered Grampa, "but perhaps we should all hit the hay."

"OK, Grampa. I'll be dreaming of you," she said.

"You go ahead. I am going to rest out here awhile and enjoy a little bit of God and me in my Molly mirror."

"OK, Grampa. Sweet dreams!" said Tony, as he led his Julie to their bedroom.

"Goodnight, Grampa Sam!" Julie offered, as she waved to him and blew him a goodnight kiss. *"All's well with the world. Isn't it?"*

"Goodnight, Julie! Goodnight, Tony! Yes, Kids,
ALL'S WELL WITH THE WORLD!"

All's Well With The World

The End

The Seventh Record

By
Francis William Bessler

— A Spiritual Short Story —

Originally written in 1980.

Revised slightly in 1987.

Revised slightly in 2005.

Introduction

Originally, I wrote this in 1980. It was intended as a gift for a friend. Kika is her name. We grew up together in the 1950s on neighboring farms outside of Powell, Wyoming. In 1975, I had written a philosophical novel I called **NEVER BE ASHAMED TO LOVE**, but was disappointed in my ending. For several years I had tried to find a suitable ending, but it had alluded me. I wanted my characters to find their souls in terms of come to understand the origins of their souls, but search as I did, I could not find the answers for which I sought. In my disappointment, Kika encouraged me to keep trying. It was the summer of 1980; and I was 38.

I told Kika that I had pretty much given up on writing a new ending for **NEVER BE ASHAMED TO LOVE**, but I would write one short story in her honor and then give up trying to write forever more. Thus, I penned **THE SEVENTH RECORD** that follows and sent the first copy to Kika. She called me and thanked me for my story and requested that I not stop trying to find the answers for which I sought and that I owed it to the world to share those answers when I did find them. I could tell she was crying too. I guess my little story touched her much more emotionally than I ever expected it could.

So blame it on Kika, I guess. Blame this little story about the love between an old man and his wife of many years on Kika; and blame all that I have written since on Kika. If it had not been for her encouragement in 1980, I may have given up searching for my answers about the soul and I may have given up writing.

I will always be grateful for Kika's encouragement as I am grateful for the significant encouragement I have received from quite a few in life – including my parents, my daughters, and a number of friends. Many friends have lent me some of their insight along the way, but most notably, one called Nancy. Early on, it was Nancy Remmenga – a former neighbor in the 1970s, married to a good friend, Rich - who chatted with me about life and helped me evolve into the particular thinking person I have become.

Nancy was and is a lovely lady and ongoing friend. Emmett Needham was like her in that he and I discussed the meaning of life constantly during the brief four years I knew Emmett. My friend died of a heart attack in 1985 at the age of 53, but his legacy in me lives on. I suppose it is possible to do it alone in this world, but it has not been my experience. I will not attempt to name the many who have helped me evolve into the me I am, but suffice it to say, there have been many; and Kika, Nancy and Emmett are among the many.

I have also had three wives along the way – to date – who have contributed to my total mindset. Dee, Pat, and Ann contributed mostly by resistance, however, as none of the three ever embraced my mindset of life being essentially divine and wholesome.

It is hard to say how to deal with resistance; but I have dealt with it by leaving the resistant behind to honor life as they wish while taking another road that allows me to honor life as I wish as well. I have always felt that any two should respect one another and only try to change one another if change is desired. I married all three times that I did expecting greater agreement than I found, but since none of us wanted to change to accommodate the other, it has been best, perhaps, that we thanked each other for the time spent together and then went along our separate ways.

Who knows? As I write this, I am only 63. I am always open to an agreeable spouse. I have risked marriage three times in the past and have been engaged three additional times as well – eventually breaking the engagement before marriage would require divorce later on. Is there a seventh engagement possible? I'd say so – and maybe even a fourth marriage.

Anyway, this is a reproduction of an old story – with some minor revision of the original. When I wrote **THE SEVENTH RECORD** in 1980, I wanted to capture a sense of growing old, gracefully and naturally. I wanted to say that all life is blessed from our days as a baby through our passage to the next life, whatever that turns out to be.

I wanted to say that old age should be embraced and not rejected, as we so often do. I wanted to say that passion should be just as much a part of the lives of the old as it is for the young. I wanted to say that death is nothing to fear – that even as we enjoy the life we have in the body, we should not keep the thought of dying too distant because we are all going to go through the portal of death someday. It's natural – just as natural as living – and we should be comfortable with it. I wanted to capture some of my feelings about the beauty of Nature and about the ideal of embracing its processes.

So I wrote this little story to tell of my feelings about life. Through their actions and intimate conduct, Maggie and her old husband tell how death should be embraced – though hopefully I will leave you with a surprise at the end of my story. I think life is like that. When you least expect it, there's a nice surprise waiting to tear your heart out and make you realize how wonderful life is and how great it is to be alive.

After writing this story, it happened like Kika hoped it would. I would find the answers about the soul for which I sought and eventually write about that discovery in several efforts. **UNMASKING THE SOUL** analyzes the origin of the soul in essay form. I finished that effort in 2003, though I wrote an initial effort in 1988 or so. Eventually, I rewrote **NEVER BE ASHAMED TO LOVE** too, fitting it with a suitable end. The rewrite was finally completed just this year – 2005 – and the new title is ***ALL'S WELL WITH THE WORLD.***

All of my written works feature very frank discussions about life. The stories, of which I have written four, including this short story, feature not only frank discussions about life, but also frank conduct within life. In a story, one can feature the ideal. In all of my stories, I try to feature the ideal as I see it. I believe that life is divine in that I believe that God is in it. Believing that life is divine, I also believe it is worthy as it is. How could it not be if God is in it? In my stories, I try to feature characters who discuss the divinity and wholesomeness of life and treat life as both divine and wholesome.

In the real world, I think lots of people claim that life is divine, but then they act like it is lacking. **It is like there is a disconnect between the thoughtful and the actual.** People "think" that life is divine and worthy as it is, but they often "act" like life is lacking and some aspects of it should be shunned. In all of my three novels and in the following short story, *I try to feature characters who connect the thoughtful and the actual.* In that, my characters may shock a bit because the standard is to refuse connecting the thoughtful with the actual. At least, that is how I see it.

Be that as it may, enjoy, if you will, my following little story about Maggie and the old man that has been her husband for a lot of years - facing the prospect of one going and the other staying behind. You might have a hankie ready, too. Unless you are one of those with a cold, cold heart, you might need one.

Thanks!

Francis William Bessler
Laramie, Wyoming
September 22nd, 2005

The Seventh Record

"Come here," he said. "I'd like to talk."

Her response was quick. "As soon as I get the pie out of the oven."

"My, how that fresh pie of yours makes this lovely house even lovelier!"

Of course she heard him; and even after all their years together, it still pleased her.

"I've been thinking," he started, after she reached his lounge chair in the living room.

"Yeah, I know," she quipped. "Whenever you start to think, the white smoke billows up and makes me think another pope has been elected."

"Ah, come on, Dear, that's just the electricity of you around my hair. You are something, you know."

"Sure, sure," she said. "Next Tuesday you will be 82; and you act like you're 32."

"That's what I want to talk to you about," he responded. "I don't want to, but I know I will – can't help from doing it, shocking you, I mean."

"What in Heaven's name, Ole Man, are you talking about?"

"Look," he said, speaking with warmth and compassion in his eyes and voice, "we have always been true to one another. Right? And we've respected each other?"

"For 43 years now," she answered, expressing the pride of a queen who had just been crowned.

"Well," he said, pausing a long moment before continuing, "let me just say it straight out like I have always done. We are getting old now, and, well, it's not likely we will live a whole lot longer."

"Now, you stop talking like that," she bristled. *"I have you to know, Ole Man, that we could easily live another twenty years."*

"But do we want to?" he asked, hesitatingly.

"Why wouldn't we?" she responded, very curious as to the object of this strange conversation.

"I'd be the first one to want to hold onto life," he replied, "but, you know, I think it would be really terrific to be able to welcome you on the other side."

"I'd like that too," she said, smiling warmly at the old dodger, "but that happens to be entirely out of our hands."

"Maybe it doesn't have to be," he countered.

"Now, you listen hear, Ole Man, you've had some crazy ideas in this life, but you're not suggesting . . . " She had trouble saying the word, but finally came out with it, ." . . suicide?"

"No, not really. Well, actually maybe a little."

"Have you gone plumb out of your mind?"

"No, Maggie, I haven't. Let's just say I have come to the conclusion we can't get there from here."

"What do you mean, can't get there from here?"

"Well, I mean if I'm to welcome you, I can't get there before you, to welcome you, I mean, unless I go before you."

"That's true enough."

"Well, let's get on with it," he said.

The brow on her forehead lowered half way to her nose. "Get on with death!" she exclaimed.

"Yes," he replied.

She didn't know what to say. The old fellow before her had surprised her a lot in life, but never quite like this. "I don't believe you," she said, after a long pause.

"Look, Maggie," he tried to explain, "it has always been my dream to be with you forever, in life and in death and afterwards. I figure it will be more assured that I can be with you at death and afterwards if I am there first. That way I can be there to welcome you."

"That's touching. It really is," she answered, "but I think I just as soon have you here."

"I'll still be here," he said, "at least in spirit. It's just that I can be there too. Think about it. We're old and we will be going soon; and if you go first, I won't be there to welcome you like it's been my dream to; and if we go together, we may get split up in the confusion. I need to be there first to make sure of what's going on. I don't want to lose you. I want to continue this love, you know."

"Why do you think there will be confusion if we die together?"

"Of course I'm not sure, but like I said, I think we would stand a better chance of avoiding confusion if one of us is there first, to welcome the other, to show the other the way, so to speak, when the time comes. It's been my dream to be the one waiting on the other side, that's all."

"And you wouldn't think of letting it be me?" She knew he wouldn't; for he had old fashioned ideas about the man taking care of the lady. So she knew his intent in this latest surprise of a long life of surprises, to die before her so he could serve her in death; and she knew there was no arguing. Like always, he would have his way. It was only a matter of how and when.

"You're a fool, Ole Man," she said. "I suppose you have it all figured out how you're gonna go before me?"

"Maggie, My Love, you know me well."

"Dare I ask how?"

"I think the best way would be a heart attack."

His offering surprised her again. Would this man ever stop with the surprises? He was as healthy as any of their sixty year old friends and had never suffered the slightest of heart trouble.

"A heart attack?" she challenged. "You?"

"Why not," he said. "I'm almost 82."

"And I have just turned 76 and have had two heart attacks to your zero," she responded. "I would be the one most likely to go that way."

"But you're not the one going. I am."

"You stubborn old man. You don't have to remind me; but tell me, you know I must be wondering. How are you, as healthy as you are, going to have a heart attack?"

"The body can take just so much, My Dear, no matter how healthy you are; and, well, my plan is to make mine take more than it can."

"You have never believed in abusing the body," she offered. "How are you going to take too much of anything without abusing yourself?"

"I guess I'm ready to make one small exception. I'm sure my body will forgive me for overdoing it, just once."

"And what are you going to do? Pray tell, I don't know if I want to hear."

"You have to hear," he responded, "because you are going to help me do it, if you will."

"Oh my! Not only are you insisting on dying, but you're asking me to help. Ole Man, you are really too much!"

"I can't do it without you, Kid, I mean the way I plan it."

"And that plan?"

"Remember when we first met, how I enjoyed dancing for exercise and how I would dance before you to the beat of a rhythmic band like ***The Glenn Miller Band*** or some good fiddler and how I'd dance at times until I'd drop in my tracks from exhaustion?"

"Yes, I do," she replied. "You did truly enjoy that, didn't you?"

"I sure did," he said. "Well, I have it figured out that at 40 I could take that, but not at 81."

"And so you plan to dance your way to a heart attack?" she exclaimed. "Not with me as your partner, I don't think."

"No. I'm not going to dance my way. I'm going to love my way; and you, My Dear, are going to be the lovee. I'm going to love you to death, Kid - my death, that is."

"You can't even get it up anymore, Ole Man. How are you going to love me to death?"

"No, not with that, Maggie – with my hands. I am going to exhaust myself giving you the best massage you've ever had."

"How can it be my best when you plan to make it my last? We've always believed the best is yet to come."

"Well, I guess we have to make another exception," he stated, matter-of-factly. "We'll have to make the last the best this time."

"Dear, I have so much enjoyed your massages over the years, but I don't think I could enjoy this one, with what you have in mind."

"Don't worry, Kiddo," he said. "I'll be gentle."

"Now you know that's not what I mean," she stammered.

"Yeah, I know," he said. "Look, I think we better get on with it – or I'm going to chicken out."

"You mean right now?"

"I mean right now."

"But . . ."

"Trust me, OK?" He spoke gently but firmly as he reached over to help her undress. In 43 years of marriage, there had never been a question of purity in this. Even with their children, now grandparents themselves, they acted the same. They had always dressed and undressed before them – and had often assisted each other in the process: **Brother Naked and Sister Nude!**

"You're asking the impossible, Ole Man," she said, glancing over his shoulders and catching the reflection of their natural outlines in the big mirror, "but I'll try to be for you again as I've always been. Sir, I'm in love with you. I want you to know that."

"I do," he said. "I do."

She held him close, moving her hands over his body like she had a million times before. Reaching over, she grabbed the bottle of baby oil on the mantle; and opening it, she poured a little on her shoulders and down her front side. The old man gracefully took the bottle from her and returned it to the mantle. Then, while still standing, he slid his gentle hands over her breasts and front side, spreading the baby oil smoothly over her; and then he repeated the action on her back.

Turning her around, his tongue met hers and became entangled for a moment; and then he reached for the bottle again. This time he poured some in his hands and applied it to her lower body, making sure as always that she was fully covered – except for those parts he wanted to kiss. The oil helped him glide over her body and prevented friction between hand and skin. Any masseur or masseuse knows the value.

"Let me make a **farewell drink**," she told him.

"Not **farewell drink**," he noted, "*until-we-meet-again drink*."

She prepared her favorite drink, gin and tonic, and another for him. He was more partial to orange juice and vodka, although the orange juice contained an acid that caused him a bit of heart burn. Meanwhile, he took a sheet out of the linen closet and laid it on the floor. Maggie claimed she could wash the sheet easier than the carpet; and anyway, the bare carpet was less romantic. She liked the feel of the clean sheet under her when he massaged her – and occasionally on warm days, consented to sleep on the floor, totally relaxed after his affectionate care - with nothing but another sheet over them to keep her and her favorite masseur warm.

"I don't like this, Ole Man!" she said. "I don't want it! I don't want to live alone! I can't live alone! You're asking too much!" She started to cry.

"I know," he replied, "maybe too much indeed, considering it's really a gamble in the first place. We don't even know for sure that life in the spirit is immortal. Maybe we don't exist after death."

"Dear!" she exclaimed. "We have never had such doubts before."

"I have never faced death before, My Love," he replied. "I mean, it makes you think. Don't get me wrong. I really do believe, but, you know, no belief carries with it one hundred percent assurance – or else it would be certain knowledge and would no longer be faith."

"But you do still believe?" She wanted reassured.

"Absolutely!" he said. "Yes, I do believe!"

"In spite of it being a gamble?" She inquired further.

"A small gamble the way I see it," he responded. "The chips are really stacked in our favor."

The talk of Belief was very comforting; and she almost forgot the reality of what her husband was set on doing.

"Here's to life!" he said, touching his glass to hers.

"And life after death," she enjoined, her toast more a thought than a feeling. "Here's to the love we have known and to the love we will always know."

They came together and embraced; and he fondly lay her down and began. So many times he had done this, giving his wife what he called *the complete treatment – the total expression*. He straddled her now, his haggard but manly form over hers, as she lay on her front side. She always began in this position and always ended face up. Often, she did him too; and he followed the same procedure.

Having closed her eyes, she was crying again, being aware that this insanity could turn into a nightmare; and yet she let him continue, saying to herself again and again, *I do believe!* She wanted to for sure; and in wanting to, perhaps she began to; but she would not deny him nor his courage to take his life and lay it down for her – or for them. How could she say 'no' to that kind of love? She knew she couldn't.

Like it often happened, the old phonograph that played the old 33 1/3 records had been turned on – and seven of their favorite records had been selected. His plan was to massage his wife and hope that by the seventh record, his release would come. He put intensity in his movements even as he kept them graceful. Recently, he had not been able to last two records long, let alone seven. It was a reasonable plan – and exit.

Up and down were his movements, like the good masseur he was – or down and up. Down the outside of her back, gliding with the baby oil, and then over to her spine and up the middle, repeating the motion again and again. The blood flows that way. The old man had long been aware of that.

Go with the flow, he had always believed, in most everything you can. Don't resist the natural – and don't try to turn it in another direction. You'll only end up frustrated and defeated in most cases. The blood of the body travels down the outside and up the inside. Go with the flow of the blood in the body – and any man could be a masseur.

Very often, the old man told his acquaintances that full body massage should be as common place as dinner plates, as simple as they are; however, they do take a lot of strength and effort and even dedication. Perhaps that's why so few people give them; but this was one man who was dedicated, dedicated to giving his Maggie all she could want, *the butterfly treatment,* he called it, claiming the form of a butterfly in his movements; and he would often call her his **Lady Butterfly.**

He had spent the time of three records on her back side, massaging every part he could. Loving every minute as he worked to become exhausted, he took special care following her flesh downwards on her legs and smoothly up the inside to her buttocks, circling up and around and down again. He was tiring, but that was the program.

Hearing the third record ejecting, gently he turned her over and bent down and kissed her on her inviting mouth, making sure the kiss was as flowing as his hands, moist and full of depth. Her tears were evident and he struggled to continue. Heartbreak was not his wish.

This beautiful woman with her gentle body had loved him throughout their life together; and he was finding it difficult to say goodbye. Still, he continued. Again, the motion of a masseur, down the outside and up the inside. He was perspiring heavily and she could see he was getting close to the point of exhaustion. It takes so much strength to continue a body massage for even ten or fifteen minutes; and he had now passed the hour mark.

She looked at him now, almost without flinching; and she loved him and who she was too. Throughout the years, his attention had been guiding; and she knew that she had also guided him. It happens that way when two people flow in the same direction and live the same ideals.

Her breasts, so feminine and endearing to him, gave way to his attention and stood a little erect. Kissing her as he could where there was no baby oil, he followed her outline with his hands, down the outside of her breasts, continuing down the outside of her slender legs, and over the toes, and up again on the inside of her legs. He could hardly move as he did so and his body ached with a pain he had rarely known.

Throughout the massage, from beginning to end, he would always include in his attention, his wife's virginity. He loved to call it that; and it pleased her as well. Her virginity was always a part of his massage. She, too, included his virginity.

It irritated him, not a little, that people would accuse a person of losing their virginity upon intercourse. From his way of seeing things, nothing could be further from the truth. Virginity means *purity;* and never in the course of true love, can intercourse absolve it. So they both enjoyed viewing their sex as their virginity. Perhaps Adam and Eve lost it; but they never did.

The fifth record had ejected and the sixth had begun. He wanted to rest, but knew he would defeat his purpose if he did. He was groaning a lot now, but neither spoke – as words would have interrupted what could not be spoken.

Then the seventh record began. It was a Mozart record, or at least someone was playing a Mozart composition. Maggie loved the flute sound and could pick it out very easily, although she had never been very good at remembering names. She knew it was a Mozart composition, but that's all she knew; and he was too exhausted to be aware of anything around him. Perhaps, though, he sensed that the seventh record was playing. His breathing was harsh and loud; and yet it could hardly be heard above the music.

Drawing himself up beside his wife and laying his head down on her breasts, he knew he could go no more. His back was afire and he anticipated the pain in his chest was the heart attack he sought. He drew himself up and looking into the tear filled face of his Maggie, he whispered, *Goodbye, My Love!* Then he lowered his head and collapsed.

As the Mozart composition began to reach its climax, she prayed: *Father, take good care of him, you hear? He's the best. He's the most wonderful love I've known; and now he's there with you to wait for me; but I don't know what I am going to do without him.*

Her tears were quieter now; and she really didn't feel alone. He said that in spirit he would remain. Maybe that was the explanation. Mozart had finished. Silence took over - and then she heard an exciting sound – the low guttural tone of a familiar snore.

Startled by the sound, but amazed and gratified, she looked down at **Brother Naked**. *"Oh, my God!"* she cried. *"Oh, my God, you're still alive!"*

Her tears were now uncontrolled. She had been reborn at age 76; and in her excitement, she cried the more. *"I have you to know, Ole Man, we could easily live another twenty years!"*

The Seventh Record

The End

From The Dark Into The Light

By
Francis William Bessler

— A Spiritual Novel —

Originally written in 1980.

Revised slightly in 2005.

Introduction

This is a combination of two short philosophical/spiritual stories I wrote in 1980. I began with a story about a lady I named *Priscilla* – offering a tale around her. No need to offer the details because that may spoil the story to come. The title of that first story was ***THE WEDDING GARMENT.***

Then based upon questions that I felt needed resolved that were stimulated by the first story, I wrote a second story and introduced a questioner that I named *Lance*. The name of that story was ***BACKING SATAN INTO THE LIGHT.*** My purpose was to attempt to clarify my own perspective of the meaning of life by virtue of having *Lance* question a bit of what *Priscilla* posed in the first story – and then offering *Priscilla* as having to resolve various confusions, felt by *Lance*. Again, I won't offer any details so as to not spoil any of the following story.

Chapters 1 through 4 and 6 of this current effort comprised the initial story – ***THE WEDDING GARMENT.*** Chapter 5 of the current effort was Chapter 1 of the second story – ***BACKING SATAN INTO THE LIGHT.*** Chapters 6 through 11 of the current effort represented Chapters 2 through 5 of the original second story offering *Lance* as questioner.

Outside of this noted minor rearrangement and a few minor changes, that which now comprises this combined current effort is often literally the texts of the first two works. In offering this story, I want to replicate the two stories told initially. I do not want to make any extreme changes so as to retain whatever integrity that was offered in 1980. As I produce this current full story in 2005, my perspective has changed a little from what it was in 1980, but I want *Priscilla* and *Lance* to remain as they were. Change does occur – and I have changed a little – but people are important for what they were too. It is almost like a form of respect for *Priscilla* and *Lance* that they remain mostly unchanged as I tell their stories in this current effort.

I am calling this consolidation effort **FROM THE DARK INTO THE LIGHT** because for me it has been that. It may not be that for anyone else, but for me, beginning somewhat in the dark and thinking my way through things, it has been almost like experiencing a dawn from a previous dark night. It is a lot like staying up for a night and watching a sunrise. I am not promising it will be like that for anyone else, but it has been that way for me. Thus I am calling it as I am.

That is not to say I would write it today just as I wrote it 1980, if I were writing it for the first time today. Oh, I can assure you, I would write it differently because I see things a bit differently today than I did then; but the basic message would be the same. I might slant things a little different, this way or that way, but the overall message would be the same.

And what message is that? *Life is good as it is. Life is without evil because life is full of God. Evil happens, I think, when we fail to appreciate the Presence of God in all things; but life is essentially good as it is.* The new *Priscilla* that I might present today might differ a bit on some detail or other, but the old and new *Priscilla* would be the same in the basic message that life is good as it is and that virtue is really only accepting our goodness and living life fully because of it while refusing to impose our virtue on anyone.

Yes, I might write the story of *Priscilla* different today than I did in 1980 if I were writing that story for the first time; but I love the *Priscilla* of old too. One does not have to tell all in one story. Does one? I have written other spiritual stories too since 1980 – though only a couple. *Priscilla* and *Lance* are not the only story in town; but I hope you can take the message of integrity that they offer seriously and attempt to imitate the idea that each of us must make of his or her own life the fulfillment of his or her own dream - or dreams.

Thanks!

Francis William Bessler
Laramie, Wyoming
September 24th, 2005

From The Dark Into The Light

1

For thirty-eight years, he had been the pastor of the small church on 53rd Street, a church that he himself had founded and for which he had paid the down payment. Legally, it was in his name, although, in spirit, it belonged to his flock. For thirty-eight years, he had preached the *Word of God,* the Gospel of Jesus, the salvation of the Lord. *"Come unto me all you who are labored and are burdened."* He had no idea how many times he had called upon his Lord and called upon his congregation to heed those same words; and certainly he believed them. At times he still cried when he delivered his sermons; and he thought his performance, though it was much more than that to him, caused his flock to keep coming.

Clutching his robe around him, he opened the door and looked out. His dog, Punch, came bounding up to him, wagging her tail and barking sharply. He reached down and fondly patted her on the head. *"Where do you get all your happiness?"* he asked. *"Do you have the Lord in your heart too?"* He hadn't meant to startle himself, but he did. *"Why indeed are you so happy?"* he asked again, suspecting that the answer may not be acceptable. Punch merely looked up at him, cocked her head, barked again, and then took off racing around the yard.

The Reverend sat down on the small step outside his modest home, a house that was surrounded with trees and flowers and life – no matter which way you looked. At sixty-six, he was sincere, as he had been all his life. His late wife, Martha, and he had enjoyed a happy life until three years previous when his lady had been taken to Heaven to spend the rest of eternity with the Lord. He had almost forgotten how it had happened. Anyway, at the moment, it wasn't important. He was caught up with the question he dared not try to answer before now. Why was Punch so happy? Why? Why? Why? He kept asking himself.

It almost doesn't seem fair, he thought. Punch could be so happy while the whole world, far greater than this funny little creature, was mired in tragedy and despair and disease. Momentarily he challenged the doctrine: *man is supposed to hurt to become purified in the Lord.* His thoughts went back to Punch, still running and bounding and panting.

"Come here, Boy," he said. He always called her 'Boy,' even though she was a girl; but regardless of title, she obeyed with the same enthusiasm as before she was called. Why couldn't he get his parishioners to respond with equal enthusiasm for the *Word* he preached? His thoughts again wandered to the edge of heresy. Perhaps Punch had the key. Perhaps Punch would make the better pastor of the two of them.

Looking up, he saw the car approaching the fence alongside the front side walk. It would be nice to see his grandkids again. Martha and he had seventeen of them, but only these three lived close enough to make visits easy. Grampa was the first in line to be hugged, but Punch was their more exciting interest; and the three pursued Punch like she was one of them.

"Hi, Dad!" she said, as she reached over and kissed him tenderly. "It's so good to see you out here in your bathrobe. In fact, it's a real joy. Mark said to say hi. He'll come over later to mow the lawn. Is the coffee ready?"

"Coming right up," he replied. "You want it here or in the house?"

"I think I'd like to sit out here with you awhile, Dad, if you don't mind."

"Not at all," he responded. "I'll be right back."

Priscilla sat down on a front step and felt good in doing so. Like usual, she wore jeans. She didn't like them tight, though; for neither she nor Mark enjoyed wearing underwear anymore than necessary; and tight pants for her was the same as wearing panties. She liked to stay loose and was very fond of her looseness; although she would be the first to admit that her motivation was far more spiritual than physical. Some call it freedom. She called it **a feeling of blessedness.**

On this Saturday morning she did not stay alone for long, as her three young ones came to show off before her and Grampa. Davy tried to do cartwheels and fell flat on his stomach. Blaming Punch for tripping him, he retreated to the back yard to tend to his wounded pride with Punch loyally at his heels.

Dawn and Marie picked some marigolds and offered them to Priscilla. "Well, thank you," she said. "My, how pretty!"

"Could you get the door for me, Dawn?" Grampa had his hands full, a tray with three glasses of orange juice and two hot cups of coffee.

"Davy, you want some juice?" Priscilla shouted.

"I'll be right there," was the response; and less than half a minute later, Punch and he came running.

"Thank you," Davy said, as he grabbed his glass; and the girls echoed his politeness.

"Is it OK if I ask him now, Mom?" Marie was spawning as a teenager and she felt it was her right to be the one to ask.

"Sure, Honey," was the reply.

"Grampa, we're going to camp out next weekend – and we were hoping you could join us."

"Now, that sounds inviting," he responded. "Give me a day or two to think it over. OK?"

"It would be so much more fun with you, Grampa," added Dawn. "Please?"

"Well, My Dear, I would sure like to, but you know I'm a preacher and I have Sunday responsibilities. It would all depend upon my finding someone to fill in for me."

"We understand, Grampa. Certainly we know that. Would it be hard to find someone?" Priscilla was as eager as the kids.

"Thanks for the juice, Grampa." Davy was ready to go back to the demanding exercise of playing with Punch.

"You're welcome, Boy," was the response.

"Why don't you girls find something too?" suggested Priscilla as she motioned as if to point to some imaginary place in the distance. "Grampa and I would like to be alone for awhile. OK?"

"OK, Mom. Come on, Dawn, let's go check out Connie if it's not too early for her. It probably isn't, though, cause more than likely she's watching cartoons." Connie was the girl next door; and they often played together. Dawn did not hesitate as she handed Mom her empty glass and ran after her older sister.

"Dad, I can tell there's something wrong. What is it?" Priscilla had captured the pensive mood of her father; and she was eager to find out his state of mind.

"Nothing's wrong, Dear, nothing's wrong – but I guess you found me thinking this morning."

"What do you mean, this morning, Dad? You tell me when you haven't done a lot of that."

"Oh, I don't know, Sweetheart, maybe not enough."

"Why, what are you thinking about anyway?" Priscilla was no closer to the truth than the moment before.

"Prissy?"

"Yes, Dad."

"Why is Punch so happy?"

"Punch?" she questioned. "Your dog, Punch?"

"Yes, my dog, Punch."

"Why not?" was her reply. This was not like Dad to concern himself with matters like this. Usually his conversation was about the kids or the congregation or the weather or Mark, anything but Punch.

"I'm confused," he admitted. "We're supposed to be happy. We're supposed to be contented and grateful; and yet, I'm willing to bet you, Prissy, that this morning the only one contented and grateful on this whole block was Punch. What does she have that we don't? I'm serious now. I really want to know."

"Well, Dad, you have kind of caught me off guard. I, I really don't know what to say."

"Oh, I think you do, Prissy. You are more like Punch than anyone I know."

"Well, thanks," she quipped. "Should I lick your face?"

"No! Just tell me what I want to know." He was insistent and refused to be sidetracked. "You know I am a preacher and I know all the pat answers and my congregation keeps coming and coming. Yet, none of them is even half as contented with his lot as Punch. Again, Sweetheart, what does she have that we don't?"

"She doesn't have what you just said you have, Dad. She doesn't have confusion."

"Confusion? Boy, that's true," he responded.

"But neither does she have the power to think, Dad. I would rather be confused and have the power to think than to be think-less and thank-full like Punch."

"You always did have a way with words," he responded. "Think-less and thank-full?" The Reverend wasn't sure. "Is it better to be think-full and thank-less than think-less and thank-full?" He was caught up with this play with words.

"Now, come on, Dad, there's nothing wrong with being think-full, as you call it, and thank-full too."

"No, there isn't, is there?" he replied. "That's what you are. You have more than most of us. You're thank-full as Punch and thoughtful as a human being should be."

"Well, I insist on knowing my own mind, if that's what you mean. To be honest, and that's what you're asking, isn't it, I can't say that any of your congregation could stand on their own two feet if they didn't have someone to preach to them every Sunday."

"You're probably right," he said. "You know, Prissy, I can't think of anything more tragic; and I am really beginning to question my usefulness, any preacher's usefulness. Perhaps we confuse more than we clarify. Maybe Punch is ahead of us, not behind us, because she can't be confused with ideas."

"I don't think that's it, Dad." Priscilla was very much an idea person, even though as much so a person of strong will. She believed in ideas; and she believed we are here on earth to find them, to discover them. The problem as she saw it is that mankind as a whole is scared of ideas, scared of new ways, scared of maybe getting lost while searching for the truth. She tried to explain. "I think Punch is ahead of us, as you say, Dad, and not behind us, not because she can't be confused with ideas, but rather because each day is a new adventure for her. She is merely caught up with her new adventure of every day. That's what makes her happy."

"But she does the same thing, day after day," countered her father. "Why doesn't she get bored?"

"Would you if you weren't in need of more dimensions in life, Dad?"

"What do you mean?"

"I think Punch can be satisfied because she's not in need of the world outside these fences that surround your yard. She can take it or leave it. She can be happy inside a fence or out-side of it. Now, if men were dogs, they could be satisfied inside of fences, but we're not. To treat us like dogs is to do a great disservice to us. What makes Punch happy can not possibly make us happy."

"You think I treat my parish like dogs?" he asked, somewhat upset at the thought.

"Or like sheep," she responded. "You treat a man like a sheep or a dog, same difference, he will act like one and he'll never come to know he's a man and not a dog or a sheep. Sheep and dogs can still be themselves with fences and dictators. Man cannot."

"Priscilla!"

"It's true, Dad. At least I think it is."

"But what about the forces of darkness?"

"We're not dogs, Dad. We're not sheep. Let us be human. Take away the fences. We can handle it."

The Reverend was hurt. Could it be he was the reason that men are like sheep and not like the image and likeness of God? Could it be the shepherd shouldn't be a shepherd? Could it be? "You puzzle me," he said, after pondering his crisis for a moment. "But even if you're right, what can I do about it now?"

"Maybe if you feel I'm right at this time next week, you can stop preaching, Dad. You won't find an argument with Mark or the kids, you know. They are hoping you can join us on our camping trip." She said this half in jest; for she certainly did not intend to suggest that he should give up his way of life.

He thought for a moment. "I hate to say it, but I have to admit that I am inclined to agree with you," he sighed. "Maybe it's true that by letting my sheep keep coming week after week, they're not getting stronger – just more dependent. I am supposed to be in the business of saving souls, of helping people fly; and all I'm doing is keeping them in their nest."

"Now, Dad, don't be too hard on yourself. You're as great an entertainer as the best of them, you know." This was no surprise. For years, Priscilla had called preachers primarily entertainers and often raised the ire of her father for her candidness.

"Entertainers!" he exclaimed. "Yeah, that's what we are. You've been right all along. Only we don't have the guts or clarity of mind to admit it. We fool ourselves into believing our voices will bring redemption to others; and all the time, we are just claiming a spotlight."

"Dad!"

"Don't Dad me," he said. "You know you are very convincing."

"I have gone off at the mouth a lot, Dad. You know that, but I'll not hear of your talking like this." Priscilla was both surprised at this change of heart and worried a little too.

"Oh, you won't, huh?" he countered. "Well, for your information, this is one entertainer who has spent his last day on stage. I'm no good for them, Prissy. You know that. I'm only prolonging their weakness by prolonging their dependence on someone outside themselves. They have the *BIBLE*. Let them find their own truth!"

"But, Dad, you need them as much as they need you."

"That's a reason to continue entertaining, Girl? Hardly! I mean it, Prissy. I founded this church and I will also close its doors."

"How soon do you plan on doing that?" she asked, still a bit unbelieving.

"I told you before, Prissy; and I meant it before. I have preached my last sermon. Maybe Punch should give the next sermon, the last sermon. **To be happy is to be yourself.** That could be her theme. Or how about you?" The Reverend startled Priscilla.

"Me? You're kidding! I haven't been to church for years!"

"That's precisely why it should be you. You have more to offer than anyone I know, besides Punch of course." He chuckled a little, and then once again, became serious. "You're independent. You're strong. You're convicted and convincing. You're in love. You're happy. Surely, someone like you should be the one to truly and properly close the temple doors."

"You're really serious, aren't you?" Priscilla was both impressed and frightened at the same time. The thought that her father trusted her was a bit overwhelming, considering their disagreements of the past. The thought of standing in a pulpit terrified her a little; and the thought that her father was even serious was somewhat surprising, although the shock of his sudden decision had already worn off.

"Dad, I can't . . ."

"Oh, yes, you can; and you are. You owe it to all of us." He promptly rose, halting further discussion, and retreated indoors.

Dumbfounded, Priscilla sat there. She couldn't be a preacher. She was a preacher's daughter, yes, but that was not being a preacher. She'd be about as much at home preaching from her father's pulpit as a cat in a bathtub. "Damn!" she thought, and lowly muttered the same while creasing her fingers over her perplexed eyebrows. What would she say?

"What can I say?" she shouted to her father through the screen door.

"That's up to you, Sweetheart; but I trust the way you have always criticized prepared sermons that you'll choose to speak from the heart."

Now that she was faced with having to talk without a crutch, her father's reminding her of her past mind was not welcome.

2

"Mark, I can't make up my mind about what to wear tomorrow." Priscilla was searching through her closet and coming up with blanks.

"You certainly have enough to pick from," was his reply, as he poked his head out of the bathroom. "I am going to take a shower and after that I'll help you pick out something. Alright?"

"OK," she responded, "but it's got to be something appropriate." She began pushing her dresses aside as she rejected each one. The blue gingham was really very pretty, too pretty, she thought. The pink and blue floor length one kept her gaze for a moment. No, she thought to herself, too formal. The green sundress was too short; and the strapless red was too bright – and perhaps a bit too risqué.

Then her eyes caught a glimpse of her wedding dress, shoved clear over to the edge of her closet. She hadn't put on much weight since the first time she wore it sixteen years ago. Maybe she could still fit into it. Soon the notion became a challenge; and she quickly disrobed for the trial.

"Mom, are you trying on your old wedding dress?" Marie had been watching her mother through the open door of the bedroom.

"I thought you were asleep by now," was her reply. "It's almost ten o'clock. What are you doing still awake?"

"I couldn't sleep, Mom. I guess I'm too excited about your giving the sermon tomorrow."

"Well, since you're still awake, you might as well come in and help me try this thing on." Priscilla did not need any help, but it gave her an opportunity to be friends again with her daughter; and she was thankful for the opportunity.

Soon Marie was standing in front of her mother, ready to be her assistant and play the judge. Both mother and daughter were without apparel; and together, they made a beautiful scene. All three of Mark and Priscilla's kids were as fond of their naturalness as their parents were of their own. Seldom did any of this family wear pajamas to bed.

Marie had lately started her stretch toward adulthood; and after the initial embarrassment, had become very comfortable with the whole process. This was a unique family in that even the normally private processes were shared. Priscilla was largely responsible; for her nature and her love of it was a force that refused to let her keep anything to herself. Consequently, her own self comfort had become contagious; and her excitement was now shared by all, from Mark to Davy.

Priscilla was stepping into the wedding gown when Mark appeared with towel draped over his shoulders and his hands moving his tooth-brush vigorously up and down. "I didn't know you were getting married," he joked. "Who's the lucky man?"

"It won't be you," she giggled. "You're too hairy and I like my love smooth like this one here." Reacting to the fond embrace of her mother, Marie was ready to say, "I do."

"God, it's been a long time!" Mark was eager to see his wife in the wedding gown. "Come on, what are you waiting for? Let's get that thing on. I think I'm falling in love all over again."

Priscilla had stopped to hug Marie and had let the wedding gown slip to the floor. She reached down and picked it up and slowly slipped her arms into the sleeves. The white collar fit snug to her neck; and Marie zipped up the back.

She looked into the mirror and made her decision. "You know, guys, I think I'm gonna wear this tomorrow."

"Mom, you're not serious?"

"I think I am."

"What on earth for, Honey?"

"Because, Babe, I feel pure. This gown even makes me look that way. I want to leave Dad's congregation with that same feeling. So, why not wear my wedding dress? I think I'll even make that my theme, I mean something to do with a wedding. It's really a glorious thing, right?"

"At least ours was," Mark agreed. "If you'll let me kiss the bride tomorrow, I'll have no objections."

"Why wait for then?" she said, as she threw herself at her naked husband. Mark's body responded against the whiteness of his wife's apparel. Marie noticed and smiled at her father.

"She did the same thing sixteen years ago, Marie. Would you believe it! When she puts on that white gown, I go crazy!" He made gestures like he was a beast and noises like one as well.

Marie joined in; and together she and Priscilla threw Mark on the floor and were tickling him. His laughter rang with enthusiasm; and Priscilla forgot for a moment about the dress;

however, recognizing that she was wrestling in her wedding gown, she halted her activity and quickly took it off.

"Keep him down, Marie, until I get this thing off." Then she resumed the posture of before and the laughter returned.

"What are you guys doing anyway?" Dawn and Davy were standing over them.

"Look who's still awake, Priscilla. Join us if you want, you two little bumpkins," he said, as he waved for them to pile in. Dawn and Davy responded gleefully to their father's invitation; and now it was Priscilla who was the one getting it. Five naked beings, tumbling and rolling and having a ball. This was ordinary activity for this family; and they never tired of it. Perhaps it was the *Punch* in them.

"Hey, I don't know about any of you, but I have to get up and preach a sermon tomorrow." Priscilla was ready to quit. She struggled to her feet and collapsed on the couch. "Let me catch my breath," she said, "and then I'll get us each a glass of orange juice and it's off to bed with you."

Mark decided to banter her a little bit. "Me too?"

"No, Mark, you can stay up and watch the late movie if you want," she replied, as she chuckled and left for the kitchen.

While Priscilla was preparing the drinks, Mark offered an idle suggestion. "Hey, Preacher!" he taunted. **"I think if you want to leave your Dad's congregation with a feeling of purity, you should wear what you have on. That's a whole lot purer than the wedding dress."** Mark did not intend his remarks to be taken seriously, but a seed had been planted that Priscilla would not easily let go.

"I wonder if I could really pull that off," she said, as she offered the four of them their drinks.

Marie was eager to tell her sister. "Dawn, Mom's gonna wear her wedding dress tomorrow!"

"Really?"

"Yeah, you are, aren't you, Mom?"

"I'm seriously considering it. I'm not sure I'd have the courage when it came right down to it, though."

Davy was puzzled. "Why would you wear a wedding dress, Mom, to give a sermon?"

"Your mother wants to leave a grand impression, Son. You should know your mother by now. There's nothing usual about her."

"But why a wedding dress? I don't get it."

"Sweetheart, it's either that or this: that white wedding dress or this natural nakedness," Priscilla said, as she motioned to her body. "How would you like your mom to stand naked in front of all those people?" But Priscilla was becoming more serious with every remark.

"Mark, would you stand by me if I did?"

"Did what? Go naked?"

"Yes. I'm not saying I will or even that I want to. I'm just asking, will you stand by me if I should choose to do so?"

"I think you do want to, don't you? Sure," he replied, nodding his approval.

"Thank you, Mark. Thanks to all of you. I love you all so much!" Her voice was breaking with emotion. "I couldn't do it without you very well. You know that, don't you?" She embraced her three little adults warmly while her bigger adult companion looked on.

"We love you too, Mom. I'd be nervous, but if you want, I'll take mine off too." Dawn comforted her mother; and Priscilla started to weep.

Her thoughts were beginning to jell now. The *wedding gown* and the *nakedness*. Both had to play a part in her sermon tomorrow. Somehow, she had to tell her secret, their secret, through these two things. Somehow, she had to find a way to tell it like she felt it, without compromise. Her family was with her, even Dawn and Davy, who had at best only a slight understanding of their mother's principles; but Priscilla didn't worry at all about their lack of understanding at this time in their lives. They would soon enough; and that was all the comfort she needed to follow through the next day.

3

Looking at his watch, the Reverend noticed it was almost 9:55, just five minutes to go before he would break the news to what would certainly be a shocked congregation. Priscilla had called him and told him of her plans. He argued at first, but later realized he had given her the green light to handle her chore the best she knew how.

Unlike usual, he had not stood at the entrance of his church to greet his parishioners. He wasn't sure why. He just didn't feel like doing it. Maybe it was because he was upset with himself for the burden he was giving his daughter.

Not normally an impulsive person, he had acted impulsively in his decision to close what he referred to as the temple. He was so sure it was the thing to do when he was sitting on the steps with Priscilla yesterday. Now he wasn't; and if he had not given the responsibility to Priscilla, he would have probably treated the day as just another Sunday in a sequence of many normal Sundays to come. Perhaps he knew that; or at least sensed it; and that's why he had delegated the responsibility to his daughter.

Priscilla always came through. She was dependable and as unbendable as the oak tree in his back yard; but he hadn't counted on her imagination.

Sharply at ten, the organ began; and the choir in the loft at the back of the church sang out loudly:

Precious Lord, take my hand. Lead me on. Help me stand.
I am tired. I am weak. I am worn.
Through the storm, through the night, lead me on to the light.
Take my hand, Precious Lord, lead me home.

Priscilla sat with her family in the front pew. Strangely, she was not afraid. If she had been alone, she probably would have been, but she had her family; and she knew she could flop and they'd still be there, comrades all. But family support or not, Priscilla would have still gone through with it, simply because she believed in her principles; and it was her principles that convicted her and gave her command of her soul.

Davy was a little disappointed that he had not been granted the privilege of sitting by his mother. The girls sat adjacent to her; and he had to settle for the left of his father. He wished a little that Dad was the one to give the sermon. He wouldn't have felt as much the outsider he was feeling now if that were the case. Still, he felt deeply proud of Mom.

The first hymn had ended and now the whole congregation was bid by Grampa to stand and sing, *I LOVE TO TELL THE STORY*. Priscilla used to know it from days when she was a regular and maybe she could remember the words; but she doubted that her family would. So, she stayed silent as the congregation raised their voices in song:

I love to tell the story of unseen things above,
of Jesus and His glory, of Jesus and His love.
I love to tell the story because I know 'tis true.
It satisfies my longing as nothing else can do.

"We have with us today some special guests." The hymns had ended and Grampa was speaking. "I am especially honored that our guests are none other than my daughter, Priscilla, and her family." The Reverend had almost forgotten the opening prayer and the readings from the scriptures. He knew it was no ordinary Sunday, even if no one else did. He caught himself in time. "Before we continue, let us remember the Lord in prayer. Let us bow our heads.

"Oh, Lord, we come before you as weaklings wanting to be made strong. We know in your grace we can." He could go no further.

Normally, he would have gone on with this prayer for several minutes and then would have read from the scriptures – but not today. He sensed he was the weakling of his prayer because he wanted to be. He wanted them to be. It gave him a sense of importance. He had wanted their dependence; and they had remained his children. He knew he could no longer want that and he knew he could not continue with words he could no longer feel.

He was put out with himself that he had not realized what he was doing before now. Why couldn't Punch have lived thirty-five years ago? Why wasn't her message revealed to him before now? The Reverend was unhappy with himself – yet insistent to get on with the process of restoring God's children to Him by letting them go free; but he was grateful he did not have to come up with the words.

"Friends," he said, extending his arms out in his familiar good shepherd gesture, "I spoke before of our guests. Well, my daughter is more than that today. I have asked and she has accepted to say a few words about a very important event in the life of this church." Without any further preparation, he motioned for his daughter to take over. "Priscilla, would you, please?"

Caught by surprise, Priscilla rose as her father bid. She hadn't expected it to be so sudden; and she fully expected her father to announce the closing himself. The crowd was before her as she walked up to her father, standing next to the podium; and they embraced as father and daughter. Not certain at all of what she would say and how she would handle it, she preferred to start at the podium. It would at least provide her some support to lean on and maybe even something to hide behind for a moment or two.

Many of the ladies in the congregation realized for the first time that Priscilla had on a wedding dress. Expecting her to make some statement about this very important event the Reverend spoke of, they mostly assumed her strange dress had something to do with that. She was a very pretty lady, always had been; but many of them thought and spoke between themselves that she was too wild and free. She had admitted to some of them that she didn't wear underclothes and that she loved to weed the garden naked. *Imagine that!*

Priscilla was a girl with a reputation, an ill one; and had it not been for her father's legally owning the church property, there may have been movements initiated years ago to ask him to leave. Not having any power to do anything about it, they chose to ignore Priscilla.

Before Martha died, Priscilla had been a good regular member of the First Congregational Church on 53rd Street. What they didn't know was that it was her mother's slow, painful death that in the end set the daughter free.

Priscilla had been having doubts about some elements of her faith when her mother had taken ill; and she was sure her mother's illness was due to her lack of faith. Throughout her mother's illness, she fought the guilt complex; though she never once gave up her love of God and her love for the precious gift of life. Her mother had held onto life long enough for Priscilla to realize that she was allowing herself to be bothered by evil spirits, who falsely accused her of treachery.

Upon recognition that the cause of her depression was from without and not from God, Who she felt to be loving and forgiving rather than vengeful and suppressing, she quietly had taken command of her soul and whispered to the evil spirits that they had been found out. **They were no more.** For the first time in months, she was able to sleep soundly. It was on that same night that her mother yielded and gave up her fight. Before falling asleep, Priscilla had asked for the same, that her mother be spared further suffering.

Priscilla often wondered if the events of that night may have actually happened in reverse. Maybe her mother had passed into the world of spirit at eight in the evening and was the comforter who had come to her in the night; yet her body wasn't pronounced dead until two the next morning. Perhaps her mother's spirit was even present on this occasion. Regardless, Priscilla was truly free.

4

Searching the faces of the congregation, Priscilla could tell the suspense was there; and she knew that because it was, it was right for her to be here. It was so apparent that these people had so little in their lives that they had to depend upon this church on 53rd Street to offer them solace. Hopefully, she could start to change that.

"My father loves you all," she began, with an emotional tone in her voice. "I love you too. You are aware, many of you are at least, of my candidness. So, let me continue with the reputation.

"This will be the last service of its kind to ever be held here in this church." The old man, bent over in the back pew, bolted upright. As usual, he had been attending service because he had nothing better to do; and he really enjoyed the friendliness of many of these good people after church service. It was, in fact, his reason for coming. In that moment, he felt forsaken.

"Dad considers himself lowly and unable to set you free himself," she continued, "and that's why he asked that I be the one to do that. He recognizes that only the free can truly dispense freedom; and he knows that he's not any more free than most of you; but he'd like to be; and in that, perhaps, he's a little ahead. On the other hand, I am free; and so I can talk to you about it.

"I'm not going to pretend to be anything more than I am. I would not have anything to gain by that; and certainly, you wouldn't either. It has been said that the truth sets us free. That may be true to some degree, but in my life, I have achieved freedom only after I have willed it. That would say that it's will and not truth that sets us free.

"The question is, do you have the will to be free?" She hesitated a moment before continuing, allowing each of her listeners the time to answer the question for themselves. Doubtless, most of them couldn't answer the question before them and were likely asking another: **is it right to be free?**

"Do you have the will to be free?" she repeated. "You all have to answer that for yourself. No one else can do it for you. You can choose freedom or imprisonment, whichever you want. It's your choice, but my father has decided that he will no longer be party to your imprisonment. If you choose to be imprisoned by another rule and another church, that's your choice, but perhaps it's no accident that the free shall seek the free and the bound will seek the bound."

Her father was impressed. Priscilla was coming through again.

Fully aware that she had their attention, and maybe even their respect, as temporary as it might be, Priscilla moved from behind the podium to stand in front of them. "Many have talked of freedom," she continued, "but few know what it is. What is it really? **It's the will to enjoy.** At least that's what it is for me. It's not the truth of enjoyment. Oh, I know truth helps – and I too seek it. I always have and I always will, but the real key to being free is having the will to be something.

"The key to becoming someone is to want it first and then to will it. *Will is more than want in that want is a desire; and will is the action to realize it.* Lots of us want happiness, but few of us really will it. Few of us really go after it. My father suspects that many of you don't will for yourselves what you want in life; and that's why he's going to take away his church, which he now views as an obstacle to your finding, not truth, but the way of happiness in your own lives.

"The truth alone does not set you free. I'm here to tell you. Truth may support the process, but the will sets you free. The will is the cake and the truth is the frosting, not the other way around. Think about your lives before you go to find another church. Is that what you truly want? Make sure it is before you do it. Think about what you want as your commitment; and then go after it.

"I am not here to command your commitment. I can only suggest. Your commitment is your own; and your commitment will become your wedding. That's why I wore this wedding dress today, because it is a symbol of will, the will any of us must have to live in freedom. It's commitment, too, but that doesn't take away from the freedom.

"You must choose your wedding. I have chosen mine. Oh sure, I am wed to Mark and my family; but the wedding I am speaking of is far greater than that; and for me, it's the greater wedding that makes the lesser wedding possible.

"My real wedding garment is under this wedding dress. It's not the wedding dress itself. I have no shame for the garment underneath, as I view it as a gift of God; and who in his right mind can be ashamed of a gift? I did not make it. God did. I'm only using it; and to be anything less than openly grateful is to be less than what I should be. We are all the same in body – for the most part. It's the soul in us that varies mostly. You cannot see my soul. It's invisible and it's mine; and even if I wanted to, I couldn't share my soul with any except with those who are like me – in terms of sharing a common perception.

"It's because of the wide variety of souls out there in the world that I cannot do this everywhere; but to make a point, I will to share with you all today my real wedding garment." She motioned to Marie to assist her.

The crowd had come to know Priscilla; and it was not surprised at what she would do next. **Poor thing! The devil was responsible!** Here in their own church, Satan was at work. So, many of them thought. Priscilla claimed no shame. They had been warned about that. A soul can be hardened beyond the point of retrieval.

Awaiting her cue, Marie had been ready since the service began. She was extremely proud she could be part of this jubilation, perhaps the only real jubilation happening at this hour in all the many services being held. She couldn't help but have unsteady hands as she tried to find the zipper head hidden beneath the collar of her mother's wedding dress.

The crowd grew tenser as Marie fumbled for the zipper. Maybe Priscilla should have said something while waiting to be disrobed, but she didn't. The silence was somewhat disturbing. Finally Marie stopped shaking enough to catch hold of the zipper head; and the rest was easy. **The gown slipped off; and it was apparent that Priscilla had no use for panties.**

Standing proudly naked in Mother Nature's beautiful gift, she took the wedding dress and tossed it into the middle of the stage. Priscilla and Marie looked one another in the eyes. Marie had tears in her eyes, tears of joy and gratitude, not tears of shame or embarrassment; and she whispered, "Mom, we love you." Priscilla smiled at her lovely daughter. Then Marie turned and returned to her seat.

The congregation sat in awe, in unbelieving awe. No one left, though Priscilla suspected that many would tell the tale differently at dinner time that evening. Many of them glanced to their pastor, sitting quietly up on the right hand side of the stage, hoping this had been a surprise to him and hoping he would put a halt to this outrage. The Reverend was aware of their petition, but he paid them no attention.

Again, Priscilla had triumphed. Again, she did not feel embarrassed, nor was she afraid in any way of continuing with her action. "This is my real *Wedding Garment,*" she said, as she cupped her hands and put them over her breasts, "and this and this and this and this." Moving from breasts to thighs to legs and up to the face, she touched her body. Just standing naked wouldn't have been enough. She had to show that extra dimension of her will; but she willed to go no further.

"This is what I'm wedded to, this beautiful thing we call our body. I have stripped today to show you I really have no bodily shame. I am not telling you that you shouldn't, though. Again, that's up to you to decide. Just don't let anyone decide it for you. You must choose your shame as I have chosen mine. I would have been ashamed not to do what I have done. For me to have finished this talk without disrobing would have been shameful because it would have been an expression of shame, a shame that I do not have; **for shame is nothing more than doing what you feel you shouldn't - or not doing what you feel you should.**

"I cannot decide your shame anymore than I can decide your will. What I have done is not an example of general conduct. Rather it is only an example of private will."

Viewing his wife from his privileged position, Mark loved her all the more. He felt proud she was sharing her gift to him with others only because it was her decision to do so. He had lost nothing; and his gain was immense; for her purity was also his own.

"I'd like to talk just a little about someone I have come to know because I first had the will to find him: My Father." Pointing to her father, she added, "I suppose you think I am talking about Dad over there, but that is not who I am talking about. I am talking about a father in spirit. *I love my Dad, but I am My Father.* That's one beautiful truth I have found in life, but I couldn't have found it if I hadn't willed it in the first place. My will set me free to find my identity. It was not the truth of My Father that first set me free, but my will to find him.

"However, in finding My Father, I also found yours. My Father and I are one like your fathers and you are one; but contrary to what I believed earlier in life, **our fathers are not one.** It's a belief I have, and I'm not telling you it should be yours, but I believe we all have one two-fold birth – one of the flesh and one of the spirit or soul. Mom and Dad provide the flesh, but an individual spirit – or maybe spirits - provide the soul. Both the flesh and the spirit exist independent of each other; and the one in no way depends upon the other for its individual existence. The soul uses the body, but has its own life.

"Like the body comes forth from another flesh, the soul comes forth from another soul; and each of us has a different soul for a father just like we each have different bodily parents. Otherwise, we would all be born the same, have the same feelings, the same disposition, the same awareness. Clearly we don't have the same disposition, the same feelings, the same awareness. So, clearly we are born of different feelings or of souls having different feelings.

"Now the spirit or soul from whom I come passes on all his or her or its attitudinal traits. Whatever he or she or it is, I become; and I am given birth to satisfy something in my parent spirit. The very reason I exist is to be an expression of My Father; and being his expression, he gives me an identity that never dies. So, to find My Father, all I need to do is look at me; for all the attitudinal traits that are in him have been born in me. Truly, My Father and I are one as you and yours are one.

"Keep in mind, however, that when I say 'father,' that can be interchanged with 'mother'. I referenced 'father' just to keep my offering simple, but my soul can come just as much from a mother soul as a father soul. In my case, since I am a woman, it would probably be better to say that I am a reflection of my mother. But that's not important. It is not an issue of sex. It's simply an issue of soulful origin in general. In general, my spiritual soulful parent and I are one, just as you and your spiritual soulful parent are one."

Priscilla could tell they did not want to hear this now. The body they could relate to, the spirit they could not; and yet they would have claimed they were in the spirit and Priscilla, with her nakedness, obsessed with the body. Marie was interested and so was Mark, but Dawn and Davy were become anxious to get on with the days activities outside the church; and their fidgeting was obvious.

Knowing it was a gamble that might lose her audience, Priscilla decided to touch on one more concept before going back to comment further on her **Wedding Garment**. "I don't know, but I believe," she said, "that what I cannot gain for my parent spirit in this life will have to be gained by those to whom I will give spirit birth. That's one reason I must do the best I can in this life in whatever I will to do. If I don't, my children in spirit will have to do what I didn't. It is for me to pave the way for them. My responsibility is not only to my parent spirit, but to my future children spirits as well. It becomes my responsibility to make a world here that I should want to send my spirit children to.

"I think it is very possible that my own soul can choose to be born again in this world, but given that my soul may give birth to children souls who come in my place, it only makes sense to make straight the way, as it were, for my children souls by doing the best I can to leave them a good world in which to enter. Even if I should be the one to reenter – and again, I personally believe that is likely – the best thing I can do for the future me is to get the current me right. I will have to inherit the world I leave behind. Who wants to inherit a mess? But if it's a mess I leave, then it will be a mess I will inherit.

"Regardless of all the details, none of which any of us know for sure, and about all of which all of us are guessing, in my view of things, you have to decide for your parent spirit and I have to decide for mine. That is why I exist as a soul – to give pleasure or expression to my parent spirit. I am bound and determined to make the most out of this experience; and I am willing to enjoy my life. This is my will as it is my parent spirit's will; but you are free if you want to be. If it's not your parent spirit's will, you can make it be. If your parent spirit did not have the vision to be correct in his or her or its life, you can have; and you can share that vision with him or her or it.

"There's nothing magic about it. It's just an act of the will. You have the power to redeem, as it were, not only yourself, but your parent spirit as well; and that's all because you and he or she or it are one. At least until one of you cuts the other off, you are each other's interest.

"Keep in mind, these are only my personal beliefs. I am not saying they should be yours. I don't wish to bore you with my beliefs," she commented, as she stepped down from the stage – slowly moving toward her family, sitting in the front pew. "I do love you as My Father loves you; and I only want what you should will for yourselves. I'm here in the flesh, but it's my soul that makes me move. My soul wills that I restrict myself to my family. I have no desire to be shared physically by anyone other Mark and Marie and Dawn and Davy."

Standing directly in front of her loved ones, she deliberately embraced and kissed each one of them, one by one. Then she returned to the stage.

Again, there were silent accusations from the crowd. **Was she agreeing to incest? Would she dare to claim as right her kids making love to her? Why wasn't she clearer as to what she meant?** Priscilla had no intentions of being so. Her relationship with her children was too an act of will for her as was everything else. It was more than a concept. It was a movement; and it needed no definition or apology.

"I am lucky," she said, as she reached center stage. "I have been blessed, or is it that my will has blessed me? Mark and I are compatible in will; or else we would not stand a chance together. I would divorce him and set him free to find one who is compatible in will with him. **Two people living together cannot live in peace going in different directions.**

"So, as you leave here today in a few minutes, think about your direction; and be sure of your acquaintances before you make them companions. Hitch-hikers are of no use to anyone.

"Talking of hitch-hikers, be aware of spirit hitch-hikers. There are many spirits who want to be parent spirits for one reason or another and can't be or don't choose to be. Perhaps there are no bodies available for use. Not having a body to use for the reason they want, perhaps they have to resort to hitch-hiking. Leastwise, reason might dictate the same. So, they might hang around you and use your body until they have a body of their own.

"What that does for us who are in the body is that we have to constantly be on the alert for the presence of spirits alien to our direction and our will. These little hitch-hikers can get to you and try to make your will their own. **The best way to avoid being the agent of another's will is to have a strong will yourself.** Wouldn't you agree? Hitch-hiker souls have us at a disadvantage because we can't see them; and we may not know they are around. That's when they can most use us.

"And they have used us too, so much in fact that they have completely deceived us for their own benefit. The world has been their captive because they have instilled in us a fear that we need an outside force to redeem us from our lost ways. **All that has been needed is the will to act grateful. That would make us peaceful and not afraid.**

"Be aware they deal in fear; for fear is the best way they can keep us in suspense and tense and angry; and that's the only way they can use us for hitch-hiking. Mostly, they love to make us afraid of ourselves, to make us suspect our natures, to keep us in fear of ourselves. That's why they don't want us to get used to our natures and recognize them for what they are – temples of natural blessedness through which we can learn to act grateful and be redeemed if necessary. That's why they don't want us to love nakedness; and that's one reason that I have become naked while they look away. Almost literally, they can't stand the brightness.

"If you're going to defeat them, you just simply can't give in to their ways. Unlike Adam and Eve in the garden, who paid attention to voices outside of them, you must ignore them while keeping your soul in peace through acts and dispositions of gratitude. If you feel that what I say is true, I bid you to go home and look at your bodies as you are now looking at mine. Be grateful! It's a fantastic gift! Don't abuse it by ignoring it. Rather abuse the spirit who would have you ignore it by ignoring it.

"Angry spirits love angry spirits. Peaceful spirits do not need others to make them complete. Therefore, if a spirit is a hitch-hiker, more than likely it is an angry spirit. If you are angry, you will only attract them. You wouldn't be angry if you felt complete. **Anger stems from a feeling of incompleteness.** If you feel incomplete, then you are essentially leaving yourself open to being completed by another; and that is opening the door to a hitch-hiker spirit. Given an opening, what hitch-hiker spirit is going to turn down an invitation? Accordingly, to keep hitch-hiker spirits out of your life, don't be angry. Anger, as an expression of sensing a state of incompleteness, is the main highway by which hitch-hiker spirits can enter and use your life.

"If you find yourself possessed or bothered by an angry spirit, and you recognize it, for Heaven's sake, don't try to exorcise it with more anger. You won't succeed because your new anger will retain him or her or it. When you exorcise or dismiss an angry spirit, say it quietly and calmly in sympathy and forgiveness. Don't cry in anger, 'I command you in the name of the living God to go to Hell!' If you do, that's precisely where you will both end."

Priscilla paused, searching the faces of her audience, before continuing. "Who are you? It's time you asked that question; and it's time you answered it. I have told you who I am. I am the sum of my beliefs; and my beliefs make up my commitment. My commitment is my *Wedding Garment*.

"Jesus said, no one can get into Paradise without a wedding garment. Well, essentially, that's what he said – though that Paradise was a wedding feast. Jesus was comparing a wedding feast with Paradise. So it's the same thing. But what did he mean by that? I think I have demonstrated here today what I think he meant. We must all be committed to something to become saved as individuals as it were. *I am what I believe.* My belief – or beliefs – give me identity and dress me with a *Wedding Garment*.

"You know what I believe. **I believe principally in three things: the purity of nature as the host of my soul, the parent soul - child soul spiritual identity, and the ongoing of life.** These three things make up my commitment; and these three things make up my *Wedding Garment*.

"Do you want to reach Paradise? Do you have on a wedding garment? Your commitment does not have to be mine, but you do need a commitment to avoid being controlled by another's will. You do need a belief. You do need a *Wedding Garment*.

"My belief will do you no good. You cannot enter Paradise on my coattails anymore than you can enter Paradise on the coattails of anyone else, including those of Jesus. I cannot do it for you. Jesus cannot do it for you. **You must decide your own will or be the decision of someone else. You must go your own way.**

"My father is closing this church because it pretends that you can reach Paradise and fulfillment on the coattails of someone else, namely of Jesus. The hitch-hiker spirits have done well to keep us convinced of that; but I'm here to tell you, it won't work.

"Find your own way. If it be the way of Jesus, fine. I too have found his way; but even if it not be in the name of Jesus and it be deserving of your commitment as a way to avoid being caught up as the commitment of another, it may prove a worthy *Wedding Garment*. If your belief is belief in needing another to make you complete, however, that is not a belief that can amount to a wedding garment. **To be free of others, you can't depend on them.** That's not to say you can't enjoy others. It is only to say that enjoyment includes them, but doesn't depend upon them. You must stand alone to be dressed in a *Wedding Garment*. Jesus said, I would rather you be hot or cold than lukewarm, or something close to that. I am sure you know better than I the exact quote. So, I say to you, be hot, be cold, but be strong."

The audience was stunned. This is what it had been waiting for. This was the blasphemy they needed to condemn her; and yet none of them had any defense. Priscilla was the only one naked in the entire assembly; and yet she alone could be certain of a *Wedding Garment*. Even Mark had yet to match the fervor of her will, the degree of her commitment, the loveliness of her *Wedding Garment*.

"I love you all," she said, "but I must go so that you can come, come to your own realization of life, that is. Thank you for letting me be part of your day. Don't be afraid of going outside the fence to find where you belong, to find who you are, to find who you want to become. The choice is yours. Don't let it be that of another; or you may never be fit with your own *Wedding Garment*. For my father, I say, Good-bye and Good Luck!"

The murmur of the crowd began slowly and grew rapidly as they filed out. For many, it was like the end of the world: a naked renegade had convicted them of trying to enter the wedding feast without a wedding garment. A mere child had pointed out their anonymity. A loose woman had preached about commitment.

Perhaps if there had been a Calvary, there would have been another crucifixion. Priscilla was glad there wasn't.

5

Lance and Jill were stunned – but for different reasons. In her sermon, Priscilla had stood naked before them and accused them of nakedness. Jill had felt like the shady and shoddy **DOLLY'S PALACE** from downtown had been transplanted in her church; and she felt outraged. As far as she was concerned, **Dolly's Dancing Dillies** may have just as well paraded before her and her children. And Lance? What about Lance?

Jill believed in family, almost to the expense of everything else. Family to her was the pinnacle of earth's finest treasures. In that way, she was like Priscilla; however, she differed dramatically with Priscilla in that Priscilla did not put family above individual worthiness.

With Jill, nothing was more important than family; and if she was truly honest about it, that would have included the God she praised morning, noon, and night. God was a convenience and a convenient addition to her needed family as well as a belief. Without the **Giant Image** – or **Image of a Giant** – with outstretched palm for one hand and righteous club in the other, she would have never been able to rule her life and those over whom the **Giant** had given her charge.

Often at night before falling asleep, she focused her thoughts, not on the lovable man beside her, but on her fantasy of seeing herself being bid by the **Gentle Giant** with outstretched palm to come to Him. **"Come to me, my faithful one,"** she hears him say. **"Come and share my blessings!"** Yet where are her children in this fantasy? They are not there, even as they are the reason she has made it home.

It was the moment Priscilla came down to hug her family in her natural *Wedding Garment* that Lance began his conversion. He had glanced over to catch the scowl on his wife's face and her reprimand for his thoughts. Quickly he had wiped the smile off his face and had sat at attention – like a private having been corrected by his sergeant. Jill would have accepted his response for any other kind of admonition, but not for this one; for the last thing she wanted was for her bodyguard to attend to the business in front of him. She promptly spilled the contents of her purse, as if by accident, on the floor, hoping her efforts would further distract her husband from the naked scandal in front.

Lance did not take the bait, as he was already taking charge; however when Priscilla first slipped out of her wedding dress to stand naked before them and proceeded to talk of her beliefs, he had reacted like the others with surprise and disbelief. His wife was one who scolded him for taking a bath without closing the door; and now she was being affronted, not by a naked man, but by a naked lady. Lance felt a little bit of justice.

By the time Priscilla turned her affection to her family, her seed had already started to take hold. Jill had good reason to worry and to feel challenged. Lance had been listening; and little did he know it then, but he would never be the same again.

After the service, Jill rapidly gathered the contents of her spilled purse and dragged her four children out of the church, admonishing Lance to follow. Lance was more interested in Priscilla and her willingly attendant children as she proceeded to dress. He was still stunned; and he felt an unnerving shame for his own timidity.

He had long sensed that God couldn't be the **Jealous Judge** his Jill believed, but he had not been able to put his thoughts into a belief like Priscilla had. He wanted to go to the front and congratulate Priscilla, but he lacked the courage to resist his angry wife's cold twitch of the head, signaling him to follow as bid.

After a moment's hesitation, Lance responded and tagged after his family, looking back several times as he sauntered out. Priscilla noticed his interest as being more than lustful. A lady can tell those things. She smiled, formed an OK sign with her thumb and index finger and held it up for Lance to see. Lance was embarrassed that Priscilla had noticed his interest; and he wiped his hand across his mouth for something to do, pretending he had an itch that needed attention.

6

The five of them were going home; but Priscilla was concerned for her father and had asked Mark to drive around so as to be able to ask him if he wanted a ride home. The church was only six blocks from his house; and he always walked; but Priscilla thought that maybe he would like a ride as an excuse to be rescued.

"Grampa, want a ride?"

The Reverend knew his daughter and he was thankful for her concern, but he also knew what he had to do. Turning away from his upset parishioners, ready to throw him into the lion's den, he just winked and said so only his daughter could hear, *"I can handle it, Prissy. I can handle it."*

As they drove away, Priscilla glanced back and noticed a new sign had been placed to the side of the church. Her father had surprised her with his quick action; and she wondered how he had acted that fast. He had told her he intended to turn the church into a community service building; but she had no idea he would act with such haste.

The old sign was already gone. It had read:

FIRST CONGREGATIONAL CHURCH
Peter Guestly, Pastor.
Closed, except on Sundays

The new sign simply said:

OPEN!

7

"Jill, do you love me?" Normally he would have routinely said, "I love you, Jill," before saying Good Night.

Jill was a bit startled by the question. His asking if she loved him rather than telling her he did almost challenged her. She was uneasy. "What do you mean, do I love you?" she finally responded.

"Do you love me?" he said again. "I can't put it any plainer than that. Do you?"

"Why? Do you think I don't?" she replied, puzzled by the implication she might not.

"I don't really know," he said. "I know I love you, but I am not so certain of your love for me." Lance turned over in bed and looked her directly in the eyes.

"After ten years of marriage, you dare ask me that? If you don't know by now, then you have a problem."

"I have a problem?" he responded, with authority in his voice. "I don't think I have a problem. You do if you can't answer it."

"What are you talking about? I can answer it," she replied, a little furiously. "Certainly, I love you. Now, are you satisfied?"

"Should I be?"

"Lance, I don't know what's got into you, but I am tired. I want to go to sleep. It's been a long day. That damned preacher's daughter carrying on like she was God's own and now you askin me foolish questions."

"I'm sorry, Jill, but I am not so sure Priscilla isn't, as you call it, God's own."

"Of course she is," she replied, correcting herself in midstream. "We all are, but some of us have let the devil in; and I think Priscilla is one of those."

"Judge not, lest you be judged," Lance responded, irritating his pajama wife the more.

"Lance, turn out the lights. I'm not in the mood to talk anymore. I want to go to sleep."

"Are you angry?" he asked.

"Dammit, Lance, you know I am. Now turn out the lights and let's go to sleep."

"Don't let the sun go down on your anger," he quoted. "I think we better talk this thing out. Tomorrow may be too late."

"What do you mean, too late? Too late for what?"

"Maybe tomorrow won't come," he replied. "What would happen if you died in the night? You'd die in your anger."

"Now that's not likely. You know that. Anyway, not all anger is bad. Some anger is justified."

"Priscilla wouldn't agree." His mention of Priscilla added fuel to the fire.

"God-dammit, Lance! Don't you bring up that bitch again! Do you hear?"

"Why didn't you leave if you didn't like what she was saying?" That, too, was dangerous territory; and Jill became angrier.

"I don't know," she answered. " I couldn't. I think that woman put a spell over all of us. None of us left; and yet, none of us agreed with her either."

"Make that one of us," he responded, startling Jill.

Neither Lance nor Jill spoke for a moment. Then Jill exploded. "That figures! Lance, I'm worried about you. You're always trying to justify your going naked, willy nilly - and now that devil's daughter stands up there so brazenly and bold and tells you it's God's wish - and you believe it."

"She didn't claim it's God's wish," Lance corrected quickly. "In fact, she made it clear that what she did was her will and had nothing to do with God."

"God-dammed atheist! That's what she is!"

"That's totally unfair, Jill. Priscilla and Mark are not atheists. They just believe that God makes us good in the first place without need of further grace. No, Jill, they are not atheists. They are theists in the first degree, I think. They don't disgrace God by believing He made their natures in need of redemption."

"That's what the devils want us to believe," she replied, "that we don't need redemption."

"Priscilla would say it's the devils who want us to believe we need redemption – just the other way around from what you say," he countered.

"Priscilla, Priscilla, Priscilla!" Jill angrily retorted. "If you want to believe Priscilla over the **WORD OF GOD**, then Dammit, go sleep with Priscilla. I can't believe one woman could be allowed to divide us like she has. I love you, Lance. Please get that devil out of your mind. Don't let her destroy you like that."

"I'd rather be destroyed now, so I can have time to rebuild," he responded, "than to find out after death that the way of redemption is the way of the devil."

"Lance!" Jill exclaimed. "Do you know what you're saying? You're letting that whore make you believe that God's ways are really the devil's ways. I hope that God doesn't strike you dead tonight!"

"First of all, Jill, Priscilla is not a whore. Secondly, she isn't making me believe anything; and thirdly, maybe the devil is so smart that he has actually convinced us his ways are God's own to keep us his prisoners. Maybe the so called **WORD OF GOD** is nothing but poetic misleading of the devil, posing as God."

Jill was crying. She felt honest hurt for what Lance was saying. She couldn't see the possibility that two thousand years could have elapsed with mankind believing its practices for the love of God were actually clever misleading of what are called devils. She resisted the idea and would not accept it. She had too much to lose. Even if Lance was right in his conjecture, the shock would be too much to bear.

"Lance, Honey, please don't talk like that. Don't gamble with your life like that. Don't gamble with mine. Don't gamble with the lives of the children."

"Jill, I can understand your feeling hurt by what I am suggesting; but you know, I think I have to find out."

"Find out what?"

"If the **WORD OF GOD** is really the **WORD OF GOD**."

"Oh, Honey! How are you going to do that?"

"I don't know, but I have got to find out. I owe it to you and the children, as well as to myself. Do you realize that if the devil is behind the **WORD OF GOD**, what that means? Do you realize what fools we are if he is?"

"Lance," she replied, in her growing desperation, "you cannot challenge the **WORD OF GOD**. No one has ever been able to do that."

"Maybe no one has ever really tried. I take that back. Maybe some who have challenged it have been burned at the stake by a loving God," he replied sarcastically. "That tends to dissuade the best of us."

"I can't take anymore of this talk, Lance."

"Are you still angry?"

She was subdued a bit now, as all this talk had begun to really exhaust her, but she was still angry. "Yes, I am. I can't help it. I'm very angry, especially at Reverend Guestly for allowing his daughter to do what she did. How many other lives will be threatened like yours because of her? Yes, you bet I'm angry."

"Maybe I owe my eruption to her," he agreed, "but I have long doubted a lot of things I haven't had the wit or will to challenge."

"And now because of her, you will challenge them and probably end up in Hell," she responded.

"Yes, somehow Jill, I'll challenge them; but I hope I don't end up in Hell; however maybe if I don't, I will. Ever think of that?"

"I can't think anymore about anything. Please turn out the lights."

Lance reached over and flipped the switch before giving his Jill a goodnight kiss. Jill snuggled up to him, perhaps hoping she could sensually distract him from his heresy. He wanted to have sex; but under the circumstance, he didn't feel right in playing with the division between him and his wife. Ordinarily, she wouldn't have wanted it; and he knew her likely intention. His response was a whisper, **"Good Night, Jill."**

8

Jill was standing in front of a kindly-looking, gray-bearded **Giant**. Lance was directly behind.

"Jill, my precious child, you had many failings in life, but you accepted my **Son** as your personal savior; and so, in spite of those failings, I give you eternal life."

Turning toward Lance, Jill blew him a kiss and said, "Goodbye, Love." Then seven men and seven ladies, dressed in white, who had been standing by the **Giant's** throne, came forth. Smiling, they led Jill away, passing out of sight behind a cloud to the right side of the throne.

"What's this man's name?" the **Giant** asked. "I do not remember my **Son's** talking about a man of his description." It had become Lance's turn; and Lance was trembling.

A tall man, also dressed in white, came forth from the **Giant's** left and said without hesitation, "I'm sorry, Father. I do not know him."

"Are you sure, for the sentence is final?"

"Quite sure, Father," was the answer.

"We must be absolutely sure," came the response from the bearded **Giant**. "Get me **THE BOOK**." Three eagles appeared with a huge book hitched to them, much like a wagon would be hitched to a team of horses. White strands of rope were attached to the body of the book and led to the team of eagles. Just at the point where they should have been attached to the birds, it appeared they disappeared. Lance wondered how that could be.

The eagles swooped down from the right side of the bearded **Giant**, sitting on his elevated throne, and made a pass around Lance as they entered from the **Giant's** left side. Lance caught the gold lettering of the book as they flew by: **BOOK OF THE SAVED**.

Having passed directly in front of the **Giant**, the eagles somehow came to a complete stop in front of the **Giant's Son**, without even the slightest fluttering of their wings to keep them in air. The **Son** of the **Giant** spoke to Lance. "What is your name?"

Lance was almost too scared to speak, for he feared his name would not be found; but he managed a timid, *"Lance Jenkins, Sir."* The son then proceeded to turn the pages from beginning to end.

"Father, it is not here."

Turning towards Lance, the bearded **Giant** said in a stern voice that almost bellowed, **"Your remaining days will be spent in total suffering because you denied me!"** Then he bid several servants dressed in black to come and take Lance away. Lance balked and resisted their fierce attempts to lead him away.

"No! No! No! I won't go!" he cried. Struggling, he repeated his words of defiance. "No! No! No!"

Then Lance awoke with a jump that should have awakened Jill, but somehow it didn't. His resisting "No!" echoed in his mind; and he was covered with sweat. In that moment of terror, he almost willed himself to the **Son**; but quickly realizing his terror to be a dream, he settled back and tried to relax. He looked briefly towards the window and thought he noticed a black winged creature fluttering in the curtain. Then he realized it had to be the ribbon that Jill tied in the middle, moving with the breeze.

Letting out a sigh of relief, Lance turned back the covers and got out of bed. Still, Jill did not stir. Momentarily, he sat on the edge before proceeding through the living room to the kitchen where he heated a cup of coffee in the trusty microwave. After heating his cup of coffee, he took it with him and moved back to the living room.

"Your remaining days will be spent in total suffering!" The last words of the **Giant** haunted him. In fact, they still terrified him. And then he asked himself out loud: Could **He** really have sent me to Hell? What right did **He** have to do that? Could this dream be a look at reality beyond – or was it just a nightmare?

He was sitting in the living room now in his favorite chair. Jill always closed the curtains at night. He opened them thinking that the act may somehow open his mind too. The neighborhood was lit only by the street lamps. If there was a moon, Lance could not see it. He looked for it, though, almost as if it were a needed angel of comfort; but when he couldn't find it, he guessed it to be on the other side of the house.

Lance began to ask himself a series of questions. Who is this **Giant** or **God** that He has the right to send me to Hell, to make me suffer for the rest of time? How can I know that He can or cannot? Why must I be afraid of loving my life? Why would a God give me a life I should hate? Why is not my love sufficient for salvation? Why do I need Jesus? Who are devils? Why do they exist?

Priscilla said she believed devils to be hitch-hiker spirits. At the moment, that didn't mean anything to Lance. His attention went back to God. Who is God? What is God? God is forgiving. God is just. Correction: God is all forgiving. God is all just – not just forgiving and just, but all forgiving and all just. Lance had heard it a thousand times from those allegedly called of God. What did these terms mean anyway?

Forgiveness means release from debt, Lance thought. Justice means demanding that a debt be paid. If God is all forgiving, then He has to be all releasing; and no man need fear not paying his debt. If God is all just, then He has to be all demanding; and no forgiveness could be considered.

Lance said aloud, "It's ridiculous, absolutely ridiculous! It is said that God is all forgiving and all demanding at the same time. It can't be so. He must either be one or the other, but not both, if He is, in fact, all that character."

Lance returned to his silent speculation. Could it be, then, that God is partially forgiving and partially just? Lance was sure it couldn't be so. Anything that could be defined of God has to be with the modifier, *'all'*. How could God be half this and half that? The very concept of 'absolute,' which God has to be, excludes the possibility. God has to be absolutely this or absolutely that, but He can't be some of this and some of that.

What is He, then, all forgiving or all just? Lance was becoming excited with his thoughts; and his hand jerked with the sudden surge of emotion, causing him to spill a little of his coffee on his pajamas. The sun was beginning to rise and Lance thought jubilantly, How fitting! He sensed he was about to emerge from the cloud of his confusion. He sensed he almost had a very important answer. He sensed he was about to find out something extremely important about God.

Is God all forgiving or all just? He has to be one or the other in spite of all the self-proclaimed evangelists throughout the world. Lance pondered further. It is reasonable to think that whatever God is, He had to be it from the very beginning. So, before there was a Creation and there was only a Creator, what did an absolute being have to be – all forgiving or all just?

To forgive Himself, God would have to release Himself from a debt; but what debt could God have to Himself? His only debt had to be His very existence. God certainly couldn't annihilate Himself. Therefore, He couldn't forgive Himself of existence, so to speak. God, then, has to be self-demanding, demanding that He continue in existence if nothing else. God, then, has to be **Absolute Justice**.

Lance trembled at the thought. Christianity teaches that God is all forgiving; and he had just demonstrated to himself that such couldn't be so. God has to be all just, being that from the very beginning. God can't forgive. The thought struck Lance like a low blow to the midsection.

We have to pay our debts and be just, like God, or perhaps suffer perdition. Lance was not ready for this, as that implied Hell for failure. Christianity was right in its teaching of Hell and wrong in its teaching that God could forgive. What a bag of worms? thought Lance.

How about Jesus? Jesus supposedly claimed to be the Son of God; and yet allegedly he died to forgive sins. If Jesus was truly the Son of Absolute Justice, then he had to be all just and unable to forgive; but he did forgive. Therefore, he could not have been the Son of Absolute Justice. Another doctrine bites the dust, Lance suggested to himself.

In less than an hour, he brought to ruin two of the basic truths of traditional Christianity: that God is forgiving and that Jesus was the Son of God. What did that do to the doctrine of salvation through Jesus Christ? There was the possibility that Priscilla brought up that the father Jesus was speaking of was not God, but rather his personal spirit father. At the moment, that seemed the likeliest explanation, that the god Jesus was the son of was only a blessed spirit, not God Himself or Itself.

In any case, the forgiveness of Jesus can have no forgiving effect on me, Lance thought, as he continued his thought process. God must still be demanding and just, regardless of what Jesus did or did not do. So, the story was still a demanding God and not a forgiving One.

As just a short time before, Lance was jubilant because of his discovery, he was now edging toward depression. There seemed to be no hope. There could be no hope for forgiveness; but forgiveness from what? What have I done that I need forgiveness for?

I have doubted the story of Jesus in the past, he thought; but what can God demand of me for that failure since Jesus is now no longer His son? I have broken the Ten Commandments, he thought, again accusing himself of another violation; but was Moses anymore a prophet of God than Jesus was a son of God? Lance was sure there was a way to determine the truth.

God is all just. Moses spoke of justice to the exclusion of almost everything else. Therefore, Moses may be of God where Jesus could not have been. Moses was rigid and demanded strict attention to rules under the pain of death for some violations. Yes, it was possible that Moses and his rules could be of God.

Could that mean, then, that the Jews are right when they claim they are a favored nation under a just God? It seemed so. At least their claim of a just God seems right as the Christian forgiving God seems to be a lie. Judaism, it appeared, was pro-God; and Christianity in its lie, anti-God.

Fast concluding that the Jews may be right under Moses, Lance had backed himself into a corner. As it appeared now, there was no way out but strict adherence to a rigid set of rules handed down to man through Moses. Lance could hardly believe it. Judaism was right and Christianity, perhaps the lie of Satan. Impossible, he thought; and yet try as he might, he could not escape from his corner.

He had demonstrated that God has to be all justice and that Moses claimed and demonstrated himself to be a strict, just man. He realized the story was not yet complete. He was missing something he was sure; but the logical evidence tended to point in that direction – the law of the Jews may well be the law of God. Lance swallowed hard, as he had not expected this.

9

Leaning against a tree in the city park, Lance was still totally bewildered. It was October 12th, Columbus Day, and he had been fortunate enough to have the day off from work; and he had spent a greater part of that day pondering his crisis of the Absolute Justice of God. Promising Jill that he would make it up to her later, he had left the house and had driven to the city park where he always received spiritual motivation and spiritual nutrition while ambling about in meditation. The normal quiet of the environment, often only broken by the sound of quacking ducks in the city park pond, lent itself to being able to concentrate on some thought at hand.

Lance was positive he had walked around the park twenty times or more; and it was well over a mile for each circuit. How could he resolve his dilemma? How could he know if he was right or wrong in his Jewish conclusions? **Who could he talk to?** Unfortunately, he did not know any Jews; and he was very reluctant to contact a synagogue.

Who was it that got him into this mess? *Priscilla!* Sure, she would be the most likely person of all, he thought. He glanced at his watch – 2:42. The day was fast passing on. Mark and he had gone bowling a couple of times years ago when Priscilla and Mark were still regular members of the First Congregational.

He liked Mark, but he had always been more impressed with Priscilla. Even back then, Priscilla carried herself like she knew of her importance; and now she had delivered a sermon that turned Lance around and upside down like nothing else he had ever heard.

Her choice of a topic to her unique delivery had impressed Lance. He admitted to himself, although he would never admit it to Jill, that he was indeed aroused sensually by Priscilla; however, he had always been aroused in that manner by her, but this was the first time he had seen her naked. Priscilla was beautiful in every way; and Lance told himself many times that he would have enjoyed leaping through the wheat field with her. She had that special something that automatically equated with nature; and Lance loved whatever it was. **God, he thought! How could he ever handle these sinful feelings if he had to become a Jew?**

Luckily, there were several phone booths in the park; and it didn't take him long to reach one. "Reverend Guestly, this is Lance Jenkins."

"Lance, how are you?"

"Fine, Reverend."

"What can I do for you?"

"If you don't mind, I'd like to talk to Priscilla."

"Sorry, Lance, she's not here."

"I know. I was hoping you could give me her number." Pastor Guestly cooperated fully, knowing Lance as one of his more thoughtful parishioners. He had long felt a friendship with Lance that was more unspoken than open. He was sure of his character too, as he would never give his daughter's phone number to just anyone; and he was also sure that Priscilla wouldn't mind. Lance wrote it down on his palm.

"I suppose you want to talk to her about her sermon, huh?"

"That and some other things, I guess," was Lance's reply.

"I hope you find what you're searching for." Reverend Guestly was fully aware of Lance's anxiety to get on with his phone call.

"I hope so too, Reverend. I'll let you know. OK?"

"OK, Son. Talk to you later."

It was almost 3 o'clock now. Lance thought, I bet I'm too late for today; but he dialed her number anyway: 422-8802. Several rings and then the voice of a mature sounding lady, "Hello!"

"Priscilla, this is Lance Jenkins."

"I'm sorry, Lance. I'm Marie. I'll call Mom. Mom, remember Lance? He's on the phone."

"Tell him I'll be right there, Marie."

"She'll be right with you."

"OK," Lance replied. He only wanted the truth; or at least that was his primary reason for calling; but as he waited, his nervousness made him suspect himself.

"I'm sorry, Lance. Are you still there?"

"Yes, I'm still here."

"It's really good to hear from you. It has been a lot of years since you have been over to the house."

"Yeah, I know. I'm sorry, but Jill has kept me rather busy."

"You don't have to explain, Lance. I'm fully aware that Jill does not think a whole lot of me. Can I help you with something?"

"I hope so, Priscilla. I need to talk to someone about some thoughts of mine that are kind of tied into your sermon on Sunday. I feel a little awkward calling you like this, but . . ."

"Why, because I'm a woman?" she interrupted.

"I guess."

"Well, if you don't have a problem, I certainly don't. Can you come over now? This evening I have to go to a P.T.A. meeting."

"I was hoping you would have the time."

"I do. Come on over. Mark will be here in a couple of hours. He'd like to see you too."

"Fantastic!" Lance was genuinely pleased. Maybe his guardian angel hadn't left him after all.

"Oh, Lance?"

"Yes, Priscilla?"

"We're friends, aren't we?"

"Yes," he replied. "Certainly!"

"Then when you come, I'll have on my *Wedding Garment*. See you shortly."

10

"I'm not sure, Lance. That's interesting speculation. Let's think about it in the back. OK?"

Priscilla and Lance had been discussing Lance's dilemma for nearly twenty minutes. Lance was enjoying the company; but he was intent on finding the answer, or answers if that they be. Surprised a little at Priscilla's suggestion to go outside, he was a bit disappointed. She seemed eager to interrupt their discussion; and he was not at all sure he should take the chance. What if he were seen with Priscilla in her *Wedding Garment;* and could he trust himself with his naked friend?

"Come on, Lance. Don't worry. The children are out back. They'll protect us." Priscilla was very aware of at least part of the reason for Lance's reluctance; and she didn't give him any time to think about his indecision as she grabbed him by the arm and pulled him toward the screen door leading to the back yard. "The neighbors know I love the natural and they have gotten used to it. Now, if it's that you don't trust yourself, I'd suggest that you take off your covering too."

"My covering?" Lance remarked in a state of amazement. "Are you serious?"

"Do what's comfortable, Lance; but I always feel much more protected in front of innocent children if I'm not trying to hide anything. And be honest, Lance, with the kids playing within eyesight, you'll be safe from yourself and me because even if I should have a desire, I wouldn't do anything in front of the kids that they can't handle. Know what I mean? Like I say, they are the best protection a lady could want."

"You're amazing!"

"Oh . . . no, just alert, Lance, just alert."

"Who would have ever thought that children could be a grown-up's best protection?"

"Then you agree?" she asked.

"Though I'm a fool in perhaps a fool's paradise right now, I can't argue with you. Thanks for the trust."

"Thank the children," she replied, "and God. Lance, people in general don't understand my love for nakedness, but let me put it this way. *I was born naked. I pray to God I'll be allowed to die naked; and I'm going to take every opportunity to live naked – simply because that is the way I have been created; and who am I to challenge the offering of my Divine Benefactor?* If I'm going to talk about God with a true friend, I just as soon be in God's natural surroundings. I can think clearer that way." She waved to the children; and the children acknowledged her attention and shouted greetings to Lance as well.

Lance felt awkward in undressing. He had not yet progressed to the stage of going without underwear as had Priscilla. His attention flicked back to Sunday when Priscilla undressed outside of her home environment too. There had been something magic about Priscilla having no panties on. When the wedding dress dropped to the floor, that was it. Priscilla did not have to go any further. She wasn't wearing panties. She had been just a touch closer to being natural not having to strip herself of panties.

On the other hand, when Lance took off his pants, there was still underwear. It was like another layer of protection that Priscilla had not had. At that moment, Lance resolved to never wear underwear again. For the instant at hand, though, there was underwear. Lance slipped it off. Given his relative youthfulness, his manliness reacted to the freedom. Priscilla noticed and smiled. Of course she had seen it a thousand times in Mark. It was natural, all Godly and all Divine. Priscilla had no desire of having a second husband, however, and was willing with eagerness to get on with simple brotherhood. Feeling quite at ease and knowing immediately the borders of freedom that Priscilla was instilling with her ease, Lance sat down opposite Priscilla on the grass.

"You know, Lance, I didn't know it in the house, but if there wasn't an opposite to absolute justice, you'd have a point."

"What do you mean?" Lance was grateful for the distraction.

"I mean we can't stop with the top side of things in this discussion."

"We can't?"

"No. That's forgetting the bottom end; and the bottom is as important as the top."

"You have lost me," he replied, with a wrinkle in his brow.

"Think about it, Lance. God is totally demanding, positive, everything that He is. Right?"

"Right."

"Well, if God is everything, what is nothing?"

"Nothing is nothing," he said.

"Or space," she replied.

"So?" he responded.

"Space is the opposite of God. Space, in a way, is total forgiveness, as it is totally lacking in demands upon itself. Space is forgiveness as God is justice."

"I guess you're right, Priscilla. I hadn't thought of it that way."

"Who has?" she replied. "I wouldn't have either if it hadn't been for you bringing this whole discussion to light. Thank you for your revelation. Columbus Day should be a day for new discovery; and you have made this a beautiful October 12th."

"October is suitable for this discussion, isn't it?" Lance remarked. "Just when you think you have found life, you find you've been reaching for death, like summer turning into winter."

"That's for sure, Lance. We are such fools for not thinking things out better than we have. Anyway, assuming that space is total forgiveness, or total lack of demand, as God is total justice, let me see you try to relate to space."

"I don't follow you."

"Well, you insisted on trying to relate to total justice and almost became a Jew in the process. Now, let me see you try to relate to space and perhaps become a Christian in the process."

"Come again, Priscilla." he replied.

"Let me say it this way, Lance. *God is to man as man is to space. Man can't begin to reach total justice anymore than total forgiveness can reach out to man who is partial justice and partial forgiveness – or at least should be. That which is space or total forgiveness or total lack of demand to be something can't possibly relate to some demand or some justice.*"

Lance was still puzzled. Priscilla tried to make herself clearer. *"Look. Something can no more become nothing than nothing can become something; and likewise, everything can no more become something than something can become everything."*

"Huh? What are you driving at?"

"I'm saying that man shouldn't try to become absolute justice anymore than he should try to become absolute forgiveness. He's in between; and he should be satisfied with that."

"But what about God in demanding justice from us?"

"God can't require justice of us, Lance. He can only relate to totality and we are partiality, so to speak. In essence, God can no more relate to us than we can to Him. He's outside of our dimension as we are outside of His. He can't reach down to an individual something, which is us, anymore than we can reach up to Him. That means we need never fear His judgment or His justice."

"You mean you think that God can't even talk to man anymore than man can talk to God?"

"That's right. It's totally outside the realm of possibility. He can only reach towards everything; and we are only something. In a way, it's very comforting. Isn't it?"

"Yes, it is, Priscilla, if it's really so."

"Well, that's a matter of opinion if it's so or not, I guess, but from where I sit now and how I am thinking now, our conjecture seems to be leading us to these conclusions. It may be truly a mystery we will never be able to figure out. Without knowing how our souls came to be, we can know they are and will continue. *Man couldn't go to nothing, even if he wanted to. It's outside his dimension. He's trapped into being something.* Man may die, but it's only an illusion. His body continues as dirt and his soul as spirit. His body came from dirt and will return to dirt, or dust, as they say. His soul came from spirit and will return to spirit; but whatever, he doesn't become nothing. It's totally impossible for him to do that."

Lance was filled with the inevitable question. **"If it has not been God who has spoken with man, who is it?"**

"I suppose at least in some cases, those hitch-hiker spirits I talked about on Sunday. Because of our ignorance of God, they think they can claim to be Him and we will have no recourse but to believe them. They work miracles; and we believe they are God because we think that only God can work miracles. The truth is, God is not one to work miracles, even if He wanted to, which I'm sure He doesn't. In truth, God is not in the business of wanting or being able to want like human beings. For all practical purposes, God is simply in everything. *Being in everything, God cannot act as if He can go into things in which He is not. To work a miracle, He would have to reach into something He supposedly cures; but if He is already in it, how can he reach into it, as it were?* Pure and simple, God can't work miracles of individual cures in terms of put more of Himself into a situation than was present before that situation. It is a total misunderstanding of God that allows for God to be outside of us in the first place. *God can't go into something in which He already is. Can He? So, if miracles are worked, it is something other than God which is working them."*

Lance shook his head. "That takes some thinking," he said, "but it does make some sense. I do think I need to meditate on that for a bit, but it is worth thinking about. Assuming you are right though, Priscilla, that one who is not God might perform some cure and then claim it was God who is doing the cure, why would anyone want to claim he is God or claim to be speaking for Him?"

"To make us fellow travelers so they can catch a ride with us."

"But why?" Lance was not satisfied.

"I don't know why, Lance. I really don't. Now, that's open to speculation. In my talk on Sunday, I speculated it was to catch a ride with a body that is living because no other bodies are available for their own birth; or maybe they find an advantage in using others and wouldn't dwell in a body even if they had the chance. Who knows? But whatever their reason, they are not going to mess with this lady." In these last words, she was particularly emphatic, gesturing with definite, repeated hand movements.

"How can we keep them away?" Lance inquired.

"By staying away from what they are," she replied.

"And what are they, angry spirits?" Lance was recalling her Sunday sermon.

"Yes, but why are they angry?"

"You're asking me?" he said.

"Yes, why do we get angry?"

"We don't get our way, I guess."

"Either that – or we get it too much. *Either way, we lack the most important character a soul between God and space, between justice and forgiveness, can have. We lack balance.*"

"You think balance is the answer? You mean, an equal share of forgiveness and justice?"

"Precisely. Let's just say the ideal is to relax between payments."

"I like that. It sounds right."

"It was there for the finding, Lance."

"Alright, Priscilla," he wanted to know, "if I act half just and half forgiving, or as you put it, I relax between payments, how is that going to keep the hitch-hiker spirits away?"

"It's as clear as the nose on your face, as clear as the . . . I was going to say, 'shoes on your feet,' but I forgot you are naked. I'll bet you forgot too, didn't you?"

"As a matter of fact, I did. How can you forget you are sitting with a beautiful naked lady? You're going to have to explain that one to me."

"I don't have to explain anything to you, Lance. Just accept it and enjoy it. It's the most beautiful thing in the world – and also the most maligned. It's called, *Innocence.* Thanks for sharing that *Innocence*, Lance; for you have blessed me greatly; and I will always love you for it."

Lance was embarrassed and glanced quickly at his genitals, as if to assure himself that they hadn't suddenly disappeared. All at once they became an obstacle to the feeling of *Innocence* he had known just a moment before. Priscilla noticed his feeling awkward.

"Did you find them still there?" she quipped, startling Lance momentarily.

Lance began to chuckle. "What are you laughing at?" she inquired, joining him in his laughter without knowing why.

"Me," he said. "I really look funny."

"Yeah, I guess you do a little bit," she agreed, "but that's alright. You're entitled to look a little funny if you want."

Lance was quickly overcome with a desire to take his funny looking torso and go dive into the kids' sandbox. "Do you think the kids will mind if I join them for a minute or so?" he asked, not having any idea how Priscilla might react; however, he should have suspected agreement.

"Why not ask them?" she said, and then she corrected herself. "Na! Just go over and jump in. I'm sure they won't mind. The shrubbery will hide you from the neighbors if you want, if you go on your hands and knees."

Priscilla laughed heartily as she watched Lance scampering bare on his hands and knees across the lawn. Dawn and Davy joined with giggles of their own; and Lance fell over halfway to the sandbox, clutching his side in near pain as he rolled over in his own laughter. "God!" he exclaimed. "It's great to be a kid again!" He decided he would forego the sandbox and quickly hurried back to Priscilla.

"What are you doing back here? I thought you were going to play in the sandbox."

He laughed again. "Are you disappointed?"

She answered with a command. "Down on all fours again," she said, as she pushed him down on the grass and climbed aboard. "Come on! Let's go together!" Smacking him lightly on his behind, Priscilla rode horseback, or if you will, piggyback, across the lawn before Lance collapsed again in laughter with Priscilla square upon him. She rolled off and let him flop himself down on his back.

"This ole man is too weak to make it to the sandbox, Kids. Why don't you bring it to him?"

"OK," they said. Soon, two red buckets of sand were being dumped on Lance. Priscilla took some from the pile on his stomach and tossed some lightly into his hair – and too, another handful at his funniness. He responded with more laughter and made no attempt to get away.

"Come on, you weird looking creature," she chuckled, "let's get back to our discussion."

"God!" he said. I enjoyed that! What were we talking about anyway?"

"The first thing that comes to mind is your *Innocence*," she said. Turning toward the kids, she told them they could go back to what they were doing. Lance and Priscilla then began their treks on all fours, though separately this time, up to the front end of the lawn where they had been sitting. Their laughter was more mute now, but just as real. Lance was glad of the children's presence; for it was confirmed that except for them, Lance may not have been free to play with Priscilla like he had. This was one smart lady, protected by her kids and blessed in her *Innocence*.

"Only with a friend, Lance. Don't ever do that except among friends, except with people you trust."

"I know," he replied.

"It's too bad we can't do it with everyone, but until the human race recognizes that we are all equal in the same God, we can't," she continued. My children could not have protected me if you had a rapist mentality. Rapists are hitch-hikers, Lance; and they are, in turn, controlled by hitch-hiker spirits. Unfortunately, the world is full of rapists, of spirits that seize rather than share."

"Yeah, I know," he responded. Then he added, "Be careful, Priscilla. Please don't get yourself raped."

"As long as I remain on guard and go naked only with friends who respect the sanctity of life, I trust, Lance, that my providence will keep me safe."

"And your children? What about them?"

"I teach them the same vigilance. They know not to trust strangers. They too will be protected as long as they stay with their own and don't go wandering with their *Innocence.* It's not easy, Lance, but it's mandatory if we are ever to rescue this world from the hitch-hiker spirits. The alternative is to keep surrendering and to keep losing."

"But how do we win, Priscilla? You say it's with proper balance; but how is balance going to keep a hitch-hiker spirit away?"

"OK, Lance, it's like this, anyway the way I see it. *A hitch-hiker spirit is out of balance, or rather, hitch-hiker spirits are out of balance; or they wouldn't be interested in using what is not theirs to have. They are either too just and demanding or too forgiving and loose. The idea is to be equally demanding and forgiving. If we have balance, they can't get in to use us. A soul of imbalance has to have another soul of imbalance for hitch-hiking purposes. One who is in the middle has no need for augmentation from a side."*

"I guess that does make sense," Lance remarked, as he stretched his body and intentionally tested his *Innocence* by brushing the sand off his genitals. "So, where does Satan figure in all of this?"

"I suspect Satan is legion. I suspect *Satan is souls of a given imbalance taken collectively.* Together, they can make quite an assault. It's interesting, because our discussion points out that souls wanting to be like God and are too just and demanding are no better than souls determined to live loose, without direction or discipline. I doubt that souls of looseness or apathy would get along with souls of too much discipline at all. They probably hang separately."

Lance hit upon what he thought was brilliant and was eager to share the thought. "Now, I can see. Judaism and Christianity are vehicles of Satan because each is too much of one thing or another. Judaism is too strict and judgmental; and Christianity is too forgiving or easy, at least when not hypocritical. Neither one strikes the ideal balance we should seek in our lives."

"That's right, Lance. You got it. I guess when I suspected there were termites in the foundation, I was right; but not until this afternoon did I know for sure why."

"Where does Jesus fit into this?"

"Not as we have been led to see him," she answered. *"Satan has used him to pave the way for his hitch-hiking and taking control.* Keep in mind, now, that I am using the term Satan in a figurative sense to specify any one or group of souls who have it in mind to control others. We have already proved that God can't work miracles in terms that God is not a person that is outside of anything, but rather an *Absolute Everywhere,* so to speak. So, if God can't work miracles because God can't deal with individual things, that must mean that spirits seeking control over others must work those miracles. And when a cured person falls down and cries, 'Thank you, Jesus! Thank you, Jesus! Thank you, Jesus!' they have a beautiful subject for use. *There is nothing that a hitch-hiker spirit likes better than a spirit that yields;* and traditional Christianity teaches that we must yield to Jesus to be saved. How clever they are to have set us up, ripened for the picking. *Our salvation may well turn out to be our damnation because in yielding to powers outside ourselves and not using our own powers, we fail to grow. We fail to strengthen our own virtues.*

"Speaking of Jesus, Lance, I think that he came into the world when the imbalance was far to the right or to the way of assumed godliness or justice. He tried to correct that by throwing the scales over to the left; and he preached that which was necessary to correct the imbalance – forgiveness. *Jesus said he came, not to do away with the law and justice, but to perfect it in forgiveness. He was right. He did have the cure; but the too just Jews wanted his life for the life he was taking from them.*

"Thus, they had him executed to save their nation of justice; and Satan led the way. After the death of Jesus, Satan struck down a fellow demanding spirit, Saul of Tarsus, while claiming to be Jesus who Saul was persecuting. *Peter was also a demanding spirit, not a forgiving one; and so he was chosen to lead the new nation which at first was only a continuation of the old – too demanding and too strict and almost totally lacking in what Jesus preached: forgiveness.*

"From the 5th chapter of Acts in the **BIBLE,** Lance, witness when two new church members, Ananias and Sapphira, who had failed to pay their financial dues to the new church, were brought before Peter. Did Peter forgive as surely Jesus would have done? No! Peter filled them with fear, not forgiveness, and they fell dead at his feet, one after the other, for the fright Peter instilled in them. The iron hand of Satan, rather than the forgiving heart of Jesus, was already at work. *Do you think that Jesus would have approved of what Peter did? Hardly!*

"Now it's interesting, Lance, that traditional Christianity suffers from too much strictness to too much looseness. One time the heavy or demanding side of Satan controls it or a faction thereof; and another time the loose side of Satan controls it – both different cults and strongly contrary to the ideal of balance. In fact, they probably use the same medium to challenge each other. They are indeed a house divided against itself; and as Jesus supposedly said, they cannot stand against a man of firm foundation, equally just and forgiving."

"Wow!" Lance exclaimed.

"Yeah, Wow," she responded. "Wow is right."

"What about the scriptures, Priscilla? How can we explain them?" Lance was thinking of his earlier discussion with Jill when he conjectured the scriptures might be of the devil.

"You knew before you asked, didn't you, Lance? *The scriptures are generally based on the idea that God can speak to man – though admittedly through some prophet who has some kind of direct line to God. Now there have probably been spirits who have inspired the various scriptures, claiming to be of God; but as we have seen, they can't be. The scriptures are no more written by God than Jesus was the Son of the Absolute Justice God.*

"It's interesting that people look at prophecy as a demonstration of God power. They don't seem to realize that scriptural predictions coming true do not make them of God. Satan can plan and make things happen under the mask of God; but regardless of any prophecies telling of his supposed entrance, Jesus lived and died to prove a point – that forgiveness is just as important as justice.

"The scripture of Isaiah tells of a man to be born who would save the nation of Israel. That man was to be named **Immanuel** – which means **God With Us**. Jesus probably saw himself as being one to offer the message that God is with us, or more specifically, in us. He may have aptly chosen the name or nick name of **Immanuel** to reflect his message. It might get confusing, Lance, but try to bear with me. OK?"

"I'm listening," he replied.

Priscilla continued. "Alright, God is without imbalance because He only has justice and is not offset with forgiveness. Now, *in a way, man can only become like God in terms of achieving balance by equal shares of justice and forgiveness.* So **Immanuel** lived to tell the truth that an ideal son of God, so to speak, has to have total balance; that his life reflected that total balance and as such, he was an ideal son of God. Now he wasn't the son of Absolute Justice, but rather the son of balance, which God is."

"And people confused his calling himself a son of God with being a son of Absolute Justice!" Lance exclaimed.

"Precisely," she answered. "***Immanuel*** probably spoke of saving the nation from its sin, meaning he lived to point out the way to perfection; but he would have never claimed to be its savior in that his blood was a once for all thing and that others don't have to work out their own salvation or balance. 'I am a son of balance' is what he should have said. 'I am a son of God' is supposedly what he did say. Unfortunately, in all his wisdom, he didn't leave any evidence behind except his followers who totally misunderstood him and called him *'Jesus'* which means savior.

"And it's Jesus who lives in the church, not **Immanuel,**" Priscilla continued. "Perhaps **Immanuel** did not do enough to dissuade his followers from believing he was their personal savior rather than his being the way of perfection; and consequently, he is at least indirectly responsible for the cults that have arisen using his name; or perhaps he was preparing the world for his justice in case the world chose to reject him, but let me keep that for later.

"For now, to add to his followers confusion, he probably spoke of being one with his father, who was not God nor the idea or action of perfect balance, but rather his own father spirit who gave him soulful birth like our spirit or soulful parents have given us soulful birth. His listeners probably confused his father God with his father soulful spirit.

"Peter, the fisherman, was probably a man of great remorse for his betrayal of his friend and then likely tried to justify himself by using the resurrection of Jesus, legendary or real, as the foundation of a new church. Unfortunately, he did not know the master and consequently misled rather than led. I doubt very much, Lance, that Judas - as the betrayer he is presented to be - ever lived. Peter was probably the betrayer in that he did not support his friend when his friend needed him. Remember? Allegedly, Peter ran out on Jesus when Jesus was being tried and probably did not return until after his friend's execution at the hands of the challenged Jews."

"Where do you get all of that?" Lance asked, completely enthralled with this version of Jesus.

"Ah, it's just speculation. It's not important. Whether I'm right or I'm wrong, who cares? *The scriptures cannot be of God in terms of having God as their author; and all who inspire the divine lie have to be of Satan in terms of having an ulterior motive of control by virtue of their tale."*

"So that's the way the devils have been keeping the world in the dark," Lance responded, "through the scriptures that pretend to be of God so that they can continue their domination through, of all things, the church? God, I am glad they are out of the shadows and into the light."

"So am I, Lance. So am I."

11

Lance was eager to continue their discussion. "How about good spirits? Are unbalanced spirits or Satanic cults the only spirits who are down here with us?"

"No, certainly not, Lance. There has to exist balanced souls who have no interest in using other souls. Their only purpose is to aid them in their search for balance."

"But how can we distinguish among them?"

"By a laying on of hands, I think, Lance."

"What do you mean – a laying on of hands?"

"I mean an evil or unbalanced spirit wants control and, as such, will eventually try to overpower a living person – or slay them in the spirit, so to speak, according to the common vernacular. A balanced soul, however, is content to stay in the background, perhaps only influencing situations rather than controlling them. A balanced spirit above all realizes that a soul in aid has to achieve its own balance and cannot be given it from outside his or her person. Every soul must have its own *Wedding Garment*. Remember what I said on Sunday?"

"Yes, I do," he replied, "but I fail to see how a balanced soul's controlling out of love could go against that end."

"You think if someone else catches the ball on the team for you and runs for the score, it's your touchdown?"

"Yes, in a way."

"The difference may be subtle, Lance, but I think it's there. The only points that count in the end are the points you score, not what another scores for you. *The saints may block a bit for you, but they won't run for you.*"

"And you believe that devils not only block, but take the ball away and make it look like your score?" Lance asked.

"Precisely; and that's how you can tell the difference. *For the most part, you won't know a saint is around, whereas a devil's presence is a lot more obvious by virtue of overt control of a situation or person.*"

"Do you think that good spirits won't even heal?" Lance was a little upset at the thought.

"They might in special cases, but ordinarily I don't think so. If someone is crippled, it is for a reason; and to cure him or her by an outside force would not enhance a lesson, only detract from it. The devils may heal just to get souls they want to forget why they are lame. Maybe a soul is here to overcome a certain burden to gain spiritual strength. So what good is it if a devil takes away the burden? Does that make sense?"

"Perhaps not," Lance responded, "but it's hard for me to accept that God could want us lame."

"*God is not in question, Lance. He's outside of the picture, although you can be sure the devils will do all they can to accuse you of blasphemy if you claim it. That is not in their favor for us to think that God is outside of the picture in terms of individual overt control.*"

"So, should we try to communicate with our balanced friends in the spirit?" Lance questioned.

"By all means, Lance, by all means. We are part of a team; and we shouldn't forget it. I trust my balanced friends will continue blocking for me; and it's not for me to be ungrateful when they do. I talk to My Father spirit or soul, though I can't see him or her. I talk with my brothers in spirit. I even talk to God for my sake, though I know God is not a he to hear me. *God is a Presence within me, not only a force outside of me.* If it weren't for His or Its existence, I wouldn't even be a mystery. I do exist, though I am a mystery; and I think I should act grateful, not only to my personal father soul – or mother soul – but my wonderful All Justice God."

"Then I'm right in believing you're not an atheist?" Lance remarked.

"*You sure are. I consider that God and I are partners, though I do not understand It or Him or Her; and It or She or He doesn't understand me. Whoever said love requires understanding? I once did, but not anymore. Love is an act of the will, more than that of the mind perhaps; and I will to love God; and though He can't hear me, I thank Him daily for what He has given – and is giving.*"

"And so will I, Priscilla" Lance responded. "It's interesting. You know, this day has shown saints as sinners and sinners as saints. Those controlled by outside intervention, thought to be of Jesus and of God or Yahweh or Allah or whatever, are proven to be helped by devils; and those written off as lost because of independence from who we thought was God in whatever name we choose to label Him are actually more in line for salvation because their commitment is their own. Do you suppose that's what Jesus meant when he said, 'the first will be last and the last will be first'?"

"Perhaps," Priscilla replied. "*I have no way of knowing what Jesus meant by those words – or even that he spoke them.* I can't believe the scriptures, at least not all of them. They turn out to be at least partially inspired of the devils – or ones who want to control or rule others. Jesus was a beautiful man of great wisdom and virtue who has been misused and misquoted more than any man in history."

"It's a real shame that if what you say is true," Lance remarked, "we can never know *Immanuel* or the real Jesus."

"Leastwise not from a book we can't," she replied. "*Immanuel* can not be found in a book – or in the *power* of a spirit that overcomes. Angel spirits, as opposed to devil spirits, know the importance of the *Wedding Garment* and would never presume to take over another's life like a devil spirit would. There is little doubt in my mind, Lance, that on the day of Pentecost the attendant disciples of Jesus were overcome as claimed – but not by whom they thought. If it had been angel spirits, white doves would have appeared above their heads rather than tongues of fire – white doves of peace saying, *Come, we will help you fly* rather than flames of fire that said, *Come, we will consume you in suffering.*

"It is indeed too bad, Lance, that we can't know the real Jesus through a book. It's too bad the world did not recognize him. It did not; and does not. *Immanuel* – or the real Jesus – was not known, nor properly translated. Maybe he suspected he wouldn't be and that's why he insisted on speaking in parables. He may have suspected that people would reject him completely if he spoke plainly. Maybe his words would then have gone to the grave with him; but in speaking in a figurative way as he did, his teachings could live in stories masked in truth. People would pass them on, not knowing for sure what they were saying.

"It is hard to know who Jesus was, but we can know his teachings through his parables. The walking Jesus who healed and rose Lazarus from the dead is a legend, perhaps the invention of well meaning men overcome by the force of devils who inspired their writings. *Immanuel may not have healed at all.* That wasn't why he came. *He came to teach the truth and show the way – the way of forgiveness, balanced with justice – or the way of effort balanced with ease – or the way of strong balanced with gentle.*

"It was *Immanuel* who lived before the crucifixion. It is often Jesus who lives after, but Jesus in this reference is not *Immanuel*. Given that Jesus is seen as savior, as one who rescues us from having to do for ourselves, Jesus is Satan, masquerading as *Immanuel. When we killed Immanuel, our reckoning became Jesus;* and it is Satan's Jesus that slays believers in their spirits and prevents them from learning to fly on their own, prevents them from finding their own *Wedding Garments*, prevents them from becoming saints. The dead Jesus, completely the opposite of the *Living Immanuel*, has been leading us around by a ring in the nose." Priscilla was showing hurt in her voice at the end, as she had honest compassion for the many souls following the blind.

"But why does the real Jesus allow it? I don't understand that, Priscilla."

"That's a good question, Lance. I do not know, but I suspect it's a little thing called 'justice'. Remember? Jesus was for both forgiveness and justice – or law tendered with kindness."

"You're saying Jesus may be letting Satan use his name as a measure of justice?"

"That's right, Lance. Now of course I don't know for sure, but do you remember the parable of the vineyard that Jesus told? Did the father in that parable forgive those who took the life of his son?"

"No, I guess he didn't; but you don't normally align Jesus with justice."

"Regardless, Lance, he was the son of both justice and forgiveness as a way of balance. He and his father or providence have forgiven the world for its treachery by not destroying it, which they may have had the power to do. They have received justice by letting the world find its own way, even though that means misusing the way they came to establish."

"You're saying, in a way, that the devils and their use of the name of Jesus and the church is our punishment for murdering *Immanuel*?"

"That's right. The father of Jesus sent the son into the world; and the world killed him. Would the law of justice permit us to go unpunished for that most miserable of crimes? What would you do, Lance, in the name of justice?"

"I don't know, maybe the same," Lance responded, "but whether it has been because of the allowance of Jesus or not, I'm more than a little angry, Priscilla, that Satan has been leading us around by a ring in our nose, as you so aptly put it. Pardon my saying it, but I want to take that ring and shove it up his intimidating ass."

"Strong words, Lance, but I sympathize; however the best way to shove it up his intimidating ass is to bind him with our will to achieve balance, as we have today, and shove him into the sunlight of truth where he can't help but cower and sag because of his own imbalance. There he can't hurt us. He can only whimper from his own helplessness."

"Maybe it sounds cruel, but perhaps it's time he did a little whimpering after what he has done to us."

"Perhaps it is," she replied, "but still, for the most part, it's our own fault."

Lance continued. "Getting back to what we were talking about, Priscilla, I really find it hard to believe that Jesus, the prince of meekness, could have the stomach for deliberately allowing man to suffer in blindness and misdirection due to our rejection of him."

"They minimized that part when they wrote his story, Lance; but it's there as plain as can be in his parables. From the forgiving father who prepared a great feast for his son who returned after blowing his inheritance to the demanding father who required justice upon those who ravaged his vineyard and killed his son. It is clear through his parables that Jesus was for both justice and forgiveness; and so must we be if we are to be rightfully called **brothers of the Christ.**

" The fake Jesus would have us believe we should aspire to be like God and be masters of the universe, rather than masters in the universe. *Immanuel* taught we should be content to be like children, never aspiring to become greater than we are, to accept the *Innocence* of life – rather than accuse it of being dirty or filthy. *We are what we are. Let us appreciate ourselves in that light and not insist on acting above or below that dimension.*

"The bottom line is that man can not be like God, nor should he be like space and do nothing. The justice devils are hard and cruel and demanding in their imbalance; and if we be led by them and used by them, we too will become as they. The forgiveness devils are soft and easy in their imbalance and inspire us to believe our salvation is in them and in their lord, Jesus, the fake Jesus.

"*The parables of Jesus have not given one indication that the real Jesus ever preached salvation through another.* On the contrary, from the parable of the virgins to the parable of the talents, it is clear Jesus preached earning your own way, buying your own oil for your lamp of vigilance, investing your own talents. It is only in the narrative about the alleged activities of Jesus and in the writings after the gospels that there is ever sustained a doctrine of salvation through another. *If Jesus believed that salvation is through another, even if that other is himself, he would have surely taught it through a parable. He did not.*

"Don't you think that's a little strange, Lance, that the accepted Master of Salvation never used a parable to teach salvation is through another? That, in itself, is a dead give away that Jesus never believed it. Don't you think it also strange that not one of his parables ever taught that the whole human race suffered a loss of innocence due to the single violation of one set of parents? If that were true, Jesus would have also addressed that condition of humanity and then made sure it was included in the gospels; for it is the basis of our alleged need of redemption. The fact is, he did not. Leastwise, we have no evidence of it in his parables – the method he chose to teach.

"'I am the vine, you are the branches.' Jesus never gave that speech, Lance. Do you know how I know? I know because Matthew, Mark, and Luke all ignored it. Don't you think a speech of such great significance would have been included in their narratives? How come it wasn't? Was it forgotten by mistake, overlooked because of human frailty? Can you imagine the fundamental speech of Christianity being overlooked as unimportant?

"Or perhaps only John was present for the occasion. Even if that were true, impact of legend would have compelled them to remember it. Or was it not part of the legend when they wrote their gospels? *Tell me, Lance, how come the greatest speech in the history of Christianity was not included in the narratives of Matthew, Mark, and Luke – who all wrote their gospels long before John?*

"And while you're telling me that, kindly explain to me why the greatest miracle in the history of the world was omitted from their narratives as well. I mean, how often is a man raised from the dead, Lance?

"*Can any reasonable person believe that three men can write narratives about the same life and simply overlook the greatest miracle of all time? How come only John writes of the raising of Lazarus from the dead?* Didn't the others think such an event was significant? Again, the impact of legend would have compelled them to include it, even if they didn't witness it – unless, of course, that legend had not yet been devised.

"*No, Lance, the greatest speech ever devised by man was never given; and the greatest miracle of all time was never performed. Immanuel would have never given such a speech; and he didn't.* However, the greatest falsehood ever imposed on man was born in those dark days following the crucifixion.

"People will say, 'Priscilla, you have a devil.' But I say to them: *Prove to me and the world at large that I am in error. Don't come to me with any miracle and claim that as proof of what Jesus taught. Show me through the parables he taught that I am wrong. Don't come to me with any feeling of ecstasy and claim that as proof that Jesus lives in you. Show me through his parables that he is expected to live through you – or you through him.*"

"Do you mind if I say something, Priscilla?" Lance offered, as he finally found a place to jump in.

"I'm sorry, Lance. I guess I got carried away; but I'm sure you know now the depth of my conviction."

"Yes, I sure do."

"What did you want to say, Lance?"

"I love you, Priscilla."

"Oh, is that so?" Mark was standing there in the back door. "Lance, is that you?"

Lance was embarrassed because of his last remark; but he recovered quickly. "Yes, it certainly is, Mark. I'm surprised you recognized me."

"How could I not recognize an old friend? Gee, it's good to see you! I must say I'm a little surprised you're naked, though I would expect Priscilla to be; and, Lance, make that two of us. I love her too," he said as he winked at him, an obvious allusion to Lance's recent avowal of love. Mark reached over and warmly kissed his lovely wife and extended his hand to his friend.

Dawn and Davy came running from playing in the sandbox and jumped on Mark. Marie joined them as she brought out an overdue pitcher of lemonade and glasses for all.

"You'll join us for dinner, won't you, Lance?" Mark asked.

"Sure, it will be my pleasure." He was thinking of his own family; and he hoped they would forgive his absence at home, but he would handle that when the time came. Knowing that

Jill could not begin to understand his afternoon, he would keep the details a secret. He wanted to give his marriage another chance, but he suspected that he would never be accepted after this day.

Priscilla was holding up her glass and motioning for Lance to match hers for a toast. *"To the single greatest Columbus Day in my life!"* she said, to the clinking of the glass.

"And to the day we backed Satan out of business in our lives," Lance remarked.

"And into the light," she added.

"Shall we celebrate with a kiss?" Lance inquired, anticipating her response.

With the children and Mark looking on, Priscilla and Lance embraced in celebration; and tears of joy and triumph fell to the grass below.

From The Dark Into The Light

The End

Summer Town

By
Francis William Bessler

— A Naturalist Musical Screen Play —

Originally written in 1986.

Revised slightly in 2005.

Introduction

It's only some thoughts about life – with a few songs thrown in. I intended it as a screenplay; but I suppose it could be adapted into a stage play. In any case, it is only a skeleton for a possible production. I wrote an initial version in 1986, but in April of 2005, I am retyping it and revising it somewhat as I do. I even wrote an additional song for this 2005 final version called **I Am Divine.** All other lyrics were written in the mid 1980s.

I believe quite strongly that we human beings are failing to embrace our divinity. Perhaps that is what this play is about. It's about a few people trying to get it right. They form a town called ***SUMMER TOWN*** that is supposed to reflect what one might call "summer time" values. In the summer we tend to let our hair down and take it off – our clothes – that is; but it's that theme of living with our hair down all year and without pretense or cover up that the name of the town – even in winter – is ***SUMMER TOWN***.

It's the story of an idealistic citizenry, of course. Perhaps you could add to that – low key. These are folks who are not interested in living in the fast lane. They are folks who have decided that being close to God is being comfortable with all that God is making – especially themselves. **These are folks who are intellectually based and spiritually motivated.** They believe in the human mind and they believe that the human mind is entirely capable of working out its ideal destiny.

There is a lot of conversation in this play, which may make it slow moving. It is not one of those fast action thrillers whose only purpose is to fascinate and entertain. It was written to promote the concept of *Divine Naturism*, although there is only one brief reference to that title as such in the play. It comes in Scene 7 via a discussion between Grampa Owens and Julie and Terry. Julie and Terry are teenagers.

Divine Naturism is a concept that says that whatever God is, His (Her, Its) reality is in Nature or expressed through Nature. So we don't need to go outside of Nature to find God – or at least to appreciate God.

The main characters of **SUMMER TOWN** are depicted as individualists who feel strongly about personally doing what they feel is right, but leaving it at that. None of them need to demand corresponding conduct from others.

SUMMER TOWN, however, is without major conflicts. There are no fist fights, no outrageous jealousies, no settling issues through violence. In the words of Julie in Scene 10, *"Summer Town is the way the world should be."* Ideally, we should tolerate our differences, even as we try to adhere to our own personal beliefs. That is what **SUMMER TOWN** is all about.

This is a screenplay featuring a town that loves nakedness. It is assumed that all characters will be naked in scenes within the town itself. The only scenes featuring clothes or the lack of apparel will be in scenes outside the town itself.

I wrote the lyrics with accompanying melodies, though I am only providing the lyrics with this screenplay. If someone wants to produce this thing while I am available to supply my own melodies, that would be fine. It would also be fine for another of interest to generate his or her own melodies for the various lyrics of this effort. I will leave it at that for now. **Hope you enjoy your visit to *SUMMER TOWN*.**

Thanks!

Francis William Bessler
Laramie, Wyoming
April, 2005

Scenes & Songs

The Characters

David (near 50)
Linda (near 50)
Frank (near 50)
Marie (near 50)
Julie (17)
Jimmy (8, Julie's brother)
Grampa Owens (late 70s)
Steve Owens (mid 50s)
Janet Owens (mid 50s)
Terry Owens (12)
Becky Owens (8)
Tom (17)
Rick (17)
Gary (early 20s)

Rest of Atlanta Cycle Club (over 30):
Biggie & Nancy
John & Sue
Danny & Betty
Howard
Bob
Ruth
Russ

Tammy
Paul
Phil
Jenny
Jason
Judy

And a town of Naturalists

Summer Town

Scene 1

Introduction (Roller Skating)

With the instrumental music of the song, *Summer Town,* playing in the background, cameras will scan a midday **Summer Town** and come to focus on the tennis courts where adults and children will be roller skating. Focus should be directed to a sign which reads:

Roller Skating - Noon – 3 P.M.
Dancing   - 7 P.M. – Midnight
Tennis   - All other times.

Among the roller skaters will be narrator, Frank, and his lady friend, Dawn Marie (Marie), and David and Linda. After a minute or so of capturing the roller skaters, Frank and Marie will move to a bench on the sidelines where a drink dispensary of some sort will be located. Frank will fill two glasses or receptacles and offer one to Marie. Marie will smile and say thanks and sit down on the bench. Frank will return her smile and take his drink and sit down next to Marie. Frank will then start talking to the camera (and the audience).

Frank: I'd like to tell you about my favorite town. Here's a toast to my favorite town. (Marie toasts with him, touching drinks together.) It's called SUMMER TOWN. It was started some 17 years ago by that couple you see there, skating so freely. (Cameras will focus on David and Linda.) They were just out of high school then, at least when they first got the idea. It would be 14 years later before they would realize their dream, though. But the idea sprouted in their mind just after graduation in 1956.

David was planning to go into the Army, but changed his mind – became a computer programmer for an outfit in Denver, Colorado. Linda had something to do with that. Linda and David were married in April of 1957. Linda convinced David that his energies were better spent makin peace, not defendin it.

Ah, David and Belinda – Linda for short – are committed to peace, makin it, that is. They figure that if people could spend their lives makin peace, then no time would be left to make war. You know I can't fault them there. Can you?

Oh, I suppose you're thinking it's not realistic. Peace is for dreamin, not livin. Right? If you would, why don't you kinda hold your judgment on that until I finish my story, or until we finish our story. OK? While you're holdin your judgment and I'm figuring out what to say next, let's allow the good folks of SUMMER TOWN tell you about their town in song. They love to sing the praises of their own town. So, let's let them do it. OK?

Song

Summer Town

REFRAIN:
Summer time is Summer Town.
Winter time is Summer Town.
Spring time and fall time too –
Summer Town lives the truth.

Life's majestic and that's the Truth.
Life's fantastic and that's true too.
Life is splendid. Life is sweet.
Life should knock you off your feet. *Refrain.*

Creation's a miracle and that's a Truth.
They are satirical who otherwise accuse.
Satire and judgment make us frown.
They don't belong in Summer Town. *Refrain.*

Nakedness inspires and that's a Truth
For those who don't look at life as crude.
If you see life as crude, then don't come around
to our wonderful home called Summer Town.
Refrain (3).

(The song will be sung with a variation of leads and choruses with all singing the refrains. Through it all, the roller skating will continue. At midway, there should be an interlude with maybe a little fancy skating going on.)

Scene 1B

(Focus back on
Frank and Marie)

Frank: Oh, I forgot to tell you. Folks, my name is Frank. I'm a Judge in SUMMER TOWN. This is Dawn Marie. (Dawn Marie (Marie) looks into the cameras from looking at the action on the court and offers a smile and a wave.) How did you like their song? Mighty fine folks in SUMMER TOWN. I think there's more happiness in our town than in any town on the face of the earth – if not more, at least as much. Know what I mean?

Before I go further, I need to tell you how SUMMER TOWN got started. I told you before that David and Linda started it, but I didn't tell you how. You see, David and Linda graduated together in a little town in Wyoming, near the Montana state line. As I told you before, David was planning to go into the Army, but something happened to change his mind. That something was a someone named Linda. This incident occurred in the beautiful Big Horn Valley in Wyoming in 1956. Now, this ain't Wyoming. It's Georgia, but let's go back there and reminisce a bit.

Scene 2

Big Horn Valley in Wyoming

(With Frank still talking, the scene goes to the Big Horn Mountains in Wyoming, to one of the big sloping mountains. David and Linda will be reaching the top of the sloping – as opposed to jagged – mountain. The cameras will scan the valley, coming to rest on David and Linda who will be sitting down at the top.)

Frank: It's June in Wyoming in 1956. David and Linda were serious about one another. David took Linda to the mountains for a picnic. He loved those mountains and went hiking there a lot as a kid, alone and with pals too. On this day when his hiking pal was Linda, he was planning to tell her about his decision to go into the Army. Let's let you see for yourself what happened.

David: Gosh, the mountains are beautiful, aren't they, Linda? Just listen! It's so quiet you can almost hear God.

Linda: You know how I feel about that, David. Wouldn't it be nice if we could stay here forever?

David: Yeah, I think it would be grand, alright, but it won't happen, will it? In just a little while, it will be off to the Army for me, as you know.

Linda: Do you really think that's for you, David? I know you've talked to the recruiter and all, but somehow I can't see you in a gray uniform, let alone carrying a gun. That's not the David I have been going to school with.

David: Oh yeah? Who's the David you think you know?

Linda: The David who was planning to be a priest – that's who.

David: Well, I figure I can be a priest and be in the Army too.

Linda: And what of me? Am I to become a nun? I am not even Catholic.

David: Linda, I wish you were. Maybe then you'd understand. I have to do what I have to do.

Linda: You're right! I don't understand! First you say you want to serve your God and then you want to defend your Country – and maybe a long way down the line, it's OK to think of me. Where do I fit in, David? I'm neither God, nor Country. Who wants third place?

David: Linda, you're not third. You're first.

Linda: Really! Then why haven't you asked me to be first?

David: Among mortals, you're first, Linda – but God is first, first.

Linda: And where is God?

David: He's here, right now! I wish people could see that.

Linda: Why don't you tell them that?

David: I want to. I really do. I want people to see themselves differently than they do now.

Linda: And how do we see ourselves that you don't like? What would you change?

David: Nakedness!

Linda: I should have known.

David: Can I help it if I love nakedness?

Linda: The Army or Seminary won't help you.

David: Will you?

Linda: Yes, David.

David: Really?

Linda: Yes, really, I will. I will admit that when you first suggested that people should go naked when we were Juniors, I almost freaked out. As fate would have it, I visited a cousin in Denver in the summer following my Junior year. They belonged to a nudist association outside of Denver and took me along. I was shy at first, but once the ice was broken, you couldn't keep clothes on me.

David: I know. You told me about that.

Linda: I think that's why I fell in love with you when we became Seniors, David. I began to share your love for nakedness.

David: I'm glad you did. And now we're here – sitting on top of the world in the Big Horn Mountains outside our home. And you are telling me you'll help me tell the world of nakedness.

Linda: Yes, I am. The Army doesn't need you. I do – and the world needs you, needs us. How are we going to tell the world, David? What are you going to do?

David: I don't know, Linda, talk to it, I guess – and maybe start a town and declare nakedness as part of the charter.

Linda: I'm now the world, David. Talk to me!

Song

Let's Look at Each Other Differently

David:
Let's look at each other differently
with a whole new respect.
Sure, we have genitals,
but why should we object?
Genitals are only muscles –
they're not so mysterious.
Touch them and they extend,
but why make it serious?
We treat sex like a thrill
and isolate ourselves with our act.
We don't stand with the world –
belong only to the human pack.
And then we run away and hide
and God we accuse.
You shouldn't have made us that way, we say,
and His grace we refuse.

Let's look at each other differently
with a whole new respect.
Let's join the stars and seas
and with Creation, let's connect.
Let's enjoy what we are –
genitals and all.
Then we won't be so weak
and won't with Adam fall.
Come on, is it so hard
to see each other differently?
I'm not alone. I'm like all men.
Enjoy the world that's in me.

Linda:
Let's look at each other differently
with a whole new respect.
It's time we had a new vision –
and new values, let's select.
The old one isn't good, I agree –
it divides the world in two
and puts on one side all that's good
and on the other, evil crews.
As a lady, I am tired
of being measured by my breasts.
Why can't I be a woman
without passing a ratings test?
And as a man you shouldn't care
about the size of your penis.
It's just a muscle, as you say,
and it doesn't measure genius.

Let's look at each other differently
with a whole new respect.
We could really fall in love
because our natures we'd accept.
And then when we'd act together –
sexually and otherwise,
we wouldn't be strangers to the world –
we'd need no disguise.
Our ebbs and flows wouldn't be
restricted within our flesh.
We'd truly be one with the world
and with everything enmesh.

David: Let's look at each other differently
Linda: with a whole new respect.
David: I am ready.
Linda: I am too.
Both: Let's take the first step.
David: I'll take my clothes off, for good, my good.
Linda: And I'll do the same.
Both: We'll stand so proud with our eyes aloft
and we'll give our souls a raise.
David: Oh, birds, can you see?
Come fly in real close.
Linda: We'd like to aspire on your wings
to become holy ghosts.
David: Well, My Friend, I think that
this is Paradise.
Linda: But only if we act as pure
and welcome our own sight.
David: Let's look at each other differently –
Oh, yes, let's do.
Linda: Feel free, My Love, to look at me –
and I will look at you.

(Allow for an instrumental interlude here during which David & Linda will undress for each other. Should be a sensitive event with touching and kissing and hugging. Undressing does not have to be continuous. Can take off an article and then be affectionate. Whatever comes natural. Once interlude has been completed, repeat last verse.)

Scene 3

Residential scene in Summer Town

(After the song, the scene will return to SUMMER TOWN, with Frank walking in a residential scene. Again, he will be talking to the audience. The camera will capture him and various residential activities.)

Frank: Well, Friends, that's how it happened, according to David. Linda doesn't comment when David tells the story, but she nods now and then. She's not one to tell a lie or let a lie be told if she can help it. So, I suspect David is telling the truth.

I guess it's no secret that women change the courses of men every day, but Linda – she's some kind of woman. I suspect that if it wasn't for her love, David would have joined the Army, may have got shot over there in Vietnam, and, well, SUMMER TOWN would not be here today.

David and Linda married shortly after that session in the Big Horns and moved to Denver. David became a programmer in 1961 and worked for four years for a firm in Denver. Brian was born in 1959. He's gone now – livin in Atlanta, a happily married man. Of course, there's grandchildren, two of them – one is three and the other just turned one. Christy, their other child, was born in 1961. She's still single, but lives in Atlanta too. As a matter of fact, she went to school and became a computer analyst. David still works as a contract programmer and works mostly in Atlanta too.

Forgive me for getting ahead of myself. As you know now, David and Linda and their two children moved to Atlanta from Denver. They did it in 1966. While living in Denver, they belonged to that nudist association Linda visited in her Junior year. As a matter of fact, that's how they came to move to Atlanta. From a friend in the nudist association in Colorado, they heard that Georgia might be a great place to found a town for Nature loving people. Not that Colorado wouldn't be right for that, but Colorado is a might colder than Georgia, you know. For that reason, Georgia seemed more practical.

They founded the town you see here in 1970 – and yours truly was lucky enough to be around. That was only 17 years ago as I'm talking to you now. It's April of 1987 right now. A lot has happened since our start in 1970. We started out just a clearing in the woods. Actually, Linda was the real momentum behind the actual founding. She doesn't know what shame is. David kept talking of the ideal town that charters nakedness, but it was Linda who lifted the process and turned an idea into reality.

She told David, why just talk? Do something. David will agree he wasn't much for doing, but he sure did do a lot of talking about what needs to be done. But Linda? She did something. She did a lot of something. David loved to bicycle; and so she suggested that they join a bicycle club and then suggest to the members about riding naked.

Well, they did. Most of the club dissented to the naked part of it, just as most of the world would, I guess. But Linda was right. They found among the cyclists who agreed, the core of their town. A few of us were among that cycle club, Dawn Marie and me included.

That's another scene worth re-enacting, I think. Let me set the scene. We're in Atlanta in 1969 – and David and Linda are about to make their big promotion chat. A bicycle club of about 20, all of us over 30, have been riding for 20 miles or so. If you look, you can see us, resting on a grass knoll beside a deserted parking lot. It's a business offices complex and it's Saturday. That's why no one is working.

Scene 4

Grass Knoll in Atlanta

(The scene is a grass knoll on a slight incline outside a business office complex parking lot – save one or two lonely vehicles parked clearly away from the building, implying they do not belong to the office complex. All participants are on the grass knoll with their bicycles parked in the parking lot below. Some will be standing. Others, sitting.

Characters: David and Linda (married). John and Sue (married). Danny and Betty (living together). Biggie and Nancy (married). Singles: Frank, Dawn Marie, Paul, Phil, Bob, Russ, Howard, Jason, Jenny, Carla, Ruth, and Judy)

Bob: It's sure a nice day.

Ruth: It certainly is.

John: How long you been ridin, Ruth?

Ruth: Off and on, I guess, since I was a kid.

John: That must be all of 10 years, then, huh?

Ruth: Lookin for a tip, John?

John: A little flattery doesn't hurt.

Ruth: (Smiling) How long have you been riding?

John: 20 years or so.

Ruth: Just out of curiosity, what's your best ride? I mean, your longest ride?

John: About 60 miles, maybe, though it's been years since I did that.

Ruth: How about you, Lindy? What's your longest ride?

Linda: I really don't know – a couple of hours worth, maybe 20 miles. David did 108, though, just last summer.

David: I'd like to try for 140 sometime, but it better be under the clouds when I do it. That 108 miles was under a hundred degree sun. I had to constantly stop and ask for water.

Nancy: Where did you do that, David?

David: On some country roads off of I-20 between Atlanta and Augusta.

Nancy: Why did you pick such a hot day to do it?

David: I didn't really. I just chose a day – and it turned out to be hot.

Russ: I never thought riding a bicycle could be so much fun. I have really gotten into it. It's nice riding alone, but it's better with company. That I must admit.

Linda: How long has this club been going?

Russ: Ask Biggie and Nancy. They started it.

Biggie: About 12 years, I guess.

David: What was your reason for starting it?

Nancy: Mostly for something to do. It almost didn't get started, though.

Linda: Why?

Nancy: I didn't see a railroad track jutting above a pavement we were riding about 13 years ago – and boy, did I take a spill! Broke an arm and was in a cast for a couple of months. Bad break it was. I guess it's a lot like getting bucked off a horse. I didn't get back in the saddle for over a year. But I did get back into it – and Biggie and I started this club about a year after my spill.

David: And you say you started it for something to do?

Biggie: Mostly. Nancy and I don't have any children; and we tend to have a lot of time on our hands.

Ruth: It's a good way to spend time, alright. It's a lot of fun and great exercise.

David: It's more than fun or exercise for me. It's an expression of freedom. We're free right now, but you're really free when you are riding without a stitch separating you from glorious Nature.

Ruth: You mean naked?

David: Yeah, naked!

Ruth: You've ridden naked? Where?

Linda: David and I do it every chance we get – especially on country roads early in the morning. I mean, you talk about freedom! Riding a bike naked is for David and I what driving a Mercedes is for a sports car enthusiast.

John: I think I'd rather drive a Mercedes.

David: To each, his own, John.

John: The only place I have any desire to go naked is taking a shower. I don't even go from the bedroom to the bathroom naked. I figure I owe it to the kids and Sue to be modest.

David: Why, John?

Sue: Because I don't want him to – and I'll thank you not to give him any ideas.

Linda: Come on, Sue. Why don't you want John to go naked?

Sue: It just happens to be lacking in dignity.

Frank: At least you didn't say, it's sinful. Lots of people believe that. I have always resented such a notion.

Russ: Me too, Frank. I tell you, nothing irritates me more than all these fundamentalists acting holier than thou.

David: And they don't have the truth in the first place. That's the amazing thing to me. They are the ignorant ones and they think they are the wise ones. I doubt that their Christ would agree with them. They are always invoking his name – and I'll bet you the real Christ wasn't anything like what they think he was - or is.

Nancy: Do you think that Christ would be against riding bicycles naked, for instance?

John: I do. I think he would find it disgusting.

David: What proof do you have for that, John?

John: What proof do you have he would approve it?

David: None, but I don't need any. I don't need Christ and he doesn't need me.

Sue: Oh, you don't, huh?

David: No, I don't. Christ taught self-reliance, using your own talents, not crying, Lord, Lord!

Linda: Don't get us wrong, Sue. We believe in Christ, but we believe he believed that we should believe in ourselves. And we believe in the freedom to follow the dictates of your own conscience.

David: And we resent fundamentalists who feel they are dirty and sinful telling us who have integrity that we are bound to Hell.

Frank: Nothing aggravates me more. I mean I believe it's great to be moral and all, but you have to understand, morality is a personal thing.

Marie: It sure is, Frank. There is absolutely nothing more personal than morality because morality or being moral is only doing what you feel is right.

Frank: I couldn't agree with you more. (After a brief pause.) Do you really go naked, David, on your bicycle? I think that's great! No, I think that's fantastic!

Sue: I think it's disgusting.

Linda: Do you want to know why we do it, Sue?

Sue: Not particularly, but I think you're gonna tell me anyway.

Linda: Not if you don't want to hear. That's your choice.

Sue: I don't. John, let's go.

John: See you guys some other time. It's getting too heavy – and we don't like heavy. (They leave.)

Marie: I'm intrigued, Linda. Why do you go naked?

Linda: Salvation – pure and simple – salvation. My soul is at stake. Our souls are at stake.

David: The way we see it, Dawn – that is your name, isn't it?

Marie: Yes, Dawn Marie Jackson, but you can call me Dawn or Marie or Dawn Marie. I like Dawn Marie the best. My mother's name is Marie and my father's name is Don. I like being named after both of them.

David: Lovely name – and names!

Marie: Thanks!

David: Alright, Dawn Marie, being civilized is dangerous to your health in a way.

Marie: Why?

David: Because someday we're going to die and we're going to have to face that great beyond.

Linda: And what better way to prepare for going past life than loving it, living it fully, not denying it.

David: It just doesn't make any sense to deny it like we shouldn't enjoy life. Someday we're gonna die and when our souls are outside our bodies, looking down or looking back, I think we'll really be sorry we denied life and nakedness when we had the chance to love it.

Linda: Think about it, like you are a star when you die. Are you going to be dressed in robes then? You wouldn't fit in the Universe. Nothing is clothed in the Universe. Why should we as human be different?

David: Anyway, we go naked to prepare for death as well as to enjoy life. And when we die, it will be an experience of tremendous degree. Think about it! Life is done and your soul is alone and free outside your body. You look down and see your naked body lying there. Won't that be nice? Think of the peace. You're a part of the wonderful Universe! You're a sister to the stars!

Linda: Now, look at the opposite, Dawn Marie. You lived your life civilized and wore clothes from birth to death. You're looking down at your clothed body, lying in a morgue. And all you'll be able to think of is – I denied life. I had the gift of life and I denied it. I had the gift of life and I betrayed it. I listened to the deaf who could not hear the sounds of Nature's symphony tell me I had no right to hear. I believed in perverts. I exulted in condemnation. Not a pretty picture, huh? What kind of future will you have? You can only hope that memory won't play as much a part because you won't have much in your bank of memory worth remembering. How sad! How terribly, terribly sad!

Marie: But no one knows for sure what will come after.

David: That's true, Dawn Marie, no one knows for sure. No one – not one single person living now knows for sure, including all the blind believers of a hundred and one prophets.

Linda: But a wise person makes plans based on probability.

Marie: So what do you think life after death probably is?

Linda: In so many ways, living naked.

Tammy: Oh, really? Why do you think that way?

Linda: What's death, Tammy?

Tammy: Death? I don't know. It's just not living, I guess.

Linda: True, but what happens when you die. I mean, what probably happens, especially to the soul?

Tammy: It is said the soul is judged.

Linda: Forget about what is said, Tammy. Is it wise to believe something just because others say it is true?

Tammy: Hardly. You can get into a lot of trouble doing that kind of thing, being blind and following the blind and all that.

David: Well said, Tammy. Well said!

Linda: Forgive me for badgering, but this is important. What probably happens to the soul after death?

Tammy: You asked me before. Now, I ask you. What is death?

David: Is it not leaving something?

Linda: Yeah, Tammy, isn't that true? At its most primitive definition, death is a process whereby one thing leaves another. Not only life leaves the body upon death, but the soul leaves the body upon death.

David: Accordingly, then, upon death, the soul is stripped of its temporary clothing; and that temporary clothing is the body.

Linda: Death, then, probably leaves the soul naked. Can't you say that?

Jenny: But it's a different nakedness.

Linda: Perhaps, but it's still nakedness. It's going without cover, without disguise.

David: Now considering that, the wise soul will go naked in life in order to prepare for nakedness after death.

Linda: What person likes to be shocked, Jenny? Surprised, yes, but not shocked. By not going naked in life, you are probably setting yourself up for a shock after death.

Jenny: Sorry, I don't follow.

Linda: It's all bound with the idea of having something thrust upon you, Jenny. In life, we don't like that, do we? We can handle things if we prepare ourselves to handle them, but we don't like things being thrust upon us. It's very, very difficult to react with grace when something is thrust upon us; and almost inevitably, we react with fear.

David: So it only makes sense to avoid having nakedness and a sense of judgment thrust upon you, upon death. No one knows when they are going to die. Zap, you're there – very often, totally out of the blue. It only makes sense to prepare for nakedness by accepting it in life, before death.

Tammy: That's a smart thought. I wonder if judgment is nothing more than having to face the truth?

Jenny: Nakedness is judgment?

Tammy: Don't you think?

Frank: I do. I think that's a good definition of it. People live their lives thinking judgment will come from someone else.

Tammy: And in reality, it may be the shock of having to face the truth, after living life desperately to avoid it. You live life terrified of nakedness and death strips you bare – or probably strips you bare, as you suggest, Linda. Then you have nowhere to run – nowhere to hide.

Linda: You're probably right, Tammy. Judgment is probably nothing more than not being able to hide or run from the truth. It's thrust upon you. It's there; and you have no way to deny it. What better way, then, to prepare for death and avoid a shocking judgment, your own judgment, than to go through life fully exposed and naked? It won't matter much if you are stripped naked in death if you live your life that way. And what a sense of continuity must accompany you if you can ease from one naked state to another.

Ruth: You're gambling with eternity on that one, kids.

Linda: Not at all, in comparison to you, Ruth. You are the one who is playing against the odds. Is it likely that a person who died rather than judge anyone is going to change and start judging? Is it likely that Jesus will judge anyone when he condemned the practice? And that's what you are counting on, isn't it? You are counting on Jesus judging me and putting me in my place, right?

Ruth: Oh, he'll judge you, alright. You can scoff at it, but you won't be able to escape it.

Linda: Judging others in terms of condemning them is for fools, Ruth. Was Christ a fool?

Frank: (mimicking) Look over there, Ruth! Can you see him? He's coming upon that big fluffy cloud. Can you see him now? Look there! What's that he has on? A white robe?

Ruth: A white robe of righteousness.

David: If he has a robe of righteousness on, Ruth, he has to be naked. You can't have one without the other. Why would Christ need to cover himself? Has he something to be ashamed of? If so, he ain't Christ because according to your own definition, Christ is sinless. Why, then, would he come covering himself? But as he stands there naked and sinless, Ruth, do you think he would have you do otherwise?

Ruth: I am not sinless.

Linda: Then you should go clothed. Indeed, if you feel that way, it's right for you; but David and I go naked because we, like Christ, are sinless – and like it would be for Christ, naked-ness is right for us. Our nakedness is an expression of our integrity and, if you will, our righteousness.

Tammy: Is nakedness necessarily righteousness?

David: Only if it's chosen, Tammy, only if it's chosen. Somebody who goes naked because they are forced to go naked will do so in shame. Going naked without purpose is not being free. Nakedness by itself doesn't mean much. It's only if you choose it deliberately and choose to love it that it's good.

Ruth: So if it's so good, why aren't you naked now?

Linda: As a matter of fact, that's why we are here today. We would like you to try it with us. You can't judge what you hav-en't tried.

David: You have to experience nakedness, purposeful naked-ness, to know it. You'll never know freedom, and we think, purpose, until you've gone naked and until you go naked consistently.

Ruth: You're crazy! I am getting away from you! I think you have a devil! Suggesting I get naked with you – you must be out of your mind!

David: You will find out if I have a devil after you die, but I will bet you probabilities, Ruth, that I'll be free and you won't be.

Ruth: I don't want to be free.

David: Congratulations, Sweetheart, you're not. You may take freedom lightly. I do not. And you who are not free when you die – who's to say that without the benefit of choice, the soul won't be forced into a kind of limbo, just hanging in there with no way to move about for lack of freedom – kind a like staring out into space and seeing nothing but a general gray mist.

Jenny: That's a gruesome thought – limbo forever. Surely not.

David: It's a possibility that I wouldn't dare risk myself.

Tammy: You mean you think we may lack the ability to adjust? I agree with Jenny. That is a gruesome thought.

Linda: Isn't it, though? That ought to be enough to scare us into living naked, and in a very real way, without sin.

Russ: I don't follow. Why wouldn't the soul be able to adjust?

David: Because the option to choose nakedness will be no more. Death makes us naked and there will be no choice to it. If you haven't chosen it before death, it may be too late to enjoy it after death because it will no longer be a matter of choice and freedom.

Linda: What experience have you had in life, Russ, where you really enjoyed something you did not choose?

David: Don't you think it's the freedom to choose it that makes it lovable? If you are given a delicious chocolate pie and commanded to eat it, do you think you will enjoy it near as much as you would have if you could have chosen between deserts?

Linda: Once again, if something is thrust upon you, normally you will lack an impulse to love it – even though it may be good for you.

David: Keep in mind, we're speaking probabilities. We have no reason to suspect that the conditions for freedom and enjoyment in this life are not also the conditions for freedom and enjoyment in the next life. Since being able to choose in this life is so important, it can be assumed it is in the next life as well. So, we should choose while we can. We can't choose nakedness in the next life because it won't be an option – or may not be an option. We will – or may – have to go naked. If you don't love nakedness before death, you won't be able to love it after death because you will lack the freedom to not have it – or again, may lack the freedom to not have it.

Linda: So, you see, it's greatly a matter of exercising your options now while you have options. If you choose it now because it is good and right and enjoy it now, in all likelihood, you will continue to enjoy it when you can no longer choose it. But if you don't choose it now and don't enjoy it now, in all likelihood, you will not be able to enjoy it later when it is thrust upon you. If it is a burden now, it will be so later as well.

David: That makes sense to us.

Ruth: What about Jesus?

David: What about him?

Ruth: Jesus will come for me.

Linda: That's the difference between us, Ruth. You will be waiting for Jesus to come and get you. David and I will be going with Christ – along with all of those who are willing to go naked while the choice is still theirs. So, now is a good time to pose it. Those of you who like the scenario of nakedness we have presented – we would like you to join us.

Tammy: And go naked?

Linda: Yes.

Tammy: Where and when?

Linda: Here and now. Let's ride naked for an hour or so and think about why we are doing it, give it purpose.

Nancy: Even if I were to agree with you philosophically, I am not sure it would be worth the risk.

Linda: What risk?

Nancy: Of getting arrested.

Linda: You're right, Nancy. If we thought we would be arrested, we probably wouldn't do it.

Ruth: Some principles. Sounds like you're nothing more than a couple of hypocrites to me. You think it's right, yet you wouldn't do it if you thought you'd get arrested.

Linda: Freedom is relative, Ruth. We would not be free to go naked at all in prison. At least in our homes, we are free to go naked. Some freedom is better than none at all.

Nancy: Why, then, do you suggest we go naked here and now? Why take the risk in an unfriendly world?

Linda: Because it's worth the risk, Nancy. The chances of our getting arrested are only as good as our chances of being seen. It's Saturday and it's not likely anyone will show up at this office complex. David and I have been reviewing this area for just that reason for several months. We used to live just a few blocks from here. So we know the area pretty well. We have ridden our bikes naked a good deal in this parking lot. If we thought we were taking much of a chance, we wouldn't suggest it.

Jenny: It's broad daylight.

Linda: No guarantees, Jenny. We could get caught. We could be seen, but from our review of the area in past weeks, it's not likely. Therefore, because the risk of being seen is low, the opportunities of freedom are high. It is unlikely anyone will see us.

Jenny: If you are so certain, Linda, I guess I'll take a chance.

Biggie: I'm not even sure I'd go naked if I knew no one was around. I'm not even sure I have a soul to worry about securing freedom for an afterlife. Na. I think this ole lad will be pushing on.

Nancy: I do believe I have a soul, but I'm with my Hubby. I'll be leaving with him, but, Linda, I am curious. I'd like to stay in touch – and maybe, later.

Linda: Anytime, Nancy, Anytime.

Biggie: OK, Nancy and I are going. Anyone else coming with us?

Ruth: Are you kidding? If I stay, I'll be burned from the Hell fire these lunatics are lighting.

Jason: I have no objection on moral grounds, but I'll be leaving too.

Phil: It's a bunch of nonsense to me. Ain't no way I'll be sticking around.

Judy: Me too.

Tammy: I'm not going to strip, but I'd like to stay and ride. You don't have to strip to stay, do you?

Linda: Of course not. We'd be delighted to have you ride with us, naked or otherwise.

Tammy: Then I'm staying.

Russ: So am I.

Howard: Me too.

Frank: This is the first opportunity I've had in a long time to do something truly sensible. I have a feeling the angels are getting out their harps. (Looking upwards.) Hello, Heaven, you can finally tap the wine you've been saving for this day!

Ruth: Yeah, the wine of wrath – God's wrath.

Nancy: (Impatiently) Come on, Ruth, let's go.

(All leave except David, Linda, Frank, Marie, Tammy, Jenny, Russ, and Howard)

Linda: Joining us, Dawn Marie?

Marie: With clothes, yes. I'm kind a shy. I am not sure I could ride naked, but I do like the idea. Give me a little time to get used to it. OK?

Linda: Of course.

David: (Undressing) Freedom is the first name for a full name that ends in Love. You can't have love without freedom; and chosen nakedness is the ultimate of freedom. Being a child of the Universe and liking it – loving it. That's real sanctity, I think. That's the only real gratitude too. Anything less is a mockery of acceptance. Freedom is the first name. Gratitude is the second name. And Love or Belonging is the last name. Is not love and belonging the objective of a happy soul?

Frank: I'm a believer, David! You bet, I am! I think I have always been a believer, but I have a feeling that today I'm beginning a ride that will take me to the stars!

Song

Freedom

(David, Linda, Frank, Jenny, and Howard undress while Tammy, Marie, and Russ begin riding around the parking lot fully clothed. David and Linda will sing the song. Linda will start while she is undressing. David will repeat the song once the ride has begun. After David finishes, there will be a musical interlude, during which Marie, first, and then, Tammy, will overcome their reluctance to strip. Marie will stop riding, as if considering the action, then ride again, then stop again and undress. Tammy will follow Marie's lead without hesitation once Marie is riding naked. Frank and Dawn Marie will each take a verse, but David will sing the conclusion alone. No hard and fast, here, though – actors should be free to follow their hearts and sing along as they wish.)

I want freedom in my life – freedom in my soul.
Freedom to be right – freedom to be a fool.
There's no way that I can be what it is that you call free
If I have to wear the garb of your society.
I want freedom for you, Dear, freedom for you, Sir.
And if you're not free to be, then none of us are free.

I want the freedom to ride my bike without any clothes,
Without the charge of indecency directed at my soul.
I want the freedom to do what I feel my soul should do,
and you ain't got the right to tell me I can't lose.
I want freedom for you, Sir, freedom for you, Dear.
And if you're not free to be, then none of us are free.

Scene 5

Front of Courthouse in
SUMMER TOWN

(Following the bike ride scene in Atlanta, the scene will go back to SUMMER TOWN. Frank will be sitting in a rustic type chair, tilted against a wall. Bike riders will be seen on a street in front, as well as other traffic and a few pedestrians, including an old man and woman crossing the street. One will have the use of a cane and the other will assist with an arm hold. Frank will be talking to the camera from his leaned back position.)

Frank: Well, Friends, that's how I first came to know David and Linda. The police never showed either. Biggie and Nancy worried for nothing – at least on that day. David tells of an earlier experience, however, when he was riding without clothes when the police did show and David was hoisted off to the Atlanta City Jail in the city's finest paddy wagon. He was charged with public indecency. David says it was really a RWC charge – riding without clothes. There was no indecency to it, but then that's the crux of the misunderstanding about public nakedness, isn't it? Unnatural is decent. Natural is indecent. Rather

308

shameful, huh? It would seem like the world has got things turned around.

Anyway, at his hearing the following Monday, no witnesses showed and Judge Barbara Harrold dismissed the charge. On the day he was caught and charged with a RWC charge, as David would call it, David was riding in an empty parking lot, too, but someone did notice and evidently complained. So, Biggie and Nancy had a right to be concerned. It just didn't happen the day that we rode. All of us who rode naked that day, except Russ, later joined David and Linda in founding our town. Here we are, 17 years later, a thriving democracy of several thousand. And we're kind of a pure democracy too. From the very start, we agreed to a real democracy. A majority vote is required on any vote that affects us all. We do not leave it up to representatives to vote. We vote collectively on every issue, from an issue like – should we put in a lavatory at the city park – to how should our town delegates vote on any issue outside the rule of our democracy where delegate voting is the process. Our delegates don't represent themselves – they represent us. So we vote as to how they should vote, then send them off to do it.

We'd like to see the day that counties and states and the entire nation – and eventually maybe even the world – would require a democratic vote on every issue before the various legislatures. Wouldn't it be grand to say that no law can be made without the specific approval of a majority of constituents. If every issue had to be put to a vote, then, number 1, fewer issues would come before the legislatures and waste our time on nit picky type issues, and, number 2, resulting decisions would truly be democratic. Isn't that what a grand ole democracy should strive for?

The way it is, the people governed by law often have no protection against ridiculous laws made by a handful who very easily could actually represent a minority of constituents. That's tragic in a so called democracy. We have stayed fairly free as a country in America so far, in spite of legislators not being bound to vote the will of their constituency, but can we continue to be free? Will someday a bright, devious, band of thieves gain control and shut down our right to be a democracy? Then our only recourse would be submission to a new dictatorship or another revolution to recover what we lost. It seems to me we can prevent that only if we wake up and live as a true democracy now and not just lazily resort to let a select few decide our destinies. With the advent of computers, there's no reason why every law can't be the actual decision of an enlightened majority. Maybe that's something to think about, huh?

But enough of that. Let's go shopping.

Scene 6

Clothing store on main street in SUMMER TOWN

(The scene will be in a clothing store. Frank will be browsing suits. Julie (17) will pass by, briefly exchanging conversation with Frank at the suit rack. Frank will follow her to the next isle at her request to help her pick out a dress from a dress rack.)

Frank: (to the camera) Sometime I have to go outside the city where clothes are still required. Do you think I'd look good in blue? Outside of the wonderful color of flesh, I guess it's my favorite color. (Julie appears) Why, Julie, it's good to see you. Looking for something to wear?

Julie: Yes, Judge Frank, I am. Tom and I are planning to go to a dance in Atlanta tonight.

Frank: There's a dance here, nightly, you know.

Julie: Yes, I know, but I'd like to see what it's like to go dancing where everyone is clothed.

Frank: I can understand that.

Julie: Actually, there's a band playing at a place called "Juniper's Triangle" in Atlanta that's the rage. That's really why we're going, although I am sincerely curious about attending a dance where everyone is dressed.

Frank: Well, enjoy it, Julie.

Julie: I intend to, but what dress should I buy? What color do you think fits me, Judge?

Frank: I'm afraid I can't help you there, Julie. You're on your own, Little Lady.

Julie: Oh, come on, Judge, you can help a little, can't you?

Song

I'll Put On A Dress Tonight

I'll put on a dress tonight –
and Tom and I will go to town.
I'll put on a dress tonight –
but why do men have to act like clowns?

They say we're living in a land that's free –
but if I were to go without
they'd point their fingers, cry insanity –
but the real insane are among their crowd.

I'll put on a dress tonight –
and I'll try to enjoy,
but no one will know my true life –
and many will tease like I am their toy.

Oh, what dress should I put on –
the red one or maybe the green?
It won't matter to my friend, Tom –
he'd prefer to see the one who is me.

But I'll put on a dress tonight –
and I'll go in a disguise.
I'll put on a dress tonight –
and go a stranger in the night.

Why, I wonder, don't people want to know –
who they really are?
Why must they hide in shadows –
and compete in darkness and in war?

I'll put on a dress tonight –
because the world is afraid
of all that's good and lovely –
and of all that God has made.

I'll put on a dress tonight –
and Tom and I will go to town,
but I can't help but cry a little –
why must men act like clowns?

Scene 6B

Cashier and store front

(After the song, sung by Julie, Julie pays for the dress. There should be an extemporaneous exchange between Julie and the cashier. Frank will be seen chatting with another person in the store. After paying the cashier, Julie takes her selection and leaves the store, bumping into Terry (12), her next door neighbor. Terry will be going into the pet store next door.)

Terry: Excuse me, Julie. Sorry.

Julie: That's alright, Terry. Hey, I'm heading home to leave off this dress. You heading home too?

Terry: Not yet, but in a minute, I will. Mom asked me to pick up some bird seed at the pet store. Will you wait for me?

Julie: Sure, Terry, go ahead. I'll wait for you.

Terry: OK. Don't go.

Julie: I won't.

(Terry goes into the pet store and Julie fingers her new dress. A boy, her age, Rick, happens by and starts to chat.)

Rick: Hi, Julie.

Julie: Hi, Rick.

Rick: See you at the dance tonight?

Julie: No, not tonight, but I'll be there tomorrow night.

Rick: (Eyeing the dress) Pretty dress.

Julie: Do you think so? Tom and I are going to a dance in Atlanta tonight. The Jason Trio are playing – and you know how I feel about Johnny Jason. He makes that sax sing, doesn't he?

Rick: I'm more a guitar man myself, but I guess he's alright. Hey, how come you're going with Tom?

Julie: Cause he offered and I like him. Why not?

Rick: Would you go with me sometime?

Julie: Maybe.

Rick: Well, then maybe I'll ask you sometime. I have to be going. See you at tomorrow night's dance.

Julie: OK, Rick. Bye!

(Julie waits for awhile for Terry, waving to several girls walking by on the opposite side of the street. Terry comes out with a bag of seed.)

Terry: Got it. Thanks for waiting.

Julie: That's OK. Was glad to.

(They walk. Scene ends.)

Scene 7

Julie's Neighborhood

(Julie and Terry will be approaching home.)

Terry: Julie, can I ask you something?

Julie: Sure.

Terry: You've changed.

Julie: It's growing up, Terry. You'll be there soon.

Terry: Do you like it?

Julie: Are you kidding? I love it!

Terry: (Looking at Julie's pubic area) Why does the hair grow there? How come adults have hair and kids don't? What makes it grow?

Julie: I don't know. I'm not sure anybody does. It's just the way it is. (They approach Terry's house. Grampa Owens is weeding out front in a marigold patch) There's your Grampa, Terry. Why don't you ask him? Hi, Mr. Owens!

Grampa: Hi, Julie. Nice day for a walk, huh?

Julie: Absolutely great, Sir. Terry and I were just talking.

Grampa: I'm sure of that. What about? Or is it personal?

Julie: No, not personal. Terry wanted to know why I've changed.

Terry: Yeah, Grampa. How come she grew hair around her vagina? How come her breasts got bigger?

Grampa: Well, Terry, that's the biggie now, huh? Why the hair? Why did her breasts get bigger? Her breasts are getting bigger because it is Nature's way of preparing a lady for nursing a baby. About the hair, who knows? Certainly not me. But, son, you should thank your lucky stars you live in a world where you can notice such things. Isn't that right, Julie?

Julie: Yes Sir, that's right.

Grampa: Terry, my boy, lots of kids your age aren't allowed to notice such things. Natural growth is kept from the eyes of most kids – most adults too, for that matter.

Terry: Why, Grampa?

Grampa: Because some folks think it's sinful to go naked.

Terry: But we don't, do we, Grampa?

Grampa: No, we don't. Your Gramma and I went naked the whole 40 years of our marriage. I think I can honestly say, we never knew sin in all that time. Sin is not the consequent of going naked. Sin is the result of misuse. It's violating design. It's going against the sacred pattern of Nature, my boy. It's planting seeds where you don't want them to grow. It's uprooting seeds that have started to grow. That's true sin, my boy. Going naked is no sin, but doing things without respect for Natural Design is. Your Gramma and I, God bless her soul, never played gardener to later rip up what we planted. We played a lot and played with each other a lot, but for 40 years we were good gardeners and not unfaithful to the Grand Design. I'm mighty proud of that. Do you understand what I am talking about, Terry? Do you, Julie?

Terry: I understand, Grampa.

Grampa: What do you understand?

Terry: I shouldn't rip out the marigolds, Grampa. I should let them grow.

Grampa: And if you don't want any marigolds?

Terry: Then I shouldn't plant them in the first place.

Grampa: That's right, my boy, that's right. And what if you were to plant too many marigolds by mistake? What would you do then?

Terry: I don't know, Grampa.

Grampa: Maybe you could let them grow and later dig them up and give them to someone who doesn't have any marigolds. Do you suppose?

Terry: I think so, Grampa. I think that's what I would do.

Grampa: How about you, Julie?

Julie: May I talk frankly in front of Terry.

Grampa: Of course, my dear. Terry knows all that marigold stuff is about sex. He can handle whatever he hears as any kid can; and what he can't hear, it's no big deal, he doesn't have to handle it either.

Julie: Mr. Owens, I must admit I'm a little confused about sex right now. I mean I want to have a baby, but not now. But then I don't want to hold back my emotions either. How do you control it? What's a girl to do? It's all so confusing.

Grampa: What's a guy to do, too, Julie? It's just as confusing for him. You will just have to talk to your fellow and work it out with him.

(During this conversation between Julie and Mr. Owens, Terry should stay, working the marigold patch of his Grampa and offering appropriate curiosity glances now and then at Grampa and Julie.)

Julie: Can I ask you a personal question, Sir?

Grampa: Of course, my dear. I encourage it. That's how we can work things out – by asking those who already have.

Julie: Were you and Mrs. Owens very active? I mean, did you enjoy sex?

Grampa: You bet we did, Julie. Maggie and I were like two violins playing together. We just weren't all that different. We never had a quarrel about sex because we saw things so much alike.

Julie: And how was that?

Grampa: I'd say, for the most part, we both respected Nature and Natural Design. If we had any question about what we should do in sexual things, we just looked at the great teacher, Nature, for the answers. Julie, Nature is a fabulous teacher. Just look at how she handles sex through other animal species and follow the pattern. That's what Maggie and I believed.

Julie: So, what does Nature say about when to and when not to – have intercourse, I mean?

Grampa: Look for yourself, Julie. Watch the animals and see for yourself. You may see them differently than Maggie and I.

Julie: But how did you see them?

Grampa: We saw them as having intercourse only when conception is intended. We saw them as having intercourse only to procreate.

Julie: And so you only had sex when you wanted kids?

Grampa: No. But we never had sex and flushed away our seeds after we did either. There were times we had intercourse without intending conception, but not many – until after Maggie went through her change of life. Then we had intercourse a lot. That's one thing about life, Julie. You can have it all in time. When we were young, Maggie and I chose to be more reserved, working with Nature and never against it. We had a wonderful time, being a partner with Nature. We wanted sex a little more than we had it – in terms of intercourse – but we respected intercourse too much to have to prevent or ignore its natural conclusions. For us, it was simple. Don't plant seeds that can grow if you don't want them to grow. I guess we're back to the marigold patch again.

(Let Terry smile at Grampa here.)

Julie: Didn't you ever use rubbers – or other contraceptives?

Grampa: Are you kidding? A rubber suit on my penis? No thanks! You can understand that, Julie. Our kind here in SUMMER TOWN enjoy life without clothes. If I'm not wearing any other kind of clothes, I'm certainly not going to clothe my penis. That's for those who think clothes in the first place – not me – and not my Maggie. I want your nakedness, she would tell me, and I don't want to put up with an awkward rubber suit.

Julie: When you put it that way, I can understand. I don't think I will allow them either.

Grampa: For what reason? To keep from getting pregnant? You can control that with your mind like Maggie and I did. A little respect will go a long way. And without respect, life is not worth a plug nickel anyway.

Julie: So when you weren't having kids, Mr. Owens, what did you and Mrs. Owens do for sex?

Grampa: We caressed each other a lot, kissed each other a lot, without reservation. It was great between my lady and I, Julie.

She'd caress me to orgasm one time – then I'd do it for her another time. Then there would be times – many of them – that we would caress each other to orgasm. And then we would fall asleep in each others arms.

Julie: I think I want it that way for me too.

Grampa: And you will have it, my dear. I'm quite sure of that.

Julie: Really? Why?

Grampa: Because you're wise enough to experiment and ask questions – as you are proving with this little chit chat about sex. You are already showing great promise. I know because I recognize maturity and sensibility when I see it. And you, Julie, are as sensible a 17 year old as I have ever known. Go for the wisdom, my dear. Go for the wisdom.

Julie: What do you think is the ultimate wisdom, Mr. Owens?

Grampa: That's easy, Julie – gratitude.

Julie: Gratitude?

Grampa: It's been my experience in life that nothing really counts in the end but gratitude. I don't care if you massage yourself on a subway – or have intercourse on a Ferris wheel – or make passionate love in your bedroom – nothing really matters but gratitude, being thankful for what you do and for what you have. If you do something with gratitude, it will be meaningful. If you are without gratitude, then I don't care if you have just cured a thousand people of cancer, it's worthless.

Julie: Worthless?

Grampa: That's right, Julie, worthless. It's not what you do. It's the attitude with which you do it that counts. Gratitude is the single rule for morality. Nothing else matters. Being grateful is what happiness and peace of soul are all about.

Terry: I'm grateful, Grampa.

Grampa: You think you understand gratitude, Son?

Terry: Is it more than saying thanks?

Grampa: No.

Julie: And you believe gratitude is also equivalent to peace of soul?

Grampa: Yes.

Julie: I think you're right, Sir. When I'm unhappy, it's when I'm ungrateful. And it's also true that when I'm happy, I'm also feeling thankful. Being at peace with the Universe is really just being happy with yourself, isn't it?

Grampa: Without question, my girl, without question. But I would like to put prime importance on being at peace with the Universe, being thankful for the Universe; and then because I'm part of the Universe, I'm at peace with myself. And if I am at peace with the Universe, I'm also at peace with God – or the Divine or the Eternal or the Infinite or whatever you want to call it. Whatever God is, Julie – and Terry – He or She or It is in it. God's in everything – bar nothing. Everything, then, is Divine and worthy. How can it be otherwise?

Julie: I guess it can't.

Grampa: It's pretty basic, isn't it, Julie? People go to war to fight for God, thinking He is out there to be fought for – and they will be rewarded by a kind old man who is strictly outside themselves. It's a pity. God is not outside them in the first place. He can't be because He's inside of everything because He's everywhere. They waste their lives looking to be redeemed, when all the time, they were never lost. But if a man thinks he's lost, in effect, he is. It's a pity. How can you take God out of Nature? But there are billions who have it in their minds. God is not outside of Nature. He's inside of Naturalings and outside of Naturalings. Because God is in Nature, Nature is Divine. Live like Nature is Divine, Julie and Terry, with an attitude of Divine Naturism, and you will always be at peace with the Universe and be grateful and happy.

Song

Be At Peace With The Universe

(Grampa will sing with either Julie or Terry or both. During the
interlude, Grampa and Julie, then Julie and Terry, will dance.)

Grampa:
**Be at Peace with the Universe,
and everything within.
Be at Peace with the Universe,
and you'll not know sin.
To be at Peace with the Universe,
accept this as a clue,
Peace can only be if you're free –
and Peace depends on you.
Peace can only be if you're free –
and Peace depends on you.**

Be Happy with the Universe,
and everything within.
Be Happy with the Universe,
and you'll always win.
To be Happy with the Universe,
listen to this advice.
Happy can only be if you're free –
and you see with your own eyes.
Happy can only be if you're free –
and you see with your own eyes.

So, open your eyes, My Friend, and look
Life should be an open book –
just sit back and read.
The pages of Nature are there for you.
Be in awe and you'll find Truth
in the grass, the sand, and the sea.

Student:
I'll be at Peace with the Universe,
and everything within.
I'll be at Peace with the Universe,
and I'll not know sin.
I'll be at Peace with the Universe,
the path I clearly see.
Peace can only be if I'm free –
and Peace depends on me.
Peace can only be if I'm free –
and Peace depends on me.

I'll be Happy with the Universe,
and everything within.
I'll be Happy with the Universe,
and I'll always win.
I'll be Happy with the Universe,
thanks for your advice.
Happy can only be if I'm free –
and I see with my own eyes.
Happy can only be if I'm free –
and I see with my own eyes.

(Instrumental interlude – with dancing)

Grampa: Repeat third verse.
Student: Repeat both your verses.

Scene 7B

Julie's neighborhood – continued

(Following the song, Grampa, Julie, and Terry will come together for a hug. Then while all three are standing, looking at one another, Terry will begin the next sequence of conversation.)

Terry: Grampa, tell me about Gramma. Where do you suppose she is?

Grampa: It's hard to say, my boy – out there some place, although maybe she's here right now. I think I can say for sure, though, she's not rocking away in some heavenly rocking chair some place. She's probably riding the wings of a bird. There, that bird (pointing to a bird). Maybe she's riding its wings. Who knows?

Terry: How come you're always visiting the cemetery then, Grampa, if she's not out there?

Grampa: Well, my boy, the way I figure it, she might visit there too from time to time. I don't suppose her soul stays at the cemetery, like a lot of folks act, but I do think she may stop by to pay respects to her bodily remains.

Julie: Why, Mr. Owens, would you think she would do that?

Grampa: Maggie was a person who loved her body a lot, Julie. She loved living as she didn't mind dying. Just out of pure gratitude I think she'd be one to come back and visit her old temple – leastwise the bones of that temple. Maybe that's why I go to the stone so often. Maybe I think she'll be visiting sometime the same time I'm there.

Julie: How will you know she's there, Sir?

Grampa: I won't.

Julie: Then why keep going?

Grampa: To keep the love going, I guess. Some day I'll die too and be buried beside her. Maybe we'll rendezvous there with our souls and we can both go riding the wings of a bird together.

Julie: That's sweet, Sir.

Grampa: Julie, after I have joined Maggie, maybe sometime you'll look up and see two birds, chirping on a nearby branch. Maybe Maggie and I will be riding their wings – and we've just come to say hello.

Julie: You sure did love her a lot, didn't you, Sir?

Grampa: I love her a lot, Julie. You don't stop loving somebody just because they die if you loved them before. Maggie and I have a pact. I expected to go before she did, but life is full of surprises – including death. It's OK. She caught the bird wing express before I. Like a bird in the heavens, she used to say. Love is like a bird in the heavens. Maggie, my love, I can hear you singing.

(The prerecorded song of *Like a Bird in the Heavens* plays while the cameras capture a whole array of bird scenes, mixed with shots of Grampa, Julie, and Terry.)

Song

Like A Bird In The Heavens

REFRAIN:
Like a bird in the heavens, I'm free to be.
Like a bird in the heavens, I can fly to thee.
Like a bird in the heavens, I'm in love, you see;
For love is just being me.

Look at the little birds. See how they fall?
In seconds, they learn about flight.
There's a lesson so clear. It should bring a tear.
Man's still at war with his fears of the night.
Refrain.

BRIDGE:
Oh, how I love all the birds of the air –
no less than I love ole sister Moon.
So, please don't blame me if I follow their lead –
and act like the whole world is my living room.

I don't need a servant - tending my needs.
I don't need the world feeling sorry for me.
I don't need your glasses - to let me see.
Just set me free – to be little me.
Refrain, followed by Bridge.

(Then repeat **"I don't need a servant"** verse,
concluding with **Refrain** twice)

(Following the song, the cameras will focus on the three watching the birds. Then Julie will turn to Grampa.)

Julie: Mr. Owens, do you believe in Heaven?

Grampa: Do you mean, do I believe in happiness? Of course, but let me put it this way. I believe that if you're happy one place, you'll be happy in another too. In that way, yes, I do believe in Heaven – but there can be Heaven after death only if there is Heaven before it. If you're not happy with life – and with life in the body – then why should you think you can be happy after life? It doesn't make sense – least not to me.

(Terry's dad calls out that it's time for dinner. Grampa signals with a wave that they heard his call. Then he returns attention to Julie.)

Grampa: Heaven is happiness. Hell is unhappiness, Julie. That's all there is to it. My Maggie! You can bet she's in Heaven. She was a very happy lady. (Grampa pauses, then continues). Well, my friends, we have been summoned for dinner. We better go and eat. Would you like to join us, Julie?

Julie: Thanks! I think maybe I will. Let me go tell Mom and Dad and take this dress to the house.

(Julie goes to her house. Grampa and Terry go into Terry's.)

Scene 8

Dinner with the Owens

(The scene will be a living room and dining room with the Owens family.)

Terry: Grampa asked Julie to join us, Dad.

Steve: That's good. Is she going to?

Terry: She wanted to take something to her house first – and tell her parents.

Steve: Mom, we need to set a place for Julie. She'll be joining us.

Janet: Yes, I know, Steve. I heard. I'll get a place setting for her while you make room for her at the table.

Becky: I get to sit next to her.

Steve: Alright, Becky. (They maneuver the setting to fit Julie in. Then Steve directs a question to Grampa Owens.) Dad, what do you think of the amendment limiting a man to two terms?

Grampa: Under the current two-party system, I think it's a good idea.

Steve: What's a good idea – the amendment or the attempt to repeal?

Grampa: The amendment, Son. Now, if this country would truly be a democracy, it wouldn't be a good idea. But we're no democracy. We're a republic; and there's a lot of difference. The American Republic sold out democracy a long time ago when it approved a two-party system.

(Julie joins them at the table with usual welcomes)

Steve: Yeah, I know how you feel about that, Dad. I also know how you'd change things.

Julie: How would you change things, Mr. Owens?

Grampa: I'd make it a democracy, that's what – not a republic. That's what it should have been in the first place. That fellow, Frank. He's got the right idea.

Julie: What's his idea?

Grampa: All elections should be determined by three rounds of voting and determined entirely by popular vote. The first round would be open to anyone who wants to be a candidate. In fact, with computers as an aid, we could make the first round entirely a write in round. Each voter could submit a choice for an office, with the top four vote getters competing in a round 2 vote, which would elect a final two for a final run-off. If we would do that, it would be more democratic and then we shouldn't limit a person to two terms. The people should decide such things. But under the current system, a party can be too powerful and opposing candidates might not have a fair chance. The Country should ban the two-party system and let it be each man for himself.

Julie: Or each woman for herself.

Grampa: I stand corrected. Pass the vegetables, please.

Becky: Julie, you going to the dance tonight?

Julie: Not the one here, Becky, but I will be going to a dance.

Janet: Oh, really, Julie, where at?

Julie: Atlanta. Tom and I are going to dance to a fantastic sax player.

Janet: You're going to dance to a saxophone?

Julie: Oh, he's not alone. He's part of a band.

Janet: I see. It's getting so I don't care to go to Atlanta any-more. There's too much crime. A woman's not safe on the streets. You be careful, Julie.

Julie: I will, Mrs. Owens. I mean, we will.

Grampa: That's another thing I'd change if I had the say – the way we handle criminals. If a man willingly murders another, he should have to take his own life too.

Julie: Take his own life? You mean, commit suicide?

Grampa: Call it what you wish, but it's justice without turning the rest of us into murderers ourselves. We shouldn't have to kill a killer. He should have to kill himself.

Janet: Now, Dad, how would you do that?

Grampa: I'd give a convicted killer an orange and an apple, maybe a steak, twenty gallons of water, and a cyanide pill. Then I'd lock him in a comfortable room for 40 days. That would be justice with mercy.

Janet: What if he survived the 40 days?

Grampa: Then, I'd set him free. But if he's convicted again of another murder after his release, I'd shut him up in a room with an orange, an apple, and a cyanide pill forever. There would be no third chance.

Steve: Wouldn't that be kind of cruel, Dad?

Grampa: More justice than cruelty, Son. Maybe Julie and Becky could walk the streets of Atlanta after dark and not have to fear for their lives. I mean if a man knows he will have to slit his own throat, he'd be less likely to slit someone else's.

Steve: Maybe.

Becky: Why do people have to kill one another anyway?

Janet: I don't know, Becky. Some people just have killing in their souls, I guess. Who knows what makes them tick?

Steve: Grampa, maybe you do have the right idea, but with a little twist. Instead of shutting up a killer with an easy way to die, shut him up with whatever weapon he used to kill his victim. That would be even more effective, I think. You suggested it. If a man slits another's throat, then shut him in a room with a knife. If a man strangles another, shut him in a room with a rope and let him hang himself. If he shoots another, shut him in a room with a gun. They could kill themselves, starve to death, or try to survive - if as you suggest they be shut up for some period of time for a first offense. At least, they would have a choice – something they denied their victims.

Julie: Kind a gruesome, Sir!

Steve: Killing is gruesome business, Julie. And what's more, falsely accusing another of a crime is equally gruesome. I mean if a man is convicted of falsely accusing another, he should have to undergo the same penalty that a falsely convicted man would have to suffer, or perhaps did suffer.

Grampa: I agree, Son.

Janet: How did we get off on this subject anyway?

Julie: Going to a dance in Atlanta is what brought it up.

Janet: I wonder why the whole world can't be as safe as SUMMER TOWN? Going to a dance here is a wonderfully free thing.

Becky: Julie, is Jimmy going to be at the dance tonight?

Julie: I think so. Do you like my brother, Becky?

Becky: Ah, he's kind a cute, I guess.

Julie: He thinks you're cute too.

Becky: Really? Did he say that?

Julie: Not outright, but he has hinted.

Becky: How? What did he say?

Julie: He said he thinks your mom makes a great peanut butter cookie.

Terry: What's that got to do with thinking Becky's cute?

Julie: Oh, it's just an indirect way of saying it. You'll find out.

Terry: You mean if some girl tells me that my mom bakes a great pie, she saying that she likes me?

Julie: Maybe.

(Of course, there are smiles where proper - and serious looks where proper - in any of this conversation. Let this scene end with a camera drawback while the diners are continuing to chatter amidst a lot of good hearted laughter. It matters not what is said, as long as it's light hearted and gay.)

Scene 9

The Park in SUMMER TOWN

(The scene will start with Frank walking his dogs by a park with a baseball game going on. The camera should show that it's late in the game. Frank will talk while the cameras switch among him, the dogs, the game, and other activity. A couple of boys will be wrestling; and maybe a couple of girls too. That would be refreshing. An older boy and girl should be sitting close to each other, watching the game too. If it can be worked in tactfully – and it can – there should be a scene of a couple engaging in affection on a blanket. Ideally, there should be a boy/girl couple, a girl/girl couple and a boy/boy couple. There should also be several bike riders going by. At the end of the scene, after Frank leaves, following his brief comments, cameras should focus again on the various activities. The scene should end with a fade out.)

Frank: That Grampa Owens is something else, isn't he? He and Maggie used to come here and watch the kids play a lot. Have you ever played baseball? I guess it was my favorite game as a kid, although I wasn't so lucky as these guys as to play it in the buff. What do you think? Do you suppose it would be more fun to play in the buff? Of course, if a ball hits you in the groin, it may not be so much fun, right? But personally, I think it's worth the risk.

Dawn Marie and I often come and watch the kids play. Sometimes we join them; and sometimes we play a little friendly tackle football too. And sometimes we will just sit here and hug and kiss a bit. Dawn Marie is really special to me. She's been after me to get married, but I've been reluctant until now. I don't want our wonderful relationship to get sour by getting too serious, if you know what I mean. To me, marriage should be playful, not serious. The last thing I want to do is to stand in front of some somber magistrate – like myself – (with a chuckle) and agree to be serious for the rest of my life.

But I have an idea that might work. I told Dawn Marie last night that I'd consent to get married, but only if it could be a playful type ceremony. So, I figure that maybe we can keep marriage playful if we let the playful bind it. You will see what I mean tomorrow.

Speaking of Dawn Marie, I'm already late. I'm supposed to be helping her set up tonight's dance. Most everyone you've met will be there tonight, including Julie and Tom. Maybe they will have something to say about last night's dance in Atlanta. So, I'll get over there and let you watch the frolics at the town park a bit. Go on now. Get down there with those kids and imagine what it must be like – frolicking in complete freedom. I'll see you later.

(He chuckles lightly, then calls his dogs and departs. The scene will end as earlier specified.)

Scene 10

The Dance

(The scene will be the tennis courts which serves for roller skating and dancing activities as well. The band will be comprised of male and female members, naked along with everyone else of course. Outside the tennis courts will be a barbecue area; and there will be considerable eating going on. Following a little extemporaneous activity, David will announce the beginning of the dance with the standard song used to start all their dances – *Let's Get Started*.)

David: Hey, everybody, it's time to get started with our jubilation exercises for the evening. Come on, Linda, my Wyoming Wonder, let's go!

Song

Let's Get Started

1ˢᵗ REFRAIN:
Let's get started to see a new world.
Let us look each other in the eye.
Let's get started to be a new world.
Let's find God. He's not so high –
He's only sublime.

If God is in everything,
then He's not just above us.
He's inside and outside the ring –
So please tell me, what's the fuss?
1ˢᵗ Refrain.

If God is in everyone,
why listen to a preacher
who sees a daughter less than a son –
and claims he is a teacher?
1ˢᵗ Refrain.

If God is in the sand and leaves,
why look for Him in a book,
a book that claims to part the seas –
and drown like rats ones claimed as crooks?

2ⁿᵈ REFRAIN:
Let's get started to see a new world.
Let us look each other in the eye.
Let's get started to be a new world.
Let's find God. He's not so high.
He's only sublime.
He's not so high. He's only sublime.
He's not so high. He's only sublime.

(Instrumental interlude with dancing)
Repeat *2ⁿᵈ Refrain* – **End strong.**

(Lots of participation needs to be worked out in this song. David will lead it, but everyone will participate, including the children. Following the song, the dance will continue. Sometime within the dancing, the following brief discussions and other extemporaneous chatter should fit in.)

(Between Julie & Tom:)

Julie: Tom, this is a lot more fun than the one last night, isn't it?

Tom: I'll say. I like your natural look much better than your dressy look.

Julie: And I prefer to see the one I'm dancing with too. Did you tell that pretty brunette you were dancing with last night about our town?

Tom: No. I didn't want to.

Julie: You didn't want to?

Tom: I guess I was feeling a little protective.

Julie: I can understand that, Tom, but don't you think we owe it to others to tell of our lives? They are pretty wonderful, you know.

Tom: I'm not so sure.

Julie: That our lives here are wonderful?

Tom: No – that we should share it with others.

Julie: I see I'm gonna have to work on you.

Tom: Did you tell anyone?

Julie: Yes, I told several. One of the guys I told was really interested. He said he'd like to visit.

Tom: I'll bet he would.

Julie: His name is Gary. He told me his biggest hang-up is that he doesn't think he will be able to control what hangs down, as he described his masculinity.

Tom: That's a common notion. What did you tell him?

Julie: That he shouldn't visit if he felt that way, that we don't want him if he can't control himself. But I added that he shouldn't cut himself short. He probably would have no problem. He just thinks he would.

Tom: With an invitation like that, when do you expect him?

Julie: Maybe tonight, Tom. I hope he comes tonight. I mean SUMMER TOWN is the way the world should be. Why keep it a secret? Gary is only a beginning.

Tom: Why? Why do you have to tell? I don't understand.

Julie: To keep something to yourself, something precious, is wrong, Tom. It's like love. Love is not love until you have given it away. We have to give SUMMER TOWN away for it to survive. Don't you see?

Tom: But in giving it away, Julie, maybe we're killing it by giving it to the unworthy. How would you like SUMMER TOWN ravaged by giving it to the wrong people?

Julie: It can't be ravaged, Tom. It's unravageable. The unworthy will not be able to ravage it because it's fiction.

Tom: What do you mean it's fiction? It's real. We are here and now – you and I. This is not fiction.

Julie: But the story we tell of it is like fiction to others who don't know it. Once they get that fiction into their blood, they can make it real. It's unreal until it's experienced. We're giving them fiction, but they have to make it real.

Tom: I'm beginning to follow, Julie. I'm beginning to see.

Julie: SUMMER TOWN can never die, Tom, because it's fiction and fiction doesn't die because it has never lived. You cannot kill that which has not lived. That's the wonder of it! SUMMER TOWN is a story that can be lived out in every household throughout the world. There is no power that can stop it. People don't need a real SUMMER TOWN. Don't you see? Tonight, if he comes, I'll begin with Gary. I'll share the story of SUMMER TOWN with Gary. And next week I'm going back to Juniper's Triangle with Rick – and I'm going to tell another guy.

Tom: And I'll take Brenda there and I'll tell a girl. I mean we can really get the ball rolling. I think I see! SUMMER TOWN is a screen play that can lift a lot of hearts and give eyesight to the blind!

Julie: Oh, Tom, I love you! I love SUMMER TOWN! Here's a toast to the fiction of SUMMER TOWN, a fiction that can become the hope of the real world!

(They toast, with imaginary glasses of something and tears of joy.)

(Between David and Linda:)

David: My Dear, you look radiant tonight!

Linda: Thanks, Sweetheart. Oh, I forgot to tell you, Joyce stopped by today. Somebody's getting married tomorrow. Can you guess who?

David: Phil and Jane have been acting rather affectionate.

Linda: No, not them.

David: Let's see – not Howie and Jenny?

Linda: No. Let me give you a clue. The two of them were with us on our first bike ride with the club – and not Howie and Jenny.

David: Frank and Dawn Marie?

Linda: Dawn Marie and Frank.

David: Well, I'll be. It's about time – 17 years and they are finally going to tie the knot.

Linda: Marie's ecstatic. Even though they have been living together for over 16 years, she's looking forward to the wedding like a Senior just out of high school.

David: I wonder why they took so long?

Linda: You know, David. Frank's been of the mind it won't make any difference.

David: No, Linda. I don't think that's right. Frank's really been afraid.

Linda: That's right too.

David: He thinks that too many people let marriage kill their spiritual unions and he hasn't wanted to take a chance on destroying the spiritual union he and Marie have.

Linda: That's worth caring about.

David: It sure is.

Linda: David, I think you'll be impressed with the ceremony tomorrow. Frank and Marie may have the answer for all time for all future weddings. Wait till you see what they are going to do.

David: It will be different?

Linda: That's an understatement.

David: I take it you're not going to tell me.

Linda: Do you want me to?

David: No. I can use a surprise.

(Between Becky and Jimmy:)

Jimmy: Becky, your Grampa helped me fix the wheel on my wagon this morning. He's sure a nice Grampa.

Becky: I'm glad. Jimmy, do you really like Mom's peanut butter cookies?

Jimmy: Huh? What's that got to do with my wagon?

Becky: Nothing.

Jimmy: Then why did you bring it up?

Becky: Cause I think you're cute too.

Jimmy: Huh?

Becky: Ah, shut up and dance!

(Between Julie and Gary:)

Julie: Gary, I hoped you'd come. Welcome to SUMMER TOWN!

Gary: I couldn't resist. The picture you painted of SUMMER TOWN last night was too good to be true.

Julie: But it is true.

Gary: I can see. And you know, Julie, I never thought I'd believe it, but what hangs down is really not important, is it? It's like in all this sea of nakedness, it melts into insignificance.

Julie: You're wrong, Gary. It's important! It's very important! And it's very significant! It's just not an obstruction. It's all a miracle, Gary! Enjoy and be aware!

(Between Jenny and Howard:)

(Jenny and Howard from the initial bike ride will be known as living together in SUMMER TOWN. Previous to this scene, they should be shown riding their bikes; and during this scene, they should be shown dancing, prior to this little sub scene.)

Jenny: Howie, Sweetheart, I enjoy dancing with you as much as I enjoy our bike rides.

Howard: Life in the fast lane sure can't compare to what we have. What a life we have, Darling?

Jenny: A life Divine, for sure. It feels so good to feel so close to God.

(Then Jenny and Howard sing the following song.)

Song

I Am Divine

Jenny:
I'm like a star in the heavens.
I'm like a sun in the sky.
I'm like a star in the heavens –
because I am Divine.

Howard:
You're like a star in the heavens.
You're like a sun in the sky.
You're like a star in the heavens –
because you are Divine.

Both:
Who knows what the life of mystery is –
who knows, who knows?
Who knows what the mystery of life is –
who knows, who knows,
who knows, who knows –
who knows, who knows?

Howard:
I'm like a deer in a meadow.
I'm like an eagle flying high.
I'm like a deer in a meadow –
because I am Divine.

Jenny:
You're like a deer in a meadow.
You're like an eagle flying high.
You're like a deer in the meadow –
because you are Divine.

Both: (Repeat Who knows series)

Jenny:
I'm like a horse on the prairie.
I'm like an angel riding high.
I'm like a horse on the prairie –
because I am Divine.

Howard:
You're like a horse on the prairie.
You're like an angel riding high.
You're like a horse on the prairie –
because you are Divine.

Both: (Repeat Who knows series)

Howard:
I'm like a man in a garden.
I'm like a lady in Paradise.
I'm like a man in a garden –
because I am Divine.

Jenny:
You're like a man in a garden.
You're like a lady in Paradise.
You're like a man in a garden –
because you are Divine.

Both: (Repeat Who knows series)

Jenny:
I'm like a parent holding hands.
I'm like a child running wild.
I'm like a parent holding hands –
because I am Divine.

Howard:
You're like a parent holding hands.
You're like a child running wild.
You're like a parent holding hands –
because you are Divine.

Both: (Repeat Who knows series)
Both:
I'm like a star in the heavens.
I'm like a sun in the sky.
I'm like a star in the heavens –
because I am Divine.
I'm like a star in the heavens.
I'm like a sun in the sky.
I'm like a star in the heavens –
because I am Divine.
I'm like a star in the heavens –
because I am Divine.
I'm like a star in the heavens –
because I am Divine.

(The scene should end with a focus upon the heavens – or the sky – as the song is finishing. It should be later in the evening by now and at least at the end of this song, night time should have arrived.)

Scene 11

The Wedding of Frank and Dawn Marie

(The scene will capture a rising sun. Soft music will be playing as the cameras will capture the entire town, landscape and sky. After a minute or so of browsing about, the cameras will focus on the town park once again. Gathered will be much of the town for this special sunrise wedding. All the principals of this story will be there, including the newest resident, Gary.

Standing in front of Frank and Marie will be Becky. As the cameras go full on the trio, Becky, the minister, and Frank and Marie will sing *The Wedding Song*. The interlude should feature a dance among the trio.

Song:

The Wedding Song

REFRAIN: Minister Becky:
We are gathered today for a wedding –
a wedding that all of us should see.
We are gathered today for a wedding –
a wedding so blessed and so free.

Minister Becky: Refrain – then:
Will you take this man to be a husband?
Will you take this woman to be your wife?
Will you take each other in marriage –
and promise to love all your life?

Marie: I'll take this man to be my husband.
Frank: I'll take this woman to be my wife.
Both: We will take each other in marriage –
and promise to love all our life.

Minister Becky: Refrain – then:
Will you love this man forever?
Will you take him for your own?

Will you love this woman forever –
and make her a happy home?

Marie: I will love this man forever.
I will take him for my own.
Frank: I will love this woman forever –
and make her a happy home.

Refrain. (sung by all)

(Instrumental interlude with dancing)

Minister Becky:
Will you search for the natural -
and love the natural in your man?
Will you stand beneath the stars –
and find equality in her hand?

Marie: I will search for the natural –
and love the natural in my man.
Frank: I will stand beneath the stars –
and find equality in her hand.

Minister Becky: Refrain – then:
Will you realize God in her life –
while embracing all her charms?
Will you realize God in his life –
while he holds you in his arms?

Frank: I will realize God in her life –
while embracing all her charms.
Marie: I will realize God in his life –
while he holds me in his arms.

Repeat *Refrain* **several times.** (sung by all)

Scene 12

The Finale

(Following the wedding, it would be anticlimactic to do anything but close with a rousing song. So, we'll end it with a rousing invitational type song – *You Can Have Your Summer Town*. The many refrains will be general choruses with everyone singing them, but between the 5th and 6th verse, there will be up to four consecutive refrains. One of those will be sung by Jimmy. One by Becky. And one by Terry. Before the final two verses are sung, widespread dancing should commence.

Considering the verses, Marie will lead, taking the first verse. Grampa Owens will sing the second verse. Julie will sing the third verse. Marie will sing the fourth verse. Howard will sing the fifth verse. And David and Linda will harmonize on the final two verses.

Following the song, the cameras should capture a still or series of stills of Becky, Frank, Dawn Marie, David and Linda, Julie, Tom and Gary. Final film credits should be worked in around this setting, with special emphasis on Becky and Julie.

The torch has been passed!)

Song

You Can Have Your Summer Town

REFRAIN:
You can have your SUMMER TOWN.
You can be a SUMMER TOWN.
If you will let your life astound,
you can have your SUMMER TOWN.

1. Life is what you make it, Friend.
You can be brittle or you can bend.
It's up to you to follow through –
to see Life itself as the Truth. *Refrain.*

2. In SUMMER TOWN, we don't accuse –
God in eternity of being a ruse.
It's they who trick who use His name –
to make others play their game. *Refrain.*

3. Don't be afraid of Life, My Friend.
We all have the very same end.
As we live we die and pass away.
Touch your life, be Happy today. *Refrain.*

4. There is no ugliness in Life.
Seeing such will cause you strife.
Reach and touch your body, My Friend.
Your Soul will benefit through the end. *Refrain.*

Repeat verse 1 – then *Refrain* 4 times.

(Instrumental interlude with dancing)

Repeat verse 3 – then *Refrain.*
Repeat verse 4 – then *Refrain* several times.

Songs

Summer Town

REFRAIN:
Summer time is Summer Town.
Winter time is Summer Town.
Spring time and fall time too –
Summer Town lives the truth.

Life's majestic and that's the truth.
Life's fantastic and that's true too.
Life is splendid. Life is sweet.
Life should knock you off your feet. *Refrain.*

Creation's a miracle and that's a Truth.
They are satirical who otherwise accuse.
Satire and judgment make us frown.
They don't belong in Summer Town. *Refrain.*

Nakedness inspires and that's a Truth
For those who don't look at life as crude.
If you see life as crude, then don't come around
to our wonderful home called Summer Town. *Refrain (3).*

364

Let's Look at Each Other Differently

David:
Let's look at each other differently
with a whole new respect.
Sure, we have genitals,
but why should we object?
Genitals are only muscles –
they're not so mysterious.
Touch them and they extend,
but why make it serious?
We treat sex like a thrill
and isolate ourselves with our act.
We don't stand with the world –
belong only to the human pack.
And then we run away and hide
and God we accuse.
You shouldn't have made us that way, we say,
and His grace we refuse.

Let's look at each other differently
with a whole new respect.
Let's join the stars and seas
and with Creation, let's connect.
Let's enjoy what we are –
genitals and all.
Then we won't be so weak
and won't with Adam fall.
Come on, is it so hard
to see each other differently?
I'm not alone. I'm like all men.
Enjoy the world that's in me.

Linda:
Let's look at each other differently
with a whole new respect.
It's time we had a new vision –
and new values, let's select.
The old one isn't good, I agree –
it divides the world in two
and puts on one side all that's good
and on the other, evil crews.
As a lady, I am tired
of being measured by my breasts.
Why can't I be a woman
without passing a ratings test?
And as a man you shouldn't care
about the size of your penis.
It's just a muscle, as you say,
and it doesn't measure genius.

Let's look at each other differently
with a whole new respect.
We could really fall in love
because our natures we'd accept.
And then when we'd act together –
sexually and otherwise,
we wouldn't be strangers to the world –
we'd need no disguise.
Our ebbs and flows wouldn't be
restricted within our flesh.
We'd truly be one with the world
and with everything enmesh.

David: Let's look at each other differently
Linda: with a whole new respect.
David: I am ready.
Linda: I am too.
Both: Let's take the first step.
David: I'll take my clothes off, for good, my good.
Linda: And I'll do the same.
Both: We'll stand so proud with our eyes aloft
and we'll give our souls a raise.
David: Oh, birds, can you see?
Come fly in real close.
Linda: We'd like to aspire on your wings
to become holy ghosts.

David: Well, My Friend, I think that
this is Paradise.
Linda: But only if we act as pure
and welcome our own sight.
David: Let's look at each other differently –
Oh, yes, let's do.
Linda: Feel free, My Love, to look at me –
and I will look at you.

Freedom

I want freedom in my life – freedom in my soul.
Freedom to be right – freedom to be a fool.
There's no way that I can be what it is that you call free
If I have to wear the garb of your society.
I want freedom for you, Dear, freedom for you, Sir.
And if you're not free to be, then none of us are free.

I want the freedom to ride my bike without any clothes,
Without the charge of indecency directed at my soul.
I want the freedom to do what I feel my soul should do,
and you ain't got the right to tell me I can't lose.
I want freedom for you, Sir, freedom for you, Dear.
And if you're not free to be, then none of us are free.

I'll Put on a Dress Tonight

I'll put on a dress tonight –
and Tom and I will go to town.
I'll put on a dress tonight –
but why do men have to act like clowns?

They say we're living in a land that's free –
but if I were to go without
they'd point their fingers, cry insanity –
but the real insane are among their crowd.

I'll put on a dress tonight –
and I'll try to enjoy,
but no one will know my true life –
and many will tease like I am their toy.

Oh, what dress should I put on –
the red one or maybe the green?
It won't matter to my friend, Tom –
he'd prefer to see the one who is me.

But I'll put on a dress tonight –
and I'll go in a disguise.
I'll put on a dress tonight –
and go a stranger in the night.

Why, I wonder, don't people want to know –
who they really are?
Why must they hide in shadows –
and compete in darkness and in war?

I'll put on a dress tonight –
because the world is afraid
of all that's good and lovely –
and of all that God has made.

I'll put on a dress tonight –
and Tom and I will go to town,
but I can't help but cry a little –
why must men act like clowns?

Be at Peace with the Universe

(Grampa will sing with either Julie or Terry or both. During the interlude, Grampa and Julie, then Julie and Terry, will dance.)

Grampa:
**Be at Peace with the Universe,
and everything within.
Be at Peace with the Universe,
and you'll not know sin.
To be at Peace with the Universe,
accept this as a clue,
Peace can only be if you're free –
and Peace depends on you.
Peace can only be if you're free –
and Peace depends on you.**

Be Happy with the Universe,
and everything within.
Be Happy with the Universe,
and you'll always win.
To be Happy with the Universe,
listen to this advice.
Happy can only be if you're free –
and you see with your own eyes.
Happy can only be if you're free –
and you see with your own eyes.

So, open your eyes, My Friend, and look
Life should be an open book –
just sit back and read.
The pages of Nature are there for you.
Be in awe and you'll find Truth
in the grass – the sand and the sea.

Student:
I'll be at Peace with the Universe,
and everything within.
I'll be at Peace with the Universe,
and I'll not know sin.
I'll be at Peace with the Universe,
the path I clearly see.
Peace can only be if I'm free –
and Peace depends on me.
Peace can only be if I'm free –
and Peace depends on me.

I'll be Happy with the Universe,
and everything within.
I'll be Happy with the Universe,
and I'll always win.
I'll be Happy with the Universe,
thanks for your advice.
Happy can only be if I'm free –
and I see with my own eyes.
Happy can only be if I'm free –
and I see with my own eyes.

(Instrumental interlude – with dancing)

Grampa: **Repeat third verse.**
Student: **Repeat both your verses.**

Like a Bird in the Heavens

REFRAIN:
Like a bird in the heavens, I'm free to be.
Like a bird in the heavens, I can fly to thee.
Like a bird in the heavens, I'm in love, you see
For love is just being me.

Look at the little birds. See how they fall?
In seconds, they learn about flight.
There's a lesson so clear. It should bring a tear.
Man's still at war with his fears of the night. *Refrain.*

BRIDGE:
Oh, how I love all the birds of the air –
no less than I love ole sister Moon.
So, please don't blame me if I follow their lead –
and act like the whole world is my living room.

I don't need a servant - tending my needs.
I don't need the world feeling sorry for me.
I don't need your glasses - to let me see.
Just set me free – to be little me.
Refrain, followed by Bridge.

(Then repeat **"I don't need a servant"** verse,
concluding with ***Refrain*** twice)

Let's Get Started

1st REFRAIN:
Let's get started to see a new world.
Let us look each other in the eye.
Let's get started to be a new world.
Let's find God. He's not so high –
He's only sublime.

If God is in everything,
then He's not just above us.
He's inside and outside the ring –
So please tell me, what's the fuss?
1st Refrain.

If God is in everyone,
why listen to a preacher
who sees a daughter less than a son –
and claims he is a teacher?
1st Refrain.

376

If God is in the sand and leaves,
why look for Him in a book,
a book that claims to part the seas –
and drown like rats ones claimed as crooks?

2nd REFRAIN:
Let's get started to see a new world.
Let us look each other in the eye.
Let's get started to be a new world.
Let's find God. He's not so high. He's only sublime.
He's not so high. He's only sublime.
He's not so high. He's only sublime.

(Instrumental interlude with dancing)
Repeat *2nd Refrain* – **End strong.**

I Am Divine

Jenny:
I'm like a star in the heavens.
I'm like a sun in the sky.
I'm like a star in the heavens –
because I am Divine.

Howard:
You're like a star in the heavens.
You're like a sun in the sky.
You're like a star in the heavens –
because you are Divine.

Both:
Who knows what the life of mystery is –
who knows, who knows?
Who knows what the mystery of life is –
who knows, who knows,
who knows, who knows –
who knows, who knows?

Howard:
I'm like a deer in a meadow.
I'm like an eagle flying high.
I'm like a deer in a meadow –
because I am Divine.

Jenny:
You're like a deer in a meadow.
You're like an eagle flying high.
You're like a deer in the meadow –
because you are Divine.

Both: (Repeat Who knows series)

Jenny:
I'm like a horse on the prairie.
I'm like an angel riding high.
I'm like a horse on the prairie –
because I am Divine.

Howard:
You're like a horse on the prairie.
You're like an angel riding high.
You're like a horse on the prairie –
because you are Divine.

Both: (Repeat Who knows series)

Howard:
I'm like a man in a garden.
I'm like a lady in Paradise.
I'm like a man in a garden –
because I am Divine.

Jenny:
You're like a man in a garden.
You're like a lady in Paradise.
You're like a man in a garden –
because you are Divine.

Both: (Repeat Who knows series)

Jenny:
I'm like a parent holding hands.
I'm like a child running wild.
I'm like a parent holding hands –
because I am Divine.

Howard:
You're like a parent holding hands.
You're like a child running wild.
You're like a parent holding hands –
because you are Divine.

Both: (Repeat Who knows series)
I'm like a star in the heavens.
I'm like a sun in the sky.
I'm like a star in the heavens –
because I am Divine.
I'm like a star in the heavens.
I'm like a sun in the sky.
I'm like a star in the heavens –
because I am Divine.
I'm like a star in the heavens –
because I am Divine.
I'm like a star in the heavens –
because I am Divine.

The Wedding Song

REFRAIN: Minister Becky:
We are gathered today for a wedding –
a wedding that all of us should see.
We are gathered today for a wedding –
a wedding so blessed and so free.

Minister Becky: Refrain – then:
Will you take this man to be a husband?
Will you take this woman to be your wife?
Will you take each other in marriage –
and promise to love all your life?

Marie: I'll take this man to be my husband.
Frank: I'll take this woman to be my wife.
Both: We will take each other in marriage –
and promise to love all our life.

Minister Becky: Refrain – then:
Will you love this man forever?
Will you take him for your own?
Will you love this woman forever –
and make her a happy home?

Marie: I will love this man forever.
I will take him for my own.
Frank: I will love this woman forever –
and make her a happy home.

Refrain. (sung by all)

(Instrumental interlude with dancing)

Minister Becky:
Will you search for the natural -
and love the natural in your man?
Will you stand beneath the stars –
and find equality in her hand?

Marie: I will search for the natural –
and love the natural in my man.
Frank: I will stand beneath the stars –
and find equality in her hand.

Minister Becky: Refrain – then:
Will you realize God in her life –
while embracing all her charms?
Will you realize God in his life –
while he holds you in his arms?

Frank: I will realize God in her life –
while embracing all her charms.
Marie: I will realize God in his life –
while he holds me in his arms.

Repeat *Refrain* several times. (sung by all)

You Can Have Your Summer Town

REFRAIN:
You can have your SUMMER TOWN.
You can be a SUMMER TOWN.
If you will let your life astound,
you can have your SUMMER TOWN.

1. Life is what you make it, Friend.
You can be brittle or you can bend.
It's up to you to follow through –
to see Life itself as the Truth. *Refrain.*

2. In SUMMER TOWN, we don't accuse –
God in eternity of being a ruse.
It's they who trick who use His name –
to make others play their game. *Refrain.*

3. Don't be afraid of life, My Friend.
We all have the very same end.
As we live we die and pass away.
Touch your life, be Happy today. *Refrain.*

4. There is no ugliness in life.
Seeing such will cause you strife.
Reach and touch your body, My Friend.
Your soul will benefit through the end. *Refrain.*

Repeat verse 1 – then *Refrain* 4 times.

(Instrumental interlude with dancing)

Repeat verse 3 – then *Refrain.*
Repeat verse 4 – then *Refrain* several times.

Summer Town

The End

Peace On Earth

By
Francis William Bessler

— A Spiritual Short Story —

Written in 2007.

Introduction

In a way, this is a sequel to another short story I wrote for friends, Russ & Liz, in May of this year, 2007. I called that one: ***Laramie Mountain.*** Mostly, it featured speculation by a single character. This short story is shorter and features two characters instead of one, but it is largely another version of ***Laramie Mountain*** – which is nearly 40 pages long as this story is only 19 pages or so. Both short stories, however, end in song.

This is a story, I think, about virtue. ***I think true virtue is the easiest thing in the world.*** Now, where have you heard that before? Almost everyone I know thinks that virtue is hard. I think that is because un-virtuous people have defined virtue as *serving other people.* True virtue, however, is not primarily *other people* oriented. It is mostly of solitary character. That is why it is the easiest thing in the world. Why is it easy? Because, in my opinion, ***True Virtue is only embracing the gift of life and being thankful for it;*** and what should be hard about that?

I shake my head at this world because it doesn't seem to have realized that lesson. Happiness is the most important thing in the world because no one in his or her right mind would actually want to be unhappy. Be honest. Do you want to be unhappy? Of course not! No one wants to be unhappy; but most people do not realize how easy happy really is – or they would never settle for unhappiness.

Am I happy? Yes! Why? Because my happiness does not depend on anyone but myself. That is why I am happy; and quite frankly, I think that is why Jesus was happy too. Sadly, we have been led to believe that we are supposed to serve someone else to be happy. Nothing is farther from the truth. I am not saying we who are happy cannot serve others. That is certainly not so; but I am saying that service of others is not the basis of our happiness. It is a plus. That is all it is. **The moment that I need to serve you to be happy myself is the day that I have taken one step – be it small or huge - toward self-destruction;** and that is the main problem in this world today. Mistakenly, people think that happiness should be *other oriented*; and then when others do not cooperate to satisfy some happiness seeker's plot, all hell can break loose.

What is terrorism if it isn't you killing or harming me if I do not cooperate with you? That is all that terrorism is. Anyone is a terrorist who thinks they have to have their own way with others. I cannot be a terrorist because I do not need you to make me happy. Because I am independent of you, I am happy without you; and because I am happy without you, I don't have to look your way to make sure you are not doing something to keep me from attaining happiness. I am already happy. I am not seeking happiness. I have it – and nothing you can do can prevent me from staying happy.

Say that I die tonight. I will take my happiness with me. **You can't prevent me from being happy or taking happiness with me because my happiness is totally independent of you; and that, my friends, is what I think Jesus was all about.** In life and in death, it is probably the same – we continue as we began. We have to reap what we sow. So, if we are happy in life, we continue happy; and if we die unhappy, that is probably the way we continue after we die. **So, why in the world ever allow life – be it now or after death – be dependent upon others?** We get other stories that turn Jesus into some messiah who is supposed to make others happy – not just lead them in the way of happiness – but those stories largely were written by the unhappy. **Why take lead from an unhappy soul who promises some great reward of happiness when he or she is not even happy him or herself?**

I may be wrong, but in reading the gospels of the *BIBLE*, I do not get the sense that Matthew, Mark, Luke, John, Peter, or Paul were happy souls – at least not of themselves. I get the sense that they wanted to be happy, yes; but I do not get the sense that they were happy. I get the sense that they hoped for happiness in another life and somehow thought that Jesus was the door to that happiness; but I do not get the sense that, per se, they ever spent a moment being happy in this life with life itself. Why? Because they missed the message of Jesus that happiness is a solitary thing.

At least I have found in life that there is but one thing that makes me happy; and that one thing is *gratitude*. That is the basis of my happiness; and I think it is the basis of all happiness. All unhappy people I have ever known or read about lack in gratitude for the moment and for what the moment has to offer. Oh, they may think that they are grateful for what is past – or what may be – but all unhappy people are caught up with a lack of gratitude for what is now. *The key to happiness is saying thank you and feeling thank you and knowing thank you.* Any moment that I spend not being thankful is an unhappy moment for me. Isn't that true for you? **No one needs another to say 'thank you'. Look around if you want to find something for which to be thankful. The world is full of beauty and mystery – starting with yourself.**

When I was young, I was taught like most are taught – to pray like this: *Bless me, Father, for I have sinned.* My problem with that prayer was that I always felt blessed. So, why was I asking to be blessed, as if no blessing was already at hand? In time, I recognized that I was being blessed because I was being surrounded by the *already blessings of life and God.* And there it was – the blessing that I was praying for in my prayer was already being given. All I needed to do was to open my eyes – and far more importantly, my mind – and see it. ***I was already the very miracle for which I was praying; and I did not know it.***

But most do not realize their prayers were answered before they even prayed. They don't see that they have been blessed and that life itself is a blessing; and so they conclude that since they have not been blessed that they are with sin; and it's all a lie – a huge lie that keeps them always asking for more blessings and just plain ignoring the blessings at hand. The prayer should not be: *Bless me, Father, for I have sinned* – but rather: ***Thank You for the Blessings, Father.*** In reality, there is no sin because there is no lack of blessing. ***How can there be sin if there is blessing?*** **In truth, the only sin is being blind to the blessing of life, demanding the services of another to be happy – and being unhappy as a result.**

So, it is really simple if you cross the threshold of wisdom. When you realize that the clothes on your back were put there, not because you were without blessing, but because you did not see the blessings you have and the blessing you are - then nakedness becomes the blessing it always was because nakedness is life itself. It is life, my friends, that is the blessing we ask for in our prayers; but so many live their entire lives not realizing that – always asking for more blessings and always ignoring the ones they have. **People want Heaven – which stands for Blessings – and they don't realize that what they want, they already have**. As Jesus said, *Heaven is at hand*! Nice, huh?

And that is what the Grampa of my story realized long ago. Grampa and his granddaughter leave out the plea for blessings in their prayer because they realize they are being blessed; and their nakedness reflects that blessing – the blessing of life itself. If only people would pray thanking God for all the blessings and would leave out the *for I have sinned*, the world would be the Paradise they want it to be.

We must stop *punishing virtue* because it seems to offer nothing toward some illusive *social good* – and realize that true virtue – and the embrace of life and nakedness – is the only true way to a happy and peaceful world.

If I might, let me offer a suggestion. My little story is strictly conversation between a grandfather and a granddaughter. It might be worth your while to read it out loud with someone – with one of you taking the role of the grandfather and the other – the granddaughter. Then read it again, with roles reversed. There is nothing sexual about it. So, it could just as well be a grandmother and a grandson. If you wish, just change Grampa to Gramma and granddaughter to grandson. The story won't change in the least – as it shouldn't.

After the story, there is a song. Personally, it sounds like a Christmas time song to me; but judge it as you will. If it does appeal to you as a Christmas time song, be my guest and sing it out. Make up your own tune. As a brother of mine would say, ***TALLEY HO! - AND BE HAPPY!***

Thanks!

Francis William Bessler
Laramie, Wyoming
July 31st, 2007

Peace On Earth

"Will there ever be peace on earth, Grampa?" the young one asked, as they sat next to one another on the couch on Grampa's porch.

"Perhaps, My Dear," the old man answered, "but if there is, it will have to depend on you."

"Me?" the youngster of seventeen replied. "Why should it depend on me, Grampa?"

"Well, not so much depend on you, My Dear, as include you. If there is ever to be peace in the world, all must be at peace – and that includes you and me and everyone."

"I guess to find peace we need to know what peace is, Grampa. What do you think it is?"

"Well, for starters, Honey, peace is not something bestowed by another. No one can find peace through another. We all must find peace from within. Peace is only from the individual outward. Peace is only being comfortable with life as a gift. It is knowing gratitude and denying despair. Peace is not something that is given by someone else. Peace is something inwardly experienced. It is something that is inspired from within, not communicated from without. No one can make you grateful; and no one can make you peaceful. Peace is something that is believed and imagined and lived by the one who wants peace. Then when that one has peace, it can be shared. When everyone on earth declares and knows peace in their own life, then, and only then, My Dear Little One, will there ever be peace on earth for everyone."

"And that's why it must depend on me, Grampa?"

"You are right, My Dear! That's why it depends on you. Without you, world wide peace is impossible. If peace can't happen without you, it is dependent upon you; but we can't make peace. We can only share a peace we already know."

"But it depends on you, too, Grampa," the young one acknowledged. "World peace requires you as much as it requires me."

"As it is said, " the old man replied, "wisdom will come from the mouths of children. You have said it well."

"You know, I am not exactly a child, Grampa. I'm seventeen."

"Well, you will always be a child to me, Honey."

"I think I will always want to be a child, Grampa." Eager to pursue their discussion on peace, she continued. "But why do people think they can make peace, Grampa? Why do nations go to war to make peace? Why do people think they can force peace?"

"That's a good question, My Dear, " he replied. "I guess people have always felt that peace is something that can be forced upon another. I think it is only that people have not stopped to think about what they are doing. I think they confuse a thing called *surrender* – or maybe strength or power - with *peace*. I think they think that if you surrender to me after I have forced surrender upon you that peace will result between us."

"But that wouldn't be peace, would it, Grampa?"

"No, it wouldn't," the gentle man replied. "But as long as people think it is peace, then I guess there will always be wars to make peace. To be honest, though, Honey, I think that people who make war are mostly only soldiers in conflict with themselves. They war with others, using others as substitutes for themselves. I really think that's true."

"Why can't the world be like us, Grampa? I love you so much; and you have never made me do anything."

"That's because I have always had peace, Little One. People who are at peace do not need to make others do anything. Why do you suppose that is?" he questioned his young grandchild.

"I think it is because you don't need me to make you happy," his grandchild replied. "At least, that's what you have always told me. I guess it is because you have yourself and don't need another to be happy."

"Well, I suppose I have said that, My Dear, but I would prefer to say that it is not so much that I don't need you to be happy as it is that I only need me to be happy because all that I need for happiness is in me. I am not so much excluding you to be happy and to be at peace. I am only depending only on myself for my peace."

"But is that not saying you don't need me, Grampa?"

"In a way, yes," the old one replied. "No, I don't need you to be at peace with myself, but I think I do need you to show it."

"Is that important, Grampa? Do you have to show your peace to others?"

"I think I do, Honey. Well, maybe it is not that I have to show my peace to others. It might be more like I just want to show my peace to others – like wanting to share something that has made me happy. I guess it is normal to want to share what makes one happy."

"You show it to me, Grampa. Am I not enough?"

"For this moment, yes, you are enough, my Dear One, but I should always be open to show my peace with anyone who is open to it. I think that is only right."

"That might be a little difficult, Grampa. The world does not think that anyone should be at peace with what one is in this world. I have had so much trouble with my friends who think you are weird, claiming that the world is right as it is and that we should embrace ourselves as we are. They say that the world is full of sin and that we can't embrace ourselves as we are."

"Yes, I know," My Dear One," the gentle one replied. "I know full well the story. Man is sinful and therefore cannot be happy with what he is because to be happy with what he is is to make sin. It is ridiculous beyond words that people believe that. It is why there is no peace in the world. How can you be at peace with yourself if you are at war with yourself? And that is all that being unhappy with life is – making war against something you don't like – yourself."

"But we do not have to make war against ourselves, do we, Grampa?"

"No, we don't, Honey! We can be at peace and love what we are because our lives are a gift from the Divine. We don't have to act scared of life like all around us do just because we are surrounded. We can be at peace with ourselves regardless of how many around us are not at peace with themselves."

"I'm glad you are at peace, Grampa; and I think I am learning from you."

"As long as you learn from me and I do not make you do something, it works just fine," the old gentleman replied, "but the moment I make a law that says you have to be at peace, then it is not peace I offer you, but coercion and surrender."

"Maybe the world will realize that someday, Grampa," the young one replied. "I know you enough, Grampa, to know that is what you think Jesus taught – that peace is not something that can be legislated. It is something that is known – and then shared."

"You're right, Honey. I think one of the great problems with mankind is that it has misunderstood Jesus. I think Jesus believed in the sacred of all and believed that no one – not even a child – is without worth; but I think they who wrote about him believed him to be a Lord – someone who was to give them what they needed rather than inspire them to find in themselves what they needed."

"Most of my friends who believe in Jesus consider him to be a lord, Grampa. They expect Jesus to give them wonderful things after death if they believe in him during life."

"I know, Honey. It is a battle I have had with other Christians all my life. I think it is really sad that someone who taught that all are worthy was turned into a lord that supposedly can make others worthy. That is a lot like that idea that peace can be made by making war."

"I think you are right, Grampa. It really does not make any sense, does it?"

"And yet, most in the world are blind to both ideas," her grandfather continued. "They think they can be made worthy via the efforts of another and they think they can make peace by whopping any who might want to whop them."

"You know, Grampa, Mom always taught me that I have to be worthy because I am a child of God. She had this little poem entitled **CHILD OF THE LIGHT** that she recited that I memorized that goes like this: *Oh, Child of the Light, play as you will. You have but to live to find your fill. You can't understand from whence you came. Just embrace it all joyfully as if it's a game. For a game life is – or should be for all. Oh, Child of the Light, have yourself a ball. Look at the earth and the sun and the moon and know that they are all in tune.*"

Grampa smiled at his lovely granddaughter. "Yes, I know," he said. "I taught her that poem." And then Grampa continued: *The wonder of all of God's great creation should fill your mind with jubilation. Oh, Child of the Light, you fit in well. So, ring as you should as one of the bells.*"

"You wrote that, didn't you, Grampa?"

"What makes you think that?"

"When I asked Mom who wrote it, she just said, *ask Grampa.*"

"I don't know why your mother didn't admit it, but, yes, Dear One, I wrote it. I guess she was just being secretive as you girls like to be sometimes."

"Well, it wasn't much of a secret, Grampa. I think I always knew. You know there's more. Let's recite it together." Grampa smiled at his granddaughter and in unison, they completed the little ditty, as Grampa liked to call what he wrote. ***So, don't fret and worry and live in fear. As God is your source, It's also your care. Be not afraid as you go forward in time. Oh, Child of the Light, you've a life that's Divine.***

The young one smiled at her Grampa after they completed the verse in unison. "Grampa, wouldn't it be nice if we all believed we are children of the light?"

"It sure would, Honey. I wish that people would take time to think about that. How can we not be children of the light when without the light we could not even exist? Take away the light of the sun and there would be no life on earth. Clearly, we are all ***children of the light.***"

"I like that, Grampa. You and me, children of the light. We don't have to know more about our lives. It is obvious to anyone with a mind to think. We should be grateful we are earthlings and thank the sunlight for making it possible."

"And I like to think, too, Honey, that we should thank God for making the sunlight possible. It is all so simple. It is almost astonishing that mankind has chosen to make it so hard. We don't think that being children of the light is very important. We act like we are children of some dark someplace. Maybe others are, Honey, but not me."

"And not me either, Grampa. I am honored to know you, my fellow son of the light; and I am happy to play with you as one like you."

"Sweetheart, play is the word, too. Play with life and play with yourself and with your friends as long as you are thankful while you play. Life is a gift – a mysterious gift, but a gift. I am so pleased you see it like that."

"How could I not, Grampa? I am the daughter of your daughter; and we are one."

"Yes, My Dear, we are one. I am so proud that we are."

"Me too, Grampa. Well, it's time for me to go. Unfortunately, I have to get dressed to leave you, Grampa, because the world thinks my being dressed naturally with what the Divine has given us is somehow indecent."

"Yeah, I know, Honey," her grandfather replied. "But we know different, huh?"

"Oh, Grampa, thank you so much for being different!"

"Not being different, My Lovely One, just thinking different. No one is different. We are all the same. It is why I can go naked with myself and it is why I can go naked with you. We are all the same in that we are all **dressed with Divinity, dressed in the light and with the light.** And no one who is at peace can ever know otherwise."

"I do wonder why we think we are different from one another, Grampa. I think it would be so much better if we all realized we are the same."

"Absolutely," My Dear, he replied. "The problem is that in wanting to be different from one another, all we see is our differences and not our sameness. If I want to be different from you, Honey, I will look for ways in which we are different; but if I want to be the same as you, I will look for ways in which we are the same."

"And then, though there are many differences between us," she responded, "we will only see how we are alike."

"Yes, for the most part, that is true; but oh how wonderful our differences are too. I love you, Dear One, because we are the same; but I am enchanted by you because we are different."

"Enchanted by me, Grampa?"

"Oh, yes, enchanted," he retorted. "I love you because we are the same; but I am enchanted because of our differences."

"And I am enchanted by you, too, Grampa, if liking being with you means being enchanted. Is that what it means?"

"You got it, Dear One!" he replied. "But being enchanted by another does not mean using another to fulfill oneself. I am enchanted by you, Honey, for what you are – not what you can do for me."

"Me too, Grampa! I like you for what you are. I don't need you to do something for me. You used to tell me, Grampa, when I was much younger, that you did not need me to make peace with the world and that is why I could go naked around you. I did not understand that then, but I think I do now. You said that people who need others to be at peace with themselves are the ones who can do harm to others because if others are needed, others can be forced into submission; and since you were at peace with yourself, I need never fear you could harm me. And you never have, Grampa."

"Thanks, Honey! And I never will. You can count on it. We will always be at peace because neither of us needs the other to be at peace with ourselves. You have learned well."

"You have taught well, Grampa!"

"Thanks for thinking so, Honey, but keep in mind that my ideas are only opinions. It is my opinion that peace is strictly within. Others are as convinced as I am that it comes from without. You need to make up your own mind on that. Am I right? Am I wrong?"

"I think you're right, Grampa. It makes sense to me."

"Does it make sense because I am your Grampa – or does it just make sense?"

"I guess I would have to admit that I am prejudiced, Grampa, but I think you are right."

"And others who think otherwise think they are right. Just listen to all sides and decide for yourself, Honey."

"I hope I am listening, Grampa, but I admit that so many different opinions makes it hard to know what is really right."

"I know, Honey. We are all in the same boat with that confusion; but I think I can show you how they could have made Jesus a lord when he was not one. Are you game?"

"You bet, Grampa!"

"Look at me, Honey. Look at your ole naked Grampa here beside you, sipping a glass of water. What do you see?"

Smiling, the young one did as she was bid. "I see my Grampa," she said.

"But beyond that, what do you see?"

"I see a man."

"No more than that?" asked Grampa.

"No. Should I see more than that?"

"My Dear, Dear One, no. But why do you see a man and nothing more?"

"I'm not sure," she replied.

"I think it is because I am naked – and you are naked, Honey. If I had been clothed, you would have seen me as something different – like maybe an American. It is said that clothes makes the man; and I think that is true. When clothed, I am an entirely different person than I really am. Clothes change me – or rather, the impression of me. When clothed, I am no longer a man. I am whatever it is you are looking for. I am a statesman or a soldier or an artist or a peasant or a king. I am no longer *just a man*. Am I?"

"Wow, Grampa! You're right!"

"And that's how they got Jesus wrong – or could have got him wrong," the old gent added.

"Because they didn't see Jesus naked?"

"That's right – because they didn't see Jesus naked – or if he was naked, they refused to look at him as he was. Instead, they did not see a man first. They saw what they were looking for; and since those who wrote about Jesus were looking for a messiah or a lord, that is exactly what they found."

"But how can we know what the real Jesus was then? If we cannot believe what those who wrote about him said about him, how can we know about the real Jesus?"

"We can't, Honey. We can only guess about the real Jesus – like we can only guess about any man of history who has been seen in outer ware. Very few in history have been *only men*. History does not record *only men*. History records men who did this or that or the other thing, but never, *only men*. History records George Washington as general and president, but it does not record George as he really was – *only a man*. History records John Paul II as a priest and a pope, but it does not record John Paul as he really was – *only a man*. And history claims to have recorded Jesus as some kind of messiah and lord, but it does not record Jesus as *only a man*. Why? Because history and mankind in general does not want *only men*. It wants heroes that do this or that and in wanting heroes that do this or that, men live but are never known; and what we have in their place are impostures of men and not men themselves."

"That's a pretty harsh statement, Grampa!"

"I think it's the harsh truth, Honey, but it should not be reason for despair. It should be just the opposite – reason for excitement and reason for enthusiasm and reason for loving life without fear of what men in clothes have dictated as truth. Take away the clothes of George Washington and you no longer have a general and a president. You have *only a man*. Take away the clothes of John Paul II and you no longer have a priest and a pope. You have *only a man*. Take away the clothes of Jesus and you no longer have a messiah and a lord. You have *only a man*. And take away the clothes of Grampa and you no longer have whatever he was in life. You have in front of you, Dear One, *only a man*."

"Oh, Grampa, I like it! And take away the clothes of your dear lovely granddaughter and all that is left is *only a lady*! Wow!"

"There it is, Honey! People know what they see, not what might have been. And since the story is the same everywhere, we can know with almost absolute certainty that not only could we have got Jesus wrong. In all likelihood, we did get Jesus wrong."

"But it is possible they got him right, too, Grampa. Right?"

"Yes, it is possible; and because every person in this world is important, it is useful to search for people in the history of words – as long as you realize that what was written may not have reflected the true story. In all that mess of words, there are some nuggets. Not everything that man has done has been folly. There is no need to take that approach; but there is tremendous need to realize that all that has been written may not be the truth – regardless of all who are willing, as they say, to stand on a stack of **BIBLES** claiming that all that has been written is the truth."

The young one started to chuckle. "Grampa, I just thought of something. I just imagined Jesus joining us on your porch naked. I guess he would be *only a man* then, huh?"

"You have that right, Honey – and I think you also have Jesus right. Not everyone who lived when Jesus lived was looking for a lord and not everyone who wrote about him wrote about him as a lord – or messiah. Only those clothed in some fashion of tradition were looking for a lord; but there were others."

"Others?" she questioned. "Who?"

"I don't know how many, Honey, but I'm familiar with two – **Thomas and Mary**."

"Grampa, I should not be taking so much time with you today. I am due for dinner with a friend at Noon. I hope he doesn't mind my being late if I am, but who were Thomas and Mary?"

"Maybe in the end, they are fiction, Sweetheart. Maybe someone wrote in their names, but it is considered by some scholars that Thomas was one of the twelve apostles of Jesus and Mary is the one known in the other gospels as Mary Magdalene."

"The prostitute, Mary?"

"Yes – the same one, although Mary may not have been a prostitute in reality. Who knows about that? Those who wrote about her in that fashion may have been simply trying to discredit her – perhaps because of her views on Jesus or perhaps because of a friendship that they did not want to honor. Who knows about that?"

"You think gospel writers could actually tell lies to discredit someone?"

"Keep in mind, Honey, that when those works were written, they may have not been what you call 'gospels'. They may have been later defined as gospels, but in the beginning, they may have made no such claim. They could have been nothing more than works about Jesus that were strictly personal opinions."

"Like the personal opinions of Thomas and Mary?"

"Exactly!"

"But why have I not heard about the works of Thomas and Mary? I had no idea they even existed."

"Almost no one in the current age has had any idea of any contrary works on Jesus, Honey. You are not alone. I did not know about them either until some friends of mine, Russ and Joe, told me about them."

"But why? Why have we not known anything about them?"

"It is nobody's fault of the current age, Honey. It's just one of those things. Things happened long ago that suppressed any works about Jesus that did not agree with what the majority of the rulers of the church believed. No one is to blame."

"But what happened, Grampa?"

"Honey, long time ago, there were lots of different opinions about Jesus. Thomas and Mary – or ones who called themselves Thomas and Mary – were just two of many who wrote about Jesus. Some like the gospels that ended in the **BIBLE** believed that Jesus was a messiah from within Judaism; and some – like perhaps Thomas and Mary – did not see him in that light. They saw him as quite special, but not as a Jewish messiah."

"Really? I thought that everyone saw Jesus as a Jewish messiah."

"Almost every Christian does, Honey. And he might have been a messiah, too. They might be right, but my point is not about being right or wrong. It's that there were other works on Jesus that did not proclaim Jesus as a Jewish messiah. There were other opinions. Right or wrong, there were other opinions."

"So, why have we not known about those other opinions?"

"Again, Honey, it's no one's fault that is living today. Call it *incidental*, but in the 4th Century before any books were collected into a single work we now know as the **BIBLE,** there was a Pagan emperor we know today as Constantine. He was a Roman emperor who was actually of the Pagan faith. Pagans believe some are gods and some aren't. Those who are gods are divinely inspired to rule and those who aren't gods are supposed to obey the gods who are divinely inspired to rule."

"Constantine was one of the gods?" the young one asked.

"Well, yes, or at least he saw himself in that light. But his mother, Helen, or Helena, had become a convert to Christianity – or the leg of Christianity that saw Jesus as a god like Constantine was a god. It was probably because of his mother becoming a Christian and because Constantine loved his mother that he decided to make Christianity a state religion.

Before Constantine ruled, Christians were far outnumbered by Pagans and were very much persecuted; but when Constantine rose to power, he changed all of that."

"That's sure intriguing."

"Yes, it is, My Dear, but it is also why books like those of Thomas and Mary were eventually banned. You see, Constantine favored Christianity because of the love for his mother, but he favored that branch of Christianity that saw Jesus as a god – like Constantine saw himself. He called all his bishops together and bid them to select books favorable to his view of Christianity and to ban those books not favorable to his view. Anyway, in effect, if not by design, that is how it happened."

"Constantine did not like Thomas and Mary?" she asked.

"That's right. He did not like their view of Jesus. So he bid the bishops of the church to collect those works on Jesus and **Old Testament** works favorable to the idea of a messiah into one work that is now called the *BIBLE*. Before Constantine, there was no *BIBLE*, but upon his command, a *BIBLE* was created that included the works on Jesus that saw Jesus as a Jewish messiah – and all other works were not only banned, but supposedly commanded to be destroyed. Constantine did not want any opinions about Jesus in his empire except those he favored – and that was that."

"And so Thomas and Mary and other works about Jesus that did not agree with Constantine were banned? Is that right, Grampa?"

"That's the story, Dear One. Constantine and his bishops commanded that all works on Jesus not favorable to his opinion of Christianity be condemned. All of those works were supposed to be destroyed."

"But I take it that they were not all destroyed."

"You take it right, My Dear. I guess you could call it blatant disobedience on the part of some who did not believe in the view of Jesus as offered in the gospels that were selected to be part of the **BIBLE.** Many of the contrary works were destroyed and we have no evidence of them; but some – like the works of Thomas and Mary – were hid from authorities and were not destroyed."

"How long were they hid, Grampa?"

"I am not sure about the work of Mary, Honey, but the work of Thomas was only discovered in 1945. So, that is how long the work of Thomas on Jesus was hid – from about the 4th Century to 1945 – about 1,600 years. That's a long time. Huh?"

"It sure is, but how was it discovered?"

"Call that *accidental,* if you like. In 1945, some peasant was rummaging through a cave that overlooks the Nile River in Egypt near a settlement called *Nag Hammadi.* He wasn't looking for anything in particular, but he happened upon this big jar that contained a number of ancient works. It turns out that big jar contained that which we now know as **The Gospel of Thomas** – among others."

"Wow!"

"Yeah, Wow! But that which is really important about this story is that it reveals something none of us living today ever dreamed happened. It revealed that at one time there were a lot of works about Jesus that disagreed among themselves about what Jesus was. Before 1945, we were mostly in the dark. I suppose some works about Jesus that had not agreed with Constantine's view of Jesus had emerged, but not many. In fact, I think the work on Jesus attributed to Mary Magdalene was discovered sometime in the 19th Century, but I am not sure about that. For now, when it was discovered is not important. That it was discovered is important because along with other works like that of Thomas, it reveals that history – or rulers of history – tried to suppress works on Jesus that were not favorable in some fashion to their outlook on life."

"Amazing!"

"I think so, Honey. It is, indeed, quite amazing to learn that once there were different opinions about Jesus. And it is wonderful that we can now review some of those different opinions."

"No longer just one version. Is that it, Grampa?"

"That's it. Which version is right, if any? Well, it probably all comes down to which version you want to be right – Constantine all over. He wanted some to be right and decided that the others were wrong – and so he probably refused to even listen to versions contrary to his views on rule and gods. And people today are no different. We all block that which we don't want to hear. Don't we?"

"I guess so, Grampa, but what did Thomas or Mary say that caused them to be suppressed?"

"I suppose it comes down to the issue of what was Jesus. Was he a messiah, as strictly a product within Judaism – or was he only a master without necessary ties to Judaism? Was he a Jew that believed in the history of the Jews – and therefore could be their messiah – or was he simply a man with a view about life in general? Was he one to represent a kingdom – or was he one who had no use for kingdoms - that is a kingdom on earth? Most interesting, huh?"

"That's heavy, Grampa!"

"Yes, it is, but I did not make it heavy. None of us living today did. None of us living today were part of the drama that suppressed a view of Jesus that did not see him as a Jewish messiah. Constantine and his bishops did that. None of us need feel guilty about it."

"I must admit it is interesting, to say the least, Grampa. I should have gone long time ago, but this story is too exciting for me to leave it behind. Wow! That's all I can think of saying. Wow!"

"Well, it's only a story, Honey. Consider it nothing more than that. Suffice it to say that it should suggest that we may have been given the wrong Jesus. Suffice it to say that it is possible that the Jesus that Constantine liked – or the version of Jesus that he liked – does not reflect reality. With the emergence of contrary works on Jesus that none of us ever knew existed, we have plenty of reason to challenge the idea that Jesus even believed in sin, let alone ever claimed to be a messiah that was to save mankind from sin."

"Are you saying that the works of Thomas and Mary may even challenge the concept or belief in sin, Grampa? Surely, not!"

"Perhaps, Honey. Let me give you a few examples. In the work on Jesus by the one called Mary, Jesus was asked about sin by Peter, I think. Peter is presented as saying that Jesus had taught them about lots of things, but what did he think about sin? What do you think the Jesus of Mary answered to Peter's question about sin – according to what we know today as *THE GOSPEL OF MARY?*"

"Oh my!" the young one exclaimed. "I have no idea – what?"

"Near as I can remember it was something like this: *There is no such thing as sin, but you create sin when you mingle as in adultery, and this is called sin. For this reason the good came among you, to those of every nature, in order to restore nature to its root.* Who knows what that all means, Honey, but it does suggest that Jesus did not favor the traditional Jewish concept of sin. It seems to me that answer is a challenge to what Peter expected to hear. Doesn't it seem so to you?"

"Grampa, I did not hear the last part of your quote, if you were quoting. I would need time to review things, but I did hear what you said that Jesus claimed there is no such thing as sin. That's enough right there to make you think. Isn't it"

"I think so, but, of course, it makes more sense to me than it would to many others because I don't believe we can be separated from God at all since God, being Infinite, must be everywhere and in everything – and I think it is that notion of separation from God that is the entire statement of sin – as traditionally understood."

"And if there is no such thing as sin as traditionally accepted, then there is no need for a messiah to save us from such a thing? Is that right?"

"How could it not be, Dear One? What happens when the entire notion of sin as traditionally understood is discarded?"

"It has to call into question the entire claim of authority on the part of the church that claims belief in sin, I guess."

"Precisely, Dear One! It allows for some very interesting speculation - doesn't it – for those of us willing to speculate."

"It sure does. What does Thomas have to say about it, Grampa?"

"Nothing directly about it, Honey, but there is plenty of room to speculate that Jesus did not see himself as a messiah. Thomas does not have him comment about sin, per se, I don't think, but he does have him commenting about him being a messiah. Want to hear about it?"

"Of course, Grampa!"

"You sure you won't be late for your dinner date?"

"Maybe, I will, Grampa, but this is more important than any dinner date. I can have dinner anytime, but how often can I hear about another version of Jesus? Dinner can wait."

"I'm glad you are so interested, My Dear. In what is known today as *THE GOSPEL OF THOMAS*, Jesus is presented as asking three of his disciples about how each of them sees him. Peter answered that he thought Jesus is like a righteous angel. One called Matthew answered that Jesus was like a wise man of understanding – or maybe it was just the opposite. Maybe Peter saw Jesus as a wise man and Matthew saw him as a righteous angel. I'm not sure about that; but Thomas answered that he couldn't answer the question, but that he saw Jesus as his master. And what do you think Jesus said?"

"How can I know, Grampa? But I am excited to know. What?"

"Jesus is presented as telling Thomas: *I am not your master because you have drunk from the bubbling spring which I have measured out.* What do you think about that, Honey?"

"I'm not sure."

"I think it suggests, Honey, that Jesus was objecting to being anyone's master. He just did not want the job. He is telling Thomas that he is not the master of Thomas, but because Thomas seems to have understood what Jesus was teaching, Thomas had become his own master. That is to say to me that it is not the grace of another that saves us from what might be called sin, but understanding."

"And it calls into question a need for a savior or messiah. Is that right?"

"That's right, My Dear. It suggests that Jesus did not want to be anyone's savior or messiah and that all he was interested in was suggesting wisdom that when believed would liberate us from what might be called sin."

"And that's what you believe. Isn't it, Grampa?"

"Yes, Honey, that's precisely what I believe – that liberation from sin, if you want to call it that, is not what another can do for you, but what you can do for yourself – with wisdom."

"Grampa, I'm beginning to think that I am going to even be late for desert. Wow!"

"I like your excitement because it's also my own, Honey. It's like waking up from a nightmare where you are being threatened with a beating to find someone smiling and reaching out to hug you. It's quite a different story. Isn't it?"

"But why would they suppress such a view of Jesus, Grampa?"

"Because Constantine did not like it, I guess – and because the bishops who decided things didn't like it. Needless to say, there is a lot to not like about it from the viewpoint of one who wants to rule others. Rulers – in general – do not want to hear about wisdom liberating anyone. They want to hear about command and the right to command. I guess it should be obvious that the works of Thomas and Mary were not conducive to command. Were they?"

"And that's why they were banned?"

"Probably. If you saw Jesus in the light of authority, would you embrace works that seem to contradict the right to rule? Hardly! As a matter of act, there is one verse in **THE GOSPEL OF THOMAS** that states directly about command. Jesus said something like: ***Let him who has power renounce it***. Now, is that something that you think Constantine – or anyone who wants to rule – would want to hear?"

"Of course not, Grampa. Who would have ever thought?"

"Yeah, who would have ever thought? There are lots of things that the works of Thomas and Mary say that are not conducive to rule and command of one over another. There is even one verse in **THE GOSPEL OF THOMAS** that says that you and I are not out of line, Honey, with our love of the natural state of ourselves. Jesus was asked by one of his listeners – or disciples – about when they would recognize him for what he was. And what do you think Jesus answered?"

"I can't imagine," the young one replied.

"Jesus said: ***When you take off your clothing without being ashamed, and take your clothes and put them under your feet as the little children and tread on them, then you will behold the Son of the Living One and you shall not fear*** – or something really close to that. What does that say to you, Honey?"

"It says that shame is out of order – that is, shame for life. It says that we should embrace our lives, I guess. Is that what it says to you, Grampa?"

"Without question, My Dear. But keep in mind that all I am offering you today agrees with my state of mind. That might be why I am so eager and anxious to believe it – just like those who are anxious to believe in sin believe that nakedness is sinful and that life is sordid and needs salvation. In the end, I think, we believe what we want based on how we perceive life."

"You think we read into various verses what we want to hear, Grampa?"

"I think so, Honey. If someone who believes in the traditional concept of sin and separation from God were to review the verse I just quoted, they would likely hear something very different than I do. In fact, I have reviewed other interpretations by others and I have been amazed that they think that Jesus is speaking only symbolically about embracing nakedness. They claim that Jesus is only using clothing as a metaphor for shame and that to know him, we must discard our shame – like taking off our clothes - but shame is in no way related to clothes. Clothes are only a metaphor for shame. Well, that is one way to look at it. Isn't it?"

"But it's not how we look at, is it, Grampa?"

"No, it isn't. Knowing nakedness as a way of life as I do, I think that wearing clothes is not just a metaphor for shame. It is an expression of shame. People who do not want to embrace life as it is excuse their need for clothes in any fashion they can. When metaphors are desired, metaphors are seen. I guess we are all the same."

"And you think that Jesus really meant we should embrace actual nakedness to know him? Is that right, Grampa?"

"To know his wisdom, yes. I don't think it has anything to do with knowing Jesus personally or needing to know him personally. I think it has everything to do with knowing the wisdom of Jesus and thereby, as Jesus spoke to Thomas, becoming masters for having imbibed on the same wisdom."

"And you think that embrace of nakedness is essential for the attainment of wisdom? Is that right, Grampa?"

"Don't you, Sweetheart?"

"I'm not sure, but I haven't lived near as long as you have, Grampa. I need some time to think about it."

"As it should be, Honey. You need to take time to make up your own mind about things – just like your ole Grampa has done. At your age, I was still wrestling with the traditional concept of sin. At your age, I had a long way to go to reach where I am now."

"Thanks, Grampa. I appreciate your confidence in me – and the freedom to make up my own mind."

"I strongly suspect, Dear One, that unless you embrace life as it is – without shame – as Jesus says directly in that verse I quoted you, you cannot know wisdom. In another verse, apparently Thomas caught Jesus naked in the desert – though it does not say so in literal terms, but Jesus said: *Why did you come out into the desert? To see a reed shaken by the wind? And to see a man clothed in soft garments? Your kings and your great ones are those who are clothed in soft garments and they shall not be able to know the truth.* I suspect that is true, Honey. I suspect that it is the actual wearing of clothes for the purpose of distinction that prevents a man from knowing the truth. And I suspect that is why Peter and all of those who believed that Jesus was a messiah never knew the real man."

"Are you saying that it takes one to know one, Grampa?"

"I think that is exactly what I am saying, Honey. How could Peter or any of the others even begin to know Jesus if they did not even appreciate the need to embrace life as it is because of its being holy? There is so much reason now to suspect that Peter never knew Jesus, but only thought he knew him. I do not want to suggest that Peter knew otherwise and only pretended to know Jesus. I think he really thought he knew him, but there being no evidence whatsoever that Peter embraced nakedness like Jesus suggested we should, I doubt that Peter had any idea about Jesus; but it's only one man's opinion, Honey. It's what I think and believe, but you don't have to believe it."

"Like I said, Grampa, I need time, but if it means anything to you at all, I am leaning in your direction. I am inclined to believe in the Jesus of Thomas and Mary, but I need time to study them on my own. Thanks so much, though, for opening a door I had no idea even existed."

"That's the key, Honey – being willing to hear more. Not many are so willing because they are so entrenched in their own views about things that, as it is said, they can't see the forest for all the trees in it. You have to stand back, withdraw from history and from mankind in general, to see mankind. You can't see mankind from within its history. You can only see mankind as it is, naked, as you are seeing it and knowing it on this porch."

"I think I agree, Grampa. I think it is possible that in one hour naked with you on your porch I have learned more about who or what I am than I could have learned in a dozen years hunched over books of history."

"I don't know about that, Honey. I don't claim to know much. I just claim that others may not know as much as they think they do – and my *not much* may be closer to the truth because I am not protecting my ignorance by assuming that which was written is the truth. I prefer to be **only a man**, Honey, but I see **only a man** as being absolutely wonderful. I am delighted to be **only a man.** I have no need to be more. I am content to be what I am and to be thankful for what I am, leaving who I am somewhat of a useless search."

"What do you mean by that, Grampa?"

"Well, Honey, I think that people get derailed from enjoying life by insisting on being personalities. I think they get so focused on being persons that they forget they are people. I think they get so focused on becoming known for some great deed that they overlook what they are. In searching for an identity, they lose sight of what is more important – life itself."

"And we are life itself. Aren't we, Grampa?"

"Ah, that we are, my Lovely Daughter of my Lovely Daughter! We are life itself. I am a reflection of life itself by being *only a man*; and it is in that in which I should find glory and happiness and contentment. I am *only a man*, but why should I be more?"

"And I am *only a lady*, Grampa! But I feel like a queen. I feel like I am ruling the universe by being *only a lady*. I have nowhere to go because I am really the best that I can be. Wow, Grampa! Wow!"

"I hope you keep that enthusiasm, Honey. It is easy to lose it in the world of clothed people because many self-ignorant don't know who they are, but they are intent on believing they are special. It is easy to lose sight of what is really important when mingling with others who have already lost sight of it. Just beware!"

"I will, Grampa. Well, gotta go out there into the world that knows little peace, but, Grampa, I will always have my own peace – and you! See you soon!" she said as she rose and bent down and hugged her Grampa and then kissed him sweetly.

"OK, My Dear One," the old gent replied, as he returned his granddaughter's affections. "Thanks for coming by. You know you or any of your friends are welcome – dressed with the world or *dressed with Divinity*. As you know, I hug, not hate."

"If only the world knew that, Grampa!" she replied, as she reached for her clothes, looped over a chair on Grampa's porch. "If only the world knew hugs and gentle and not hate and force. "But maybe someday it will," she said, as she began to cover her light with the shroud of clothes that mankind has chosen to prefer over the light itself. "Maybe someday, Grampa, we will all realize we are all *children of the light* – and really come to know *Peace on Earth*."

"I hope so," he replied. "I hope so."

Peace On Earth

A Song
By
Francis William Bessler
July 31st, 2007

REFRAIN:

There can be peace on earth – for all the world to see.
There can be peace on earth – but it must begin with me.
There'll be peace on earth – when we all see Divinity.
But there can be no peace – without me.

What is peace, my friends?
It's knowing that you belong
and it's knowing that we're all the same.
That is peace, my friends
as we're singing in this song;
and it's not holding anyone to blame.
Refrain.

What is peace, my friends?
It's loving what we are
and it's knowing that all life is a gift.
That is peace, my friends
and if we're ever to stop war,
we must believe that all life is blessed.
Refrain.

What is peace, my friends?
It's failure to hold a grudge
and it's forgiving to be forgiven.
That is peace, my friends
and it's the only way to nudge
our way into that lovely state of Heaven.
Refrain.

Repeat *Refrain* a few more times.

Peace On Earth

The End

FIVE HEAVEN ON EARTH STORIES

The End

About the Author

Francis William Bessler was born in 1941 on a small farm outside of Powell, Wyoming. The second youngest of eight children, he has always felt close to nature—and thus to God. He graduated from Powell High in 1960 and attended Catholic seminaries in Wisconsin and Colorado for six years. After studying for five years at St. Thomas Seminary in Denver, he was terminated from further studies because, according to the school, his thinking was not that of a Catholic priest.

He considers himself a "Divine Naturist" (his own term) and believes that separation from God is not possible because an infinite God must be within all things. Heaven exists everywhere, because God must be present everywhere.

Books
by
Francis William Bessler

(Main Theme: Life Is Divine, Sinless, Sacred, & Worthy)

See www.una-bella-vita.com
or enter "Francis Bessler"
in the search bar of Amazon.com
for availability.

Prices vary from $14 to $28 - depending upon size of book.
See www.una-bella-vita.com or enter "Francis Bessler"
in the search bar of Amazon.com for availability.

All books also available via Kindle

1.
WILD FLOWERS
(about 270 pages)
(essays and songs mostly written as website blogs from
2012 to 2014)
Printed in a smaller font 2 type.

2.

FIVE HEAVEN ON EARTH STORIES

(about 420 pages)

(Featuring 5 philosophical stories written from 1975 - 2007)

Printed in a larger font 4 type for the benefit of an easier read.

3.

EXPLORING THE SOUL -
And BROTHER JESUS

(about 200 pages)

(Featuring an analysis of several theories about the origin
and destiny of the soul - and supplying an original idea too -
originally written in 1988.

Also, featuring a new look at Jesus via an essay series
written in 2005)

Printed in a larger font 4 type for the benefit of an easier read.

4.

JOYFUL HAPPY SOUNDS

(about 470 pages)

(featuring all of my songs and poems written from 1963 to
2015; total: 197)

Printed in a smaller font 2 type.

5.

LOVING EVERYTHING
(WILD FLOWERS # 2)

(about 350 pages)

(essays and songs mostly written as website blogs from
2014 to 2015)

Printed in a smaller font 2 type.

6.

JESUS -
ACCORDING TO
THOMAS & MARY -
AND ME
(about 240 pages)
(Featuring The Gospels of Thomas & Mary
and a personal interpretation of each)
Printed in a larger font 4 type
for the benefit of an easier read.
Compiled in 2017.

7.

IT'S A NEW DAY
(WILD FLOWERS # 3)
(about 250 pages)
(essays and songs mostly written
as website blogs from 2016 to 2019)
Printed in a smaller font 2 type.
To be published in early 2019.

Made in the USA
San Bernardino, CA
26 July 2017